I dedicate this work to those beloved individuals who
once having entered my life, changed it irrevocably;
Penelope, Peter and Charlie.

They, like the little girl who had a little curl right in the
middle of her forehead; when they are good, they are
very, very good, but when they are bad, they are horrid.

Virtue Hathaway

Buying the Ranch

An Adventure Story

BOOK I

Facing Real Life

WRITTEN AND ILLUSTRATED BY
VIRTUE HATHAWAY

LA HACIENDA PUBLICATIONS
JALISCO, MEXICO

Buying the Ranch

An Adventure Story

BOOK I

Facing Real Life

COPYRIGHT© 1996 • VIRTUE HATHAWAY

PUBLISHED BY

LA HACIENDA PUBLICATIONS
APDO. POST. 20, MASCOTA, 46900
JALISCO, MEXICO

ISBN 970-91841-0-5

Who will I marry?
Rich man, poor man,
Beggar man, thief,
Doctor, Lawyer,
Merchant, Chief

School Girls's Jumping Rope Chant

ACKNOWLEDGMENTS

I would sincerely like to thank those people in my life who have worked so diligently, who have encouraged and helped me immeasurably, inspired me and in a very real way, have saved my life, allowing me to make this book a reality.

My beautiful granddaughter Galia Plasencia Boccaccio, my daughter Penelope and my sons Peter and Charlie, my grandsons Giovan and Gaston Plasencia, John Youden and the original graphic artist Paul McBroome, Maricruz Montes de Oca the current graphic artist, the staff at the Café Cyber Gallo, my editor Joy Eckel, my friend Jan Lavender and finally Herminia Rosas and her father Susano, María Tovar and her husband Héctor Pércz.

CONTENTS

PROLOGUE

Aunt Minerva is laughing as we stumble down the rock-strewn path to the old clap board outhouse. I am four years old and was born in Chicago. I know nothing about outdoor plumbing.

The traditional sliver of a moon is carved through the top of the door, the significance of which is lost to me. She drags open the sagging door to the rustic construction within—a wooden plank, with two large holes carved side by side, big enough to accommodate the ample rear ends of some of my larger relatives. The gassy, putrid stench of decaying human waste assails my delicate childish senses.

As Aunt Minerva swings me up and over one of the holes, I quiver in terror of falling into the unspeakable mess below. With my small arms and legs I grip the plank, anxious for it to be over so I can go out to play with the dog in the peach orchard. Next to me hangs an old Sears catalogue. It is suspended with a rusty wire from a nail hammered into the old wood of the outhouse. It is meant to be used as toilet paper. It seems a travesty to condemn those beautiful, elegant models in their Sear's ready-to-wear to such an ignominious use.

Aunt Minerva, or Minnie as she is called, is a large, ample woman. She fills the doorway as she watches vigilantly over me. She always wears ankle-length black dresses, still in mourning for the death of her parents. She swings me off the hole and lovingly cleans my butt, my head tucked between her legs during the process.

Then tossing me up and over her hip, she walks up the slope to watch the men harvesting the peaches. "It is good for you to learn to live in the country, away from the city luxuries that can be taken away from you," she says in her foreign accent. She is scornful of flush toilets, running water, electric lights, telephones, pavement, automobiles, and streetcars.

The year was 1939. My still youthful parents were off on a month-long vacation with another couple to an exotic, far-away place called Mexico. They left me with our Italian relatives on their peach farm in Makanda, Illinois. Except for the outhouse, I was perfectly happy there.

The farmhouse, a simple wooden construction, was badly in need of paint. The ground floor consisted of a living room and a kitchen with a large handmade wooden table for dining, while off to one side were two dim, musty-smelling bedrooms. The rough wooden floors were covered with cracked and decayed linoleum scattered here and there with hand-crocheted rag rugs to relieve the squalor.

A wooden ladder led up to a sleeping loft where guests and children spent the nights. There was no electricity. The beds in the loft were creaking affairs of iron springs and feather beds made from the soft down of poultry that had been sacrificed to feed the family. The down feathers were encased in cotton sheets and were wonderfully warm during the chilly nights.

Water was supplied to the kitchen from a hand pump secured to the side of a copper sink. Although I tried to pump that thing, ultimately I would end up hanging from the pump handle by my two little hands unable to raise a drop of water. My aunt would triumphantly put her strong arm to the task, and soon a torrent of fresh water would gush from the spout. The water had a slightly iron taste. Perhaps that was what made my aunt so strong.

In the evenings after the work was done, the family and the farm hand, Shorty, would gather on the front porch to rest and talk about the farm, maybe gossip a little, or just sit in silence. I loved to sit on the old porch swing—wired together where the links had broken—squeaking constantly as we swayed gently back and forth. We listened to the wind, looked up to the sky for weather signs, and remarked on the names of the different birds singing their twilight songs.

At night when the house was lit with kerosene lanterns, the humble home took on a warm, cozy glow. The light softened the weathered faces of those around me. After supper, my aunt would escort me and any other children present up the ladder to the loft. Being a good Catholic family, we would all kneel beside our beds to pray for our communal well-being. She would then tuck us in and arrange the white enamel chamber pot for easy access under the beds.

She would descend the ladder with the lamp, plunging the loft into total darkness until dawn. We had been blessed and were asleep before she reached the bottom of the ladder. As a consequence of those experiences, I never feared the dark, rather welcoming it, feeling secure in its velvety cloak.

It was a large extended family. The older members had been born in Italy—or the Old Country, as they referred to it. Both my parents were from Europe. My other aunt and uncle lived on a farm near Carbondale, and the clan visited each other frequently. I had four cousins at that time: Aunt Minerva's two sons and Aunt Margaret's two daughters. They were adults, however, and one cousin was even married. They would bring the children of their friends to play with me on the farm and spend the night.

My Uncle Joseph was the opposite of my Aunt Minerva. He hardly spoke a word and would spend the evenings scowling over a newspaper in his overstuffed chair. This was during the economically difficult time of the Great Depression, and he may have regretted the drastic move from his beloved Italy. I dimly remember my elders being forced to work for the government out of necessity. Disillusion hovered over them as they left with their lunch pails for whatever the WPA had planned. My mother disdained public works.

My various companions who came and went are amorphous in my memory, like fantasy children that appear and disappear in dreams or like children you imagine having someday.

But the dog is engraved in my childish memory forever. Palsey Walsey was his name. He was a big, white, shaggy dog that allowed us to ride him a few steps before shaking us off. He seemed huge to me but kind and careful with small children, a noble beast, for sure. I vowed that as soon as we got back to Chicago, I would ask my mother for a dog just like him. I loved that dog, but my mother was adamant—no animal in the city. She was right, of course, but I would cry for a dog and vowed someday I would have a great big dog of my own.

Sometimes, I would follow Shorty around the farm. In the mornings he would milk the cows, and I learned to pick my way around the dung. He would set a three-legged stool alongside one of the cows, usually the one with the large, swollen udder, and while she was eating, he would wash her teats and begin milking her by hand.

"Joanna, open your mouth," he would say and then would direct a stream of warm, sweet milk into my wide-open mouth. Much of it would dribble down my dress, the sight of which would have appalled my very tidy German mother. I loved this unconventional way of drinking milk and would beg for more. After Shorty filled several buckets with milk, we would return to the house, where I would receive the first of many changes of clothing for the day.

The killing of the chicken for lunch was both repelling and fascinating at the same time. Aunt Minnie would stride forth in her black dress, with a tattered and stained apron tied around her ample waist. Wielding a small but heavy ax in her right hand, she looked like an ancient goddess of death. We children would tag along, following her into the chicken yard, where she would close the gate behind us, locking us in with her and the creature she would select for the stewpot.

She would stride with great authority into the swarm of flapping, squawking hens and a few roosters to make her selection. With a strong hand, she would grasp the screaming bird, which seemed to be aware of its fate, and lay the creature down on a leveled tree stump. Strands of black and gray hair would fly from her chaste bun, making her look even more ferocious. She raised her arm, ax in hand, and struck. With one swipe, the chicken's head would fall from its body.

We watched wide-eyed as the chicken's headless body began a macabre dance of death around the yard. Flapping and running in all directions, it would run toward us, sending us screaming to one corner. The creature would finally run itself out, like a fire slowly extinguishing for lack of fuel, and then collapse in a filthy, bloody heap. My aunt would slip the chicken head into her apron pocket to give to the cat then scoop up the carcass into a bucket.

We would troop behind her into the kitchen to see what would happen next. On the wood-burning stove, a pot of water was boiling. She would plunge the chicken into the water for a few seconds, pull it out, and begin plucking the feathers. At this point, we children would lose interest and run outside to play hide-and-seek in the barn, climb trees, or play with the kittens and the dog.

Then there was the henhouse. It was a real surprise for a city child to see that eggs were not manufactured in cartons but came from the bottoms of hens! We would walk slowly and quietly so as not to disturb the hens as they went about their business, clucking softly at our intrusion. Aunt Minnie entrusted me with the egg basket while she would carefully work her arm beneath the hen, ignoring the pecks and bites while taking an egg away from the distraught mother hen. She would hand me the warm, stained, brownish-white eggs, and I would carefully arrange them in the basket.

Breakfasts were huge—served later in the morning, after the early daily chores were finished. There was ham and bacon, bred and cured on the farm, fresh eggs, scrambled or fried, and corn on the cob in season. Aunt Minnie brought to the table fresh, homemade cottage cheese, peach marmalade, and freshly baked bread, all topped off with butter from the churn—food fit for the goddesses and gods. The aroma of home-smoked bacon, sausages, and ham cooking is unforgettable.

The pigs ate slops—all the leftovers from the meals mixed up with the whey from the butter and cheese-making. It was an awful-looking, gooey mass that we would consider garbage, but the pigs love it—like dining on lobster tails or filet mignon with a glass of champagne.

When I think back, I marvel at how ecologically correct it all was. Nothing was wasted. It was all recycled back into the land or re-eaten in different forms. My ancestors had a natural, symbiotic relationship with each other, the land, and the animals. Although, I must say, some of the animals did get the worst of it.

We were treated in the same manner as children were treated in the Old Country, as precious little treasures. We were small time capsules of the future, carefully nurtured.

On Sunday mornings, after the sun had been up long enough to warm the cold water, we would be bathed in a large, galvanized iron tub. We wore underpants as modesty dictated when boys and girls were bathed together.

Aunt Minnie was blessed with abundant good humor and an operatic singing voice. I loved to hear her burst forth with an aria or an old Italian love song or a Venetian boating song. Her hair was very thick, black streaked with gray, and worn in a severe bun slightly above the nape of her neck.

She must have been beautiful when she was young, as her two sons were very handsome. With age, her face had become blemished by thick, dark moles, some of which sprouted black hairs. She had a mustache and eyebrows that almost met in the middle. She did absolutely nothing to enhance her appearance.

Her voice was loud, and I think she used a lot of vulgar speech, which would provoke my mother. I would have loved to spend more time with these relatives, but I think my mother felt they were a bad influence on me. My mother was determined to make a gracious, refined "lady" of me, although even then I was showing signs of possessing a determined will and an adventurous spirit. This was not acceptable in the '30s. "Ladies" were not spirited, adventurous, or determined.

My father named me Giovanna in memory of the thirteenth-century Italian author Giovanni Boccaccio. Father's family name was Botticelli, who was a great Italian artist. My mother objected strongly to my name, insisting that Giovanna combined with Botticelli was way too foreign-sounding and that I must be called Joanna, the Anglo equivalent of Giovanna. I always thought the name Joanna paled before the strength of Giovanna. And then there was the fact that this writer's work was iconoclastic, erotic in form, exposing the social and religious hypocrisy of the time—radical. However, Mother ruled, and I am called Joanna.

Sunday afternoon the whole clan would gather for their weekly picnic at Starved Rock State Park. They would load the wagons with food and drink, hitch up the horses, and everyone would pile into the hay for the bumpy ride to the park.

The legend behind the name of the park was intriguing. In the late 1700s around Fort St. Louis, as the white man pressed his conquest westward, a lone tribe of Illinois Indians held out here, close to the confluence of the Mississippi and the Ohio rivers. The militia who were sent to capture or destroy the tribe found their retreat into the monolithic rocks and caves to be impenetrable, so it was decided to besiege the Indians into submission. The Indians decided to starve rather than surrender, and all perished amid the remnants of what was once their land. It is said the ghosts of those Indians still wander the cliffs and caves waiting for the time when their lands will be restored to them by their gods.

While my aunts and cousins organized the outdoor feast, consisting of *polenta* (cooked corn meal), meat sauce, cheese, sausages, bread, fruit, and much whiskey, homemade beer, and wine for the men to wash it all down with, I would wander off to stare up into those mysterious rock formations and imagine seeing the ghosts of the Indians still abiding there.

My sympathies lay with the beleaguered Indians who were so heroic to die by starvation rather than lose their tribal lands and live in submission to the white man. The whites were driven by crass ambition, the hunger for money and land. At that age, my feelings were instinctive and uneducated but very real. Concepts of right and wrong were forming that would surface later in my adult consciousness.

Hiking around that park—over and around the huge boulders, hopping over crevasses, staring down at the river rushing below and the granite cliffs soaring above—imparted to my young senses a spiritual awe and respect for nature that has lasted all my life. Monolithic rock masses seem to have divine power, and they remain fascinating to me to this day.

My parents, as children, had lived on neighboring farms in southern Illinois. Their families had immigrated from Europe right after the turn of the century, selling everything to take the great risk of starting over again in this "new" world. They sought to escape the great social and political upheavals taking place in Europe at that time as the continent moved slowly and inexorably toward World War I.

The powerful forces of the industrial state were mobilizing to convince the masses, by hook or by crook, that freedom did not lie in owning your own land, farming it, and passing it on to your children, but in having a nine-to-five job in a factory. Pamphlets circulated among the European dispossessed promising cheap farm land and unlimited opportunities for gaining wealth in the United States, and my forebears took the hook.

Both families had farmed for as long as there was recorded family history. However, in the new world, farming was hard work. There was no extended family to help, and the returns were small. As a child, my mother had to milk the cows and then sell the milk to neighbors. In order to supplement income from the farm, my father as a boy worked with his father in the coal mines of Illinois. My grandfather had worked as a blacksmith in Italy and used his skill to weld and repair mining equipment.

The lure of the big city proved irresistible. As soon as the younger generation reached their late teens, my parents, along with various sisters, cousins, and uncles, fled the farms and headed for Chicago to seek their fortunes.

Finally, after what seems like an eternity, my parents return from Mexico to the farm in Makanda to reclaim me and rejoin civilization. There is a great uproar as their Oldsmobile sedan struggles up the hill and turns around to park.

My parents emerge, laughing and gay, a handsome couple with a magic aura about them—something they had brought back from their journey—it was Mexico. I adore them. They are the most wonderful people I could imagine in the world. I am swept up, kissed, and given a small bag to carry, while they lug huge, colorful hemp bags filled with treasure.

The treasures are carefully emptied onto the kitchen table of my aunt's house. And it was all so *"cheap,"* my mother gushes as she hands me a lovely, dark-skinned clay doll with black eyes and a mouth like a rosebud about to open. Her expression is quite serious. She has a long, black braid down her back tied with a red ribbon, and her head is topped by a tiny woven-straw *sombrero*. She carries a miniature basket of paper mache fruit. Her dress is embroidered with red, ochre, green, and blue flowers and leaves, and her full skirt is edged in delicate, handmade white lace. On her little feet, she wears leather huaraches. I try standing her up on the table, but she falls over, so I have to lean her against something. She is very beautiful, and that is the most important thing.

The family crowds around the table, admiring everything as it spills forth. A large hand-embroidered tablecloth and napkin set in pale beige cotton is unfolded and ceremoniously handed to my Aunt Minnie. "But it is too beautiful!" she protests. "Here on the farm, it is just going to get so dirty." The gift represents a painful challenge to their rustic way of life. A set of hand-painted dishes are for my other aunt, Maggie, and several lightweight woven wool serapes in brilliant colors with patterns of birds, horses, and haciendas are presented to the men.

"And here, Jimmy, is a real guitar. You are the musician in the family," my mother states as she hands my handsome cousin a rustic Mexican guitar.

"Guess I'll need some lessons now," he comments as he begins to strum some chords, looking rather Mexican with his dark hair, mustache, and dark eyes.

My uncle fixes drinks for the men and women—whiskey and water—while the story of the trip to Mexico continues to unfold. Mother holds the attention of all.

She wears her blonde hair in the current fashion, called an *upsweep*. All her hair was swept to the top of her head and there ends in big curls held together with blonde bobby pins. In her excitement, strands become loose and fall around her shoulders. She is quite pretty, a German beauty with large blue eyes with fluttery dark lashes. She prides herself on being one of those modern women of that era who copied the style of the famous movie queens like Carol Lombard and Marlene Dietrich.

Next come the photographs, before the ultimate gift is given. "Look," my mother continues, "here we are on the road just outside of Ciudad Victoria. Just look at those mountains! Aren't they breathtaking? Black-and-white really doesn't do the scenery justice." We dutifully pass the photos around, staring at the misty tones of gray, white, and black, making out vaguely the soaring mountains of eastern Mexico.

"This is the hotel we stayed at, high in the mountains. I have never been to any place so beautiful, with great verandahs, stone pillars and arches, gorgeous views wherever you looked. The bedrooms were huge, with hand-carved wooden furniture and fireplaces that worked. We ate food I have never tasted before—fruit called a mango and papaya they say is good for your digestion, thin, flat pancakes made from corn they call *tortillas*, chili peppers so hot you could burn your whole insides and bring tears to your eyes, then something called, uh, artichokes—looks like a big thistle, and you eat only the bottom part of the leaves."

"The bad thing is the plumbing. They could use a fulltime welding repair man." My father chuckles.

Mother holds up another blurry photo. "And here we stopped to go to the bathroom—you know, how you do on the road—and all of a sudden all of these children appeared from nowhere begging for money. Can you imagine? They think we are *rich*." In this series of photos, my parents, their friends, and the Oldsmobile sedan were surrounded by around fifteen or twenty children looking like variations of my doll, but most were smiling with their hands out. "We gave them a few pennies, and they were happy and finally let us get back into the car."

"Oh, here we are in Xochimilco in Mexico City. These are floating gardens, and the little boats are totally decorated in fresh flowers."

"Floating gardens?" my aunt interrupts skeptically.

"Yes, right outside the city. It was fantastic with all the colors and floating flowers all around you. And here we are still in Mexico City, and you can see the two famous volcanoes in the background. One is Popocatepetl, and the other is Ixtaccihuatl. The legend is that Ixtaccihuatl is the sleeping maiden and Popocatepetl is her husband. Look, you can see a small plume of smoke coming out of Popo," she explains.

Later, I would learn that Popocatepetl was the *lover* of the sleeping maiden, but even if my mother had known that, she would have insisted on legalizing their relationship.

Reaching into the bottom of the last hemp bag, my mother produces two bottles of a clear yellowish liquid. The labels were artfully designed, featuring drawings of cactus around the borders, while two burros were hauling a small cart full of spiky-looking plants. Next to them was a beautiful Indian maiden carrying a basket of fruit on her head. In the background was a sprawling hacienda with arches and the two volcanoes behind that. It was another world entirely. And there in large, classic lettering was the word *TEQUILA*.

"Oh, better be careful of that stuff," warns my father as the men turn the bottles around in their hands, curiously examining this gift from South of the Border. "Mexican firewater, a few snorts of that stuff will put you right under the table!" He produces some small clay cups and fills them to the brim for the men to sample.

"They make this from cactus, if you can imagine," says my mother in her travelogue voice. "Agave cactus I think it's called, and they drink it straight with salt and lemon chasers."

The afternoon passes into evening, and the men congregate off to one side of the living room. I imagine they are discussing the worsening political situation in Europe, the economic depression in the States, events that were leading up to the Second World War. The women are busy in the kitchen cooking and serving supper. After eating, it is time for bed.

The next morning, after breakfast and packing up, my parents and I take leave of the farm. "Hurry back! Come for Christmas," exhorts my aunt. We all kiss goodbye while my father loads the trunk of the sedan. I kiss the dog when my mother isn't looking, as she seriously disapproves of kissing dogs.

We are on our way back to Chicago, speeding along the two-lane highway. I feel sad as the magic aura slowly fades away into the distance and the flat Midwest plains stretch out to what looks like eternity.

The fortune my parents sought in the big city was difficult to find. My mother worked nights as a telephone operator, one of those women who in the early days of the telephone would ask, "Number pleeze?" My father was out of work, but somehow we managed. He stayed home to take care of me during the afternoons and evenings, while mornings he studied master welding in a trade school.

On Saturday nights we would attend the country music concerts, called the Saturday Night Barn Dance, in a great theater on South State Street. The whole family would pile into our first automobile, a Model T Ford that had a rumble seat in the back. Merrily, we drove off to see the leading country music celebrities of the time, names like Pat Butrum, Gene Autry, Patsy Montana, and many others.

The huge stage was like a big barnyard, and some of the best singers would bring a horse on stage with them. The horse would whinny along in harmony. There were chickens off to one side clucking away; it was past their bedtime. And sometimes goats would wander across the stage. The audience would applaud uproariously when one of the animals would relieve itself during the performances. It was wild, raunchy good humor.

Some of the singers specialized in yodeling, while others played bluegrass banjo from the Appalachian Mountains or sang cowboy songs of the West. Others sang songs of unrequited love and had the ability to cry profusely while singing. They were my favorites. It was most exciting to be allowed backstage after the show to meet the performers, get an autograph or maybe a kiss from these glamorous artists. I told everyone I wanted to be a cowgirl when I grew up, and they laughed at my infantile ambition.

Another form of entertainment in those days was to walk with my mother's beautiful younger sister, Aunt Henrietta, and Cousin Jimmy to the municipal airport, which was just a few blocks from where we lived on the South Side of Chicago. There, we would hang on the chain link fence spending the afternoon watching the big propeller planes take off and land. We would be covered with dust from the backwash, but it was thrilling. I dreamed of someday becoming a pilot. It seemed to me to be the ultimate freedom to be able to fly a plane.

I often wondered why Aunt Henrietta did not marry Cousin Jimmy; they were so attractive together. Later in life, she told me she wanted to marry a wealthy businessman and Jimmy was from the farm, a working man. She eventually did marry a successful businessman, and together they lived a happy life of travel, yachting, and high society. For better or for worse, they never had children.

The highlight of my week was my mother's day off, usually a Wednesday. We would dress to the hilt.—she had a fur coat of some kind, raccoon maybe, and me in some fancy concoction she had sewn up from family hand-me-downs. We would take the streetcar downtown to Marshall Field's on State Street. She would buy some little things, but mostly we would look at all the beautiful products for sale. Then, we would have lunch in the Redwood Room.

After that, we went to the movie theater across the street and spent many hours watching a double-feature film program. I saw *Gone with the Wind* when it first came out, although I had not much of an inkling of what was going on, less for *How Green Was My Valley*, but I loved Disney's *Fantasia*. Then there would be live performances with magicians, comedians, country singers, and dance routines, followed by cartoons and a newsreel. It was dark when we came out of the theater.

When the war was gaining momentum in Europe and Japan, the newsreels would cover that action in grainy black-and-white film. Most dramatic were scenes of men fighting and planes bombing cities and people. The war affected us profoundly with great feelings of patriotism and inspired people to sacrifice for our threatened country. There did not exist the bitterness and anger that accompanied the later war in Vietnam. That engagement was suspected of being fostered by special business interests of the US and resulted in the heartless destruction of a small country's way of life.

The Second World War changed everything. My farm relatives were forced to sell their land. It was the same woeful tale of farm families. It cost more to produce the peaches and to ship them to Chicago than what they could receive selling them. They all relocated around Pontiac, Michigan, and took jobs in the automobile industry and in the production of munitions to fuel the war.

My father was drafted into the army and sent to Europe. Toward the end of the war, he wrote that his company was fighting in North Africa. Then, we received a terrible telegram reporting that he was missing in action. And we never heard from him again. Adjusting to his loss was extremely painful for my mother and I as well as the rest of the family.

My relatives from the farms did not prosper, because the jobs they once held in the auto industry were phased out or relocated to other countries where labor was cheaper. My aunts and uncles are long-dead and my cousins in ill health. One of them succumbed to alcoholism. However, I did hear that one of my second cousins is a music and voice teacher in a high school somewhere in northern Michigan.

CHAPTER ONE

San Francisco

Vincent Franklyn Cooper swings his big white Buick into a parking space overlooking the southeastern part of San Francisco. He is almost too nervous to notice the spectacular view from the top of Upper Terrace, but he always said that no matter how difficult your life may be, one must take pleasure where one finds it.

After locking the car, he stands for a moment gazing up at the dull gray, two-flat building that was soon to be his home. It was situated on the last curve of the street before ascending to the top of the hill and dead ending. Another chance in life for him, a gray phoenix rising from the ashes. Why does Kelley have such terrible taste in colors, he thinks to himself as he opens the street door and makes his way up the dirty green-carpeted steps to the first flat. He unlocks the door.

Two young women are seated at a card table in front of the picture window in the dining room. They are noticeably startled at his unexpected entrance. One, a long-haired brunette, stands up and stares at him in surprise. She must be the occupant I have to evict from here, he thinks as he arms himself for the confrontation, with his lawyer's air of authority. The place is a mess and smells like fish.

"Hi, sorry, I didn't know anyone was here. I am Vincent Cooper, Dr. Kelley's friend. I imagine he must have told you that I am renting this flat as of yesterday."

I brush my hair back nervously, assessing this intruder, this invader of my present home. "I'm Joanna Botticelli. Uh, yes, Dr. Kelley mentioned something about that, but they haven't finished the work downstairs in, uh, my apartment." I am disconcerted, striving to know who or what he is.

""You don't mind if I look around the place now, do you?" he asks as he moves off with a youthful stride after nodding politely in the direction of Donna, my friend from college. He trails smoke from his cigarette as he moves from room to room.

He is an attractive man who looks to be in his late forties, though I am no judge of age. He has a high forehead, with thick grayish hair swept back across the top of his head and keen blue eyes that droop slightly at the corners while taking everything in at one glance. He is on the tall side and wears a rumpled gray suit and a bowtie.

The nostalgic mood of the afternoon is irreparably broken. The flat is a mess. The dust balls dance about the virgin oak floors when they are disturbed and now are illuminated by the slanting rays of the late afternoon sun filtering in through the drifting fog. My only broom has vanished in the chaos of my present life.

An improvised table on one side of the dining room holds my oil paints, turpentine cans, brushes, and paint rags. Next to the table is an easel with a half-finished painting of a Mexican boy kneeling in the market next to a basket of fruit. Around the room are my other paintings, some finished and some in process, leaning against the dull brown walls of the dining room. They are all of children, some Mexican and some Chinese, with serious faces that either stare out into space or look directly at the viewer as if wanting answers to some unknown question.

"What does that guy want?" asks my friend Donna in a low voice. She was having lunch with me while her husband attended a corporate conference at the Fairmont Hotel downtown. We have been talking about our old friends, old times at college and looking at photos of her children.

I begin to gather up the remains of our lunch: Dungeness crab, sour dough bread, and Napa Valley Chablis wine—some of the edible treasures of the city. "He's a friend of the doctor, the man I was telling you about who has been so kind to me since the divorce. The doctor is also being divorced, and his wife was so pissed at him that she reported my downstairs basement apartment as illegal, which I guess it was, to the downtown housing code bureaucrats. Consequently, he had to have workers come in and lower the garage ceiling under my apartment then lower the floor in order to have the right amount of space to satisfy the code—something like that anyway. They have been working down there for two months now. He let me stay here until they finish for the same rent, $70 a month, if you can imagine. Dr. Kelley does complain about how much money it costs him, so I guess he wants me to feel gratitude."

I wrap the crab shells in an old *Examiner* newspaper and drop them into a box under the sink. The smudged wine glasses are rinsed under the tap briefly, and the plates get piled up for later. Returning to my friend with two cups of steaming instant coffee, I look out the window at the beautiful view of the city. We can see all the way down Market Street, across the bay to Oakland, and the hills behind.

"It looks like he is measuring something or other," Donna whispers to me as we sip our coffee while Mr. Cooper bustles about with a measuring tape and a little notebook.

"Dr. Kelley told me this man is also getting a divorce and wants to move in here with his next bride-to-be as soon as possible." I laugh lightly at this rampant deterioration of marriages.

"Jeez, Joanna, this sounds like Deevorce City or something. You better watch out for him, honey. He looks like a ladies' man to me, you know, like he's God's gift to women," she says cryptically, shaking her blonde head, her Midwestern sense of propriety somehow offended by what she sees going on here at the top of San Francisco.

"Why do you say that? I'm twenty-six years old, you know, and I want to see what life is all about after getting married at the tender age of nineteen. You know what I mean?"

"There's just something about him, that's all. Be careful is what I mean to say. He's big city, and you are small town, and he is much *older* than you." She offers me a cigarette then lights mine and hers on one match.

"Chicago is not exactly a small town, Donna," I say defensively as I exhale, feeling very unqualified to comment on this man's ability to conquer women.

"Compared to here, it is," she says, tilting her head back and narrowing her eyes in a know-it-all manner.

Vincent Cooper has by now finished his tour of the flat and taken his measurements. He reenters the room, still trailing blue smoke behind him. We wait expectantly for his next words. "You don't mind if I have some furniture moved in here tomorrow, do you?" he asks me.

"No, the place is practically empty. I have very little furniture myself. I, uh, am sorry the place is such a mess. I use it as a studio and don't seem to get around to cleaning very much." I laugh nervously, wondering inwardly why I am feeling so flustered in this situation.

"Can we plan on moving Saturday?" he continues, ignoring my apologies, putting his cigarette out in my potted philodendron.

"I don't know. Today is Tuesday. Maybe the workers will be done by then, but the bedroom is still missing half the floor." I stare at the sputtering cigarette butt in my plant, annoyed.

"I'll phone you during the week. Here is my business card in case you need to talk to me. Tell Kelley to get those guys working down there—you know, lay off the booze and finish the job."

"Oh, don't worry about your plant," he says as he picks up the still smoldering butt from the dryish dirt, opens a window, and throws it out. "Ashes are actually good for plants—fertilizer, you know."

There is silence.

"Say, you don't paint too badly," he says, positioning himself in front of my easel. "You could use some more detail—I mean, in the hands. Hands always reveal whether an artist is good or not."

He is too much! "I paint in the Impressionistic style. You don't use too much detail. Everything is rather misty and unclear, suggested rather than drawn explicitly," I say with all the authority I can muster at this point.

He continues to study the painting, almost as if he were about to make his own changes to the work. His arrogance is blatant, but not without charm. "Don't lose that card now, you never know when you may need a lawyer." He smiles brightly toward us as he leaves the flat, aware of his effect on women.

I watch him surreptitiously from the window as he opens the door of a big white older-model Buick sedan with a chrome bumper as thick as a man's thigh curling around the front of it. He glances up at the window and catches me watching him. Perhaps I only imagine a smile of satisfaction as he gets into that big thing, turns it around, and rolls down the street.

There is a moment of uncomfortable silence, as the thread of the past has been broken and the new, unpredictable future takes precedence.

The small Midwestern liberal arts college that Donna and I attended was very clear about its aims. The young men were being groomed for positions in various corporate entities that proliferated in and around Chicago, while the women were being educated to be proper and entertaining wives for these men. I didn't realize it at the time and managed to absorb an education, to the detriment of wifely accomplishments like serving tea to important people, etc.

But marriage at that time was the only conceivable move for a woman once she finished college. Even though I majored in art, I never imagined myself as an artist in the world, so I became an art teacher after my marriage, while my husband went to law school at Northwestern.

Donna suddenly seems stodgy and boring, a wifely slave of a corporate slave, their lives managed and scrutinized by a stuffy board of rich old men. Her husband had to move about the country at the will of the board of directors, their friendships limited since they could not hold any opinions contrary to company policy. They could trust no one since information in the slightest way damaging could be used against the employee in the ongoing struggle to rise upward in the corporate hierarchy. Gossip, slander, demotion, or the loss of a job, it was a tenuous way of life despite the high salaries, the perks, and probably the prestige involved. It was totalitarian in spirit.

I suddenly feel grateful that I was not caught in the web of big business even though my life is a disaster at the moment. I am alone, short of money, and I fear the future on the one hand. On the other hand, I am feeling the thrill of something new, some excitement right around the corner, the possibility of great adventure.

Donna stands up and brushes off her skirt, takes her handbag from the back of the chair. "My goodness," she notes, "it is 4:30 already. Where did the time go? I have to pick up Fred at the Fairmont around 5:00, and I hate driving in strange cities. Then, there is a wives' meeting tonight after dinner. It's fun, but it can be exhausting, too."

She goes to the bathroom, while I stare out the window at the fog coming in, blotting out the view. Her life is all so predictable, I think. Just as long as her husband produces for the company, it is all secure for her and the children. Children—I wonder if I will ever have any. For that, I envy her.

She emerges from the bathroom freshly lipsticked, hair in place, smiling warmly. "Thanks so much, sweetie, for everything. It has been wonderful seeing you again. I sure hope everything goes well for you. Be a great artist, and I can say I knew you way back when."

She fumbles in her handbag for the rental car keys as we walk arm in arm down to the street. She unlocks the car, slides in, and rolls down the window, prolonging the ritual of saying goodbye. She extends her hand, and we pause a moment. "I really, truly hope you find some nice guy around here that you can be happy with. Really, honey, that's the only life there is for a woman."

"I don't know, Donna. I just got out of a marriage. I'm not sure I want to rush into a commitment anytime soon. I may just want to play around for a while, see what it's like to be a single woman. I never really did that."

Donna pulls her hand away from mine. "You're not getting any younger, sweetie," she says as she starts the engine.

I feel the distance between us widening into a chasm. "Give my love to Fred!" I shout as she begins the roll down the hill. The car disappears around the curve. That is the last we ever see of one another.

I pace about the spacious old flat with its beautiful views of San Francisco. Late afternoon, the worst time for me—depression sets in with a vengeance. The beautiful, old hardwood floors are covered with dirt and dust, and I do nothing about it. I mourn the unused fireplace, the feel of old elegance that I will have to give up when I move down into my cramped quarters below.

Lighting a cigarette, I survey this little corner of my life. Oil paintings clutter the walls, leaning against each other, an outward sign of my struggle to survive. The sad philodendron is probably doomed for lack of care. On the crude table littered with tubes of oil paint, there is a palette of half-dried paint hardening into uselessness. Only the brushes are tended to. I always cleaned my brushes after a painting session—they were so expensive, but then so was the oil paint.

You are not organized, I think, hoping that by scolding myself I will remedy the situation. I would work in spurts and then at other times succumb to a debilitating lethargy and do nothing. Could Donna be right? Do I *need* a man? Am I condemning myself to a series of sporadic acts with no meaning? Am I wasting my time? Am I truly an artist?

The dust balls dance and drift lightly over the floor. My movement stimulates them, and I pause a moment to contemplate them—fluffy things, rather cloud-like in their formation, the enemy of the good housewife while harmless themselves. Sad—how some of us dedicate our lives to eliminating harmless elements from our existence.

Out toward the northwest soar the twin towers of that majestic cadmium-orange bridge, the Golden Gate. They peak up above the roiling fog coming in from the Pacific Ocean. The beauty of it all is entrancing, and I decide that if I am going to be alone and depressed all my life, it is better to be in so beautiful a place than an ugly one.

In my little Triumph sports car, I would speed along the bridge suspended in space by those cables above the cold, death-beckoning waters below pouring in and then out of San Francisco Bay. The bridge reminded me of a musical instrument, and sometimes with the top down on my car, I could hear the cables vibrating, like a harp, from high to low pitch.

Now, the sun is low in the west. The fog creeps up the hills and eliminates even the tips of the bridge towers. With the fog comes the chill air of the sea. It presses me down into the solitude that accompanies me into the evening.

I clean up the remains of lunch and wash the dishes. In order to revive myself, I pretend that I am an art collector. I change the paintings on my easel, deciding if one is worthy of purchase. The setting of the scene is a marketplace in Mexico. I had spent the previous summer in Mexico City studying art, language, and the culture but also using the time to decide whether I should go through with the divorce after five years of wedlock.

The business card on the table distracts me from my fantasy art collecting. A simple white card announcing Vincent Franklyn Cooper, Counselor-at-Law, Aviation Specialist, a phone number, and an address on Post Street. *Counselor*, not lawyer or attorney. What is the difference I wonder.

I return to my paintings. Hmm, I need a fine brush to work over the palette knife work to bring out the detail of a small boy next to a basket of tropical fruit. Perhaps his little hand could use more detail. He doesn't look just right. He has a sweet, childish face, indigenous, though maybe too sentimental for some tastes, I think. Maybe it needs to be more abstract.

But no, I don't like abstract art, most of it just seems fake. I like to paint from life. It gives me pleasure to craft a subject so it is recognizable. My studies in Mexico City had helped me enormously in that vein. My instructor, Raul Anguiano, a well-known Mexican artist, had encouraged me to draw accurately from what I saw, a concept totally contrary to my art education in college.

There, one was graded down for drawing what you see. An accurately rendered hand holding a mango was the object of derision by my instructor. It was all an education in frustration. We were expected to express ourselves but at 17 years of age I couldn't think of anything I wanted to express except perhaps a desire for independence. I had no idea how to paint independence. I wanted to paint like Titian and then maybe to evolve into Renoir. The great examples that were held before us as students were Picasso's weeping, hideously dismembered women. We were victims of that great movement to dehumanize art. But I persisted in realism despite my dim prospects for success.

Taking a pencil in hand, I note down some materials I will need to buy during the coming week. I look again at my work and like what I see. I begin to feel better, art as life as hope. Even the dust balls are bouncing around more happily around my feet.

After dark, I decide to take a walk. The top of Mount Olympus, the name of the hill that I live on, is totally enveloped in the damp, chilling fog. I contemplate the eucalyptus trees dripping in the light of streetlamps as I zip up my old ski jacket from better days. I wish I had a dog to accompany me on my walk into the night. Maybe someday I will have a dog. No, not maybe, I *will* have a dog someday.

The wind is cold as I make my way up the hill to the top. There is a broken monument there, its original form now unrecognizable in its decay. I pick my way through the weeds and cracked pieces of concrete to a small bench that was once part of the statue. I look out over my fantasy queendom, through the drifting patches of fog, Market Street cuts straightaway through the city to the waterfront of the Bay, the Ferry Building sitting there like an exclamation point, the lights golden and enticing.

My life is in bits and pieces, scraps and leftovers. Perhaps I can make something beautiful out of it still—even though I am getting old, twenty-six—like a beautiful patchwork quilt constructed of leftovers. I vow not to return to Chicago, that flat, dull city. I only miss Lake Michigan and the Art Institute.

The fog closes in again, leaving this little hill, Mount Olympus, alone and isolated. I think a fire would be nice in that big old flat, but I have no firewood, nor have I ever built a fire in a fireplace. I stand and stretch, beginning the short walk back. I pass some apartments and townhouses along the way. The lights are bright through the large picture windows. People pass in front laughing and talking, carrying drinks. I catch glimpses of fine furniture and candelabras. The smell of food cooking wafts through the air.

Back in the flat, I turn on a light, making the dinginess more apparent. "Tomorrow they are bringing some furniture," he had said, I think as I stretch out on the bed, feeling a bit better after the walk.

Lately I have become aware of an inner voice. The voice is a "counselor" like my neighbor-to-be. More and more I listen to it. Sometimes I feel removed from my own life, as though I were standing somewhat outside myself observing me and my actions. A strange thing.

I don't know how to refer to this voice. Is it my soul, voices of my ancestors, God, or my conscience? All that I really know at this point is that if I ignore my inner counsel, I do so at my peril. The voice dictates my actions and is a hard taskmaster, at times insisting that I do what I logically consider impossible, that I must reach for the unattainable, which means suffering, loneliness, hard work, and discipline!

I am awakened early
Saturday morning by the screeching
hydraulic brakes of a huge moving
van that has parked outside of
my living room window.

CHAPTER TWO

Moving Day

I am awakened early Saturday morning by the screeching hydraulic brakes of a huge moving van that has parked below my bedroom window. It is barely dawn. I scramble into a robe just as the door opens and Mr. Cooper stands there, looking more disheveled than before.

"Good morning, Miss … uh … what is your name?" he asks with a crooked smile on his face.

"Botticelli. Didn't Dr. Kelley tell you? Joanna Botticelli."

He brushes past me, a man in a hurry. I follow him to the kitchen, where he stops, staring in displeasure, his hands on his hips. "Why, you … you haven't moved anything out of here! All your stuff is still …"

"They have barely finished my apartment below, and I, well, just haven't had time to …"

He stares at me, the annoyed half smile returning to his ruddy face, then he wheels around and goes on to direct the movers.

As fast as possible, I throw on some jeans and a sweatshirt, brush my long hair and gather it into a ponytail with a rubber band, pull on some socks and sneakers, then rush to the kitchen to begin putting my things in boxes. As I wrap plates and take out pots and pans from the cupboard, I realize I don't want to live in the tiny apartment below.

I *like* this space, the fireplace in the living room, the great views. I enjoyed living here for the past three months. I hate being poor.

Mr. Cooper barges into the kitchen with a box of *his* stuff, which he sets down on the floor. I wish for calm in my dealings with this man and do not wish to feel that he is pushing me around unmercifully, bullying me as though I don't matter. Another man stands behind him. There are two of them watching me now.

A cup slips from my hand and shatters on the floor. Cooper chuckles. "There, there, don't get so nervous, little girl. We won't bite. This is my good friend Dr. Ted Burkhart. He's kind enough to come and give us a hand today. And you are, uh, Miss Bocciball, did ya say?"

"No. *Botticelli*. It's Italian," I manage, wishing I were far away from this situation and these two arrogant men who don't even know the name of the famous fifteenth-century painter Botticelli.

"Pleased ta meetcha, Miss Bootesely. Ah can't pronounce those dago names, ya know, bein' pure English mahself," drawls my new acquaintance Dr. Burkhart.

"Just call me Joanna," I snap at them, bristling at his ethnic slur.

He has a leering smile and talks like he is from the South. He is tall and skinny, with a receding hairline. His posture is bad, his shoulders droop, and he has a little potbelly.

Who *are* these guys? They move past me and begin tossing my things into the old toilet tissue boxes I had brought from Cala Foods for this purpose. I hear them muttering between themselves about the delay. They step on the broken pieces of my cup, and they break further.

In a little more than half an hour, they have packed up all my belongings and moved them downstairs into my little studio apartment: clothes, easel, paint table, paintings, my few pieces of furniture, and my bed.

Down in the depths of the building in my own apartment at last, I throw myself on the bare mattress. I feel like crying but I don't, fearing someone will come in and see me in tears. The place is even filthier than the flat upstairs since the workers did not clean up after themselves. My paintings are tossed here and there as though they lack any importance. I am shaken by it all, too depressed to be angry.

The bed sits on a platform, which is right above the garage of the owner, Dr. Kelley. The apartment now conforms to the building code of the City since over 60 percent of the space has an 8-foot ceiling. I have designed bookshelves as a divider between the bed and the small space I planned to use for my painting.

There is a tiny kitchen at one end of the bedroom/studio and a bathroom on the other end. The living room is next. One entered the apartment through the living room, there is only one outside entrance, off the living room at street level.

On the outside, there is a small garden in which nothing grows. It faces north and is encircled by a brick concrete wall. The soil appears to consist of grayish gravel. Below this garden wall, I park my little sports car, my pride and joy, a TR3 painted fire-engine red.

There is a heavy, constant noise above me as the movers unload the van with Vincent Cooper's belongings. I peek through my living room window at this monstrous vehicle. "Butterfield Auction" is written in large, elegant letters along its side.

Sighing heavily, determined not to feel sorry for myself, I mobilize. I start digging into a box and find my bathroom articles, makeup, towels, brushes and combs, washcloths, etc. Next, I locate the kitchen box. I wipe the dust off the shelves and, as my mother had always taught me to do, begin to cut and lay shelf paper to line the shelves—a tedious but necessary female ritual establishing a woman's territorial rights much as a male cat sprays all over to let everyone know the space is his.

It all seems so small. I suppose I should be grateful for the speed with which those men dispatched my belongings, but the whole experience has left me feeling like a mere impediment to the grand furnishing of the wonderful first-floor flat.

The day passes between organizing my place and rushing to the window to see what is happening next in the ongoing drama unfolding above me. I remember that I still have some things in the hall closet upstairs but decide to save that for later as an excuse to go back and see what Mr. Cooper has wrought.

I am utterly alone in the city. I have no family here. They all live in Tucson, Arizona. Seven years after my father was killed in the war, my mother remarried. I have not been very close to them. She had two sons with her new husband, and her life revolved around them.

Her remarriage had essentially orphaned me, even though I had lived with them for several years before I left for college. My mother had paid part of my education, while I worked summers to pay the rest. Her husband, white Anglo-Saxon Protestant, was a successful businessman with a prosperous tool and die factory in southern Arizona, so my mother and half-brothers were well-off financially.

And now, my ex-husband took all of our friends—his friends, actually—with him after the divorce, so I am friendless, a total tabula rasa ready to become a born-again San Franciscan—a new beginning. I must make friends, become a successful artist, a totally new human being created out of this raw, female clay.

Was I a Democrat, a Republican, a socialist, a fascist, an anarchist, or something else totally new? What criteria did I have for friends, career, politics, or a lover? And children? Would my belly swell some day with new life inside me? Would my breasts fill with milk for a lovely little baby? "What is going to happen to me?" I wonder as I spy my old broom in the back of the small bedroom closet. I moodily begin to sweep up the debris of construction.

By late afternoon, I hear the van start and begin the struggle to turn around in the small space on the curve of Upper Terrace and then drive off down the hill. The banging and thumping of furniture being placed, dropped, or dragged along the floor continues above, stimulating me to get my own house in order.

I hear the special murmur of a sports car driving up and parking. I rush to the window to see who it is. A tall, slender, blonde woman dressed in a powder-blue pantsuit and high heels steps out of a yellow Austin-Healey. She walks toward the doors to the upstairs flats. She does not look wife-like.

I think she must be the new fiancée. I imagine her greeting Mr. Cooper, kissing him warmly on the mouth, then breezily giving her opinion of the décor. Maybe the work will stop for a while and they will have a drink together—a beer or a highball or even champagne. It is Saturday afternoon.

Now, the signals change from above. I hear the clomp of a woman's high heels on the floor above, and then things quiet down. I look for a cigarette in my purse. There is one left in a crumpled pack of Kent filters. I could go upstairs and borrow a cigarette and take my winter coat out of the closet, but they might just give me a cigarette and not share their sociability with me. I light the cigarette and sit down on the window seat, surrendering to self-pity. I pace about, trying to figure out what to do next. There is no husband now to tell me.

The view from my kitchen window is of the Pacific Ocean and the top part of the Golden Gate Bridge, the same view as that from above—just less of it. Upstairs is everything: a gorgeous view, probably lots of great furniture, space, and love, a working fireplace, and although I do not admit it to myself at this time, a very attractive man, older and probably prosperous.

There is a loud, authoritative knock on my front door, and I rush to open it. Again, it opens before I have a chance to unlock it. "Oh, sorry, I thought no one was at home, and I wanted to see how the place is. I mean, I wanted to see if those lazy bastards finished or not before I pay them." There stands my famous landlord, Dr. Thomas Kelley, chief of orthopedic surgery at the University of California Medical School. He has a kind of sheepish look on his face and wipes his hand across his mouth as if trying to erase it. "I'm not disturbing you now, am I?" he continues, looking around the living room, taking in the lack of furnishings. My ex-husband had taken the hide-a-bed that had served as a living room sofa.

"Oh, no," I say, "not at all, Dr. Kelley. I'm just sorry the place is such a mess and there is no place to sit down. The people upstairs just moved all my stuff down here since—"

"Please, honey, don't call me Dr. Kelley. Makes me feel like a boring old fart. Just call me Thom, okay? After all, we are going to be living here together like one big happy family. You don't mind if I take a quick look around the place. Did they finish painting the walls?"

"I think they finished everything. Patched the holes. I remember it was in pretty bad shape."

"Was the son-of-a-bitch sober?" he asks. He swears with such gusto, pleasure really, so at odds with his patrician bearing. He seems nervous and jokes a great deal, a kind of sardonic, ironic humor that must be his habitual way of dealing with life.

His face is long and narrow, with a fine, straight nose, his skin very white, almost transparent. Adorning his head is a shock of still thick gray to white hair. There are vestiges of a once handsome man lingering about his presence. His eyes are pale blue and seem to twinkle as though he is very happy about something.

He is tall, over six feet, and lanky, thinner than he had been when my husband and I first moved in here. His hands are constantly in motion, running through his hair, smoking a cigarette, or just waving about to emphasize his pronouncements. His fingers are long, like an artist's—or more appropriately, a surgeon's.

Moods pass quickly across his face. He goes from amusement to peevishness in moments and then back again.

In an effort to answer his questions, I struggle to remember the men working during the past week, and I do vaguely recall the man in charge of painting the walls. "I think he was sober," I say, giving the person the benefit of the doubt, for I couldn't really tell who was sober or drunk or how old they were or if they were criminals or honest, law-abiding people. Either it was a reluctance to pry into people's lives, or I didn't care to pay that much attention.

"You don't mind if I take a load off my feet now, do you?" he says in the bedroom/studio, where he plunks down into an old Morris chair we had bought used at Goodwill. I carry another chair from the kitchen and sit down facing him, wondering what is going to happen next. "Oh, say, you don't happen to have a drink around this place for a thirsty old doctor? I could use a belt right now."

I have nothing—no beer, wine, whiskey, gin, vodka—nor money to buy such amenities to entertain interesting older men. I feel compelled to please him for some reason; he is being so kind and helpful to me.

"Ah, hell!" He chuckles after my moment of perplexed silence. "I guess your stock is low now. Wyncha come up to my place for a drink? It's not in as good shape as Vincent's, with his instant household, but it's not too bad. Oh, say, ya have any ice down here?" He goes to the small apartment-size refrigerator and drags out some frost-covered plastic trays of old ice. "Say, you could use a new refrigerator. The door is off this goddamned freezer compartment. Better complain to your landlord." He laughs.

"I would like to clean up a bit. Moving is such dirty work. I'll come up to your place in a little while," I say, suddenly feeling part of the human race again. My company is *desired*.

"Come up the back stairway. It's shorter," he says as he leaves with my old ice.

I begin hurriedly to search through the boxes for my clothes. This is my first foray into society as a single woman. I become excited and begin to think how to present myself for the evening. After a quick shower, I put on some tight jeans, huaraches, and a hand-embroidered lace blouse from Mexico.

I arrange my long chestnut hair so that it falls in waves and curls around my shoulders, lightly apply makeup, and then make a final analysis of my efforts. The androgyny of the tight boys' jeans and the lacy, feminine blouse pleases me. I am very thin. Due to my failed marriage, I've had trouble eating, plus the lack of money to buy food.

I look good, I decide. The makeup emphasizes my Latin bone structure. My eyes are large and greenish blue, enhanced by the mascara. To finish the job, a few drops of carefully hoarded perfume from better days, and I am off to the upper realms.

Entering the basement through a door right outside my entrance, is like being in the bowels of the building. It is cool, almost cold. Huge white-taped and insulated ducts curl and wind their way from the big gas furnaces upward to the living areas of the building. The sounds of water sloshing down drains or rising in the pipes accompany the huffing of the furnaces. Electrical conduit seems to be going everywhere and nowhere.

The lighting is bad, with one lonely lightbulb hanging by its wires to fend off the dark, mysterious shadows lurking beyond the cobwebs.

I go through another door to the wooden steps. Striding past the kitchen door of the first-floor flat, I catch a glimpse through the window of people congregated in the kitchen, laughing and talking where just this morning I had lived.

The top flat is a replica of the one below, but with more kitchen amenities and a more spectacular view. I had been up here a couple of times in the past to pay the rent when the doctor was still married to his exotically beautiful, red-haired wife, Veronica. The furniture is all gone, and it has the look of a barracks, or how I would imagine living quarters in a war zone to be.

Thom Kelley is in the kitchen slicing limes. My ragged, pitted ice cubes are in an old corrugated bucket. There are gin and vodka bottles on the sideboard beside a dish of peanuts. "Hey," he says, "sorry this place is so shabby. Veronica cleaned me out. But say, what the hell? Let's make a fire and forget about our past mistakes. I bought some fake fireplace logs at Petrini's. Whaddya drink?"

I stand there for a moment trying to think what I drink. I remember: Seven and Seven. "Seven and Seven," I say, recalling the highball of choice in the '50s when I was in high school.

The doctor pauses, his knife suspended above the shiny green lime. "What the hell's that?"

"I, uh, think it's 7-Up with whiskey or something like that. We used to drink—"

He laughs at my lack of West Coast culture. "Well, sorry, babe, but I ain't got that. Look, what's really good—I mean, you should try it—is vodka tonic. Goes down real smooth, and ya don't get too drunk—unless, of course, you drink too many."

The knife descends, and within moments he hands me a vodka tonic with a twist of lime. It's still the same: I drink what the guys drink. Maybe, someday, I will decide what *I* drink. "Thank you, Dr. Kelley, I, uh, mean, Thom."

He smiles at me indulgently, pleased somehow by my faltering. Drinks in hand, he leads me to the living room. There, we sit on an old beat-up sofa his brother had found for him at Busvan Storage, so he informs me.

The fireplace has glass doors. He opens them and leans his lanky figure to the task of lighting a fire to spread a bit of cheer over our disordered lives. He wads up some old newspapers, stuffing them around the synthetic logs, then strikes his cigarette lighter to ignite the papers. When the lighter goes out, the flame just sputters and dies. I hear him swearing under his breath as subsequent efforts also fail. "Shit!" he exclaims, staring angrily at the uncooperative fireplace. He stands up to his full height, his hands squarely on his hips over his sagging trousers.

His frustration unnerves me. I feel somehow responsible, but that is impossible. I know nothing about fireplaces.

"Well, I know what I am going to do to get this goddamned thing going. Wait a minute!" he exclaims as he strides toward the kitchen, his face scowling and his head cocked to one side.

Immediately, he returns with the vodka bottle and begins emptying it all over the papers and the fake logs. He strikes his lighter to the alcohol-soaked papers, and it all flares into dancing flames. Smiling happily, he shakes out the last drops of what I assume to be expensive liquor. "Don't worry. I've got more," he says. "At least those Russian commies make *something* worthwhile." His arms cross against his chest as he watches his handiwork with satisfaction.

Waste not, want not, echoes somewhere in the back of my brain.

He turns and picks up his drink as the dimness of the living room recedes from the glow of the fire. "Cheers!" He is almost giggling with pleasure as he sits down beside me, sinking low into the old sofa. "Well, whatever works, you know. I gotta do something about this dump. Divorce is a bitch, you know."

"Yes," I agree, sipping my drink cautiously, "but Veronica was so interesting—such a beautiful, elegant woman. It does seem a shame that you two would divorce each other." I am out of my realm.

"The old battle between the sexes," he continues. "Yeah, she was a looker all right. Smart as hell, too. She wrote for *Flying* magazine and was one of the Ninety-Nines, the women's flying club. They used to race cross country, and she won a couple of times. Damn good pilot."

"Then?"

"I dunno." His face drops. "Maybe I shouldn't talk about it." But he does. "I guess I didn't screw her enough." He hangs his head and wipes his hand across his mouth as he continues. "There I was, working my butt off every day at the office and at the hospital and coming home beat, and she'd be all perfumed and ready to get laid. It was like coming home every night dog tired and having to start digging a ditch or something."

"So, she started running around with an old boyfriend of hers, a Pan Am pilot. So after a while, it didn't seem to make any sense to stay married. I was just handy to pay the bills, and she had this fellow to make love to her. Now whadya think of that?"

I was utterly shocked at what he was telling me. It was all so remote from any experience I'd ever known or had or heard about. Usually, it was the girls fending off the boys in the ongoing struggle to maintain some semblance of propriety, and now he has revealed to me a vision of a sexually demanding female preying upon the man. It boggles my mind. I want to hear more of this.

He smiles, sensing my prurient interest in his life, and continues with relish. "Oh, hell, I suppose I shouldn't be telling all this to you. You're just a babe in the woods. Anyway, I met her through one of the pilots. I do medical exams for the FAA, ya know, for pilot license renewals."

"She was piss yellow when she came into my office for her annual exam, so I took a sample of her pee. That dame was in an advanced stage of infectious hepatitis. Her damn liver was about to go out on her. I gave her a thorough physical, and she was a gorgeous gal, I tell you. I must have been the first guy in her life to put my hands all over her and not make a pass. Then, she fell in love with me for some goddamned reason. I made her stay in bed, stop screwing around so much, and cured her hepatitis, but those house calls really trapped me. Of course, I was married at the time, but my wife was one of those nags, you know, possessive types, always crying about this and that. And here was Veronica, something altogether new, kinda wild, undomesticated, couldn't cook worth a damn. She was more fun than a barrel of monkeys. I mean, Jeezus H. Christ, she was a writer, she had her own airplane, she *supported* herself. And I don't know how, but I ended up divorcing my wife and marrying Veronica."

We sip our drinks silently for a few moments, staring into the fire and contemplating life's complexities.

"Yes, she was very interesting, kind of aloof, I thought." Interjecting my humble opinion, I rather admired the woman, but try to sound as though she was dead and gone and that it is all for the best.

The doctor rises to this new challenge. "Humph, she may have been elegant and all that crap, but she had the most vicious temper I've ever seen in a dame. See that gouge there in the wall?"

I look through the gloom of the living room to see where he is pointing. There is a three-inch dent in the dull green paint, exposing the white plaster and a bit of the lathe underneath.

"She threw a Steuben glass candleholder at me just because I walked out on her at a medical society meeting. She loved those goddamned shindigs, and I just hated them. All those bleary-eyed medical students drooling around her like she was a bitch in heat really pissed me off, so I just left her there, like that!" He snaps his fingers for emphasis. "She just barely missed hitting me in the head with that thing. Imagine, me, the genius of the orthopedic department of the University of California, with brain damage. Tore hell out of the goddamned wall."

"She must have been very angry," I comment demurely, recalling my own fits of violent temper against my ex-husband during our marriage. The dented stainless Wearever pot would forever remind me of my own personal marital discord.

"Women are fierce as hell," he continues, standing abruptly and pacing back and forth in front of the fireplace, his head cocked curiously to one side, his expression bitter and angry. "They can tear a man apart any time they want if they just get mad enough. Scares the shit out of a guy, ya know. Don't believe that 'helpless little woman' theory for a minute. Oh, say, how's your drink? Ready for another?"

"Oh, yes, sure, thank you very much, Dr.—I mean, Thom." I gulp down the last swallow of my vodka tonic, feeling much better than I have in a long time.

During his absence, I muse over his words. Like caged tigresses, women look tame and docile on the outside but contain a terrible fury just waiting to be unleashed, and then all hell breaks loose. It's the stuff of comic books, of Wonder Woman, my childhood heroine. Thom Kelley seems to know more about women than I do, and I am a woman, twenty-six years old, after all. Why don't I know these things?

We settle into fresh drinks, and the conversation somehow turns to our new neighbor in the building, Vincent Cooper. "Whaddya think of old Vincent?" he asks, eyeing me carefully as though a lot hinges on my response.

I clear my throat to gain a moment or two. "Well, I, uh, hardly know him. I mean, I just met him last week. He does work fast, though. He moved me out of his flat in half an hour."

"He's really quite a guy, you know. We've been friends for years and years. There's not much that Vincent can't do. Flew the Hump during World War II. Got a dozen or so medals, champion aerobatics pilot, a whiz at trial work—no one can beat him in a courtroom. Lloyd's of London just threaten to bring him into court on one of their aviation disasters, and all those ambulance-chasing personal injury attorneys settle right then and there. He makes more money than he knows what to do with, real talent."

"Excuse me for sounding kind of ignorant, but what does it mean to fly 'the Hump'?"

"You mean, you don't know what the Hump is?" He smiles even more broadly, revealing nicotine-stained teeth. I shake my head no. "Why, those are the Himalayan Mountains, the highest in the world, between China and India." He doesn't exactly say "uneducated" of me, but it is almost implied.

"Oh, hell, I'm sorry. I guess you were just a baby at the breast during the war in the Pacific. Vincent piloted one of those big C-57 transports between India and China. The planes loaded up with aviation fuel in India then flew over the Hump to China. They unloaded the fuel in the unoccupied parts of China where the Allied air strikes originated."

"Tough duty, they flew without any defensive arms since an air battle would ignite those drums of fuel, and, well, there was no hope of retaliation. A lot of those guys didn't come back, ya know. They were the cream of American manhood." He reflects an inner sadness at all those deaths.

"Who was that woman with him?" I ask, changing the subject, as I didn't want to feel sad about anything at the moment.

"Oh, her? I think she's his secretary. It's hard to keep up with him. Vincent loves chasing skirts, ya know, 'Loves women'. He's been married four, maybe five times. I lost count a while back."

I gasp. "Four or five times? How can that be? I can hardly stand going through one divorce, let alone considering ever going through that again."

"Oh, you get used to it. The first one is the hardest. They get easier after that—experience and all, you know."

His attitude outrages all that I have been taught about proper respect for the institution of marriage, but I plunge onward, unable to resist him. "It, uh, seems everyone is getting divorced these days, that the vows have no meaning. 'Until death do us part' should be changed to 'till divorce do us part.' It all seems so absurd. If you have been divorced so many times, marriage really has no meaning. My whole life as a wife is a kind of blur, as if I were a robot, part of an institution that tells me what to do and think, not a real person."

The doctor sets his drink down with such force on the old coffee table that some of it spills. He doesn't seem aware of the miniature mess he has created.

I feel I may have said something wrong. I want to wipe up the spilled drink, somehow to atone. At the same time, I am thinking about Vincent Cooper, the romantic pilot. He rather reminds me of Terry of the "Terry and the Pirates" comic strip, which I loved as a child. Now wasn't that set somewhere in Asia I wonder. The square jaw, piercing blue eyes that showed up in the colored Sunday edition of the paper, dusty blonde hair swept back over his head in a dashing wave, that aura of handsome, masculine, heroic strength, a man a woman could fall in love with, but I don't think "sexy." I don't think that way… yet.

"Yeah, Vincent has always had the babes after him. He is a good-looking guy, but you should have seen the men we lost in that goddamned war. I was Stateside during the whole thing, a captain in the medical corps stationed on the East Coast, Baltimore. We had to put all those wounded, dying sons-a-bitches back together again. It made me sick sometimes, you know. I even cried, it was all so depressing. The best of American manhood being slaughtered, maimed, and forgotten eventually. We doctors did the best we could, working twenty-four hours a day and struggling to stay awake long enough to do the work. The only way we kept going was with food and amphetamines. Damn, it was the closest thing to hell I could ever imagine." He rises from the lumpy sofa, wipes his hand across his face, and again begins pacing the living room as if trying to dissipate the bloody memories.

If he thinks he is impressing me, he is. I had never known heroism before, only lives lived in quiet desperation, the likes of which I was determined to avoid at all costs. I can think of nothing to say. He goes to the kitchen to fix himself another drink. My father may have been a hero, but I never was told how exactly he was killed.

When he returns from the kitchen, I decide not to continue the conversation of World War II, having been only five years old at the time of its outbreak. I pick up on the secretary and Mr. Cooper, uncontrollably curious about people who live and love together and aren't married.

Thom seems to respond to my choices of subject matter to discuss. His moods change so rapidly according to the conversation, it is like watching a film at high speed.

"So, this secretary of Mr. Cooper, what is she like?" I venture.

"Oh, her, uh, yeah, Mary Belle, I think she's called. Well, ya never know about Vincent, like I said. He says he is going to marry her as soon his divorce from Phyllis is final. I think Mary Belle is actually a lawyer herself. Seems to me Vincent mentioned something like that."

I decide to return to flying. "I've always liked the idea of flying, myself, even when I was a little girl. I remember in first grade when the teacher asked each of us what we wanted to be when we grew up, most of the girls stood up and said they wanted to be nurses. I said I wanted to be a pilot. The whole class laughed at me, which really puzzled me."

"Aha!" Thom chuckles. "Your first experience in life with the social cost of nonconforming."

"I suppose so. Since that time, I have pretty much toed the line except for becoming an art major in college. My mother urged me to become a teacher—in case something should happen, something to fall back on. I imagine she meant in case I never married or my husband left me to fend for myself, I would have a way to earn a living. But a nurse? Can you imagine what that must be like? Oh, of course, you can. But to me, it seems quite repugnant, emptying bedpans for total strangers, dealing with illnesses and all those unpleasant aspects of sick bodies. Yuck!"

"Well, somebody has to do it. As an artist, you prefer to deal with the more aesthetic aspects of human existence, right?"

"Right." I love how he expresses things, as though he understands me entirely even though we barely know each other. "Or a stewardess, for instance," I continue, "that's pretty glamorous, but you are still just a glorified waitress. But now, up in the cockpit, that really must be exciting."

"When I was a child, my aunt used to babysit me, and for fun we would walk to the municipal airport, which was near our tenement on the South Side of Chicago. Hanging on the cyclone fencing, we would watch the big propeller-driven planes take off and land practically right in front of us. Dust and dirt flew all around us, and our ears would ring from the noise, but it was thrilling. I vowed to myself—I think I was around four or five years old—that someday, somehow I would fly an airplane. I would become another Amelia Earhart. The planes symbolized freedom to me although, of course, I didn't know enough to express my thoughts or even know who Amelia Earhart was."

Thom smiles. "Yeah, that's how it starts, you know. But you were too young to know the reality of it—how much it costs to learn to fly, to buy a plane, the upkeep, the insurance, the fuel and oil, and so forth, all of it. Then to be a professional pilot can be just like any other job, like driving a bus even, or just a means of getting from one place to another."

"You know, I have never been in a plane in my life, not even a commercial plane."

"That's amazing in this day and age! Say, I bet you would like to fly. I have a plane down in Half Moon Bay Airport, just a small tail dragger, a Piper Super Cub. If you like, we can take her out for a spin. It's been ages since I've flown, myself. Vincent actually taught me to fly. He's a licensed instructor, ya know. If you are serious about flying, you can learn in it. You know what a tail dragger is?"

"No."

"It's an airplane with a tail wheel, rather than a nose wheel. In order to land it, you have to stall it a few inches above the landing field. Where other conventional landing gears have the third wheel under the nose of the plane, the other two being under the wings, of course. Get me?"

"Yes. So, it might be easier to land the kind with the wheel under the nose, right?"

"Right, you can at least see where you are going."

"Oh," I sigh, excitement welling up inside me like oatmeal about to boil over. I catch my breath. Finally, I am going to *live!*

"It is a really safe plane," he continues, "lightweight, canvas-covered, like what you use for your paintings. If the engine quits, it's like a glider or a big butterfly—just put it down anywhere. Great little aircraft!"

"You mean, if the engine dies out, like sometimes your car engine just stops, the plane doesn't just fall to the ground?"

"Naw. I see you don't know your aerodynamics, young lady. If the engine quits on you, and hopefully you have enough altitude, you just push the nose down to keep your airspeed until you decide where to put her down. Sure, if you keep the nose up and you are losing airspeed, she'll stall. And then, right, you fall to the ground like a wounded bird. Oh hell, I'll have to show you what I mean."

"That would be very interesting," I say with forced calm, trying not to betray too much enthusiasm, for fear he may change his mind.

"It's really a little, bitty aircraft. I sure hope you won't be disappointed. Now Vincent has a real beaut of a flying machine, a G Model Staggerwing Beech. They only made about twenty-five of them. Classics they are. Vincent treats his like it was made of gold. I swear he loves that plane more than his women. It seats five people and has the range of a Bonanza. It is a biplane, ya know?" He sets his drink down to demonstrate with one hand above the other what a biplane is. "Except the lower wing is situated slightly in front of the upper wing. That's supposed to provide more lift and shorter landings along with the stability of the two wings."

Even though he is going way over my head, I feel like a bird in a cage about to be set free, to take wing.

"Say, if you're free tomorrow—it's Sunday, you know—you might want to take a drive with me to Half Moon Bay. I need to bring some airplane parts to Jake, who owns the flight service there. If the weather permits, we could go up in the Cub. That is, if you think you might enjoy something like that. I could give you a few pointers on flying. I'm not the expert Vincent is, of course. He is a licensed flight instructor. But I do know a thing or two about aviation."

"Well, I have nothing planned for tomorrow, maybe just to organize my apartment, but that can wait a while. Actually, I would very much like to."

There is a knock at the door, which is ajar anyway. Dr. Ted Burkhart pokes his head in. "Hi, kids, can I come in?" Typical of the men I have met around here, without waiting for an answer, he is already in and striding toward us. "I ain't interrupting any ole thing now, ahm I?" His Texas drawl is intense.

Thom smiles. They seem like old friends and cohorts. "Hell, no, Ted. Sit yourself down on any packing case or windowsill. What can I get you to drink?"

"Oh, any ole thing is fine with me. I am already stewed on Vincent's champagne. I ain't hard ta please, ya know." He looks at me with a cross between something like a wide grin and a leer like a Cheshire Cat. His whole face is engaged in the smile.

I shift a bit on the sofa and cross my legs, wondering if maybe I should offer to help Thom with the drinks. But he goes to the kitchen, deliberately leaving me with this cat-like man who sits there continuing to smile. There is a silence between us of interrupted social discourse. It all feels like the men's fraternity house in college.

Thom returns with the vodka tonic for Ted. "To yer health," he says, and we grab our drinks dutifully and drink.

"Jeezus," exclaims Burkhart, "that Vincent is incredible! There's a whole load of furniture down there. Yesterday, he just went to Butterfield's Auction and bought a whole houseful of furniture and installed it. Didn't pay all that much either. He's got a set of crystal, everything for the kitchen—pots, pans, dishes, you name it. There's paintings, rugs, chesterfields, chairs, tables, dining room set—complete, mind ya—bedroom set, fireplace outfit, towels. He's even got drapes and curtains. Ah swear, the place looks like he's lived there for thirty years."

We take in this information without comment.

Burkhart continues wearing what appears to be a perpetual grin. He needs a shave. Something about him makes it appear as if he is always thinking of a dirty joke to tell but thinks the better of it and keeps it to himself.

He is slightly stooped at the shoulder, as though he may consider himself a little too tall. He sits with one leg crossing the other, swinging the leg back and forth in constant nervous motion. His hair is dark and receding, with touches of gray. His eyes squint as though he may have spent too much time in the bright Texas sun.

When he stops smiling, his mouth droops into a pout. As he talks, he frequently licks his lips, and he obviously likes to talk. "Y'all should go down there and see the place. You'd be mighty impressed, ah tell ya."

"We haven't been invited," Thom comments with mock hauteur. "Besides, we might interrupt him in the sack with that new broad he's got with him."

"So what? We're all buddies. Let's go down and see the place. Hell, you're the landlord, for Chris' sake. Don't you agree, Joanna, that we should all go downstairs and see Vincent's new flat?"

I nod uncertainly, having no authority in the matter.

"Come on! Grab the vodka, and let's pay a social call on your new neighbor."

Propelled by this irresistible force, with drinks in hand, Thom clutching the vodka, we file down the dirty green-carpeted stairs to my former flat. The door also is ajar. The changeover is truly astonishing. It does look like a place that has been lived in for a lifetime.

"Hi, there! Come on into my humble abode. Sit down anywhere you like!" exclaims our new host, Vincent. His face is flushed from the champagne.

He winds up the cord on the vacuum cleaner then drags it into the hall closet where my winter coat, ski equipment, and ice skates still reside in a cardboard box. He doesn't seem to notice my belongings, and I am reluctant to say anything at the moment.

I catch a glimpse of the blonde woman doing something in the kitchen, maybe preparing supper. I think, a wifely thing to do.

We ease onto the flowered chintz-covered chesterfields. I was taught to call them sofas or couches, but here they say *chesterfield*. It sounds rather imperial, and I decide to call them that from now on.

The décor is early American, colonial. A huge round hooked rug covers the whole living room floor. The furniture is arranged in a cozy manner all around the room. Heavy carved-maple tables are carefully placed next to the chairs and chesterfields. Sheer, ruffled curtains hang from the picture windows, somewhat obstructing the view of the entrance to the Golden Gate.

Glancing into the next room, where just this morning my artist's studio had been, I see a formal dining room with a large table and chairs for twelve people. The buffet holds a complete set of wine, champagne, water, and cognac, cut-crystal goblets, also for twelve people. The walls are covered with antique prints of horses and old-fashioned airplanes. A large oil painting of a violinist lovingly playing his instrument hangs over the mantelpiece. It is painted very realistically, the hands rendered in a difficult position holding the bow and fingering the strings. The place is spotless, my charming, rebellious dust balls consigned to permanent exile.

"Well," humphs Thom for emphasis, "you certainly got this all together real quick, I'd say." He smirks a little as he speaks, brushing his hand over his mouth as though to keep from saying something he shouldn't. There is a cynical attitude at work here in this man, one that seems out of keeping for a man of his stature, his position in life, a defense against … what?

The drinks continue to flow like water over a dam. "Mary Belle, get your lovely ass in here. Fix us some Tanquerays on the rocks if you don't mind. You don't mind, do you?" orders her boss, Vincent, who is slumped down into a big overstuffed chair covered with rose-patterned chintz. He seems incongruous with all the old-fashioned frills, the ruffles, the lace, the roses, but somehow it does nothing to dispel his manly aura.

Thom goes to the kitchen with his vodka and leaves it with Mary Belle, who is now in charge of serving drinks.

"How can you drink vodka when there is Tanqueray gin on the premises?" asks Vincent, offering us all cigarettes. They are unfiltered Camels.

I take one, and he immediately produces a lighter and lights my cigarette. This is indeed fun!

"Ah, hell, I'll drink rubbing alcohol if there ain't anything else," says Thom, lighting one of his own Chesterfields.

Night has fallen. The dark and the fog take hold, surrounding the building high on the hill. The fire blazing in the fireplace is keeping the room warm and cheerful. The streetlight outside the window shines on the swaying eucalyptus trees, their long leaves dripping moisture glistening brightly through the sheer window curtains. The drinks, together with the wispy fog floating by, make me feel as though we are all drifting along somewhere together—an unlikely crew.

"Say, y'all, even with the fire, it's chilly in here," notes Burkhart.

"Talk to my landlord. The heater's on the bum," says Vincent, exhaling luxuriously.

"Ah, hell, I'll have someone come next week to fix the thing. Throw some more wood on the fire and put on a sweater. The little lady here never complained," says Thom, the lord of the manor.

I smile self-consciously, shrinking back into the stuffing of the chesterfield, aware of being used as a distraction.

I catch Vincent looking at me every so often. He does frighten me a little, or maybe more than a little. I have nothing to contribute to the conversation, which revolves around certain legal cases, hospital politics, and planned vacation trips in their airplanes.

Mary Belle carries in the drinks on a tray, with little plates of peanuts. Tall, with rather gaunt features, she looks intelligent but angry for some reason. She does not smile as she serves the drinks and doesn't speak to me. And no one bothers to introduce us.

She hurries back to the kitchen. Vincent jumps up and follows her, and I hear them arguing in muffled tones.

"Oh, say, Ted, I'm going down to the airport tomorrow. Ya want me to take anything to Jake?" says Thom, lighting another cigarette.

"Yeah, to get that oil leak fixed on my Beech Bonanza. Ah'm gonna have to make a trip to mah ranch this month. Lotta cattle to sell off, and Ah don't trust those bastards working for me. Jake sure takes his sweet ole time. Does his own stuff first, and then finally gets around to poor little ole you and me."

"Whadya think of all this furniture?" asks Thom, his smirk more pronounced than ever.

"Ah think he got it all so cheap cuz no one *wants* this funky, ole-fashioned stuff anymore. Oh well, it does the job, right?"

They continue talking aviation, law, and malpractice suits, while I struggle to stay sober. I feel the day is portentous, that something going on here is critical to my blur of a future, but as to what it is, I have no idea.

Having married at nineteen, I feel I had atrophied emotionally and intellectually ever since. As a good wife, like my mother, I did, thought, ate, and looked the way my husband wanted. Now, I am forced to think for myself, take responsibility for myself, make decisions all alone, and it is more than a bit frightening. I was never prepared for this. I decide to go slow and easy.

Vincent returns, but the woman stays in the kitchen. I study these men as best I can through my alcoholic blur. The feeling of helplessness is familiar and reassuring. After all, aren't women supposed to be helpless, at the mercy of men?

These are professional men in their prime. They appear to be very successful and enjoying their lives in this beautiful city. They seem to me to be enormously self-confident. They laugh, joke, and take lovers as they please. They are attractive and interesting. I have had no experience with men like these, but something tells me I will in due time.

I take a sip of whatever is in front of me. All of a sudden, I am drunk. The living room and its occupants fade from view, and I vaguely realize I am lying passed out on the new/old chesterfield. The face of Thom fades and refocuses in front of me, and at times I see two of him.

"Oh, say, there, are you okay?" Nothing exists for me at the moment except that florid, smiling, Irish face with the white hair now falling forward into his incredibly blue eyes.

Somehow, someway, he guides me gently down the back stairs, past the furnaces that need to be fixed, the pipes, and the gurgling tubes and drains, the fat, snaky air ducts, to the street level, through the basement door, into my tiny entrance hall.

He fumbles for the key and lets me in. I stagger shakily toward the bedroom, manage to climb the three steps to my bed on the platform, where I promptly collapse—an ignominious end to my first foray into my new life.

CHAPTER THREE

The Flight

The phone ringing on the floor next to my bed awakens me in the morning.

"Hi, there. How ya doin'?" Thom speaks in a sweet, concerned tone of voice.

How nice to have someone worried about me! "I, uh, don't feel too good. Actually, if you want the truth, I feel horrible." My voice is raspy from smoking unfiltered cigarettes, and I am weak from what I recognize to be three sources: lack of food, a hangover, and the onset of menstruation. I rub my hand over my ribcage, which resembles that of those unfortunate refugees in concentration camps during the war. I crave eggs and a steak sandwich right now.

"Oh, my, do you still want to go flying with me?"

"Well, of course, I do!" I do not want to miss out on this great opportunity to continue my new life. "I suppose I just drank too much yesterday. I'm not used to that, you know. My husband and I lived very temperate lives. That all seems to be changing somehow for me."

"Don't worry about it. I'll be right down there and have you in flying shape before you know it, okay?"

I drag my emaciated body from the bed and stagger to the bathroom, still in my tight jeans and Mexican blouse. I feel as though I am going to throw up. I sit on the toilet, my head cradled in my hands, bleeding profusely. The bed is probably bloody, too, I think to myself as I toss the soiled clothes in a heap behind the door. I put a robe over my nakedness, get a drink of water in the kitchen, and answer the knock on the door. How nice of him to knock first!

"Jesus Christ, you do look pretty awful—white as a ghost and skinny as a rail. We better get some food into you," Thom says as he follows me to my bed, where I collapse again. He stands over me, hands on his hips, a slight smile about his mouth, surveying the damage.

I pull the blankets up over the blood spot, but he has already seen it. "I got my period, on top of everything else, and the cramps are killing me, Thom." I mean, after all, he is a doctor and must know about women's cycles.

"Ah, yes, the cry of the unfulfilled womb!"

"Huh?"

He laughs. "That's an old wives' tale, you know. The older nurses at the hospital are skeptical about modern medical theories and claim that cramps are nature's way of punishing selfish young women who don't want to be bothered having children or else they don't want to ruin their nice figures by becoming *enceinte*." He is fumbling about in his shirt pocket and produces two small vials of pills.

"What does *enceinte* mean?"

"Pregnant—that's how they say it. Now, open your lovely mouth and swallow these little pills, and you will feel like a new girl."

"But Dr. Kelley—I mean, Thom—I don't take pills. My mother is a naturalist, and she raised us to—"

"Don't be silly! Forget your mother. I'm the doctor. Mankind is superior to animals precisely because we know enough to take medicine for our pain and illnesses. Now, open wide!"

He is irresistible. I swallow the pills with the leftover water.

"One is for your headache, and the other for the pain in your gut. Don't worry. They are compatible. Now, in a few minutes, you will feel better. Take a bath. You don't smell too good right now. Put on a nice dress. And come upstairs. I will fix you a great breakfast, and you will never know anything was wrong with you. We'll take a nice spin in my T-Bird down the coast. I might even put the top down—all that fresh sea air, ya know. Just wait and see."

He leaves, and I linger in bed waiting to see what happens. Gradually, I do begin to feel better. The cramps seem to recede. They are still there but farther away and don't bother me anymore. My headache also goes. How wonderful! I think as I slowly rise and float to the bathroom in order to shower.

Afterward, I languidly search for something pretty to wear on this, the second day of my new life. I want to look beautiful, womanly. Could I be falling in love, I wonder, "with this kindly, interesting man?"

I choose a sheer, lacy silk blouse and a full denim skirt. The skirt hangs on my bony hips, so I cinch it all together with an elasticized belt. I put on some sandals from Mexico, the usual makeup, and then the final appraisal in the mirror. I am pale and look sick, but in a romantic way, like Garbo in *Camille*. I find a handbag and fill it with necessities.

Before going up the back stairs, I look out the front window to see if the Austin-Healey is still parked there. It is, so I lock my door and drift up the back steps to Thom's kitchen door. It is open, awaiting my arrival.

"Hi, there! Feel any better?" he asks cheerfully as he carries a frying pan heaped with scrambled eggs to the kitchen counter.

"Yes, I do, a lot better."

The eggs fall heavily onto the two plates. They are quite overdone. He takes two pieces of semi-burnt toast from the toaster, slathers them with margarine, and adds some twisted pieces of bacon alongside the yellow eggs. My stomach heaves, but he is right: I must eat.

"Hey, would you please grab that pineapple marmalade there? And let's eat in the living room. It's hell not having a proper table, but I will get one."

We sit on the old sofa and eat. The empty glasses, overflowing, smelly ashtrays are shoved to one side. I force myself to down the eggs, toast, and bacon. He brings two cups of instant coffee with powdered cream, something I had never seen before since we always used real coffee and real cream and real butter. My mother would be appalled at this synthetic diet, but it does give me a little strength.

His black Thunderbird sports car is parked in the garage underneath my bedroom. He presses a button in the hall as we leave, and the garage door begins slowly to open to reveal the shiny black, slightly sinister-looking vehicle. I am thrilled. It looks like a kind of Batmobile. He puts the top down, and I have the feeling I am in high school again.

He has prepared himself well. He wears a light-blue cashmere turtleneck sweater and a dark-gray wool sports jacket. The blue sweater accentuates the blue of his eyes.

He sends me for a warm coat while he takes the car out to the street. I put on a full-length black wool coat left over from the frigid winters of Chicago. I match the car. The fall weather is chilly, typical October climate in San Francisco, with perhaps a threat of rain. He helps me into the car.

We swing around the Austin-Healey and are soon winding our way through the quiet Sunday morning streets to the coastal Highway 1. I wonder how we must look—the dignified, silver-haired physician and his dark-haired, much younger companion. I feel I am not me.

He drives rather fast, and we are almost screeching around the curves, the cold sea pounding right below us, the ocean spray fogging the windshield. I am enchanted, as I always have been with this part of the California coast. He turns the radio on to '50s rock music and smiles at me briefly to see how I am taking to all of this.

Half Moon Bay Airport is set on a windy plateau some twenty-four feet above sea level. He parks in front of the coffee shop. This establishment appears to serve multiple purposes: office, flight communication, and restaurant. "Hi, Jake! How ya doin'?" Thom waves in a jovial manner to the sturdy, rather swarthy man behind the desk wearing a worn, dark brown leather flight jacket, a blue work shirt, and jeans.

A cigarette dangles from the corner of his mouth. His black hair is thinning. Green eyes glower beneath a bushy thatch of eyebrows, and his scowl appears to be fixed. When he manages to smile briefly at Thom—a client, after all—it is as though he had changed faces for a moment. He badly needs a shave.

"Hey, I'd like you to meet my new tenant—well, old-new tenant in the building. She likes flying! Now isn't that a kick? Joanna, this is Jake Morenetti, commander-in-chief of the Half Moon Bay Airport and flight service."

Jake comes around from behind the desk and shakes my outstretched hand in the briefest possible time, averts his eyes from mine, mumbles something like, "Pleased ta meetcha," and with the formalities over, proceeds to ignore my existence. "Goddammit, Kelley, tell those two bums Cooper and Burkhart I am doing all I can to get their goddamned planes flying, like I don't have enough work as it is. I work more on their equipment than I do on my own—overtime and at night."

"Parts don't just appear like magic. I gotta wait till they send the stuff from Wichita if they ain't got it at San Francisco International. And tell Ted Burkhart it ain't no simple oil leak. The pump is on the blink, so I had to order a new one. Now I don't want to hear anymore shit about their goddamned planes!"

"Jake, calm down now. Say, that's between you and them. You know I respect your opinion. Hell, you're the best goddamned aviation mechanic on the West Coast! You know that, and we all know that. Oh, here's the parts you wanted. I hope they're all right."

"Thanks, Doc." He takes the brown-paper package. Jake's anger subsides as fast as it rose.

His outburst is both frightening and familiar. He strikes me as an honest man, Old World hard-working Italian, a bit leery of women. I have known a few of those.

"Oh, say, Jake, I was thinking of taking this young lady up for a spin in the Cub. How's the old bird these days?"

Jake's expression softens. "Well, gee, Doc, you ain't been flying in quite a while. You feel up to it?"

"Yeah, sure, no problem. That thing is so easy to fly, why— you know, yourself—it practically flies itself! Right?"

Jake frowns and shakes his head as though trying to eliminate some insidious doubts concerning Thom's flying ability. "Tell ya what, let's go check it out first, before you take off and land in the drink." Thom indicates that I should stay behind, have some coffee, and wait for them.

I order some black coffee. The woman who serves me is a pretty, round-faced lady, who smiles at me in a most friendly manner. Her hair is reddish-blonde and pulled back into a bun.

She appears to be about to start up a conversation with me when the radio begins to crackle and a voice struggles to make itself heard. "Half Moon Bay Airport," she identifies herself to the pilot, then gives the wind direction and velocity, barometric pressure, and general conditions of visibility, then clears him to land. She terminates the report and goes back to the lunch counter to make the sandwiches for lunch.

I am impressed by her technical knowledge. I stare dreamily out the window as my coffee cools. A small plane is landing, probably the pilot who just called in. I see another plane taxiing for position to take off—a very small plane.

"Oh!" shouts the woman. "That's them. That's the Cub going to take off." Jakes' voice cackles over the radio. "All clear!" shouts the woman into the radio, and I watch as the small plane becomes airborne.

There are many planes parked and tied down outside the hangar. They are varied, the colors and sizes quite individualistic. Some are painted with flames, like the hotrods the guys had in high school to show their power. However, fire must be the most feared element as far as these very vulnerable planes are concerned. I sip my coffee to keep my spirits up as the pain relievers wear off. I await the next developments.

After a while, the two men return, laughing, Thom's face now reddened by the gusty, coastal wind off the Pacific. "Hey, Annie, fix the doctor here up with a flight plan. He's going to make like a bird," orders Jake. The woman, Annie, is Jake's wife. She stops in the middle of a ham and cheese to begin filling out the flight plan form at the desk.

My stomach begins to turn nervously. We are really going to do it. Amelia Earhart, wherever you are, we are really going to do it! I am on the verge of my maiden flight. Stay close by, I silently intone to Amelia's ghost.

"This little lady has never been up in a plane in her life, now whaddya think of that?" he says to Annie as he shows his pilot's license registration number as Annie continues filling out his form.

"Destination?" she asks.

"Oh, I dunno." Thom waves his hand in the air. "Just here and there, not anywhere in particular. We'll be back soon."

Annie smiles in a friendly way and introduces herself. "Nice ta meetcha."

"Joanna," I say, giggling a little, as we seem to be getting closer to take off. "Yes, this will be my first time, but I have always been fascinated by flying since I was a child and I—"

"Oh, gawd!" she exclaims. "I'm so sick of flying. Jake *forced* me to learn so I could co-pilot with him or bring planes here for repairs from other airports, from Sacramento or Stockton. Jake is the hero around here, the best aviation mechanic on the West Coast. But flying, for me, is just another day's work."

I am shocked. It's like someone saying they don't believe in God.

There are some customers at the counter from the plane that just landed, and she excuses herself to wait on them.

"That's Annie, for ya, always complaining—she don't know how good she got it," sighs Jake. "Well, good luck. Keep it straight and level, and don't fall out of the sky whatever you do." He chuckles as he hands Thom the keys to the Super Cub.

My stomach gives another lurch.

Out on the tarmac, there is a brisk late-morning breeze wafting over the airport. The planes bob around on their tie-downs as if they want to fly, bored being parked here endlessly by their hard-working owners.

"Oh, there's Vincent's plane over there. See that big orange and white biplane?"

I look over to where he is pointing, and yes, there it is, bigger than the rest of the planes, kind of bulky-looking, with an old-fashioned nose to it where the propeller is attached. Curious.

Thom stops a moment to give me a lecture on the plane. "Only about twenty-five or thirty of them ever made—the G Model Staggerwing—really famous now. A couple of them have gone down. Makes the ones that are left more valuable. I don't know how many are left. Vince can tell you. He's a real aficionado."

He takes my arm, and we stroll over to the plane. "Now the whole plane is canvas-covered, like my Cub—hell, like the canvases you paint on. Stretched on a wood frame, strong and lightweight—same idea—then coated with glue then painted—same goddamned thing."

"Really!" I am surprised, never having given a thought to what planes were made of, only entranced by the romance of aviation.

"Here, get up onto the wing step and look inside." He pushes me up.

The seats are plushly upholstered in beige leather, the flight panel covered with a multitude of unfathomable—at least to me—dials and gauges of different configurations. Could my brain ever master such a conglomeration of technical information and actually fly this beautiful creation, his great canvas bird?

Thom continues, "Now this color is not orange, mind you. It is *international* orange and plain white. Vincent is a stickler for that kind of thing—call a spade a spade, you know. That's a lawyer for you. The engine is a Pratt & Whitney supercharged radial, those nine cylinders arranged in a circle around the nose, right out there in front."

The nose points skyward. It's huge propeller seems to be praying to the sky; it has spiritual quality. Perhaps that is what accounts for the reverence with which men speak of it.

Thom delights in imparting details. "Has quite a range, you know, for a single-engine aircraft. We flew to Cabo San Lucas in it without stopping once. Had to pee in big pickle jars—rough on the women. Five of us made the trip: Vincent, his wife, me and Victoria, and Ham Sado, the Japanese flower farmer from Half Moon Bay Valley."

We keep walking among the planes. "Now over there is Dr. Burkhart's Beech Bonanza. See the tail on it? A butterfly tail it is called. Real efficient, but hard to fly. Vincent likes to joke about it—says if you overstress the thing in a right turn, the wings come off. Ha-ha, he likes to scare people, you know."

The wind off the sea is refreshing, and soon we stop in front of the smallest aircraft on the field—a mosquito among the big moths. "Uh, this is my Super Cub. Kind of little, doncha think?" He laughs apologetically. "You get to love these after a while—really safe little aircraft. Put it down anywhere—a pasture, a highway, even the beach where the sand is still wet from the waves."

He begins to untie the ropes holding the plane down. "Why don't you get in before I untie it—weigh it down a bit so it doesn't take off by itself." He chuckles happily as he helps me into the back seat.

I squeeze in around the stick protruding from the floor. What is this for I wonder.

There is enough drugginess left in my body to project my anxiety into the distance—not far enough, however. It hovers there, reluctant to ruin this whole experience. Despite that, the thoughts tumble around my brain: I hope this man knows what he is doing. If we crash, my newly planned life of "great meaning" and "artistic success," my future, my unborn children will all come to nothing.

Thom glances back at me, grinning as he squeezes into the front seat. "You're not scared, now, are ya?"

"No, of course not. This is going to be fun, something I have always wanted to do."

"Okay, belt yourself in there. Too bad we are getting a late start. A little earlier and we could have gone to the Nut Tree in Sacramento for lunch. They have a landing field right next to the restaurant. But we don't want to take the chance of getting caught in the fog."

"Fog?"

He clicks into his seatbelt and starts moving dials, switches and shaking the stick around. "Yeah, the fog rolls in around 4:00 or 5:00 in the afternoon and you can't see a thing. Look out over the ocean."

There, on the western horizon, far in the distance, hovers the fogbank, stretching from north to south as far as the eye can see, getting ready to roll in this afternoon. I think the fluffy, white, vaporous clouds look like cotton stuffing suspended above the cold, tumultuous, gray sea.

"You strapped in?" he shouts as the engine begins to roar. "Clear!" he shouts, and the plane begins to tremble. I hear him talking on the radio, but the noise makes it impossible to hear what he says.

My anxiety abruptly overcomes the sedatives to warn me that there is *no turning back!* Thom's left hand slowly begins to move the throttle forward, and we begin to taxi toward the runway. My heart is pounding hard, adrenaline rushing to prepare me to fight or flee from this apparent folly, but I can do neither.

We stop at the beginning of the runway, and he talks over the radio to Annie, who is the closest thing to an air traffic controller here. I imagine her, mayonnaise jar in one hand, microphone in the other, giving him the weather and wind conditions and then finally permission to take off. The engine roars louder and louder as the plane strains at the brakes. The rudder pedals move up and down. The stick between my legs goes back and forth, obeying the commands of the pilot as he goes through the checklist.

"Say, now," Thom shouts back at me, his mouth skewed in my direction, "ya wanna fly to Marin County? We can fly over the Golden Gate, a really pretty trip."

"Sure, Thom, that would be great. I'd love it," I say after taking a deep breath, hoping my voice doesn't quaver. I am in his hands for better or for worse. How many of his patients have felt this way before going under the anesthesia/knife for surgery I wonder.

"See any other aircraft around? We don't want to hit anyone, ya know."

Oh, he is giving me some responsibility for this flight, so if we run into someone landing at the same time we are taking off, it will be a fatal error we both share. I crane my neck forward and to the sides and see nothing but blue sky with a few patchy clouds. But maybe there is someone behind us where I can't see, you never know. I worry, but tell him there are no airplanes visible.

He slowly moves the throttle forward until the roar of the engine equals the roar of my pounding heart. Then, abruptly, he releases the brakes, and we begin to roll down the runway. The grass and the weeds alongside of us whiz by, jackrabbits scatter, and the coffee shop is left in the distance with the tied-down planes. The sea is pounding on the rocks practically next to us.

Suddenly, the plane gives a little lurch, and we are in the air! He points to the airspeed indicator and informs me that we became airborne somewhere between fifty and sixty miles an hour. Why, my little Triumph sports car can go faster than that!

We gain altitude over the steely gray sea, the huge waves rolling and crashing below, the spray leaping many meters into the air. The plane bounces up and down erratically, tossed about like a feather in the irregular air currents above the surf. I glance out toward the west, and the fogbank looks much larger and closer from the air than it did from the ground a short time ago. Gradually, as my panic subsides, the excitement and pleasure of the experience take over.

"Don't worry about the rough air! That's normal here! I'll get my airspeed up, and we will gain some altitude, find a level where it's not so turbulent!" Thom shouts over his shoulder.

The bouncing around begins to affect my stomach, and I say a little prayer not to vomit all over this lovely little airplane. Soon, it all calms down, my stomach and the air turbulence.

I notice we are flying over a populated beach. There are people running around or sunning themselves, dogs frolicking, and some young people playing Frisbee. Looking more closely at these sun worshippers, I realize they are all stark naked!

Thom drops the plane down to a lower altitude to give me a better look at this phenomenon. We can make out the exposed pubic hair, breasts, and penises bouncing along happily with their owners. It looks as though some of them are waving and shouting at us, but of course we can't hear a thing. Some deliberately expose themselves, the men cradling their organ in one hand and calling our attention to it with the other. Some women spread their legs gleefully, others arching their backs to show off their breasts. Sort of flashing, but without any clothing the effect is rather diminished. Thom turns to catch my reaction. He is smiling impishly. "Nude beach!" he shouts. "You can't wear clothes there."

I return a weak smile, somewhat shocked at what I had just seen. I look back at the fading figures on the chilly beach, so fragile in comparison to those great monolithic rock formations surrounding them and the relentless pounding of the merciless sea. It all reminds me of some paintings we studied in college in my art history class—kind of a rendition of hell, but cold.

We are now flying along about the level of Highway 1, the cars traveling at a speed not much slower than ours. The passengers gawk and gesture in our direction. I begin to laugh. This must make a fairly outrageous scene. I wonder if we are breaking any laws flying so low. I feel better and begin to really enjoy it all. This is fun!

We begin to climb. "Pedro Point!" shouts Thom, a conscientious tour director. Pedro Point is an extended outcropping of rock. The strata indicate it had been turned on its side, probably in one of the huge earthquakes that must have taken place along here. On the southern border of the point is an inaccessible cove. The surf hits the point and splits violently. It is fascinating, and I vow one day to return here and make a drawing of the cove. A drawing, though it cannot equal reality, can be a way of coming to terms with what is inexpressible in any other form except, perhaps, music.

Soon, off to the right stretches the seemingly endless rows of identical little houses—Daly City, the developer's dream and the ecologist's nightmare. Thom continues the climb.

I have become accustomed to the bouncing around. I have taken on a fatalistic attitude. If we go down in this plane, at least it will be an interesting death. It's not like succumbing in a sterile hospital room, punctured by myriad intrusive needles and tubes, or a stroke at the sink while washing dishes or a heart attack polishing the silver. This is exciting.

We overfly Fleishhaker Zoo. "San Andreas Fault!" shouts Thom. I try to identify the famous fault line but see only an unremarkable rock formation extending into the ocean. There are some bent-over cypress trees marking the fault line, but civilization has successfully blotted out its visibility.

Twin Peaks jut up into the air below us. I know he is going to fly over the house on Upper Terrace, our house. The whole city of San Francisco spreads out below us, almost like an island surrounded by water on three sides. Market Street slashes diagonally from Twin Peaks down to the bay, ending in the Ferry Building. The rolling hills are a series of peaked roof tops flowing down toward the high-rises of downtown and the financial district. The skyscrapers are not too tall; the city is still young.

We circle over Mount Olympus. I see Vincent's Buick parked where it was this morning and behind it the little Austin-Healey. I imagine the lovers spending Sunday morning in sensual bliss. Thom continues circling, hoping someone will come out and wave at us, but no one does. Thom levels the plane out and heads toward the Golden Gate Bridge and Marin County.

As he climbs, I notice the stick between my legs moving back, and when he descends, it goes forward. In the turns, it goes from one side to the other. A ha, I think, this is what guides the plane!

There are pedals on the floor that also move according to the maneuvers of the plane. The rudder is at the back of the plane, and that goes from side to side, while the small wings attached to the bottom of the structure go up and down. I must carefully study all of this in order to be able to fly a plane one day.

Thom reaches his cruising altitude at about 3,500 feet, which he indicates to me on the altimeter. He lights a Chesterfield and passes it back to me then slides the side window open slightly and lights one for himself. We both relax.

"Chrissy Field!" he shouts over his shoulder. It is the Presidio airfield next to the Golden Gate. "You can use it for an emergency landing if you need to," he informs me. In the three years I have lived in San Francisco, I never knew it existed.

The thought of making an emergency landing there is titillating. I dreamily begin to imagine myself flying my own aircraft alone, when suddenly the engine begins to sputter, and the plane loses altitude. There I am, out over the ocean, but I can see Chrissy Field just ahead and pray for enough altitude to make an emergency landing there.

I radio ahead that I am having engine failure. A man's voice tells me to stay calm, that they have me in their sight, and with some luck, I can make it. Skillfully, I let the nose drop enough to keep from stalling. The controller affirms the straight-in approach I am planning to make.

"There is a slight crosswind, but we know you are an expert pilot, Miss Botticelli. In any case, we are all here to cheer your safe landing. Remember to drop your left wing to compensate for the crosswind, which is coming in at a heading of about fifteen degrees at five knots."

I see the south tower of the Golden Gate Bridge looming straight ahead. I can't risk losing too much altitude, so I maneuver my plane just slightly to the right, barely missing the tower and the cables. The cars below slow down to see what is going on. The engine is now completely dead, but I see the runway ahead of me and begin to drop.

The plane touches down at the beginning of the runway without even the slightest bounce to betray any fear or incompetence. It rolls to a stop. Amid the scream of an ambulance—obviously not needed—and a host of reporters, I step down from my disabled aircraft. I dab the perspiration from my brow with my white silk scarf. Wan and pale despite my successful landing, I am very beautiful in my triumph.

I am ready to greet the hordes assembled to witness my perfect emergency landing. However, I faint into the strong arms of the very handsome captain of the Presidio, who obligingly carries me to the waiting ambulance. All around are reporters from the city newspapers eager for details of my heroic landing.

The captain, of course, has fallen hopelessly in love with me and soon leaves his boring, frumpy wife to marry me. We live happily ever after—

"Hey, you okay?" shouts Thom in my direction, interrupting my romantic daydream.

"Uh, sure …"

"Look at those Sunday sailors down there on the bay!"

Obediently, I look down on the murky, choppy waters of San Francisco Bay. The sailboats are like flocks of white butterflies, fluttering about in a random fashion.

San Francisco glistens behind us, washed clean by the sea winds and the fog. The downtown office buildings appear to be engaged in a power struggle with the hills: which will be higher? The high-rises dominate the city to end abruptly at the bay waters. Landfill has made it feasible for their intrusion into the bay, but nature can be insidious with her destructive potential.

Why do corporate kings, owners of these monolithic, modern castles built to defend their wealth, insist on putting these monuments to their egos and greed on such untrustworthy land? Earthquakes, fires, rising sea levels—at every turn, nature is there. Though under unrelenting attack herself, she continues to seduce poor mortals with her beauty, ever ready to destroy that which man has created.

Thom continues to call out instructions to me. I pull myself away from my reveries and scan the surrounding skies for other airplanes, a constant necessity, he informs me. The Golden Gate Bridge is clogged with traffic returning to the city after a weekend in the beautiful country north of San Francisco. How elegant I feel above the plebian crowd imprisoned in their automobiles, confined to their roadways, forced to inch along Highway 101 through their own self-induced miasma of carbon monoxide.

And look, there is Sausalito nestled within the skirts of Mount Tamalpais rising majestically to the west. It looks like a toy village. Perhaps it is. Many boats cling to its wharves, which jut out into the bay, like filings to a magnet. I watch the cars creep along the waterfront road, and then I am ordered to switch my attention to the mountain to our left.

"Sleeping Woman!" yells Thom, his head half-turned in my direction, his mouth skewed.

"What?" I yell back. This man is going to be very hoarse after this tour, I think.

"The ancient Indians from this area called this mountain the sleeping woman or maiden ... or whatever. From this angle, you can't see her too well, but from San Francisco it really looks like a woman stretched out resting."

The ancient Indians from around Mexico City, the Mayans, called their sacred volcano Ixtaccihautl, also the sleeping maiden. Across a small valley was her lover, the erect volcano Popocatepetl, all 17,887 feet of him. "The Mexicans had it right," I think, "placing the lovers next to each other." Here, this poor North American maiden, Tamalpais, was alone and unprotected through the millennia.

We fly over the mountain, making out the hiking trails to the transmitting tower at its uppermost peak. Thom makes a slow bank over the Lucas Valley and some of the softest, most sensually beautiful mountains of the California coastal range—female mountains, all curves, fecund clefts, and sinuous limbs extending down into ravines with clumps of dark, bushy oaks flourishing in their axes.

To start my pilot's education, Thom hands me an air chart of the area, indicating that I should attempt to find our location on the map, a confusing document similar to a road map but with Omni stations and their radio frequencies, elevations, landing strips, and special flight information for different airports. The differing shades of green indicate the contours and elevation of the land. This I would have to study and understand if I were to become a real pilot.

"Hey, there's Santa Rosa!" Thom exclaims, pointing ahead to the burgeoning urban center in the middle of a great, extended agricultural valley. We seem to be following Highway 101. "Let's head out to the coast!" he shouts. On the air chart, I follow our progress. Thom points to the compass heading of 235 degrees, and we will soon be over Tomales Bay, a narrow bay of water cutting into the Point Reyes Peninsula toward the southeast.

"There, look, that's it! That's the San Andreas Fault! Now, you can see it real good. Tomales Bay is right on top of the fault line." Thom, boyishly excited about this, is practically jumping up and down in his pilot's seat. "And after Point Reyes, it goes out to sea and reenters land at Fleishhaker Zoo, like I showed you. Ah, look, you can see how the mountains are slightly shifted along the fault line. Our neighbor, Vincent, lands *his* Super Cub in that pasture next to the bay and buys fresh oysters right from the oyster farms there. Quite a trick, landing in a little pasture like that, but he's an aerobatics pilot. That's like acrobatics, but with a plane, ya know."

The stick continues to move slightly forward as we descend over the surf of Stinson Beach. Many people are picnicking. Children and dogs run about, and even a few brave souls swim in the bone-chilling water. No one is nude except for a few individuals under six years of age. We are down even closer to the surf than at the nude beach. Children wave at us as we skim over the breakers, the windshield wet from ocean spray.

I feel like we are in a boat and wonder how we get out of the thing if his rather reckless flying lands us in the waves. I imagine the doctor wants me to admire him. To my aeronautically challenged mind he seems to be an adequate pilot. I revel in the outrageousness of it all and don't even care if we do crash. I am feeling invincible. This older, sedate-looking doctor is showing off like a teenager in a hotrod, and I am flattered. I love the spontaneity of my new life.

Thom points toward the west. The fogbank is rising and coming close into land. "We better head back, sweetie. We don't want to get caught in the muck." The stick begins to move back, pulling my skirt as we begin to climb and bank for the return trip.

We are quite high now, around 4,000 feet. The engine putt-putts over the most dangerous part, the entrance to the Golden Gate and San Francisco Bay. Tamalpais is behind and to our left, and we are over open sea. I imagine that if the engine quit now, we could make it to Chrissy Field, the way I did in my romantic little daydream, but the truth is that I don't know. I just hope the little engine keeps putting along.

The panorama of Land's End and Baker's Beach begins to unfold beneath us. There is the Palace of the Legion of Honor, looking very small from this altitude, nestled within its tiny park on the bluffs overlooking the Pacific. Then comes the long stretch of Ocean Beach, the reverse of our earlier flight but now at a higher altitude.

The fog is rolling in thick and fast. Thom shouts back to me, "Make sure your seatbelt is cinched good and tight!"

He turns on the radio, fiddles with the dials, and gives his plane registration and number. I hear what I suppose is Annie's voice through the static giving him the wind velocity, direction, and barometric pressure. Then a male voice intercedes: "Get your goddamned ass in here, Kelley, because in five minutes this runway is going to be socked in." That must be Jake I hear through all the crackling. "I don't wanna lose no customers!" he adds as he signs off.

Wisps of fog are drifting over the highway as we rapidly descend, barely clearing Pedro Point. We are still under the approaching fog, and Thom doesn't bother entering the landing pattern, aiming for a straight-in approach no matter what. He continues to give our position on the radio.

We dodge the larger accumulations of seemingly innocent condensed moisture that are thickening at an alarming rate. It is close to 4:30 in the afternoon, and the sunlight is obscured now. I see the hills fly by us through the puffs and crane my neck in an effort to see the runway at Half Moon Bay.

There it is, in the distance. I feel we are in a race between us and the drifting fog. We pass through several dense formations where I can see nothing at all, as though we are buried in gray snow, then we are out again and the runway is directly in front of us.

The rudder pedals are moving up and down erratically, and the stick jerks back and forth in short, tense movements. I shrink from their activities, fearing I might interfere inadvertently with the delicacy of the landing and kill us both. My invincibility has vanished along with the visibility.

Within moments, we hit the runway then bounce back into the air, the stick and rudder continuing their frantic movements. We hit again and bounce again, but this time not so high. The plane stops flying, and we thud to the ground and stay there. The stick is in neutral, and the brakes are screeching. We have landed!

Thom taxis to the tie-down, wheels the plane around into the wind, and turns back to me, grinning broadly. He is sweating profusely, his face quite pallid. My ignorance serves as a protection from fear. "Jeezus Christ, that was a sure shit-in-your pants landing. Sorry, I guess I need some practice. Pardon me, but the other thing is that in another minute or two, we wouldn't have been able to land here. We would have had to go over the mountains to San Francisco International. And maybe we couldn't get in there, either, without instruments, and then you can flat run out of fuel, get lost in this muck wherever …"

Everyone in the coffee shop turns to stare at us as we make our way to the counter to close Thom's flight plan. Jake is shaking his head back and forth. "I can't believe you, Doc! Why don't you keep in touch with the radio? Look at that stuff out there!"

From the big picture windows, nothing is visible but a solid mass of thick, grayish fog. "I fuckin don't know how you made it here. You should have called in earlier. You should have been back here an hour ago. Oh, pardon my language, miss."

Thom is all smiles; he is enormously pleased with himself. It was a wonderful little adventure for him—the risk, the pretty girl, the attention. "A miss is a good as a mile,"so they say. "All's well that ends well" and so forth. "Say, we're going over to Dan's for a nip or two. We have to celebrate the little lady's first flying lesson. See ya there!" Thom waves jauntily.

We leave Jake shaking his head. I get the feeling he doesn't think much of the doctor's flying ability or his judgment.

Dan's is an Italian roadside restaurant along Highway 1 on the way back to the city. The bar is at the entrance, and my first impression is one of excess. There are pinball machines and soccer-playing machines crowded up against one another. A glowing jukebox takes up a corner space.

The walls are covered with stuffed and mounted animal heads—deer, bear, mountain lions, and eagles. There are paintings and posters of Italian pastoral scenes, adorable babies, churches, vineyards beside aviation posters of classical old airplanes, the Red Baron, Charles Lindbergh, and of course my heroine, Amelia Earhart. Interspersed are paraphernalia like goggles and helmets, parts of wrecked airplanes and non-functioning, obsolete instruments. Plastic flowers and pinups of sexy, voluptuous women complement the odors assailing one's nostrils upon entering. The place smells of booze, sawdust, oregano, garlic, bathroom deodorant, tobacco smoke and women's perfume.

Thom indicates I slide onto a barstool. Part of the dining room is visible through a wide, red-draped doorway. There, large families are assembled at tables, eating from huge plates of delicious-looking food. Hunger is tugging at my senses. The bartender smiles as he wipes the shiny wooden bar in front of us and waits. Thom orders us two vodka martinis, which arrive along with a bowl of peanuts and popcorn.

The drinks are cold, and beads of condensation form around the cone-shaped goblet. There is an olive with a red touch—a piece of pimento is stuffed into it—at the end of a toothpick. It strikes me as beautiful and I stare, fascinated by the lovely drinks. Everything is so vivid, so new to me! I feel I will remember this day for the rest of my life.

"Here's to your health and, of course, to your first flight! May there be many more!"

We sip our drinks. I am enjoying the doctor's formalities. Hmm, strong stuff! I think as the liquor hits my stomach. I munch some popcorn to ease it all down my throat.

"So, whaddya think of the flight? Fun, huh? Sorry I scared you there at the end. You just never know when you take off what you're in for. I guess we were lucky we turned around when we did at Santa Rosa. I had a hunch we'd better get our asses back to Half Moon Bay. Sometimes, it pays to play your hunches."

I dab my mouth delicately with a paper napkin. "I guess I really don't know enough about flying to even be scared," I lie. "To tell you the truth, ignorance can be bliss, right?"

"Wrong. Knowledge is power, and don't you ever forget that, sweetie. Say, you look like your blood sugar is down, scraping bottom there. How about some chow?" I assume he is inviting me to eat, which we haven't done since this morning's scrambled eggs.

The waiter seats us at a table in the brightly lit dining room. The table is covered by a clean white cloth embroidered in delicate rose and leaf patterns. It looks like it was done by hand.

Momentarily, I think of my Italian aunts and their endless output of beautiful hand-embroidered and crocheted tablecloths, napkins, towels, bed sheets, and pillowcases—an ancient domestic art that is vanishing.

Somehow, I have crossed an invisible line into another world and can only hope for the best at the moment. Two more martinis appear.

"Drink up! The best thing for a hangover," declares Thom, grinning profusely, his face animated. He shows his age, but a sense of controlled, quite abundant nervous energy makes him intriguing. He is happy now.

The waiter arrives. "How are you, Dr. Kelley?" He asks if we would like fish or steak.

"This is a family-style restaurant, you see," Thom explains. "There is this huge dinner with antipasto, Italian bread and butter, soup and ravioli, salad, then the main course, which is the only choice we get. Fish or steak, which is it?"

"Fish."

"And would you like wine with dinner?"

I nod yes, and he orders a bottle of vintage Zinfandel. He orders fresh salmon for me and steak for him. Then he settles back in his chair and looks at me, more like he *studies* me.

I squirm a bit and say I should probably go to the restroom and fix myself up. He points the way.

"Hey, Joanna, you look pretty good there with a little powder and paint!" He stands and helps me back into my chair on my return. "You know, flying isn't really as dangerous as people make it out to be. Once you understand the principles of flight and theory, you can dominate your natural fear of being suspended in the sky without any visible means of support."

"And if the engine really does quit?"

"I won't misrepresent the situation and say there is no problem, but part of your flight training—that is, if you decide to go ahead and study for your private pilot's license—is going to consist of the instructor turning off the engine, and you will have to put it down safely without power somewhere—corn field or a road or the beach, wherever."

"Oh," I murmur. Just like my fantasy daydream today, but for real.

The waiter sets a big platter of antipasto in the center of the table. There are heaps of olives, pickled herring, cheeses, vegetables—such as carrots, celery, chilies, and green onions—crackers, anchovies, pastrami and salami slices. I can hardly restrain myself from plunging into this bounty.

Then the waiter sets shining wine goblets in front of the silverware and salad plates. He then pours a small amount of wine into Thom's glass then stands back. Why so little I wonder as I watch the ritual unfold.

First, Thom swishes the wine around a bit in the goblet, then he sniffs it! Strange—I am indeed in foreign territory. He drinks it then nods his head to the waiter, who immediately fills his glass and mine three-quarters full.

I wait for a signal. He raises his glass, indicating that he wants to touch my glass. Our glasses clink together. We both drink the wine at the same time, and I carefully gauge how much he is drinking so we simultaneously set down our glasses. It is very good, nothing like the cheap stuff I was used to.

Thom picks up the bottle and studies the label. "Napa Valley Zinfandel 1959—a good year, by the taste of it."

We eat. It is all so good. "Hey, there, sweetie, you better save room for the main course now," he cautions me as he piles another pickled herring with sour cream on top of a tasty round cracker.

The dinner is meant for fieldworkers who have another five hours of hard labor ahead of them. Halfway through the salmon I give up, even though it is obviously just freshly caught that day and sweet as dandelion nectar.

"Don't worry. The waiter can put that into a doggie bag, along with the remains of my steak, and we can take it back to the house. It's great heated up for breakfast in the morning. Really gives you a good start."

The house, he says, as though we live in the same house. Well, we do in a way. As Alice remarked, "Curiouser and curiouser."

Dessert is a big dish of spumoni in three colors, with coffee and cognac. I feel stuffed and would like to sleep. "I really do intend to fly someday, Thom," I say, stifling a yawn as he takes out a credit card to pay the bill.

For me to offer to pay would be beyond ridiculous, so I just keep talking. "It is something I have wanted to do for a long time, but my husband would never permit it. And I want to thank you. It was such a beautiful day flying over the countryside like we did! You feel so, well, free, I guess, like you could go anywhere in the world just on a whim."

"Yeah, whim and a hefty bank balance. Flying isn't the cheapest pastime in the world, you know, not like roller skating or checkers."

"I do really hate to worry about money all the time. It is such a drag," I say, wishing I were home in bed.

He laughs at this. "Don't we all? But that's another fact of life, sweetie—paying the goddamned bills every month and taxes every year."

"But it's so inhibiting! Before you can do something wonderful, you have to count your pennies or worry about losing what money you may have or if someday you will be submerged in hopeless debt. It makes life so dreary when you have very little money. I just wanted my freedom and a nominal amount from my ex-husband, to be compensated for the years I worked while he studied Law."

"I sure wish I had ex-wives like you." He laughs. He says it in such a way I am not sure whether he admires me or thinks I'm pretty stupid.

"I, uh, I just don't want to spend my life gouging money out of people close to me or to work at something I hate doing just for the money. I want to be motivated by *life!* Do you understand?"

"Oh, sure. Hey, finish up your spumoni ice cream. You need some flesh on those bones."

He helps me on with my coat, and I stuff the doggie bag into my purse, which I hope won't smell like fish in the morning.

On the way out, we see Jake sitting at the bar with some other men. Thom puts his arm around him in a friendly fashion. "Hi, Jake. Say, would you fill up the Cub for me? Just put it on my account."

Jake is still hung up on our fogbound landing. "You guys are lucky to be alive, you know. A Beech Baron tried to land about fifteen minutes after you and had to go to San Jose. Just barely made it on the fuel he had left." Jake snarls his words, then adds, "I don't like nobody takin' chances like that, ya know. I need my customers."

Thom is anxious to change the subject, feeling rather humiliated by Jake's public criticism of his flying ability. "Speaking of customers, I've got one for you here. This little lady wants to learn to fly."

"Well, humph," Jake snorts, "she better be serious. I don't want no students who just take a few turns around the field and then tell everyone what a great pilot they are. If you start with me, ya gotta finish. I mean, ya gotta solo, fly all alone, all by yourself, one day. Got that?" He looks me straight in the eye and then through the eye into my mind, heart, and soul to see if I am serious or just another dilettante student.

I nod my head. "Yes, Mr. Morenetti, I really do want to learn to fly."

"And right now, I want to tell ya I don't want any of this Mr. Morenetti stuff. The name is Jake, short for Jacob, if ya wanna know the truth."

"Yes, Jake, of course. I assure you I—"

Thom interrupts, "Jake talks tough, but he's really just a big pussycat inside, right, Jake?"

Jake pulls himself up and points his finger at Thom. "Listen, Doc, I talk like I talk—ya know me by now—and I ain't no pussycat, neither. Eighteen years you been comin' around to the airport, and I never heard you or anybody call me a pussycat. What's with ya?"

"Oh, ferget it. Listen, if this girl is serious, she should phone Annie next week for an appointment." Then he turns around to laugh at something the fellow next to him says. I wonder if it is about me or the doctor.

Outside, the sea air is pungent. The mussels, oysters, starfish, anemones, and urchins are all going through their lifecycles on the rocks with the tides. We hear the waves crashing along the cliffs above the beach. The fog is so thick now. It feels as though we are in a rain cloud. The black Thunderbird, now with its top up, is glistening with moisture.

Thom opens the passenger door for me, and I slide in, reaching over to unlock his side. "I like that," he says, smiling as he starts the engine.

Driving back along the Coast Highway, the fog envelopes us. Thom puts on his fog lights—low, yellow light that is supposed to illuminate under these conditions—but they seem to make it worse. The headlights and the fog lights play off each other.

He turns the radio on to '50s music. The soothing tunes of "Peg o' My Heart" and "Some Enchanted Evening" play, among others. It feels cozy and snug inside the low-slung sports car. The heater hums quietly on low. Over it all, however, the sea can be heard thundering below—cold, menacing, and unyielding.

I can barely stay awake. Thom slowly takes my hand and places it on his thigh. I can feel the muscles of his leg working the accelerator. I can think of nothing to say. I feel my blood rising, pulsing in my neck. Inadvertently, I sigh. We drive along in silence with my hand resting on his thigh.

Only when we are in sight of the towering flats of Mount Olympus do I remove it. He turns and smiles.

We pause a moment on the sidewalk in front of my entrance. "Here, Thom, let me give you half of this doggie bag."

"Don't worry about it. Keep it for tomorrow. Your cupboard is quite bare, I noticed."

I look forward to sleep. The Buick is no longer parked in front of the building, but the Austin-Healey is. I wonder why I should even bother to notice. God's gift to women was how Donna had described Vincent Cooper.

"Say, why don't you come up to my place for a nightcap. I'll light the fire in the fireplace to warm you up a bit before you go to bed," says Thom, smiling by the light of the streetlamp.

He is so kind, I think. Yes, I will go up for a few minutes and relax with him before going down to my apartment.

Up in the flat, Thom busies himself with the fireplace logs.

He directs me to his stash of wine, a box of premium Napa Valley Chardonnay lying haphazardly on his pantry floor. I take out a bottle, the first to be removed from the carton.

I then poke around his kitchen drawers for a wine opener of some kind. The whole place is as messy and disordered as mine. The cold leftover eggs and toast from this morning's breakfast sit in mute testimony to domestic sloth.

A fire is roaring in the living room fireplace, spreading warmth throughout the fog-infested flat. The fog permeates everything— houses, clothes, cars, food, businesses, and life in general.

"You need another codeine for your tummy?"

"No, a glass of wine will do just fine. I really don't like taking too many pills."

"Didn't I tell you that mankind is superior to animals since we take medicines for what ails us?"

I pour the light yellow, glittering Chardonnay into two wine glasses, set the bottle on the so-called coffee table, and plunk down on the old sofa. Thom sits beside me, rather close. We clink glasses and drink it down. It is wonderful wine, cool but not chilled, and wakes me up.

"So, you got a kick out of that little Super Cub of mine today, eh?"

"Very much so! It's the most fun I've had in a long time, to tell the truth."

"Well, you seem very young not to be having fun, you know."

"Why doesn't everyone fly?"

"Well, like I said, it's damned expensive and hard to write off on your taxes no matter what angle you take. And then people have an innate fear of flying. They think they will fall out of the sky like Chicken Little."

"Didn't Chicken Little say that the *sky* was falling?"

"Oh, something like that. But once you understand the principles of flight, you lose your fear. Like I said, knowledge is the great liberator. Then it seems there is a certain kind of person attracted to aviation, something of a loner, usually with a spirit of adventure and a lot of self-confidence. And of course, you need a high school diploma at least. There's a lot of mathematics involved. You can't be a lame brain and fly a plane."

I laugh. "You made a rhyme."

He stands up abruptly and begins pacing. It is as though he were a professor in front of a class of—what? lame brains? Sipping the wine, he shuffles and pokes at the fire, trying to coax more cheer from the flames.

I wonder if I have said something to upset him. His mood changes seem too fast. He is actually more relaxed than he probably has been in a long time. The divorce has worn him down. I study his face by the light of the flames as though I were going to paint him.

He must have been very handsome in his youth. His features are fine and well-proportioned, his aquiline nose, aristocratic, his face long, like the old portraits of Englishmen I recall from my history classes, but of course he is Irish. Today's outing has restored color to his pale skin.

"I must say, I felt so superior while flying around up there with all those cars backed up on the freeway and we as free as a bird in your Cub," I comment in an effort to break the uncomfortable silence.

"You are right. We are superior!" he retorts imperialistically, warming to the conversation once again. "If you don't have a good strong ego, you can't do shit in this world, and don't you forget that. Most people don't use a fraction of their native abilities or intelligence. They just do enough to get by. Haven't you noticed that?"

I stare at him mutely, unwilling to admit that I had never really thought about it.

"That's what I try to get across to my students—to push themselves beyond what they consider their limits—and by god, it works! Now just look at you, for instance—the time and effort you put into your painting. You are getting better and better at it. I remember the amateur stuff you used to do when you first moved in here with your husband—or, pardon me, your ex-husband."

"You mean, you really like my work?" Praise for my artistic efforts has always been as scarce as mice in a lion's den.

"Damn right, I do! I think it's great, and it can be greater. As a matter of fact, I've been thinking of talking to you about doing some work for me. Have you ever thought about doing medical illustrating?"

He lights a cigarette and passes it to me then lights another for himself. The bottle of Chardonnay is almost empty.

"I really know nothing about medical illustration. I have no training in it. I was taught to move paint around on a canvas with a palette knife, and that's about it. The work just didn't have to look like anything recognizable, and then it was okay."

"Well, that's good training for plastering houses, but not for an artist, if you ask me. Hell, I can't draw a straight line, but I can show you what to do. I have some excellent books by the great medical illustrator Netter. He does all the work for the pharmaceutical companies. I'm gonna have to look for those. I had a whole collection for teaching anatomy."

He goes to his bedroom and comes back with a stack of books. I am tired but make the effort to see what he is aiming at. I suddenly want to be as good as he says I am. He makes me want to succeed, to triumph. He is, I suddenly realize, inspiring me.

He lays one of the books down on the table and begins turning the pages, all drawings of human anatomy, some in color and others in black-and-white. They appear extremely complex to me, an interweaving of nerves, muscles, bones, tissues, veins, capillaries, fat cells, and glands of various types, all organically and functionally interconnected.

"Like I told you, this is Netter's work. He is both an artist and an MD. He does all the work for CIBA. There are others probably just as good, but he has the name in the field."

"Now there are staff artists at UC Medical, but I have always dreamed of having my own artist to work exclusively for me. It is something you could do apart from your oil paintings and make some good money right off."

"Gosh, Thom, I don't know. It all has to be so precise. It is complicated, and I am used to making things up as I go along—self-expression, you know, and all that—creativity ..."

"Well, now, I think it would be good for you to forget all that masturbatory art and try a little self-discipline for a change and see what happens."

"Uh, what do you mean exactly by masturba—?" I know what masturbation means, but masturbatory art?

"I can see, young lady, that you are going to need a few lectures. Oops, where'd all that wine go?"

"I'll get another bottle."

"While yer at it, get some ice. This stuff is supposed to be chilled, ya know. Put a couple of bottles in the refrigerator for breakfast."

Wine for breakfast? I think to myself as I place three bottles of wine in the refrigerator and take out the ice. Where is all this going to lead? Self-discipline and masturbatory art, anatomy lessons, this is obviously not going to be a typical Midwestern college supplemental education course upon which I am embarking.

There is no more fake wood for the fireplace, so Thom is stuffing old magazines, junk mail, calendars, and newspapers, along with pieces of an old packing crate, into the fire to keep it going. "Cheers!" he says, and we continue drinking, ice cubes clinking around in the wine goblets diluting the delicious fermented Chardonnay grape juice.

"Now I want you to get over all those mental blocks you have. Hell, you can do anything you want to do, and don't forget that. I don't want to be bored by your petty self-doubts. That's what can destroy you. I see what you can do. You're good. You're gonna be great!"

I can't deal with all this, I think. The wine is making me drunk, and I must keep my head about me. This man is offering me something—a job, an education. Exactly where will it all lead? I wonder.

I plunge on, "But this anatomy, I mean it exists there in our bodies. It has to be represented correctly. For instance, if I can't draw a hand well, I can fuzz it up a bit, make it rather indistinct, Impressionistic, you know. But you can't fuzz up where a nerve intersects with a muscle and how it all connects to the vertebrae. It all has been well-thought out, so clear. Oh, god, you know what I mean—I would really have to *think* about what I was doing, concentrate, you know."

"So, what's so wrong with using your old noodle? That's what it's there for. I don't think it would do you any harm to use your brain."

"But, Thom, I don't know what goes on under a person's skin. In fact, I get faint just thinking about it. At times in art class, the instructor would bring in a model, and we would make rough drawings of limbs, postures, expression on faces, things like that, but not too realistic. We were encouraged to depart from what we saw, to paint what we felt, like Picasso. I swear, at seventeen years of age, I had about as much to express as an earthworm."

Impatiently, Thom waves aside my protests, my fears of failure. "Listen to me. In November I begin an anatomy class for first-year medical students. We will be working in the morgue at Saint Luke's Hospital doing dissections of cadavers. Specifically, I want to concentrate on the brachial plexus, since that is my field of specialization. I would like you to come along, take a sketch book, make notes and drawings for me. I need the information for some surgery I have scheduled a few months from now."

I moan unhappily. "I haven't the faintest idea what a *bralias plesnos* is."

"*Brachial plexus!*" he snaps at me as though I had uttered a blasphemy. "Here is a copy of *Gray's Anatomy*, the medical student's bible, so to speak, a basic text. I want you to study it and to make practice drawings, especially in the area of the cervical and upper thoracic vertebrae."

I take the book in both hands. It is a very large, thick, heavy tome, utterly serious. I am overwhelmed by his expectations of me. If I should refuse, would he think less of me? Would I be missing out on something very important in my life? The voice of my inner self answers me yes—or as my mother would say, "*Don't be a dodo.*"

"Now just look at this." Thom has the book open to a drawing of a human skeleton. "You study that now so you know how the human body works. Aren't you aware that every great artist has studied anatomy? Michelangelo knew more about the human body than any doctor of his time. Now you are Italian. It's in your blood to be creative. It's not that you are lazy now, is it?"

"No, I'm not lazy, Thom. I am just very tired right now. Maybe in the morning all this won't seem so difficult. Do you really think I can do this?"

"Shit, I know you can!"

Is this man a nut or a prophet? I think to myself.

I have lived by the rules up until now, accepting as gospel what my parents did and said to do. I was a good wife until it didn't make sense anymore. Then there were the books, films, my mediocre education, the newspapers, popular culture in general that influenced me. And of course I was aware of a social revolution going on, centered on the coasts of this country. I have never striven for anything on my own terms. Up until now, everything I did had been for my husband and our marriage.

Could I trust this man in front of me and what he was saying about my capacities to learn new technical applications of my art? Or did he have some ulterior motive behind his apparent good will? Why were women so protected from social and economic realities as long as they belonged to a man, but if suddenly they are separated from that man, they become vulnerable prey? This unwelcome thought strikes me as being an extremely dishonorable aspect of our society.

Thom brings another bottle of slightly chilled Chardonnay, which I don't want or need at the moment. "Lousy fire, huh? Say if it's not too much to ask of you, why don't you pick up some firewood for this joint for tomorrow?" He digs around in his pocket and comes up with a twenty-dollar bill, which he hands to me.

"This is too much for fake firewood."

As he pours us more wine, he says, "Pick up some steaks from the Chinaman down the street, if you don't mind, that is. I invite you to dinner tomorrow evening, and we can talk more about this medical drawing business, that is, if you don't have some hot date with one of those stockbrokers or insurance salesmen around town."

"No chance, Thom. Sure, I'll pick up some food for dinner tomorrow. I would be happy to."

He sits down next to me again, close but not close enough to be touching. I can't leave yet, no matter how tired I am, so I just keep drinking and listening and talking to this unusual man. I look around the flat—potentially beautiful, but dingy, like the battleground it had become. "Thom?"

"Yeah?"

"I really appreciate how much you are trying to help me, and I'd like to help you fix up your place here. A man in your position should have a decent place to live, where you could entertain people for cocktails, for dinner, a place you could be really proud of."

"You mean, you don't like my monkey-puke green walls with their battle wounds? That was Veronica for you— everything green to match her red hair she was so proud of. *Everything* was green—walls, food, clothes, rugs, furniture, car, even her underwear—like a goddamned hospital."

"You should have regal colors, Thom. After all, you live on Mount Olympus. Maybe you are Zeus reincarnated." I giggle at my boldness.

"You mean, Zeus would never have tolerated monkey-puke green walls in his palace even if Hera was a redhead?"

I am finding that Thom is such a wealth of information, an expert on ancient Greek mythology.

"Hera was a pretty independent dame. Gave Zeus hell for chasing after all the nymphs and minor goddesses there in the Greek pantheon."

"Maybe I'm Hera."

"No." He thinks about it for a moment, both of us being pretty well plastered by now. "You're a lousy housekeeper, and Hera was keeper of home and hearth. You are probably—"

"Who?" I question anxiously, desperate for a divine identity.

"You are probably... Athena! She wasn't even born from a woman, you know. She came right out of Zeus's head, his daughter. The Greeks and Romans were a lot more civilized about many things than we are."

"And what was Athena all about?"

"She was the goddess of art and wisdom. She promoted and defended civilization from the vulgar hordes. She was also the goddess of the warriors. Tall and beautiful, she led them into battle.

A powerful broad she was. You need to go to Greece and Italy to see the temples, the sculpture, architecture, and art of that time. It takes your breath away. Makes more sense than Christianity any day."

"I don't imagine Athena ever had to cook or clean toilets and floors or wash dirty socks and underwear or togas. Maybe that's why I got divorced, I must be a descendent of Athena. But, Thom, aren't you Catholic?"

"Well, shit, sure, Irish Catholic, born and baptized. But as I got older, I just couldn't buy it—original sin, for instance. How can a baby be born sinful just because his parents had to fornicate? I mean, how else do you make a kid? And then there's confession. You can do the worst things, like kill your mother, and go to the priest, confess, and ask for the Lord's forgiveness, and you are assured that God forgives you. Does that make sense?"

"When I studied catechism in Berkeley, they taught us kids that women don't have souls. I mean, Jeezus Christ, these seminary students would come into our classes and get into this long debate about whether women had souls or not."

"I had a great mother, real tough lady from Utah. My father didn't know shit from Shinola. He worked on the railroad and was drunk the rest of the time. My mother decided we were all going to be educated, come hell or high water. She wrung every cent out of Daddy that she could before he drank it away, just so we could study. I went to Berkeley Medical School before they built the medical center here in San Francisco. My other brother studied law, and my sister became a teacher."

"You must have had a wonderful mother, Thom."

"Then there is this problem of guilt."

I laugh. "Oh, I know all about guilt. I felt guilty the whole time I was married. Even though I worked like a slave and was as faithful as a dog, it seemed I could never do enough for him to be rid of the guilt."

"Guilt is what keeps you in line. Don't you know that? Every slave dreams of escape. In Catholicism, even thinking about sinning is a sin."

"It's hard to control what you think."

"But not impossible. The whole thing dovetails nicely with the rise of mercantilism and the industrial society. The pain of life here on earth is compensated for by this promise of a heavenly life, free of work, just floating around on clouds somewhere and listening to the angels sing. I remember reading Mark Twain saying something like he would prefer not to go to heaven when he died because they prohibited fornication. He'd rather be in hell with all those promiscuous sinners."

"He really said that?"

"Yeah." He raises his glass and drains it.

"I'm exhausted, Thom."

He stands, yawns, and stretches his arms, turning them back and forth. "Let me get you some codeine before you hit the sack."

"No, I don't need anything more. I feel numb all over."

"You'll sleep like a rock." He shoves the dark red *Gray's Anatomy* into my arms, a bunch of pills into my hand, then walks me down the back stairs to my apartment, all the while talking about how much he is looking forward to teaching me medical illustration and how great I am going to be.

I fumble for keys and open the door to my place then turn to give him a friendly kiss goodnight. Somehow, I find myself in an embrace with my mouth on his, but abruptly he pulls away from me.

"Later, sweetie. Goodnight." And he is gone, disappearing through the maze of air ducts, gas pipes, and drains, his footsteps echoing as he goes back up the stairs of this dim labyrinth.

I close the door behind me and lock it, wondering if something has just gone wrong here. Outside, under the light of the streetlamp is parked the little yellow Austin-Healey behind the big white Buick.

The handful of pills lie carelessly thrown on the floor next to my bed as I fall into a deep sleep.

CHAPTER FOUR

Vincent

The merciless ring of the telephone bores through Vincent Cooper's dulled consciousness. Even half-asleep, he knows he would rather not pick up the intrusive object. One arm is still around Mary Belle, and it feels a little numb from the weight of her head. She begins to stir, and he gently pulls his arm out from under her. Pins and needles race through his arm as the blood rushes back.

"Aren't you going to answer it?" she mumbles, propping herself up on one elbow, her wispy blonde hair falling over her half-opened blue eyes. She looks charming at the moment.

"Yeah, I will. I thought an unlisted telephone number would give me some privacy. Should I change it again?" he asks as he sits up and rubs his right arm to restore circulation.

"Vince, just answer it. It may be important."

"Hullo."

"Vincent!" a gruff voice shouts loudly into the phone. "The CPA is here in the office. He's been waiting for you over an hour. What the hell have you been doing?"

"Damn, I forgot about him. How the hell did you get my number, by the way?" As he speaks, he pulls the sheet over his naked bottom half as though his caller could see him. "It's Sam from the office," he whispers to his bedmate.

""I just called your house, and Phyllis, your wife, gave it to me. She sounds kind of upset. How the hell are we supposed to do business if you have an unlisted phone number?"

His wife somehow got hold of this new number, he thinks to himself. This hideaway here would now offer him no peace.

"Vincent?"

"I'm here, Sam, just thinking. Is he on to the missing trust fund money?"

"Well, I don't know, maybe. This guy's been working here since last Thursday on the accounts. Walters has been shitting in his pants. Where have you been?"

"Busy—auctions, moving, and all. Listen, I'll get down there as soon as possible. Take the CPA out for coffee or something. Thanks."

Mary Belle is now sitting up in bed. "What was that all about? How is the audit going?"

Vincent fumbles for a cigarette from a crumpled pack of Camels, lights up, and inhales deeply. "The shit is really hitting the fan. He's been there all weekend. Get some coffee going while I shower. We better get down there and face it. Goddamned Walters turns out to be a thief, and he was just about to be appointed judge in the district court."

Vincent showers quickly, barely noticing the leaks in the bathroom plumbing. He eyes himself critically in the cracked and stained mirror of the medicine cabinet. He still looks good enough he thinks, as he studies his image, good enough for what?

Blonde hair mixed with gray, blue eyes still clear, a few wrinkles here and there, but they add dignity, he decides. His shoulders are broad and his body lean. This despite a third broken marriage, not counting the short one he had when he was nineteen years old.

The serious downside is a law practice of twenty-five years now in dire jeopardy, two young children from the marriage before last to support, alimony to two ex-wives, and a mistress pressuring him to marry.

He leans farther into the mirror, opens his mouth wide, and digs out his dental plates. Carefully, he scrubs them with toothpaste so they won't smell. He avoids looking at himself at this point. His face sags and shortens, his lips collapse into his mouth, and in seconds he looks like an old man. He is forty-nine years old. Quickly, he puts the plates back into his mouth, grateful for what they do for his appearance.

He dresses in a new, lightweight beige suit that he bought this past week at the Bashford-Wilkes men's clothing store. The homosexual salesman who had supervised the minor alterations had admired him profusely.

Vincent, born and raised in San Francisco, didn't know what to make of the recent influx of homosexual men. He didn't know if he should be flattered by the fawning salesman and his suggestive touching or punch him in the nose. Thinking as a lawyer, he decided to pass it over as inconsequential.

Not like in the good old days when men were men and women were women, he thinks as he carefully knots a new dark blue and white-striped silk tie. Used to call them 'fairies'; now, they say 'gay.' Strange, since they don't seem all that happy to him.

Mary Belle, dressed in a pale blue, flowered dress from Magnin's, has coffee and sweet rolls arranged on a tray on the terrace overlooking the city. Nice touch, he thinks as he sits down. The Oakland Hills shimmer in the distance across San Francisco Bay. The day would be warm. Fall is always the nicest time of the year for him.

"Honey, I'm going to get some things together before we leave," says Mary Belle as she sips the last of the coffee and disappears into the kitchen of the flat.

Vincent stands up to admire the view. He is happy with his new home. Then he sees the girl from downstairs getting into her little red sports car. He smiles and waves to her; after all, they are now neighbors. She is actually a rather pretty thing, now that she has ceased to be an impediment to his plans.

Apparently, she does not see him. He watches as she attempts to start her small sport's car. The starting motor grinds and grinds without results. She's running down the battery, he thinks, not too smart.

The girl emerges from the car after her futile attempt to start it. He hears Kelley's automatic garage door opening, and out slips the black Thunderbird. The girl walks over to talk to Kelley. Vincent imagines she is describing her plight, then she gets into the T-Bird, and they drive down the hill.

"Vincent, it's after 9:00." Mary Belle looks very pretty with her blonde hair pulled back into a severe bun behind her head. She is almost as tall as he is and looks every inch the competent lawyer she is.

As he maneuvers their way through the heavy morning traffic, weaving, passing, cutting off other drivers, Vincent alternates worrying about his problems at the office and speculating about Thom Kelley and that girl.

"What do you think about that girl who lives downstairs in the studio? I think she calls herself an artist or something?" he asks Mary Belle as they wait for the light to change at Gough Street.

"Not too much really, Vince. She's like so many that flock here to San Francisco looking for glamor and excitement. She'll find out soon enough that it's not all that easy. I kind of feel sorry for her, poor thing. They usually end up going back to where they came from." Mary Belle comes from Nebraska.

"I heard she was married. She took off with Kelley this morning."

"Oh, really? He's way too old for her. He's in his fifties, isn't he?"

"Yeah, around there. He won't say his age—funny about that."

Vincent himself would turn fifty in April of next year: fifty years, half a century, over the hill, inexorable succession of years.

"She might go after his money. Lots of those types do that sort of thing, you know—lonely old man, lots of property around town, lucrative medical practice." She lights a cigarette for him and then for herself.

They stop again for a red light. "What about you, honey?" he says as he reaches toward her. "Are you after my money or my cock?" His hand runs up her inner thigh to her crotch. She is wearing a garter belt and no underwear. His fingers slide into the soft hair and warm folds. Her legs spread slightly. The light changes. A car behind them honks rudely. The Buick lurches forward onto Van Ness Avenue.

Vincent lets Mary Belle off at city hall with instructions: "Be sure to file those papers for BOAC before noon and check on the tax payments while you are there. We'll go to lunch at Jack's around one." Vince never asks, he commands.

As he enters the office with dread, the receptionist looks at him, a troubled expression on her face. "Good morning, Mr. Cooper."

"Hi, Sara. Is Sam here with the state auditor?"

"No, they're not back from breakfast yet. Here are your messages." She hands him a sheaf of papers, which he riffles through rapidly. Routine calls.

"I'll be in my office. If anyone phones for me, just take the message unless it's from London." Vincent needs time to think. He is up against a wall and can't see his way clear to get around it or over it. A possible felony here in the office, other debts, rent raised, salaries raised, and the only way to pay is to borrow more and more money until ... what?

He stares down at the rushing crowds going in all directions. Where are they all going? Union Square gleams like a jewel in the clear, sea-washed air and bright morning sun. He loves to look at the statue at the center of the park in the square. The winged lady angel is eternally leaping forward gracefully on her pedestal, thrusting forward her torch of truth.

His eyes wander from the statue to the group of derelict men gathered about the park passing a whiskey bottle among them—dressed in rags, scruffy growths of beard and mottled hair, eyes red and watery, their days numbered before their ignominious deaths in the bushes or under a park bench.

He shivers slightly and goes back to his desk. He slumps down into the big, soft, leather swivel chair he loves. At least those bums have good clean San Francisco air to breathe before they buy the ranch, he thinks. Now, to business—he has his own hide to save.

There was no way to avoid it. His law partner, Ralph R. Walters, was a thief. He had very quietly stolen—or borrowed, as he called it—over $60,000 from one of their most important trust fund accounts. The family of the trust was demanding an accounting of the funds due to some perceived irregularities in the tax returns.

Walters had blamed his wife for the mess, saying she had insisted—forced him, no less—to take the money from the account in order to redo the kitchen in the old, rambling mansion they had just bought in Palo Alto. Walters promised to repay the money, but when and with what?

Their bonding company would repay the missing funds, but they would never receive new bonding until they repaid, and their reputation would be destroyed once the news got out.

They are the largest unincorporated law firm on the west coast of California. They bill hundreds of thousands of dollars every month. Their cash flow reached over a million dollars last year, but unfortunately much of what came in went right back out again.

There was the Staggerwing at Half Moon Bay Airport, as well as the Super Cub that he owned with Jake. There were alimony payments to Evelyn, child support for the two kids, and now separate maintenance for Phyllis.

Then there were the office expenses: the well-paid staff of lawyers and consultants, the current up-to-date law library, and the rent, which keeps going up for these large, grand suites of offices on Union Square. Taxes, restaurant expenses, and yes, he had to face it, he loved to live "high on the hog," as they say.

At least twice a year, he would get his friends together and they would fly to British Columbia to hunt duck and quail, or go salmon fishing in northern California along the many rivers, or South of the Border to Central America, Guatemala, or Mexico. He had planned a trip to Panama early next year, but now this problem loomed over him like the shadow of doom.

Ralph Walters, who actually consumed the larger part of the office income, had fled to Hawaii when they were served notice of the state audit. Damn him, Vincent thinks, he's trying to avoid the embarrassment and maybe even a prison term. Why, the son-of-bitch is probably lolling on the beach in Maui with some Hawaiian beauty drinking piña coladas while he, Vincent the Innocent, had to face the music by himself.

And oh, what a sad tune this was! Tragic chords of economic collapse and dissolution of a lifetime of respect, accompanied by unwelcome aging, play on his heartstrings. The work and dedication of twenty-five years being sucked down into a meaningless vortex, his high-flying lifestyle on the verge of crumbling, he listens to the sad dirge, maybe even a funeral dirge.

The specter of those destitute, lost men in Union Square fleetingly passes through his mental vision, but he willfully blots it out. There has to be a way, he thinks, pressing the palms of his hands down forcefully onto his desk blotter.

Now, he begins to pace. They could borrow the money to pay off the bonding company, but that might be hard to do under the circumstances. He already owed the bank, and he was behind in alimony payments. Evelyn was hounding him.

Then there was his reputation. He is not just any attorney around town. He is *the* legal specialist in aviation law in the entire United States. He represents Lloyd's of London in all their aviation cases. He is the darling of the insurance companies and the scourge of personal injury attorneys. He is very hard to beat in a courtroom trial. Usually, opponents settled cases beforehand at the mere mention of his name. Widows and orphans of plane crash victims hate him. His mother used to say that he could find an excuse for anything.

This dark reverie is interrupted by the insistent ringing of his telephone. "I'm sorry to disturb you, Mr. Cooper, but your wife is on the phone, and she says it is an emergency."

He sighs. "Okay, put her on." He steels himself for the verbal confrontation.

"Vincent, oh, Vincent, sweetheart, is that you? Are you there?" Phyllis says in a breathless, faraway, weak voice. "I know you are busy and Lord knows I don't want to burden you, but I'm here at Saint Luke's. Dr. Burkhart is here with me. He brought me in this morning. He says it is very serious this time."

He wants to scream at her. How did she get his phone number at the new flat? Why can't she leave him in peace? But he can't say any of that. He must feel sorry for her. She is sick. "What's wrong?"

"The usual, my blood pressure, it's way up there."

"You been drinking?"

"Just a little. It's not that. It's—"

"Lemme talk to Burkhart."

"Vince, how y'all doin'? Yep, she's pretty high alright. Wants to go right off the scope. She asked me if she could talk to you. Might not be a bad idea to get yourself down here— calm her down a bit."

"Ted, I'm lying in a pool of blood here myself. Purcell spent the weekend auditing the Bryan Folger trust fund. The money just ain't there. And with interest, I hate to think how much we owe. Can't you give her some pills or something? Walters took off for the islands and left me with all of this. I'm waiting for the auditor. He should be here any minute. I'll be in conference with him till God knows when."

"Come on, Vince! She's your *wife.*"

Phyllis is back on the phone. "Vincent, darling …" She sounds like a child. "They say I may die. You know why I'm dying—I still love you so much. No matter what you have done. I forgive you everything. Just come home to me. Please, tell me you know I forgive you and I love you. And you must still love me after all we have been through together—"

"I know that, Phyllis, I know that. I love you, too. Now, you just rest and try to get better. I'll be over there this afternoon to look in on you. Do you need anything?" That was a mistake.

"Only you, my darling, you are the only thing I need in the world. And I want you to leave that slut you are living with. Remember, I am your wife for better and for worse, and I love you very much …" The voice trailed off.

"Vincent, I think she fainted," says Burkhart. "Got to work on her."

"Do what you can. I'll get by there in the afternoon. You sure she's not faking it?"

"See ya later, pal."

The phone call unnerves him further. He looks up at the clear blue sky. Perfect day to fly away in his Staggerwing, maybe to British Columbia, and never come back. Maybe get himself a beautiful Indian maiden and live off the land, fishing, hunting, or trapping—something simple. He reaches into his liquor cabinet and pours himself a stiff shot of Tanqueray gin. He never takes a drink in the morning, but this particular morning calls for it. The gin hits his stomach and then spreads out in concentric circles of mild euphoria throughout his body. It is very welcome.

He needs time. He needs time to talk to Walters. Their last meeting had been stormy. Before, they had always managed to work in harmony. Walters presented himself as the solid, serious member of the partnership, while Vincent was the sociable, flamboyant, charming, charismatic half. They had complemented each other, attracting a wide range of clientele.

Superficially, it appeared that Ralph R. Walters was the more fiscally conservative, while in reality Vincent made the greater effort to be cautious with their funds. Vincent always covered himself as far as money management went. To him, it was like flying. You took risks, but you always had an emergency landing site in mind in case all else failed. Walters didn't do that. He had a pie-in-the-sky attitude.

He had blithely explained to Vincent that he had only "borrowed" the money and would immediately return it to the trust before anyone would miss it. He acted as though he were entitled to it.

"It was for home improvements," he said. The mansion had an old-fashioned kitchen geared to servants and cooks, so he and his wife modernized it with all the latest appliances. They redesigned the gardens to make them more maintenance-free, renovated the façade and one wing. And as a little extra—"a very practical idea," he insisted—the coach house was converted into an apartment that would bring in money. "You see, it was all money very well-spent, and no one would ever miss it."

Vincent recalls the conversation vividly. "Of course, you are aware, Ralph, that it is illegal for attorneys to withdraw funds from trust accounts under their jurisdiction without proper authorization," he had commented drily.

Ralph R. Walters' thick facial features had reddened, and his large, paunchy framed trembled. "No one would have found out if that damned Butch Folger hadn't gotten nosy. I was just about to balance up the account and start paying back when he had to poke his nose into it."

"Why'd you do it, Ralph?"

The big man just suddenly collapsed into one of the oversized, leather-upholstered chesterfields and began to cry.

Vincent had been stunned at the time to see this paragon of jurisprudence dissolving into wracking sobs like a child. He had been utterly embarrassed and could say nothing, just handing the sobbing man a tissue.

Finally, Walters had gained a measure of composure. "Okay, sure, Vincent, you have a right to ask." He dabbed his pale, flabby face with the tissue, his eyes reddened and swollen. He looked horrible. "Vince, you know my history as well as anyone. My family was poor, and remember, my dad was a lowly street cleaner. He died just before we put this partnership together, right after you quit Rollins, Beckett, and Goldberg. He would have been proud to see these offices after the sacrifices he and my mother made to put me through Berkeley and Hastings, even with the GI bill helping to pay costs."

"And well, you know how Irma, my wife, is. She's a good woman, but, well, let's face it, she's a social climber. She wants to be the richest lady on the block come hell or high water. Water! That's how she spends money. And you know she thinks you take more out of here than I do."

"Goddammit, Ralph, we can go over the accounts, and you know that."

"Yeah, yeah, I know my take is more. Irma found that damned mansion, and we picked it up pretty cheap. Believe me, she was going to be the queen of Palo Alto."

"At first, I was paying for the remodeling out of my own pocket, and the thing began to get away from me. She just kept those decorators coming and going—brick layers, the plasterers, furnishings from Sloane's, all new stainless-steel kitchen appliances. I'd come home and say, 'Honey, I don't have the money to pay for these bills you are handing me—$5,000 here to this contractor and another $9,000 to this plumber and another $10,000 to the architect—and look at this, my god, $25,000 to Sloane's!' And it just kept going on and on like that. I couldn't seem to reach her. It was like she was possessed or something. The place is gorgeous, but really I don't want anyone to see it. So then, I began to take money from the Folger trust just to keep the wolves at bay, and I planned to pay it all back as soon as Lloyd's sent us the money they owe us. But they pay so late, and Irma, like a mad woman, kept tearing out walls, ripping up floors, piles of old tiles all over the place, which was crawling with workers."

"Finally, one night she hands me another heap of bills and tells me flat out that the contractors can't go on unless we pay what we owe. I sat down at the adding machine, and when I saw how much it was, I wanted to die. Even with what I took out of the fund, we owe twice that much at least."

Vincent sighed deeply. "You know you are going to have to sell the place."

"Yeah, yeah, I know. Give me a brandy. But listen, I need a vacation. I know it's not the time to leave on a vacation, but my damn ticker is acting up, and I don't want another heart attack. I'll make it all good, Vince. Don't worry about it. I promise, as soon as we sell the place, I'll put all that money back where it belongs, I swear." Hand trembling, he lifted the half-full, good-sized brandy snifter to his mouth and downed it all in one gulp.

Poor pussy-whipped son-of-a-bitch, Vincent though at the time.

That was that, and they might have had time to replace the funds if that Folger kid hadn't demanded a formal audit. There may have been someone in the office who tipped him off.

Rotten luck, he thought, resting his head in his hands. Ralph and Irma Walters, socialites par excellence, always in the local society news attending the opera, various fundraisers and benefits for one charity or another, Vincent hated Irma Walters.

She was a phony bitch who condescended to him as though he were no more than a mischievous brat they had to tolerate because he was the one who brought the big money into the law firm. She gossiped incessantly about his expenses, about his girlfriends, his trips, his airplanes, and his flamboyant manner.

At one point, Irma had tried to involve Vincent in the peninsula social life, but he had been bored, particularly by the women, which was not usual for him. They were either stiff and cold or wildly promiscuous, and he had found nothing that satisfied him after making the rounds. After the initial ego satisfaction of making a few conquests, their annoying pursuit of him with telephone calls, invitations, and planned accidental encounters turned him off.

He didn't like their Elizabeth Arden veneer, like something that could easily be peeled away. At a certain point in his life, he realized he liked beautiful women, but only if they were smart. Yeah, he liked intelligent, accomplished, ambitious women. It was a secret vice that he had that he did not discuss with most of his men friends. Those friends generally avoided self-reliant, educated women like the plague and worse still if they were attractive—too threatening to their egos—but his ego was sufficiently robust, beyond all that.

The phone rings again, interrupting his reverie. "Sam is back with Mr. Purcell, the state auditor, and they are ready to meet with you, Mr. Cooper."

"Seat them at the conference table in the law library and serve them some coffee. I'll be right there."

The three men sit stiffly at the long mahogany conference table situated in the center of the extensive law library of the firm. The secretary enters with her notepad, but Vincent motions her to leave, that he will take notes of this very private conference. After the formal greetings take place, Vincent clears his throat, smiles weakly, and begins. "Well, we all know the problem by now, right?"

"Right, Vincent," responds the auditor coolly, "the problem amounts to $148,702.32 that should be in the Bryan Folger trust account but is not. This is money for which you and your firm are responsible. Now can you tell me what has become of these funds?"

"Well, at least it's less than $150,000, but not much less. The truth is that this money is now residing in a lovely French Country-style mansion sitting on five acres of gardens and woodland down the peninsula on Riviera Boulevard in Palo Alto, California. In order to remove those funds from said mansion, said mansion will have to go on the real estate block as soon as possible."

The auditor spoons some sugar into his coffee, stirs, and then tastes it, frowning. "How quickly can that be accomplished?" he asks, setting the cup very carefully back into the saucer.

"Ralph Walters is not well. He has taken off for Hawaii to rest. He has a heart problem. He should be in contact with me this afternoon. He phones in regularly. We have talked about selling the house, but at the present time he has not taken action." Vincent offers the two men a cigarette. The auditor refuses, but Sam and he light up unfiltered Camels.

The auditor taps his pencil on his legal pad. "These things happen more often than we like to admit. And of course, it is better for everyone concerned if the money is replaced as soon as possible. The interest continues to accrue, and I believe it is around 8 percent at present." The auditor finishes his coffee.

"Um-hum," responds Vincent, who is doodling on his pad—clouds, round and fluffy, some lengthening into storm clouds, darker than the others. He puts in more shadows and a little bird flying. He puts in more birds among the clouds. "And what happens if we can't get the money back quickly enough? What are the time limits?"

"I truthfully cannot say at this time. I will have to turn all of this information over to my superiors. Then, we will have to meet with the lawyers of the family involved. I guess, this isn't exactly your field, Mr. Cooper, nothing to do with airplanes—pure dollars, cents, and time. Of course, you realize it is quite likely we will have to do extensive audits of the other trust accounts under your administration, and you will have to pay the cost of those audits as, of course, you have to pay for my time."

"Of course. I assure you everything else is in order, but you are welcome to the books anytime," says Vincent.

"As I said, if this can be handled quickly, it is possible your firm can retain its integrity." Stephen Purcell, the state auditor, scribbles some notes on his pad. A thick, pudgy man of medium height, he wears glasses and is balding—the archetypal bureaucrat, the auditor, holding the rein of power over the whole law firm. There would be no negotiating if he decides to shut them down at once. A large diamond ring sparkles on a plump little finger as he writes.

Vincent stares at him, loathing him. He is despicable. Had he ever really loved a woman, even a woman like Irma, who meant everything to her foolish husband? Somehow, he, Vincent, had to get to this man. He felt that Purcell wanted something from him, but what? If he tried to bribe him for more time, it could be even worse. These days, state auditors took home big salaries from Sacramento.

Vincent realizes that for the time being, they are being taken off the hook. He continues doodling, adding a small plane among the clouds and the birds then some mountains below, while Purcell goes over the dates of the illegal withdrawals.

Vincent decides to charm him. Yes, that might just work. Vincent is fully aware of his own mystique as a dashing pilot-lawyer around San Francisco and its surrounding environs. He was often mentioned in the gossip columns. He threw away invitations to fancy parties in Pacific Heights for lack of time or interest. Yes, he would work on this ugly little worm that now held his destiny in his chubby, short-fingered hands.

Purcell glances up, sensing Vincent's scrutiny. His eyes appear larger than normal through his thick glasses. "Well, what do you think of my terms so far?" he inquires flatly.

"Frankly, we both know it doesn't matter a damn what I think about the terms. I appreciate the chance to make good on the missing funds with as little publicity as possible. I believe what you have proposed is fair. Walters and I have more or less agreed to the sale of his home. I am not sure he can recoup what he has put into it. Those big places are hard to sell—upkeep and all, you know."

"If you fall into an alligator pit and someone throws you a rope, you don't tell him to get a ladder instead, ya know what I mean?" Vincent laughs nervously and continues, "As a matter of fact, I personally know a judge on the circuit court bench who stole over a hundred grand from a trust account to buy a ranch in Lake County. He really hustled to get it all back before the loss was discovered, and he did. No one knows the difference except for a few of us."

"Say," he looks at his watch, "it's getting close to lunchtime. What say you join Mary Belle and me for lunch at Jack's—relax a little while you're here?"

"Oh, no." Purcell looks disconcerted for a moment. "I, oh, no, I really should get back to Sacramento."

"Oh, come on, Steve! They have the best filet mignon in town. You have to eat anyway. Come join us! You've been holed up in this office all weekend. Take in a little bit of the city as long as you are here."

"I, I was just going to get a hamburger along the way. I—"

"Some of the best-looking women in town hang out there, the real high class ones, you know, the beautiful ones. And they just love guys from the country."

"Country? Sacramento is the capital city of California."

Sam joins in, sensing his bosses' intent, "Come on, Steve! You deserve a little fun. All work and no play makes accountants dull—you know the saying."

"But it's Monday. If it were Friday ..."

"So what? Monday is a good day to party a little. Everyone is rested up from Sunday."

"Oh, golly, I don't know, well, maybe. I have to eat anyway, and crossing that valley, geez, it's hot as hell. Oh, what the heck? Yeah, I'll go. I'm starving. Skipped breakfast trying to lose a little weight—you know, doctor's orders."

When they arrive at Jack's, Mary Belle is already seated at the bar, sipping a vodka martini. She looks very elegant, very feminine in the blue flower silk dress. She has let her hair out of the bun, and it falls around her face and shoulders like a golden cascade. Vincent slips his arm around her waist, and she raises her mouth to be kissed.

Instinctively she knows this tubby fellow straggling along with a worried look on his face is the auditor in whose hands lies the fate of Vincent's law practice. As they are introduced, the auditor grabs her hand and shakes it vigorously, almost painfully.

His face lights up, and he suddenly appears happier. His eyes glisten behind the thick glasses. Sacramento does not sport such beautiful women. Vincent orders a round of drinks while they wait for a table.

A second round is ordered at the table, and Stephen Purcell appears to be on his way to tipsy. His face has turned bright red. He shakes the ice cubes around in his empty glass. "You people sure have it great here in Frisco," he gushes. "Everything shuts down so damn early in Sacramento. Too tame for me, ya know. I'd give my right testicle to live here. Oh, pardon me, miss." He looks in the direction of Mary Belle, who is not paying any attention to him.

By the time they finish lunch, it is 3:30 in the afternoon. Snifters of cognac and espresso coffee accompanied by gooey pastries top off the meal. "Say, Vince, I hope you have the money to pay for all this. My expense account doesn't cover three-martini lunches—or how many martinis were there? Sorry, I know you aren't too well-off, yourself, these days," comments Purcell, now sitting back in the big comfortable chair, his face more crimson than before, verging on purple.

"Easy come, easy go, as they say. But hey, why don't you stay overnight at my flat? Phone your office. Say you were unavoidably detained. You can drive back early in the morning when it's still cool. I'll introduce you to some real beauties around town. I'd love you to stay," he lies.

"Oh?" says Mary Belle, her eyebrows raised at the prospect of being hostess to all of this. Vincent pats her thigh under the table to be quiet.

"That'd be great!" Purcell slurs, obviously too far gone to drive. He is now theirs.

"Now don't you worry about a thing, Steve. My lovely lady, Mary Belle here, and my trusted employee Sam, who holds his liquor very well, will pick up your car, and all three of you drive to my new flat on Upper Terrace. Don't you worry," he repeats himself as he signs the tab without even looking at the amount.

He feels beyond adding up dollars and cents at this point. It has all gotten out of hand. He will just keep signing and signing until he can no longer sign. He smiles as he helps Mary Belle out of her chair.

They ease the state auditor into a standing position, gently guiding him into the late afternoon sunlight of Montgomery Street. They take the auditor's keys and his parking receipt. "Sam, just leave them both at my place, you know, where I had the furniture shipped, Dr. Kelley's place. Then, phone a couple of girls, maybe Suzy Wong or Stella Dallas. One or two is enough for the evening. Take care of it, okay?"

He turns to kiss Mary Belle, who backs off. "Where are you going?" she asks, frowning.

"I, uh, have to see a sick friend at the hospital. I won't be long." He hands her a hundred-dollar bill. "Have Sam stop at Petrini's on the way home. Pick up something for supper tonight, some booze for the house, whatever. I'll leave it up to you. It's our first party at our new house."

"Tell me the truth."

"That is the truth," he says. Damned women, he thinks, always suspicious. And Mary Belle hates whores, but they all have to sacrifice now.

"Pray tell, Vincent, who is this sick friend?" she persists.

"If you must know, it's Phyllis. She's having another attack of hypertension, and Burkhart says she is really sick this time, might even die. Save us a lot of problems now, wouldn't it? Oh, hell, I don't mean that."

Mary Belle's face twists in anger. She is not pretty now. "This has been going on for over a year and a half now. Every time she thinks you are going through with the divorce, she has a damned attack. Don't you see how she is faking it just to keep you? She is making fools of both of us, and frankly, I'm getting fed up with it!"

"Please, don't say that. You know how I feel about you. No matter what, we are going to get married, believe me."

She turns away from him toward the swaying state auditor, who is propped up against one of the granite walls of California's great financial institutions waiting for something exciting to happen in old San Francisco.

Saint Luke's Hospital sits like a huge, sprawling monument to failing human health in the inner Mission District of San Francisco. The lobby has the familiar hospital smell of antiseptics and drugs. There is a faint sense of a lack of breathable air, as though all the available oxygen has been collected to fill tanks in order to be dispensed by the medical staff to the sick and dying. People bustle about or huddle in corners speaking in muted tones.

As Vincent makes his way through the maze of corridors to the elevators, he muses on the deteriorating conditions of his life despite his most valiant efforts to keep the wolves at bay from his legal door. He has always been fortunate. They used to say he lived a charmed life. Things for which other people worked and sacrificed came easily to him. People generally did what he wanted them to do, tried to please him. Money had never been a problem since his trial work brought in more than enough to support his style.

But now, he has this problem with his wife. Mary Belle was probably right: Phyllis uses her poor health to control him, to make him feel guilty. She had been his mistress during his previous marriage. Without any qualms whatsoever, she had insisted that he leave his two young children and wife of fourteen years.

Phyllis had become pregnant during that time and bore the child, but he never acknowledged the child as his. He said it was from her former marriage. Phyllis resented that, but in time, his marriage ended in divorce, so he married Phyllis. That had been a mistake.

Once married, she became a nag and a burden, but worse, she began to bore him, so he started to play around again. Phyllis, instead of raging at him, took to her bed and to her doctor. Her tirades were whispered through a veil of suffering and tears. Doctors, nurses, children all looked at him accusingly. He could hardly stand it.

And now, Mary Belle is standing in the same place Phyllis had been five years ago. It is like a long, drawn-out game of musical chairs, with the available chair representing the amorphous security of marriage to the women. Phyllis is not going to give up her chair without a struggle, and he doesn't know how long Mary Belle will continue the march around the chairs waiting for the music to end.

She is younger than he, more than fifteen years younger, and she wants a family. He doesn't want to lose her, yet sometimes she can be abrasive, sarcastic, and yes, she knows how to get to him. He would prefer that she were more gentle—strong, yes, but different somehow, sweet-tempered. He ardently wishes he could create the perfect woman for himself.

The elevator jerks to an abrupt halt. Everything is old here. As he exits, he almost collides with a gurney being wheeled along the corridor. The passenger is an old man who looks dead, but in passing Vincent detects a flutter in the frail white hand attached to a bottle of intravenous solution.

He locates Phyllis's room. He is grateful for the drinks he had at lunch to reinforce him for this ordeal. Phyllis is lying back on the bed, gazing wanly at the ceiling. Her red hair is spread out around her pillow like a flaming halo. She smiles at him as he enters. Her eyes look glazed, probably from the drugs. The lids flutter faintly. She wears traces of makeup. A pretty woman, she somehow always looks her best when sick. However, there are dark circles under and around her eyes. Her hand is cold to his touch.

"How ya doin', honey?" He bends over and kisses her cheek.

"Not too well, but better now that you are here."

"Where's Burkhart?"

"I think he's still here around the hospital somewhere. He said he would come back to see me before he leaves for the day. Honey?"

"Yeah?"

"Please hand me that tiny bottle of gin that's in my purse on the chair. I just need a tiny sip to feel a little better." She takes the not-so-tiny bottle and takes two large swallows then lies back on the pillow waiting for it to take effect.

Vincent takes a swig himself and replaces the now-almost-empty bottle in her purse.

"I need some mouthwash. Dr. Burkhart has forbidden me to drink."

He helps her to her feet. She is wearing a sheer negligee right out of a 1940s film. Her breasts, body, and red pubic hair are temptingly displayed through the gauzy mesh. They shuffle to the bathroom, where she hangs over the washbowl and repeatedly gargles, spits, and gargles again.

Vincent stands behind her, supporting her. Absently, his hand wanders to one of her large breasts. He becomes aware of his erection, which is pressing against her as she bends over the washbasin. She bends further, and he realizes she is presenting herself to him.

She stops the gargling and bends over further and waits. He lifts her negligee, exposing the cleft between her two large white, exquisitely rounded buttocks. She bends farther, if that is possible, and thrusts toward him his choice of ecstasy. He pulls the bathroom door closed, but he cannot lock it, so it stands somewhat ajar, but he is too aroused to care. "Vincent, darling, here, use this." She hands him a small jar of cream of some sort, already open.

He unzips his trousers, frenzied with desire for that pink rosebud orifice that is contracted slightly. He loves the forbidden place, the forbidden act, and the possibility of discovery enhances his arousal. If a nurse comes in, he'll do her, too. He slathers the cream from front to back while Phyllis writhes, clinging to the washstand. He dallies in the folds and crevices, tickles her hard little knot back and forth until she is moaning for him to enter her. His finger enters her vulva, then two fingers. Her pelvis is pumping as is his. He finally takes his now engorged penis in his hand and slowly guides it into her, thrusting back and forth, each time going deeper.

In small, circular motions his fingers keep rubbing her clitoris. He knows her body so well and how to bring her to orgasm. He pulls her against him so that he is buried up to the hilt, her buttocks flattened against his thighs. By now, his pants have fallen to the floor. He feels her clitoris engorge, so he thrusts harder.

Her head is thrust backward and her breathing is deep and heavy. She moans and strains against his hand so they nearly topple over. She cries out as the wet, velvety folds and muscles begin their involuntary contractions. He rubs her hard to keep her coming, and the cries turn to screams.

"Well, well, well, what do we have here?" It's Dr. Burkhart, who has opened the door and stands watching them. "Don't let me interrupt."

Vincent can no longer hold back. He ejaculates into her body with strong thrusting movements. His howling joins hers, both oblivious to their spectator. His semen overflows, trickling down her inner thigh. It fills the bathroom with a heavy, earthy, slightly acrid smell that overwhelms the sterile hospital odors.

Phyllis now hangs her head over the basin, spent. Her red hair flows down and around her face while Vincent slowly and gently withdraws from her. Burkhart folds his arms, fascinated, wanting to join in but remaining the doctor in this case.

Vincent turns to look at him, unable to speak for the moment. He reaches for a towel, wiping her first, tentatively drying her crotch, and then himself. The negligee drops discretely into place while he tucks his now flaccid organ into his trousers and zips up. "Got us en flagrante, huh, Ted? She's my wife, you know. That's what happens when you open closed doors without knocking first. Don't you have any manners?"

"Well, she's my patient, ya know, and sex is not in the prescription. Besides, we doctors have the unquestioned right to go anywhere in the hospital. That's why there ain't no locks on the doors."

Phyllis's face is now quite flushed as she totters back to the bed, the two men supporting her. Vincent draws the blanket and sheet chastely under her chin. "Now, doesn't she look better? Got some color back into her face. I mean, I have to be just what the doctor ordered, right, honey?"

With apparently great effort, she reaches her hand out from underneath the sheet and touches his hand. Her hand is now warm. "I'm pooped, darling. Let me sleep, please." Her eye lids flutter and close.

"Y'all know that screwing is strictly against hospital rules. I could have y'all put in jail if I wanted to." Ted Burkhart smiles sardonically.

"You won't be the first person to threaten me with the slammer today. I just might be doing something wrong here." The thought crosses his legal mind that if, in fact, he is planning to divorce this woman, fucking her is the last thing he should be doing. There is even an eyewitness, if that would make any difference. He feels he is losing control of things.

Burkhart becomes all doctor. He wraps the rubber cuff around Phyllis's limp arm to take her blood pressure. He pumps it up expertly and then scrutinizes the gauge. "Pressure is still up, but not as much as this morning. Looks like it's coming down. Hey, y'all may be right—a roll in the hay keeps the doctor away." He chuckles at his little rhyme.

Vincent stands to one side as the doctor continues to administer to his wife. She might not be sick at all, he thinks bitterly. She might have the psychic ability to control her blood pressure just to control him. She plays on his horniness, he decides. Maybe Mary Belle is right.

Later on, in the hall, he and Burkhart discuss his wife's condition. "Vincent, I know you think it's all psychosomatic with Phyllis—and to be truthful, I do too—however, I have known the lady for quite a few years now, and she can literally bring herself to death's door if she wants to. You have to face the fact that she is suicidal. She will do anything to keep you, I mean *anything*. I had the staff psychiatrist talk to her, and he agrees with me."

"But she wants *you* to go into analysis. She thinks you will come to your senses. I mean, hell, why do you want to divorce her? She's a damn good woman, faithful to you, and she loves you. You obviously have a good sex life together. Lordy, you do it anywhere, doncha?"

Vincent frowns. He hates examining his life and motives. "Well, the thing is that Mary Belle is putting pressure on me, Ted. She wants to be a wife, my wife."

"Goddammit, Vince, you are already married! Face it!"

"You don't understand, Ted. Mary Belle and I have a professional relationship, as well as personal. I need her help in my law practice cause she is smart as hell, dynamic. Phyllis doesn't know shit about the law, nor does she care. She just likes the money coming in."

"Yeah, yeah, I know. Don't look at me like that. Phyllis is a great woman, a great lay, and she'd do anything for me. But sometimes, I mean, sometimes, I wish she'd leave me alone. She clings so tight, I feel like I can't breathe around her. And then there's the drinking."

Burkhart shakes his head. "Sure glad I ain't in your shoes, buddy. What you need is a fuckin harem, that's what!"

"Hey, I wish I weren't in my shoes either, believe me. Say, by the way, I'm giving a little cocktail party in honor of the respected auditor of the State of California, Stephen Purcell, at my new place. Why doncha come up for a few drinks? Bring your girlfriend."

"Which one?"

"See ya later, Ted. Thanks for everything."

It was late when Vincent drove up Market Street toward Mount Olympus. He'd stayed at the office returning phone calls. He had made a call to London, and Lloyd's had promised to make a substantial payment on the work he had billed them for in the past. It would be deposited to his account by the end of the week. That had calmed him down somewhat. He did some work on a brief for a trial coming up. He needed Mary Belle at the office, but he also needed her with the auditor preparing their little party.

She was so many things to him—legal consultant, lover, hostess. Now, how could she also be his wife and perhaps a mother in the future? Really he thought, maybe Ted was right. What he really needed was a harem of women. Obviously, one was not enough for him. He begins to think of the passing years. Almost fifty years old, he never thought this would happen to him. As he got older, his girlfriends got younger. How long can this go on he wonders.

He tries to be a good father, visiting his two children in Redwood City every Sunday when he gets a chance. He would soon bring them to his new flat, something he couldn't do in the house he bought for Phyllis. She would not allow them there.

There had been some times when his children had expected him and he couldn't make it—a party, a hangover, or a woman. There were times he didn't even phone to say he couldn't visit them to take them out somewhere. His ex-wife had angrily told him how the poor children waited for him all day long, rushing to the window to see if every passing car might be the big white Buick about to swing into their driveway. Finally, when they knew he wasn't coming for them, they cried with the total despair that only children are capable of expressing. Well, he thought, they'll get over it. May leave a few scars, but that's life.

He has scars from his insatiable ego, from his all-consuming efforts to succeed in the world of male competition where a few emotional scars don't matter. Women, children, emotions, none are important in that world. With enough money, everything can be taken care of quite nicely. Men who cling to those sentimental impediments never make it. Come to think of it, Vincent doesn't know anyone who was committed to family who had become rich and famous. All his friends are divorced—multiple divorces, in fact, with children by one and then another. That's just the way it is these days.

Vincent always makes a point not to think of these things and resents their intrusion into his mental processes. He is the first to say he always sends the alimony/child support check on time. It is just that he is so busy practicing law, he doesn't have much time for the kids. After all, there is just so much time in the day, and Vincent tries to make the most of every minute.

Everything he does, he does well. He is admired and envied. No one can top him or emulate him. His office is adorned with trophies won from the air shows he had participated in, along with framed photos of him from newspapers, smiling out at the world of inferior beings.

At fourteen years of age, he was the youngest person ever to solo out of Mills Field Airport in a Gypsy Moth. Mills Field is now San Francisco International Airport. He had earned his two hours of flight instruction by washing planes for their owners. Great gleaming cups testified to his skill as an aerobatic pilot. He was a regular at the air shows in Reno, Las Vegas, and San Diego. He won first place in an air race with an AT-6, a World War II training plane. He could fly upside down in an open cockpit six feet above the ground, do loops above and below the Golden Gate Bridge. The general chief of staff at the Presidio was his good friend and would cheerfully ignore reports of his highly illegal maneuvers. Then there were the medals for his many missions over the Himalayan Mountains during the Second World War. He was one of the last of a certain kind of man, possibly a soon to become extinct species.

Then with all these achievements, why does he feel this discontent, the awareness that no matter what he does, he will still feel unfulfilled in his lifetime? On rare occasions, he will admit to himself that he never has been happy. Come to think of it, the closest he ever came to a feeling of peace and contentment was a couple of years ago on one of his trips in the Staggerwing down the west coast of Mexico.

His mind drifts back to that time, the details still vivid.

CHAPTER FIVE

South of the Border

They took off at dawn from Half Moon Bay Airport. Vincent Cooper was accompanied by two of his good friends, Ham Sado, a Japanese man who raised daisies in a foggy valley up a few miles from the airport, and Jake Morenetti, who owned the flight service out of Half Moon Bay. Their destination was Puerto de las Peñas, a little fishing village on the west coast of Mexico. Their object was escape from the relentless demands of modern life in California.

Puerto de las Peñas was a very popular destination during the 1950s with the social elite of San Francisco. Louis Benoit, owner of Almaden Wineries, had a hotel called the Oceano on the malecon that he used for his parties. There were no roads into the village. One either arrived by private plane, a Mexicana DC-3 from Guadalajara, yacht, canoe, burro or mule, horseback, or on foot across the towering Sierra Madre Mountains east of the village.

Vincent had been here once several years ago to visit an old World War II buddy, a drop-out from San Francisco high society who had married a dusky native Mexican girl and settled there for good. His name was Roland Adams. The landing field was dirt and gravel next to a rutted road north of the village. A pilot had to first buzz low on the field to scare off the cows and horses usually grazing there.

Puerto de las Peñas was a small village. It served as the agricultural and fishing center for that part of the coast of Jalisco, Mexico. It was almost totally self-sufficient. The town was situated north of the center of a wide, sweeping bay called the Bahia de Banderas, the Bay of the Flags.

It was ringed with beautiful beaches. To the north, the beaches were long and shallow, sometimes with huge breakers, but to the south, where the moutains slipped down to the sea, the beaches were smaller, forming enchanting rock coves of cream-colored sand fringed with palm trees and thick tropical vegetation. The rivers that flowed down from the high mountains formed pristine little deltas of crystal clear water, except during the first rains of the rainy season when they swelled with leaves, dead wood, and debris from the forested mountains.

The sea teemed with life—fish, turtles, whales, lobsters, oysters, serpents, dolphins, and enormous manta rays bigger than the fishing boats that plied the rich, blue-green waters.

Indigenous people had thrived there in pre-Colombian times, living in thatched huts of palm and mangrove saplings in a barter economy of abundance. They lived off the sea—fresh-water lobsters, oysters, fish of all kinds, turtles providing the protein base of their diet.

In addition, they planted small plots of corn, orchards of bananas, mamey, papaya, green tomatoes, chilies of all kinds, beans, and cactus. Aside from creating the *mestizo* population by interbreeding with the natives, the arrival of Europeans, essentially from Spain, introduced the cultivation of small orchards of citrus fruits such as oranges, lemons, and grapefruit.

The families, in general, kept cows for milk, cheese, cream, and butter. Some had pigs and chickens. Burros, mules, and small horses served for land transportation, and *pangas*, a form of dugout canoe, sufficed for water travel.

For their fiestas and celebrations, they brewed a potent distilled alcoholic beverage from the lechugilla cactus that grew profusely throughout the area, called *raicilla*. For these Indians living along the coast, it was a hidden remnant of the Garden of Eden.

The great rotary engine of the Staggerwing Beech hummed reassuringly as the vacationers flew down the wildly beautiful west coast of the North American continent, a trip that Vincent loved dearly. After passing through Mexican customs at Hermosillo, they stopped at Guaymas to rest for the night and to refuel.

Early in the morning, with Jake flying co-pilot, the three men resumed their journey into another time. Late that afternoon, the great Bay of Flags, Bahia de Banderas, loomed shimmering on the horizon. The men leaned forward in anticipation and soon saw the tiny village of Puerto de las Peñas creating an almost insignificant terrestrial change in the sweep of white beaches and thick jungle reaching down to the sea.

"Let's start our descent!" Vincent shouted, pulling back on the throttle and preparing to fly over the town to announce their arrival.

"We are going to say hello to Roland. You know, tell him to meet us at the airport," said Vincent. As they came down closer to the beach, there was the bar and restaurant that Roland owned, La Ramada. They roared over the thatched roof. People ran out onto the beach to see who it was. "There he is! That's Roland. He's there, hands waving! Let's make another pass!" shouted Vincent over the noise of the engine. The beach surged with semi-inebriated adults, dark skinned children, and dogs dancing about in uncontrollable excitement as the plane roared over their heads. Flocks of pelicans rose en masse from the breakers, removing themselves from this very unwelcome disturbance.

Vincent banked the aircraft for another sweeping buzz, rocking the plane back and forth sideways to wave the wings in greeting. Then he pulled back the ailerons and turned toward the landing field, anxious to join the crowd below. Vincent turned and smiled at Jake and Ham, whose dark, round Japanese face was bathed in sweat. "I sure hope they come and meet us. It's a goddamned long walk back."

Vincent lined the plane up with the field, pulled 15 degrees of flaps, and lowered the nose. The field was rutted and looked as though no one had used it for quite a while; weeds were encroaching onto the landing strip. A few inches above the surface, Vincent pulled back the throttle and gently raised the nose until it settled into a perfect minimum speed stall and touched down. Jake clapped his hands. "Pretty good landing—for a Sunday pilot, that is," he muttered gruffly. Compliments were painful for Jake.

Vincent taxied into the weeds on one side of the strip, turned the plane into the wind, and shut the motor off. They all got down stiffly from the aircraft, stretched, and urinated gratefully after the four-hour trip. "Let's get the luggage down and get organized, so when they come we are ready to go," commanded Vincent, ever the leader.

Vincent and Ham unloaded the plane while Jake carefully locked and secured it to some rusty tie-downs buried in the burrs and thistles. There were suitcases of clothes, two hunting rifles stowed away so customs didn't see them, boxes of fishing gear, and a small generator for Roland.

They lugged it all to the entrance road, sat down, lit cigarettes, and waited. "Sure is peaceful here," commented Jake as he drew deeply on his unfiltered Camel cigarette. They could hear the distant roll of the surf and the screaming of shore birds. Insects of all kinds and shapes chirped around them. The clouds were building up over the bay, and it looked like rain. They heard thunder in the distance.

Vincent exhaled long and fully, his eyelids drooping. He felt like sleeping. "Yep, the rainy season should be just about ready to end here. Rarely rains after October... what's the date?"

"Is October 8. Me like rainy season," said Ham in his awkward English.

"Good thing, Ham, cuz there's a hell of a lot of it in the summer in these parts of Old Mexico." Vincent stamped out his cigarette with the heel of his boot, accustomed to the dry California climate and fire danger.

Way off, they heard a car motor. They all stood up, straining to see who it might be to rescue them. Soon, a rickety old taxi pulled up alongside them and rumbled to a halt. It was a beat-up 1948 Dodge sedan brush-painted a canary yellow, missing one back fender and all the windows. The hood was wired down to the chassis of the vehicle, but it could have been a late-model Cadillac stretch limousine they were so happy to see it.

Roland Adams hopped out beaming at them. He was a tall, lean, handsome man with light blue eyes and prematurely white hair. His face was crisscrossed with fine lines and slightly puffy. He could have stepped out of a novel by Somerset Maugham. "Vincent, you old son of a gun, how the hell are ya? Great god, you made it okay!" He threw his arms around Vincent in the classical Mexican men's embrace.

Vincent, at first surprised then recalling the custom, returned the big bear hug with pats on the back of his old friend. "Say, Roland, you know Jake here. And Ham Sado, he grows daisies in the valley up from Half Moon Bay," said Vincent.

"Here, we call daisies *margaritas*." Roland laughed.

"Isn't that what we drink?" said Vincent after the men shook hands and began loading the luggage and gear into the open trunk of the taxi.

The cab driver stood aside and watched them work. He was a short, dark Indian man, rather plump, with a sardonic smile. He kept shaking his head. "*No cabe*," he stated. (It won't all fit.)

"Okay, the fishing gear and the generator in the trunk, then we'll put the rest up front with the driver. And what doesn't fit we can tie to the roof. That's how we do things here," declared Roland, "whatever works."

Finally, they all squeezed into the back seat, Ham Sado sitting on Jake's lap, and began the bumpy ride to town. "Goddamn, I need a drink. How's the Oceano these days?" asked Vincent, opening the buttons on his shirt as the sweat began to trickle down his face onto his clothing. They bounced over the dirt road through the thick jungle, crossed a stone bridge onto some cobblestone streets, and suddenly they were in town.

The cab came to a lurching halt in front of the Oceano. Since the cab had no brakes, the driver relied on the handbrake to stop the vehicle, and that was just about shot, so he finally used the curb to assure that the forward momentum was arrested.

The passengers were all flung forward, along with the boxes on the front seat, and some luggage tumbled from the roof onto the cobblestone street, but they had *stopped*.

"Christ, the trip from the airport is more dangerous than flying here," grumbled Jake, frowning and wiping the sweat from his brow with a grimy handkerchief as their belongings were taken into the hotel.

"*Cuanto*?" asked Vincent of the smiling taxi driver, using his meager high school Spanish proudly.

"*Doce pesos*," replied the driver.

"Roland, is that right? The guy's not screwing me now, is he?" Vincent hated to be cheated in any way.

"Yeah, that's about right, a dollar from the airport. Think of gas and maintenance."

"Gas, maybe, but maintenance, no. Shit, let's get drunk and look for babes."

All their belongings were piled up in a corner of the bar/restaurant. They sat on sofas under the large unglassed windows in front of a low wooden cocktail table. Across from the hotel, the sea crashed and roared onto the beach below the malecon, the beach walk that ran along the ocean wall. Salt spray hung suspended in the air almost as if one were partly submerged in the sea. Roland ordered them double margaritas: tequila, fresh lime juice, Cointreau, and sugar syrup served in champagne glasses rimmed with lime and salt. They had beer chasers.

"Goddamn, it's great to be back down here, Roland! How the hell have you been? How're the wife, the kids?" They were into their third round of drinks and Vincent signaled for another. He was feeling a lovely, painless euphoria that he never wanted to end.

The beautiful, little, hand-painted pottery plates of peanuts and homemade potato chips were constantly refilled. Then came plates of cucumbers with salt, lemon, and chili.

"Didja see the generator I brought you for the house? You can run a blender, a few lights at night, maybe a wash machine for Hermalinda so she doesn't have to go down to the river to wash clothes." Vincent laughed, knowing that Hermalinda, Roland's wife, once having worked as a maid herself, now had her own maids to do the household chores, having married what she assumed was a rich gringo.

The sun was setting over the horizon of the sea among the rain clouds, the sky exhibiting an orgy of artist's colors, from lemon yellow to viridian green, cerulean blue, and bright cadmium red, pinks shaded with dark menacing purples. The thunder was now growling close. Lightning bolts shot up and down between the sea and the clouds.

Vincent rose to take a photo. These natural displays moved him, and he could only express himself by taking a picture of it all, which never really did justice to the real thing. "Sure glad we're not up in that soup," he commented as he replaced the camera in its case and slid into place to resume the gossip of San Francisco.

Roland loved to hear about the social life there since he had renounced it all to become an ex-patriot, the black sheep of the family. He had married a dark, native Mexican girl. Worse, he had babies with her.

"Same old thing. Cahill's getting another divorce. His wife caught him with Doris Layhey. Dirk Adam's father died of cancer, your second cousin I believe, and it turns out there was no money after all the debts were paid. And they say the Reinhardts are going bankrupt. I guess everyone has their day of reckoning," commented Vincent as he lit another cigarette after passing the pack around to the others.

"So, maybe I'm not so bad off here after all. Sounds like what goes on in Puerto de las Peñas." Roland leaned back in his leather *equipale* chair, smiling with pleasure at being somewhat vindicated.

"Hey, they're selling corn on the cob out there. Anyone want some?" asked Vincent, referring to the women standing around steaming kettles of fresh corn cooking over wood coals on the malecon. The waiter was sent out to bring them the corn. The fresh, sweet, tender ears were slathered with mayonnaise, grated cheese, and ground chili. The men ate with gusto, smearing themselves happily with the concoction, the waiters attending them with hot, wet towels.

The tide was coming in, waves crashing wildly against the stony beach creating a rhythmic background to all the exotic sights, sounds, and smells. The surf roared with the tumbling of countless millions of stones smashing violently against one another.

Together with the tequila, the sultry atmosphere soothed their frazzled urban nerves. It was what Vincent loved about the place. His eyes began to droop, and he needed to go to sleep.

"Say, Vince, wake up there! How long can you stay? I've got a great trip planned for you all." Roland was happy to be among his countrymen, speaking English and especially to see his old friend Vincent, once again.

"Uh ... oh, five days maybe, let's see how things go. My partner, Walters, is in charge of the office at the moment. No problem, just a phone call if we feel like staying longer."

"Let's fly up to the ranch country. I've been up there a few times. It's fabulous, almost untouched by, uh, civilization. Hermalinda's family comes from an old ranching village from the days of the haciendas—El Valle Encantado it's called. I have a friend there, Don Francisco Ochoa. He owns thousands of hectares, something like seven ranches in all, scattered all over the valley—beautiful. There's a big volcanic crater lake, where ducks land during their winter migration. It's great duck hunting. What d'ya say?"

Vincent perks up. "How much time do we need to do it?" He lights another cigarette as he begins to imagine the place Roland is describing.

"The roads to the lake are pretty bad. They wash out all the time. Let's see, now. Arrive day one in the plane, organize the trip, and sleep in Don Francisco's house in town. Drive into the mountains the next day, with horses on the back of pickup trucks. That is, if Don Francisco is agreeable to lending the horses and trucks to us. But he loves me, and he will love you, too. Wait till you see how hospitable these people are."

"Then camp next to the lake for two or three days. You can practically live off the land up there—lots of fish, wild game, pheasants, and quail. We just take along some salt, beans, bacon, tortillas, and chili. Then another day to pack out, sleep overnight in town. And the next day, fly back here. That's *minimum* days, Vince. It's better to count on another day or two. Something could go wrong with the trucks. A horse could fall. One of us could get sick or injured. Who knows?"

"That's five days. Roland, I'm not sure. It takes us two days to get back to San Francisco."

"Aw, hell, Vince, call your fucking partner, Walters, and tell him you're staying over a couple of days. He goes all over the place, and you're the balls in the partnership. Call him and tell him!" Jake slapped his hand on the table for emphasis. He was dying to go to this wonderful-sounding place.

"They have phones here yet?" Vincent remembered when they didn't.

"There's a central radio telephone office. We can call out from there," replied Roland, happy to be able to take advantage of this visit from his aviator friend. He was seldom able to leave Las Peñas himself.

What for these men was an escape into paradise was at times a prison for Roland. He wasn't really a rich gringo, having been disinherited for his Mexican adventures. He lived rather frugally on his military pension, much of which went into liquor, and his restaurant income, which varied with the season.

Suddenly, deafeningly loud thunder seemed to crash all around them, rattling their margarita glasses. The rain let loose with a fury, as though the heavens were spilling over. The rain poured through the lobby entrance's roof of thatched dried palm fronds and turned the floor into a little river within moments.

Vincent, Jake, and Ham stared in fascination as people retreated to the bar, ordering drinks to wait out the tropical storm. The waiter rushed frantically to close the shutters on the windows, which had no glass and were open to the elements. Everything was wet. Paper napkins blew about frivolously. It was a dramatic display of a rainstorm. Vincent looked at Ham to see if he was frightened, but his round, plump face glowed with pleasure. "Me like lain time." he affirmed.

A mariachi group of musicians began playing the classical *corridas* and romantic *boleros* of Jalisco, unfazed by the storm and happy for the captive audience. "Let's eat something before we get too plastered. What's good here, Roland?"

Roland smiled, by now his face quite flushed, as he replied, "the specialty tonight will please you all. By grand coincidence, they are serving turtle steak teriyaki. Japanese style, but the turtle is straight from our Mexican waters." Ham smiled happily, his face by now a bright, shiny orange color, his eyes like tiny slivers of black almonds.

They moved to the dining room, where they ate heartily—turtle steak, refried beans, rice, guacamole, and fresh, hot, handmade corn tortillas with chili. The meal was consumed with great relish and washed down with large quantities of lukewarm Bohemia beer.

After the dinner, Vincent paid the bill and a generous tip. They leaned back comfortably in their *equipale* chairs, contemplating the evening ahead. The rain had subsided, and the air felt clean, cool, and refreshed. "How about if we go to Margarita's dance hall? It's the only nightclub in town, and Margarita can get us anything we want." Roland winked and lifted his beer mug, draining it. His face was now a bright red, which contrasted strikingly with his thick white hair.

"Ta tell the truth, Roland, I'm pooped. I don't know about Vince or Ham, but I would sure like to hit the sack." Jake Morenetti knew what his needs were.

Vincent sat up straight, studying his watch. "Good lord, it's 11:30 already. Where did the time go? Where are we going to stay tonight?"

"At our house, of course. Hermalinda would be most insulted if you didn't stay with us." Roland was adamant about his acquired Mexican hospitality.

"You are inviting us to stay at your house on that beach? How do you call that beach again?" asked Vincent.

"Los Muertos, the Beach of the Dead." Roland smiled drunkenly.

"Well, better we sleep at the Beach of the Dead and not go nightclubbing tonight. *Mañana*, we'll hit Las Margaritas, okay?" Vincent called the waiter over and ordered a round of cognac as a nightcap. Then, they hailed a cab, loaded their belongings, and took off for Los Muertos.

Hermalinda was in the smoke-blackened kitchen as they made their noisy arrival. She was frowning. A little girl crawled around her feet on the brick floor as she stirred beans in a sooty pot. She wore a stained smock. Her long, straight, black hair hung loose around her shoulders, reaching down to her protruding, very pregnant waist. She was a typical Indian woman of this region, with dark skin, wideset high cheekbones, and brown, almost black, slightly slanted eyes. She could have walked out of a painting of the South Pacific native women by Gauguin.

"Hermalinda, how the hell are ya?" yelled Vincent, embracing her ample body and kissing her on the cheek. She recoiled slightly, reversing her frown with obvious effort into a polite smile. He swung the little girl up into his arms. She immediately screamed in terror, reaching out for her mother, who took her back like stolen treasure. Vincent looked rather crestfallen at his reception.

"She's afraid of strangers," said Roland, "nothing personal. Let's sit down," he continued, "Hermalinda, make some coffee," he ordered in Spanish, holding onto the rustic wooden table for support.

Hermalinda cast a withering glance his way then went out to the pump on the patio to get water for coffee.

Roland reached under the concrete kitchen counter and pulled out an unlabeled bottle of clear liquid. He leaned forward on the table, his eyes bleary and half-closed. "*Raicilla!*" he announced reverently as though it were some heavenly elixir.

"Siddown, siddown," he ordered. "You guys can't quit yet. Ya gotta taste this stuff. Nothin' like it nowhere. Linda, *sal, limón*, the glasses."

The woman's frown continued as she cut up slices of limes, poured heavy, grainy salt onto plates, then placed four-inch-tall, thin, little glasses before each man. She seemed especially upset by Ham Sado and kept looking at him furtively. She brought more peanuts and then prepared a large plate of cucumbers and a common root vegetable, Jicama, cut into cubes and sprinkled with salt, lime, and ground chili. The cubes were speared with toothpicks, which acted as eating utensils.

"Count me out." pronounced Jake, who staggered over to an old couch covered in torn, flower-printed plastic with chunks of foam rubber rupturing out of it, and there he collapsed. In a moment, he was snoring.

"This stuff is great, man! They make it from cactus, kinda like tequila, only better—the lechugilla cactus. Pure shit—the best." Roland slurred as he poured the clear liquor in the little glasses.

"You don' mind if I go sleep," muttered Ham as he rose and left the kitchen.

They heard a noise outside in the area of the patio garden, but it didn't seem to matter. The dark tropical night, the cool, rain-washed air, and the fragrance of the night-blooming flowers all closed in around them pleasantly, embracing the two men sweetly. Somewhere, a night bird sang softly.

The woman and child left, and the light from the oil lamp became dim, so they could hardly see each other. They drank two more rounds in silence except for Jake's soft snoring.

Roland gathered all his remaining forces and stared hard at his old friend. "Vince?"

"Yeah?" Vincent replied, his head swaying slightly.

"We go, or we don't go?"

Vincent sipped from the little glass and struggled to think what Roland was talking about. He carefully set the glass back on the table.

The snoring to one side of them stopped abruptly. The sudden silence caused their heads to turn in unison.

"Yeah, Vince, whad ya say? Come on, let's go!" said Jake, sitting up on the couch.

"Oh, yeah, the mountains, Shangri-La. Yeah, what the hell? Walters can take care of business, I need a vacation. We'll go. We'll save Las Margaritas for the next visit." Vincent settled it.

They smiled at each other. Roland filled their little glasses with more *raicilla*, while Jake dropped back down on the sofa and resumed snoring.

The flight from Puerto de las Peñas to El Valle Encantado took a little over twelve minutes. It was all up. The Sierra Madre Volcanico Transversal soared from sea level to more than 10,000 feet above the little fishing village. They left late due to the debilitating hangovers of Vincent and Roland.

Once above the mountain village, El Encantado, that commanded the beautiful valley, they dropped down over the house of Don Francisco Ochoa. Roland bounced about excitedly as they swooped over the large, sprawling house, waving frantically as the plane banked in a vertiginous circle.

"Hey, Vince, straighten her out, or I'm gonna throw up," gasped Roland after the fourth circle. "Look, that's him. That's Don Pancho. He sees us. Look!"

"I thought you said he was Don Francisco!" shouted Vincent.

"*Pancho* is the nickname for *Francisco*, got it?" said Roland, his face quite white.

The cobblestone street in front of the house filled with people of all ages jumping about, some waving their sombreros at the plane. Vincent and his entourage were arriving from the sky, and that made them god-like.

Vincent turned back to the dirt air strip at the edge of town. He lined the plane up with the field and made a roaring pass over the cattle grazing tranquilly on the grassy runway. They scattered in terror. Then, Vince, silently praying they would not return to block his landing, made a final approach.

The Staggerwing bumped and skidded to a halt. Vincent quickly unbuckled his seatbelt, leaned out the door, and vomited profusely. Roland followed suit, while Jake and Ham laughed.

Partially recovered, they began the ritual of unloading, tying the plane down, and locking it. Once again, they sat on their luggage, waiting. The flies buzzed around them. Vultures and hawks flew lazily around the clear blue sky above. Birds of all colors and sizes chased insects and each other through the air. After about five minutes, Vincent commented, "Maybe they didn't know it was you—or us, I mean." He lit a cigarette.

"They know. Maybe they just have to crank up the pickup. Ya gotta be patient here in Old Mexico, you know. Forget the clock and just relax," counseled Roland.

After ten or more minutes, they heard the sound of a motor, and a badly dented, scratched old Ford pickup rumbled up to where they waited. Children began jumping from the back of the pickup like so many grasshoppers. The men stepped out. They were dressed in trousers, elegant white shirts, sombreros, and high boots. They all sported prominent Pancho Villa mustaches, big bellies, and huge smiles that displayed large, white, serviceable teeth. The women wore flowing, colorful dresses and were very overweight.

The two incongruous groups met on that cool, windy field with great enthusiasm and excitement, like friendly delegates from far flung outposts of the world. Roland embraced Don Francisco warmly in the typical Mexican *abrazo*. *"Compadre, como has estado?"* he shouted as though to include everyone in his greeting.

"Rolando, mi hijo," answered Don Francisco, tears welling up in his eyes and tracing clean little paths down through the dust on his cheeks. *"Que bueno que regresaste con nosotros. Y Hermalinda?"*

"My wife couldn't come," Roland explained in Spanish. "Ah, and Maria, how beautiful you are!" he continued, standing back and smiling profusely at Don Pancho's wife. Don Francisco's heavyset, unremarkably endowed wife giggled at this lie as Roland embraced her, kissing her on each cheek.

Two small children hid behind her skirts, peeking out from time to time at these strangers assembled before them as though they had arrived from another planet. Roland introduced the men to the family.

Ham remained almost mute, suffering enough in English, and now to be confronted with Spanish further thwarted his desire to communicate. They all climbed into the back of the pickup with the infinite number of children and headed for town.

The town of El Valle Encantado was over 200 years old. It was laid out in the classical Mexican colonial tradition, with a large central plaza dominated by a lacy kiosk surrounded by gardens of roses, petunias, and gladiolas. Tall date palm trees bordered the gardens, interspersed with jacaranda trees that flowered in April. The blossoms of the jacaranda are a stunningly beautiful shade of deep lavender, and when they fell to the ground, the carpet of pale purple would extend beneath the trees. It was so lovely that the blossoms were never swept up until they dried up and turned brown.

The homes around the plaza and on the streets radiating out from the plaza were also traditional. Windows were large and tall, protected by shutters and intricately worked wrought iron. The homes were lavishly adorned in elegant architectural detail borrowed from Spain and France. Entrances were grand, with huge art nouveau iron gates through which a leafy private patio could barely be glimpsed, only enough to admire the interior but not enough to intrude on family life.

The homes were built of sun-dried adobe bricks and then plastered over. Some of the homes were older than the town itself and spoke of grand architectural aspirations. The moldings were fashioned in shapes of flowers, leaves, and vines, with much attention to detail. The upper floors and high ceilings were supported by the columns of Doric, Ionic, and Corinthian influence. The structures were topped by the traditional red clay tiles, clay existing in great abundance in El Valle Encantado. A few of the houses here and there were old and crumbling, abandoned by former affluence, serving only as a monument to glory found and lost, a testimony to what must have been a robust, proud, and ambitious people.

The Ochoa family home was large and spacious, with a central courtyard open to the weather. The second-floor bedrooms were on a terrace surrounding the courtyard and overlooking it. The dining room opposite the entrance had a large kitchen off to one side, as befitted a people who valued ample sustenance as of utmost importance. A great candle chandelier hung on a thick chain from the wooden beam of the dining room, electricity having arrived only a few years before.

However, in all else the Ochoa family had opted for modernism. Theirs was to be the first post-colonial house in El Valle. Instead of the fluting, the intricate plaster moldings, and classical pillars, it was all flattened out, smooth and straight up and down. Only the basic design was traditional.

Next to the house was the original corral and stables for the cows, horses, and burros. Pigs and chickens were kept to provide for the household consumption. The stables were made of stone and wood, with cobblestone flooring. Vincent found it difficult to think that all this existed within the city limits.

The town itself seemed part town and part ranch. The streets were all cobblestone and ran off here and there at odd angles, unlike the urban grid with which the Americans were familiar. Fertile fields surrounded the town, slowly ascending upward toward the high, brittle mountains covered with pine and oak trees. Vincent found it all excruciatingly beautiful but, in true macho fashion, could never express his excess of feeling to his friends.

The men settled into the great dining room. Bottles of *raicilla* and tequila were placed upon the huge, heavy, carved-oak dining table. It was cool inside the room though there were no windows, just the high double doors with glass panes and an opening in one wall that allowed food and dishes to be passed back and forth between the kitchen and dining room. They could hear the women bustling about in the kitchen.

Don Francisco fanned his fat, florid, perspiring face with his big *sombrero* then handed it to a young girl to hang up for him. He was smiling and obviously very pleased with his guests. He introduced the other men gathering at the table.

There was his cousin Don Trini and an aged man who was an uncle, two younger men who were the eldest sons of Don Francisco, a neighboring rancher who had come to buy a horse, and the local mayor, who was a distant relative. Don Francisco sat at the head of the table, while Vincent and Roland sat on either side of him. Ham was regarded with curiosity but accepted respectfully by the host. He sat next to Roland, while Jake was next to Vincent.

Jake was not accustomed to Mexican formality and rubbed his hands together nervously, wondering how he should behave here. He felt slightly intimidated, as though they might be making fun of him since he could not understand a word they said.

The Mexicans laughed and joked with each other in Spanish, of course, forcing Roland to translate as much as he could. Then suddenly, Don Francisco stood up and began to make a grand pronouncement. All fell silent to hear his words. *"Compadres, buenos amigos queridos,* welcome to El Valle Encantado and to my humble house, which I want you to know is also your house. *Mi casa es tu casa."*

The Americans smiled as the outrageous offer was translated.

"We are most honored by the presence of our great friends from the North who have come to share a small part of our lives here in El Valle." All eyes turned to the visitors from *el Norte* and they were applauded. The men shifted uncomfortably, unaccustomed to patriarchal speeches honoring them around the dining table.

The women—Doña Maria, her two daughters, and a serving girl—brought out large plates heaped with sliced cucumbers, sweet papaya, syrupy, bright orange mango, and rich, buttery avocados, all seasoned with ubiquitous coarse salt, ground chili, and lime juice, planted with a tiny forest of toothpicks with which to eat it all.

There were tostadas smeared with spicy combinations of meat and refried beans. Piquant sauces arrived in bowls that appeared to be carved from volcanic rock. A tray of the tall, thin, exotic little glasses, more limes, and salt were brought to the table. Vincent leaned over behind Don Pancho, nudging Roland. "Why don't the girls come and sit down with us?"

"Women never sit down with the men. It's not the custom. They wait on the men while they eat, and then they eat in the kitchen. That's the way it is done here."

"Wow!" commented Vincent, finding this particular aspect of local male supremacy intriguing—women happily dedicated to serving the men, no thought of emancipation. They probably never even heard of such a thing.

Don Francisco continued dedicating his house, his ranches, and his family to the service of his guests. *"Salud! Y otra cosa, hoy es mi cumpleaños!"*

"Whad he say?" queried Jake with his usual scowl, perhaps more profound for his frustration in not understanding Spanish.

"Don Francisco says that today is his birthday and that he is very happy that we are all here for the grand celebration, which will begin this afternoon and probably continue for a few days. Ah, and that they have sacrificed many pigs and sheep for the event and that you should save room in your stomachs for lunch," explained Roland.

"Salud!" shouted Don Pancho again, and all the men raised their little, thin glasses and gulped down the stinging, clear *raicilla*, which was immediately refilled. Vincent was recovering from his hangover by getting drunk again.

The large table laden with cheeses, head cheese of pork, and lots and lots of alcohol, populated by these vigorous men with pistols hanging from their belts who were laughing, joking, drinking, slamming the table with their fists at their own outrageous gossip—it all seemed surreal.

Then the women working, screaming, and shouting at one another, giggling in the kitchen, and the sounds of dishes and pots clanging together, knives chopping, grease sizzling, dogs barking, cocks crowing, pigs grunting and squealing became a disorienting cacophony.

Then there were the flies that settled on everything and everyone, the strange, strong smells of the cooking, of unwashed bodies, of the corral and the animals, of flowers, and finally the thunderclouds that were gathering and rumbling overhead—all of it began to seem unreal and dreamlike to the visitors from the North, creating within them a general sense of culture shock.

Don Francisco was shaking with laughter, his stomach bouncing, at some choice bit of malicious gossip concerning a special enemy of his, all the time waving a well-used red handkerchief ineffectually at the flies that swarmed mercilessly around them.

Vincent downed his raicillas in order to cope with all of it. A lovely young woman dressed in ruffles, flowers, and lace kept his glass filled, flashing a large smile with even, bright white, beautiful teeth. "Roland, the flies ... What do we do?" Vincent's sensibilities were affronted by the quantity of these annoying insects.

"I'll see if there is a flyswatter in the kitchen."

"How d'ya say *flies* in Spanish?" grumbled Jake, waving his hand around in a futile effort to disperse them.

"*Moscas*," said Roland, vainly trying to swat a couple of the black pests with a rolled-up old newspaper.

"*Moscas, moscas*," said Jake to Don Francisco as though he should eliminate the scourge on the spot after having promised them so much.

"Ah, si, si, muchas moscas. Es por los animales," replied Don Francisco merrily as he puffed on a huge cigar, flies being an integral part of life on the ranches during the rainy season.

"Believe me, after a few more raicillas, none of this is going to bother you at all," stated Roland flatly. "And say, if you want to wash up, rest a bit for the party, I'll take you to your bedrooms. Don Francisco is very pleased that he can offer you indoor plumbing, one of the few houses in town with flush toilets."

Vincent rose and walked unsteadily over to Don Pancho, eager to take leave of this fantasy world for the time being. "*Gracias, gracias, Don Pancho."* He managed to recall some basic high school Spanish.

Don Francisco stood up and embraced him again. Vincent felt a bit embarrassed by this unaccustomed demonstration of masculine affection, which was part of normal life here in these mountains. *"Rolando, quiero a Vicente mucho, mucho. Va a ser mi gran amigo, de veras,"* declared Don Pancho/Francisco.

"Whad he say now?" asked Jake.

"That he likes Vince very much and that he is going to be his lifelong friend," replied Roland, wearying of his task.

"That's cuz of yer blue eyes, Vince. Spics love blue eyes, ya know," said Jake, laughing at his own travesty of manners.

"Don't talk like that, Jake. We're here in Mexico, guests of these people, and you don't say things like 'spic,'" admonished Vincent.

"So what? He don't know what I'm saying."

"Just the same, like Roland says, Mexicans know what you are saying even if they don't understand it. Now, let's go get some shuteye so we are in shape for all the beautiful *muchachas*."

Their bedroom was huge, with a high ceiling made of thick wooden beams with planks of wood traversing them. The walls were painted a bright shade of pink. Crude paintings of *charro* horses and riders adorned the walls. Great bouquets of various-colored plastic flowers sat on the bureaus and chests. Several crucifixes hung over the beds to protect those sleeping. There were three double beds lined up for occupancy.

"Someone is going to have to double up. We are four," said Roland.

"I'll sleep with Ham, if y'all don't mind. I can trust a Jap more than you guys with all your damned huggin' and kissin' and blue eyes, and all. I don't want no hanky-panky," snorted Jake as he pulled off his shirt, exposing his very hairy chest. They laughed and began to open their suitcases to organize their clothing.

After a few hours of deep sleep, the men took turns showering in the bathroom down the hall. The second-floor corridor overlooked the patio, where a multitude of activities were taking place. Wooden tables were brought in and set up end to end, surrounding the little garden in the center of the patio. Chairs were unfolded and benches put into place to accommodate the guests for Don Francisco's birthday party. Musicians were intent on tuning up their instruments. The church bells were tolling loudly and constantly. People were coming and going. Children ran all over, screaming and chasing each other, wild with excitement.

The family returned from a mass performed in honor of Don Francisco. Out on the street, horses were being tied up, wagons and pickups were unloading their passengers, who stopped to talk to one another, gossiping or joking for a few moments before entering the festivities.

"Say, I'm gonna get me a cowboy hat to wear for the party. What about you guys?" said Vincent as he slicked his hair back, checking his image in front of a cracked and stained mirror, imagining how he might look with a mustache and a pistol swinging from his hip.

"Yeah, good idea. One for Ham and Jake, too, so we kind of, you know, fit in."

"Ah, cut it out. A Japanese cowboy? Who are you trying to kid? You trying to make us look ridiculous or something? I ain't wearing no cowboy hat," declared Jake vehemently.

"Why the hell not? When in Rome, do as the Romans, they say," asserted Roland, though he knew he was not going to convince Jake.

"First place, we ain't in Rome. And the second place, my head's too big for the cowboy hats here cuz I tried one on once. And the third place, I ain't no cowboy. I fly airplanes, and horses scare the shit outa me."

Roland and Vincent went out into the town in search of cowboy hats, or *sombreros*, as they were called here. They went from one country store to another trying the hats on, but none were large enough for their big gringo heads.

Finally, in an out-of-the-way, dim and dusty hardware store almost out of town, they made their last attempt. An old man sat in a corner and eyed them curiously from among the spurs, saddles, machetes, and miscellaneous ranch items.

Roland made their needs known to the old man, who rose with great effort and disappeared into the dark bowels of the establishment. From there, he produced two dusty, handwoven straw hats. He smiled at his success, brushing them briskly and then handing them over to their potential owners.

"Tight," muttered Vincent.

"The fellow has a way of making them larger," replied Roland, returning the hats to the storekeeper, who once again vanished into the dark. There were some loud hammering noises, and he returned with the hats, which now fit perfectly on their heads.

They swaggered back to the house and the festivities, joking about how they must look, like 100 percent gringo dudes. "All we need now is a horse. I used to pack out in Camp Mather in Yosemite when I was a kid, you know," said Vincent.

"Jeezus, Vince, there are horses all over the place. Wanna ride one, just say something to Don Pancho. He thinks you're great—the plane and all. He's got more horses than he can count. The guy is *rich.*"

"What I want is a drink—bad. Why doesn't he look rich? I mean, like Dudley Forsythe or Winston Cahill's old man."

"It's all about land here. Ranches and cattle, that's what makes a fellow rich. This ain't San Francisco, where all the money is insurance, real estate, banks, law, medicine. This is a whole new ball of wax. And you're fortunate that Don Francisco took to you. You are now in the inner sanctum of his friendship here in the mountains, and he will do anything for you—I mean anything. All that he has is yours."

"Really now." Vincent pulled himself up a notch as they walked along the cobblestone streets.

"Well, of course, he knows you are a professional and have a few bucks yourself and won't abuse his friendship, take him literally. But basically, that is the way it used to be around here. Tell me something. is Jake happy here? He acts so gruff, and he wanted to come up here."

"That's his style. It may be a bit too much for him all at once, but he'll adjust. When are we going duck hunting? That's what he loves. Social affairs drive him crazy."

"Tomorrow, *mañana.* Don Francisco is lending us his

pickup truck and some horses, since there is no road all the way into the Laguna de Juanacatlan."

"How'd you say that?"

"It's an Indian name. Don't worry about it."

"Jeezus, look at all the people going into the house! I guess we start drinking again. Looks like here on the ranch we are going to be either drunk or hungover," observed Vincent.

The main-floor patio and corridors of the house of Don Pancho were arranged with tables and chairs. The wooden tables had been covered with white tablecloths hand-embroidered with colorful flowers, while here and there were vases of roses. But the most striking thing was the amount of alcohol sitting around on the tables waiting to be consumed during the festivities: brandy, rum, tequila, and something called *ponche*, a homemade liquor. Women and young girls bustled around the tables, carrying plates of snacks, chattering and joking with the guests as they began to take their places.

The twelve musicians had finished tuning their instruments: violins, guitars, trumpets, clarinets, and a huge bass guitar. They were dressed in black and gray *charro* suits, with silver buckles adorning their jackets and riding up the sides of their pants. Nonchalantly, over their thighs dangled pistols in their holsters. Real bullets encased in leather belts circled their hips and crossed their chests in menacing elegance. Their handmade boots gleamed as they stamped and shuffled their feet, anxious to begin.

When the first notes of the mariachis began loudly, the whole party came alive. They played *corridos*, classical ballads, the traditional music of Mexico that tells the stories of the past, of love, death, and bravery. There were songs of the Revolution and its heroes—men, women, children, and horses—of the great haciendas and how they were destroyed; of rich men falling in love with beautiful young women, of being thwarted and dying for their love; of the noble horses who had gained fame in history in their own right. Through the songs, the horses became as famous as Pancho Villa.

As Vincent and Roland entered, everyone turned to look at them curiously, whispering about who they were. Roland and Vincent passed through the crowd of people and tables smiling amiably at everyone, nodding their heads from side to side.

"Now, don't they just look like idiots with those dumb hats on? I can't believe them," grumbled Jake to Ham. They were seated in the most inconspicuous corner Jake could find, as though he wanted to be invisible.

"*Oh, Señor Rolando and Vicente, por favor sientense con Don Pancho,*" gushed Doña Maria, her face flushed from the excitement and the social coup of having Americans in their home. No one had ever had real Americans as guests in their homes in El Valle. Doña Maria led them to the head table of men—sons, cousins, uncles, and friends of Don Francisco—the table of honor.

"Is this the Dark Ages or something, Roland? All the men at one table, and the women at the other or else doing all the work?" said Vincent, lighting one of his last Camel cigarettes and worrying where the next pack was going to come from.

"Nah, nothing like that. The women are revered here. Without the women, there would be no ranches. The gals always get together and gossip like this at the parties, apart from the men since the men are a big part of the gossip—you know, the usual stuff—who is getting married, who died or is sick and going to die, who ran off with whom, who left for the States to work, who is going broke, who had a baby. People here live rather isolated lives, without telephones, televisions, or newspapers. They don't see one another too much, either. So, at these big parties everyone finds out what's going on in the valley and over on the other side of the mountains. After a while and a few drinks and some chow, they all get back together again and dance—lotsa dancing."

The music was loud, and the vocalists had to sing many decibels above the volume. They changed often to relieve the strain on the vocal chords. The food began to arrive: platters heaped with pieces of fried pork, blood pudding, pork skin fried in deep fat, and much, much more.

Vincent stared curiously at how people ate all this bounty. First, lime juice was squeezed over the meat, then a hot sauce of tomato, onion, chili, and cilantro, then the beans all on top of a fresh, hot, handmade corn tortilla that served as a plate. This was all folded up and carefully guided to one's mouth, one's little finger serving as a brake, tipping up the other end of the tortilla to keep it all from falling out the back part. Some of the lucky few had plates. There were no knives, forks, or spoons, only toothpicks stuck into the meats. Fingers were indispensable.

There was an endless supply of tequila, rum, beer, and brandy to wash it all down. Faces were becoming quite flushed and greasy. Laughter exploded around the assembly like little firecrackers. The mutual teasing, jokes, amiable insults, and uproarious stories, exaggerated to the point of lies, became more outrageous.

Next came plates of fried chili peppers and cheese, refried beans and pork intestines and tongue. Deep-fried pork intestines was the favorite dish of Don Francisco Ochoa, his special treat from the overheated, pulsating *comales* of the ranch kitchen.

He slathered burning hot sauce over his birthday taco, topped it with slices of avocado from his extensive orchards, and ate the whole thing in one huge gulp. He smiled at the surprised expressions of his foreign guests. *"Es comida fuerte. Bueno para un hombre, para coger. Cometelo, Vicente, tu, Rolando, y tus amigos."* He smiled broadly as he tucked another taco into his wide mouth, shoving the platter of fried intestines toward his guests, sauce dripping from the side of his lips onto the lace tablecloth placed there at the table of honor.

"What did he say?" asked Vincent.

"He says you should eat one."

"They are guts. They eat that? A gut taco?"

"He says they make you strong, good for fucking, give you a great hard-on every time. Here, let me make you one." Roland picked up the pieces of twisted, crispy pork intestines, placed them on a tortilla, topped it with the avocado, and sprinkled a touch of hot sauce so as not to offend Vincent's uninitiated palate.

"Your forgot the lime and salt."

"Oh." The final touches were administered, and the taco was handed over to Vincent. "Here's to your love life. You better eat it, or you will insult Don Francisco."

All eyes were upon him as he dutifully devoured his "gut taco."

"What's with Jake and Ham? They better come over here. They are being antisocial or something," said Roland.

Vincent leaned over on the table in front of his two friends. "You guys got your period or something? You look like a couple of wallflowers sitting here brooding. Come on over to the table. Join the party, for Chris sake!"

"I can't understand what they are saying," grumbled Jake. "And what is that stuff they are serving? It looks really weird to me."

"This is a great party! And you are being rude to our host, who is providing us with a pickup truck and horses for us to go up to the lake tomorrow, spend the next couple of days camping out, hunting, fishing. And his sons are going to be our guides. Now, you can't come over and sit with us, have another drink, eat something, ask a *muchacha* to dance?"

"Dance? Me dance? You gotta be off your rocker, Vince. I'll go over and sit with those guys. I might even eat some of that stuff, since I am pretty hungry and that's all there is to eat. But I sure as hell ain't gonna dance!"

In the bedroom off the corridor, teenage girls were applying a bit of makeup, not too much so as to be criticized by their elders, and endlessly combing their own and each others' hair, arranging their hair ornaments, twining fresh roses and gardenias into their braids, adjusting their dresses and undergarments. They giggled nervously among themselves about the boys they had taken a liking to, hoping they would catch their eyes.

Don Francisco stood and invited all the young people to do the traditional dances: the *baile folklorico,* the *jarabe Tapatio,* and the *Sinaloense.* The young people lined up facing each other, boys on one side, girls on the other.

The music began, and the dancers swung into rhythmic motion, tapping their feet, swaying, circling, their figures lost in the rush and swirl of the girls' colorful skirts. At times, the boys stamped the ground like young bulls in heat, the girls approaching coquettishly, their faces almost brushing the boys' faces, then retreating. The boys swept the air with their charro hats, then at the end of the dance placed them on their heads. They all stopped as if frozen, the girl leaning back over the arm of her partner, her skirt held out to the side, a glorious arc of red, white, and green flowers and lace, the boy leaning over his "conquest," all of them smiling and breathless as the guests applauded vigorously.

"Now, Jake, didn't you like that? Now, tell me the truth. Wasn't that dancing just beautiful?" asked Vincent, smiling with pleasure at this astounding performance in this culturally isolated place.

"Yeah, that was nice. I have to admit it. Now, pass me a bottle of tequila and some more pig guts, and let's get on with it."

The party shifted gears after that.

Children began chasing each other around the pillars and flowerpots, hiding from one another, screaming with laughter. The little boys grappled and tussled on the floor like puppies, ruining their party suits, the adults now too inebriated to stop them. The little girls were dressed like animated dolls in frothy colors of pink, pale green, blue, white, and lavender with lace trimming every conceivable place—hems, collars, sleeves. They too tussled, the lace getting torn. A few fights broke out, and they all danced in imitation of the adults.

The men and women began to get back together. They danced heated polkas, waltzes, and the traditional *danzone*. Couples swayed back and forth, locked together in a public embrace of love. Vincent felt touched by the scene before him, as though he were privileged to look in on an authentic reflection of our tribal past.

The young women were painfully beautiful to him, with their dusky skin; long, thick, black hair, and dark eyes. He wanted to make love to all of them. His throat caught in a desire that was not altogether sexual but more a desire to possess their beauty, youth, and innocence born of the traditional way of life on these ranches. And those gorgeous teeth! Industrial processed food had not yet arrived to this valley.

The contrast between his life in San Francisco and life here overwhelmed him. He could not describe his feelings; he did not have the words. He could only reconcile how he felt with reality by deciding right then and there, as soon as he could, he was going to buy himself a ranch here. He was going to cleanse his soul with hard work, clean living, mate with one woman for life like the geese and the wolves. He was going to be born again right here in El Valle Encantado.

The party lasted through the night and into the next morning. Vincent and his friends gave up around 3:00 AM and went to their bedroom to sleep briefly. They were awakened around 5:30 AM to more mariachi music and people singing.

A replacement band was loudly playing "Las Mañanitas," the traditional birthday song of Mexico, for Don Francisco.

These are the early mornings
That King David used to sing of.
Today, since it is the day of your birth,
We sing them to you.
Wake up, my loved one.
Look out. A new day is born.
And listen to the little song birds,
For they also sing for you.

The day that you were born,
All the flowers bloomed.
At the fountain of baptism,
The song birds sang.

The band was playing outside the ground-floor bedroom of Don Francisco and his wife. Drunken friends and relatives from the night before had linked arms and joined in the singing. Jake was out in the corridor in his shorts and tee shirt, leaning over the railing in amazement. "Hey, Vincent, the party's still going on! They're still drinking. What about our fishing trip?"

Roland took over once more as orientation leader. "Let me explain all this. The party will probably go on for another day or two then taper off over the next week. I think that today is the actual birthdate of Don Pancho, but they started yesterday because some people had to come from so far away. They will probably change the menu, and I believe they will serve *pozole*."

Except for Ham Sado, who had wrapped himself in a blanket and continued to sleep, the other men began to dress groggily while Roland continued his dissertation on Mexican customs. "*Pozole* is an Indian dish, a corn soup made with pork and chicken. They use what we call *hominy* in the States. They serve it in big clay bowls very hot, and you put all kinds of condiments into it, like chopped onion, cabbage, lime juice, radishes, and, well, it just keeps going. It's really good and can feed an army. They eat it with *tostadas*, which are toasted tortillas."

"I feel hung over, if ya want the truth," muttered Vincent, sitting half-dressed on the edge of the bed, holding his head. "That *raicilla* really does it, and ya hardly feel it going down."

"You all need a Bloody Mary or 'Bloody Maria,'" said Roland.

"Good god, is that possible here?" said Vincent as they made their way down the stairs to join the early morning festivities. Their eyes were quite bloodshot and their manner subdued.

The women of Don Francisco's family were already busy sweeping and mopping the floors, dressed in modest work dresses. They cleaned the tables and replaced the cloths and the flowers. The oldest girl came over to the Americans, smiled, and said, *"Buenos dias,"* then kissed each of them on the cheek. The gesture had a calming effect on the men. "*Oyey, Vicente, quieren algo ustedes?*" she inquired most charmingly, her dark lashes fluttering over her sparkling black eyes. Roland stepped forth gallantly, his Spanish rolled off his tongue as he explained what a Bloody Mary was to the girl.

They sat down at one of the tables and were served what looked like Bloody Marys, followed by plates heaped with scrambled ranch eggs, fresh, steaming yellow tortillas, refried beans, cheeses—grated, sliced, or whole—and different styles of sauces prepared with various hot chilies, herbs, and tomatoes. There was no electrical power at this hour of the morning, so the sauces were prepared in the kitchen by grinding the ingredients with coarse-grained salt in a mortar and pestle carved from black volcanic rock, called a *molcajete*.

The Bloody Marys had small bits of tomato in them, along with the *raicilla*, chili, and lime juice. They were delicious, and soon the second round was in place on the table.

Roland lit a cigarette and exhaled upward, the smoke forming a mystical halo around his white head. He smoked Mexican cigarettes, Faros, and offered the pack to his friends.

Vincent continued to feel like he was living in another world, another space and time. He made an effort to concentrate on what was happening, to try to reconcile all this with his past experiences, which had all been more under his control. He decided to let go of all his decision-making impulses and hear what Roland had in store for him. To put himself in the hands of another person was an unfamiliar role for him. The cigarette he was smoking was sweet and spicy—strange, nothing like a Camel.

"Okay, here's the plan," stated Roland with authority. "We will hang around here until after lunch, maybe walk around town and get supplies together for the next few days—we will need some kind of grill to cook on—and get the fishing gear together. Don Pancho is having the horses brought down from his ranch in El Ocotillo. Early tomorrow morning, we lead the horses onto the truck. His two sons are freed from family obligations for the duration of our stay. And we will then drive up to the Laguna de Juanacatlan. We stay as long as we want. Lots of ducks migrating now, and that's their main stopover. How does that sound?"

Vincent and Jake looked at each other and shrugged. "Great plan!" they chimed in unison, as there were no alternatives to the plan. They were happy captives of these very generous people.

The next morning, three battered pickups lined up in front of the house. The *vaqueros*, or cowboys, patiently coaxed six reluctant horses up some improvised wooden ramps onto the trucks and then tied them securely to the iron railing surrounding the truck beds. Manure fell damp and steaming from the nervous animals.

Saddles, boxes of food, and camping equipment were packed into one of the trucks, while the Americans and one of Don Pancho's teenage daughters and two of his sons squeezed into the cabs.

The vehicles dated from the early '40s, and they looked as though they were held together with glue and bailing wire. The mufflers had long ago given out, and the suspensions were in dire straits. But for some reason, no one seemed concerned about the dilapidated condition of their trucks. On the contrary, they were talking and laughing with each other in anticipation of a wonderful trip up into the beckoning green mountains.

"Do you really think these rattletraps are gonna take us up into those mountains?" queried Vincent nervously, his right shoulder squeezed against the truck door and the other up against Roland in a painful kind of togetherness.

"Don't worry about a thing. These people know what they are doing. They have lots of experience improvising. Just relax and enjoy the scenery," Roland counseled as they waved *adios* to the family gathered in front of the house to see them all off.

The horses tethered behind them heaved from side to side as they began to leave the village behind, following the dirt roads riddled with potholes at a snail's pace in a northeasterly direction.

Abruptly, they were among the big ranches, the *haciendas*, as they were called before the Revolution. Fields of tall corn, just forming ears, stretched out to where the mountains began.

Just a few years before, all the cultivation had been done with teams of oxen, but now modern tractors and plows sat beside the lovely old adobe houses and outbuildings. The mottled, moss-covered, dark-orange tiled roofs, running into one another, sloping and careening from house to servants quarters to pig pens to stables to chicken coops to milking sheds, seemed to form one great consecutive building. Flowers adorned the corridors of the houses—rows of bright blossoms rooted in oil cans, old clay pots, lard containers, buckets with holes, whatever was available. Geraniums, lilies, roses, daisies, and an infinite variety of succulents gave vibrant color to the reddish clay-colored haciendas.

Hens wandered across the road, clucking angrily at the vehicles invading their territory. Flocks of tiny chicks scurried rapidly behind their mother hens, almost seeming to float en masse over the road.

People were working in the fields, their sombreros dipping and rising as they weeded or fertilized the crops. Endless rows of freshly washed clothing hung on barbed wire fences, waving in the breeze like domestic flags signifying a well-run household. Children played in the corridors, in the fields, beside the roads, laughing, running, chasing, riding burros and horses, confiding their secrets to each other with the limitless energy and joy of childhood. Wood smoke curled lazily up from the kitchens of the haciendas, spreading delicious cooking odors over the countryside.

A silence descended over the Americans. Vincent began to snore softly while the trucks began their noisy struggle to ascend the mountains. They crept along in first gear past the first stand of pine and oak trees, which gradually turned into a great tall forest as they began to navigate the tortuous switchbacks, back and forth at an ever increasing angle, the old motors heaving, whining, straining to obey the merciless accelerators.

"Hey, Vince, wake up! Look at the view!" exhorted Roland. Looking back, they saw the village at the upper end of the valley, the church spire dominating the low, level houses of the town.

Halfway up the mountain, they stopped the trucks to let the engines cool and pour water into the radiators.

Vincent got out and ambled stiffly to one said of the road to relieve himself. Staring up at an enormous *higuera* tree, he saw that it was laden with delicately colored orchids. Look at that he thought to himself. I think I'll just go up that tree and cut me some orchids. Carefully, he climbed the tree. With his pocketknife, he hacked a thick growth of the orchids away from its host, and it fell to the forest floor. "Jeezus, look at this! There must be forty orchids in this plant! You know how much this would cost in San Francisco? Why, four or five hundred or maybe more. And my God, here you can just pick 'em off the trees." They all returned to the trucks after Vincent had carefully set aside his precious treasure of fresh orchids.

The road ended abruptly in a tangle of rocks, bushes, and trees, dwindling into an obscure path through the heavy mountain growth. The sons of Don Francisco leaped out of the pickups and led the horses down from the trucks then began tying the camping gear to the burros. They saddled the horses and held them still for the visitors to mount.

"I no go on horse. I walk please," announced Ham, striding with purpose into the forest.

Vincent overtook him. "Ham, it's easy to ride. You just swing up there on that saddle and sit on it like a chair. The horse does all the work, and all you do is tell him what you want him to do, okay?" Vincent did not think the small Japanese man should walk the three kilometers to the lake.

"Horse don't know me. and me don' know horse," Ham asserted.

"The horse is very well-trained. Believe me, he won't do anything like buck or try to throw you. Look at that trail there, will ya? Rocks, weeds, holes, snakes—you can't walk that, but the horse can easily."

Ham's face twisted in anguish. "Vince, you no terr me that I ride horse. I never, never ride horse. "

Vincent stroked the horse's neck while the Mexicans looked on in amusement to see what would happen.

"Here, now, you touch the horse. Go on, touch him. He won't bite. Touch him, goddammit!"

Ham extended a quivering hand and slowly placed it on the warm, damp fur of the horse's neck. The horse twisted his head to see who was touching him. Ham leaped back in alarm, while the horse resumed staring straight ahead, thinking of all the nice, fresh, ungrazed grass that lay waiting for him.

"Here, up you go." Vincent and Jake heaved the frightened man onto the saddle then stood back. The horse stood motionless except for a small shiver passing over his flanks. "Okay, Ham, now just hold these reins lightly, not too hard. No, no, don't pull on them, or the horse will go backwards. Don't grip the saddle horn like that. These horses are very docile, right, Roland?"

"Yeah, he'll be fine. Now, Vincent, you go ahead of Ham, behind Arturo, and me behind him. Gustavo goes last, behind Jake."

"I ain't so sure my horse is all that crazy about me, neither," said Jake, his horse stamping the ground and shaking his head up and down. Jake's face was grimacing as he held the reins tightly.

"*Sueltalos!*" shouted Gustavo.

"Whad he say?" yelled Jake, his voice close to panic.

"Loosen up the reins!"

"What's the horse's name? Maybe if I talk to him, he'll be nicer."

"*Pirata,*" replied Arturo as he effortlessly swung himself into place on his mount.

"*Pirata?* Ain't that like a pirate or something?" muttered Jake as they struggled to line up the horses according to plan.

"Aiyeeee!" screamed Ham as his horse reared up, Ham pulling back on the reins, his gardener's cap flying to the ground. Vincent leaped to grab the reins violently away from Ham, who was lying on his back across the rump of the horse. "Get me down, now. This horse gonna make me one dead Jap."

"Okay, you translate this, Roland. I am going to walk him so he gets used to it. He's gonna ride this goddamned horse, or my name isn't Vincent Franklyn Cooper III."

Ham righted himself while Vincent untied the lead rope, handed the fateful reins of control back to Ham, and they began to walk along the path past the trucks. Vincent smoked as they made their way up the mountain. "See, that's not so hard, now, is it? he cajoled his friend. Quit shaking and calm down. The horse knows if you are scared. See, that's fine. The horse is just walking, one step at a time. Just relax there in the saddle and pretend you are John Wayne. *Don't pull back on the reins."*

"Vince, if I die, I leave to you my fowers. You are good friend. I think I gonna lide this horse. You watch see."

They turned to go back. Ham sat straight up in the saddle, adjusted his gardener's cap advertising flower seeds back onto his head, his face set as he proudly returned to the group. The Japanese man had proved himself by imagining himself to be John Wayne in his favorite Western film, *Red River*. They rode the three remaining kilometers up the mountain without incident.

The boys began to make a camp under the pine tree, erecting a tent, spreading out the sleeping bags in the sun, and collecting firewood for cooking and for warmth during the cold night ahead. The area was almost untouched except for occasional grazing cattle that strayed this far.

It was known as *ejido* land, land freely granted to the peasants after the Revolution of the 1920s. There was no tourism, an area isolated from the hordes except for the intrusion of Vincent and his friends. Local people would occasionally come on Sundays to fish in the lake and cook out with their families.

Once the camp was comfortably organized, Gustavo, Arturo, and their sister Letti drank some *raicilla* with the men, each taking a hefty slug, then announced that they must walk down to the trucks in order to be off the mountain before dark.

"Thanks a million, or, ah, *muchas gracias*," Vince called as they waved goodbye to the young people. "And don't forget to come back for us in two days, or I lose my law practice. Oh, what the hell? Maybe that would be all for the better." Vincent laughed sardonically.

The men were left with four horses and two burros. They were instructed to tie the burros to a different spot every day to graze and to partition the grain they had brought along in gunny sacks. The horses would serve as transportation for the next few days.

The boys and their sister turned and waved once more as they left. Nice-looking boys, strong with those sturdy white teeth illuminating their smiles. The girl, her black hair flowing down her shoulders, loving the outing into the mountains, lifted the *raicilla* bottle in salute, took another swig before passing it on to her brother Arturo. And then they disappeared into the forest.

The campers, unaccustomed to the strenuous exercise and high altitude, almost without speaking crept into the tent and were sound asleep within minutes.

Vincent awoke startled, wondering where he was. He had slept more soundly than he could remember in a long time. It was pitch dark. The others were snoring loudly around him as he carefully crept out of the tent to survey the situation. The sky was covered with an infinite number of stars.

He found his flashlight and matches and lit the campfire. The boys had doused the wood with kerosene, and it leaped into flames. The silence was profound. Somehow, the sounds of the crickets, the owls, and night birds, the occasional squeaking of bats swooping about in search of their insect supper did not count as noise, nor did the howling of the coyotes later in the night count as disturbing the silence. A few clouds drifted overhead. It might rain tomorrow. They were ill-prepared for heavy rain, and he silently prayed to the unknown god of these parts that it would not rain.

He lit a kerosene lantern and put away his flashlight. Then, he rummaged through a box of food that Don Francisco's daughters had prepared for them. There was a large stack of tortillas wrapped tightly in two towels, still slightly warm from the kitchen, two large cheeses, coils and coils of *chorizo*—the Mexican sausage, dried, salted pork meat, a large bag of dried beans, lemons, salt, onions and chilies conserved in a jar. There was also a can of pork lard, extra matches, and simple cotton towels. How kind of these people, he thought to himself as he began to construct a simple outdoor cooking stove with rocks and an old iron grate they had packed for them.

He walked down to the lake shimmering under the stars to fill a bucket with water. Some frogs leaped in the little lapping waves as he dipped the bucket into the cold mountain water. He got his feet wet in the water, but he didn't care. He had a desire to strip and swim in this magical place, but didn't. It was too cold, and he was concerned about drying off.

Back at the campsite, he rinsed off part of the beans and placed them into the cooking pot. When they began to boil, he threw in some of the sausage, salt pork, a little extra salt, and a couple of dried chilies. He realized that he was very hungry and nibbled on some cheese while the beans bubbled over the fire.

Time seemed at a standstill except for the movement of the stars. He took a drink of the lake water to assuage his thirst. It tasted of algae and perhaps a bit of cow dung thrown in. It was fine, good for the immune system.

He became inspired by the outdoor meal preparation and soon had the aluminum camping plates and utensils set out for his buddies. He grated cheese for the beans and chopped up some onion. The tortillas went into a special covered pot, and he set that at the edge of the fire to heat them up.

There was something missing—oh, a cigarette. He hadn't smoked since walking Ham around on the horse—rare for him, four or five hours without a smoke. Sometimes in San Francisco, he woke up two or three times just to light up.

Jake and Roland woke up. They wandered off to relieve themselves, returning with great enthusiasm for the boiling pot of beans. "Son of a gun, Vince, you think of everything now, don't you? I'm so hungry I could eat a horse!" said Roland, rubbing his hands together to demonstrate his enthusiasm.

They took the warm tortillas and threw them over the fire for a few seconds then prepared sausage tacos topped with the cheese, chili, and onion. The conversation, the smell of food, and the laughter of the men roused Ham, who joined the circle of voracious taco eaters.

"Now, how come this is so good, and in San Francisco we would never think of ordering beans and tortillas. I mean, this is like surf and turf, chateaubriand, and lobster tail. Ya know what I mean," commented Vincent philosophically between mouthfuls.

"What's to drink?" asked Jake.

"*Raicilla* and water. That's about it."

"I'm all boozed out. I'll take some water if you don't mind." Jake drank deeply of the pungent lake water.

Ham cleaned up after their simple supper, and they sat around the fire talking and smoking, feeling the luxurious calm of urban escape, reveling in their wilderness existence.

Vincent exhaled, watching the smoke dreamily, thoughtfully. "Don't you kind of envy men like Don Francisco? Think about it. They really don't work too hard. The women adore them, wait on them hand and foot. They are treated like gods, actually. They own all that ranch land, feed their families from what they produce— no supermarket bills, no mortgages, no alimony, no office expenses. They pay jack shit to those cowboys, but then the cowboys don't have any expenses, either, to speak of. And all that time to party. They can afford to be generous. I think it would be a wonderful way to live."

"Yeah, yeah. But just you wait! It's all gonna change. Bet my bottom dollar on that!" exclaimed Jake cynically. "Ten, fifteen years from now, they'll be hotels around this lake, the ranches all sold, kids run to the city for money and drugs, turn bad."

"I seen it happen in California. When I was a kid, Santa Cruz, Watsonville, Salinas, it was all kind of wild, agricultural, like Mexico here—big family ranches, big families, everyone nice as hell, clean air, the rivers, the lakes beautiful, almost private, you could say. Now, try to drive down the Coast Highway on a Sunday afternoon, and ya go nuts with the traffic. Ranches all sold out to big business. Nothing is the same."

"There still aren't any paved roads into this valley," commented Roland, squeezing some lime juice into his drink of *raicilla* with lake water and a pinch of salt.

"That'll come. Progress, ya know," continued Jake with his usual cynicism larded with nuggets of truth.

Vincent slapped a mosquito that landed on his arm. "I don't know. They say it's progress, but then when you see how the agricultural land is all used up, the lakes polluted and the rivers, less and less fish every year. I like money as well as the next guy, but still, I like things, you know, virgin."

They all chuckled at this, knowing Vincent's penchant for seduction. "Don't laugh. I'm serious," he continued. "I'd love to buy part of the Rancho Ocotillo. Don Francisco says he's getting tired, and his sons don't really want to work the land. They want the easy money, maybe a little lazy."

"They don't look lazy to me. They were working their asses off from the time we got there to the time we left and then took us up here. I hope my sons are as hard working," Roland said as he poured himself another *raicilla*. He liked to drink.

"Now, imagine, Vince, what it would be like to buy a ranch at your age, yeah, the ranch. It would really kill you."

"Well, now, I think that rat race in San Francisco is going to kill me. I'm still not over the hill. Forty-nine isn't ancient. But I know what you are saying. I would need a woman willing to work like hell. Unfortunately, my wife would not like ranch life. She needs her doctors, the restaurants, her shopping, her friends—a city girl. I would probably need to divorce her and get myself a country girl, someone who grew up on a ranch or farm, maybe even a Mexican woman!"

They all stared at Vincent as though he were crazed.

"You seriously thinking of divorcing *again?* This time you only been married a couple of years. Hell, I don't know how you guys afford all the divorces, I'm stuck with Annie. Can't afford to dump her, if you want the truth." Jake ground out a cigarette in the forest loam under his foot.

"The truth is, you really love her, Jake, and you know it. You couldn't function without her," said Vincent.

Roland continued illustrating his point of view on the matter of ranches. "You also need children to help out," he said thoughtfully. "There's lots of physical labor. If you can afford it, you hire *mozos*. Those are hired day laborers, guys with strong backs and weak minds who don't do much more than tote, lift, cut weeds with machetes, and take care of animals. Don Francisco teaches them to drive tractors and to plant, but sometimes they wreck the equipment."

"Oh, and another thing about life around here: did you see that baby boy the girls were carrying around and fondling? Well, that's a baby Don Francisco had with another woman. He got this girl pregnant, and she couldn't afford the baby, so he took the child into his household for his wife and daughters to take care of. Now how about that?"

Vincent raised his head, shocked again by this strange place. "You mean, his wife takes care of his child by another woman?" He could not conceive of his wife taking care of *any* baby, let alone one of his by another woman. It was unthinkable, but here was this woman …

Roland, enjoying his superior fund of knowledge, continued with his cultural education of his friends. "Children are highly valued here in rural Mexican society, and men are given a lot of leeway, a long leash, as they say. A wife can actually be flattered rather than jealous that another woman had fallen for her husband. It gives her a kind of prestige. I suppose it could be likened to a harem situation, but not exactly."

"So, these men are polygamous here?" asked Vincent then continued without waiting for an answer. "Well, I guess we are in a way, also, but serially. Since it's illegal to have more than one wife at a time, we just keep divorcing. Hell on the bank account. This way sounds a lot more economical, if you ask me."

They laughed at Vincent's eternal pragmatism.

"I do want to come back here, Roland," Vincent continued. "This place fascinates me, and to tell the truth, I haven't felt this good in a long, long time."

"Say," interrupted Jake, "I don't know about you guys, but I'm pooped. I'm gonna hit the hay. Tomorrow?"

"Tomorrow, we better shoot some ducks or catch some fish or we're gonna get real tired of eating beans and tortillas," said Vincent as he took out his dentures and plunked them into a clay cup of water for the night. He didn't care if his friends saw him toothless.

They fluffed up the sleeping bags and unfolded extra blankets. Ham and Jake in the tent, while Roland and Vincent curled up close to the fire. The four men fell into a deep sleep. Not even the nearby howling of coyotes nor the hooting of night owls, the scruffling of wild rabbits, field mice, and opossums cautiously approaching to nibble on cold, discarded beans and tortillas could disturb their slumber.

She smells of booze, perfume and cigarettes, but he likes it.

CHAPTER SIX

Party Time

As Vincent swings the big Buick around the last turn of Upper Terrace, he sees that there is indeed a party going on. There is nowhere to park, so he has to drive almost to the fallen monument at the top of the hill to find a space.

The street door to the flats is wide open, as is the door to his place. He can hear his Al Jolson and Bennie Goodman records blaring. As he enters the smoky hall, a female voice screams, "Vincey, darling!" And the woman flings her arms around him, kissing him warmly and wetly on the mouth. She smells of booze, perfume, and cigarettes, but he likes it. "How'd ya like that, you gorgeous hunk of a lawyer?" the woman gasps and kisses him once more so he will be sure to get the message.

Mary Belle is there in a moment, almost but not quite shoving the drunken party girl to one side. "Where the hell have you been?" she demands angrily. "Everyone is asking for you. Well, they're all soused by now." Her hair is hanging in clumpy blonde strands around her head, and she looks like she has had a few herself.

"Working, honey, getting that case ready for Friday. Now don't be so grouchy. This is a party. Be a good girl and bring me a Tanqueray on the rocks. I don't like being sober when everyone else is drunk." He pats her on the behind as she turns obediently toward the kitchen. Women, he thinks, are so damned easy.

"Hi, Vince! Everyone's been waiting for y'all. I see ya like mah girlfriend, Suzy Wong. She ain't really a chink, ya know, just one of mah girlfriends, works at Magnin's. I brought her here for Purcell. Hope he goes easy on ya." Dr. Burkhart stands before him, rocking slightly on his heels, his face twisted into his customary half smile, half sneer. "Hey, that was quite a show you put on in the hospital with Phyllis. I loved it. Let's do it again sometime."

"Forget it, Ted. It's just one big problem. How is Purcell doing?"

"Drunk as a skunk, I am happy to say. Kelley just came down to join the party. Hey, why don't you invite that little girl downstairs, make it a building party? She's all alone, poor thing. Don't you feel sorry for her?"

"Mary Belle will have a fit. She is so goddamned jealous! She's pissed as hell that your girlfriend smooched me."

"Well, the hell with that. I'll go down and invite her myself. She's kinda cute—a bit too serious, probably could use a laugh or two. I'll bring here to the party out of the kindness of mah big ole Texas heart."

I am busy cleaning my oil paintbrushes in turpentine then washing them in hot, soapy water, rinsing them, and carefully drawing the soft sable bristles to a fine point to dry in perfect shape for tomorrow's work.

During the afternoon, I had bought steaks and firewood for Thom, and now I wonder if I should just wait for him to call or if I should call him. The noise of the party above is incessant— shoes clunking on the oak floors, shrieks of laughter, loud music. I imagine the wonderful air of conviviality, champagne, handsome, flirtatious men. It all accentuates my aloneness, the proximity of this wild human joy.

I wallow in my self-pity. I pour myself a glass of red wine and settle on the window seat of my small living room, staring out at the street. The fog is beginning to roll in. There are cars parked all over. I see the back of my little Triumph peeking out from behind the garden wall, a tiny space for a tiny sports car.

Unexpectedly, someone knocks on my door, startling me. The doctor would have phoned. I leap to open it, and there is Dr. Burkhart, the cynical satyr, still curiously attractive man I had met that momentous moving day. "Hi, there! How yáll doin'?" he asks, his teeth bared in a glinting smile. He takes my hand as though to shake it and then places his other hand over mine. I feel unnerved by him.

"I ... I'm fine, I guess. Just finished working for the day."

"Really, now? Can I see what yáll are doin'?" Without waiting for an answer, he strides past me and into the bedroom/ studio where I have my easel set up. "Say, now, yer pretty darn good, at that. Little Chinese girls, aren't they? Howdya get them to pose?"

"Oh, I take photos of them and then work from the photos. I love to go to Chinatown. It's like going to another country."

"Well, now, little lady, maybe someday I'll take you to Chinatown to eat. The food is great. Yáll look like you could use a good meal."

I wish he hadn't said that. I am both skinny and poor. My divorce left me with very little except the agreement that I could continue to rent the apartment with its precious, tiny slice of a view of the Golden Gate and a meager alimony settlement of two thousand dollars a year for three years. I am having trouble scraping together the monthly seventy-dollar-a-month rent.

"Why doncha get yourself fixed up a bit and come to the party. They're making charcoal steaks, French fries, a big salad, plenty of champagne, any kind of booze you would fancy. Doc

Kelley and I got it all together, a party every night so no one gets depressed. Vincent just showed up."

I decide he is probably right, and I discard my funk. Burkhart leaves through the back basement stairs, and I begin the task of getting myself into party shape.

A slinky black sheath hangs in my closet. A dress my ex-mother-in-law had bought for me wholesale years ago. She hated my homemade clothes, which is what I was accustomed to wearing for most of my life. But the truth is that now I have to go back to sewing my own clothes due to my reduced circumstances.

After a quick shower, I slip into the sheath, hook my nylon stockings to my garter belt, then fasten a string of real pearls (thanks again to my ex-in-laws), a pair of old-fashioned, black suede opera pumps, and my dressing is complete.

I put on some makeup, clamp some painfully tight earrings to my lobes, dab a few drops of almost empty Chanel N°5, brush out my long hair, and survey the results in the mirror. I vainly think I am beautiful, ready to take on the party. Who knows what adventures await me right above my head?

Entering through the back door into the familiar kitchen, I almost collide with the beautiful blonde woman, slightly inebriated, and a short Oriental man filling plates with steak, French fried potatoes, butter, and salad. There is a big basket filled with hot instant dinner rolls. The Oriental man and the beautiful blonde woman look up at me in surprise and then return to their tasks as though I do not exist.

I feel a chill, unwelcome, but make an effort anyway. "Hello, there. I live downstairs. Dr. Burkhart invited me. My name is—"

"Oh, fine," says the beautiful blonde woman as she sweeps past me out of the kitchen, laden with several plates of steaming food.

I enter the dining room, feeling terribly out of place. People stare at me. My beautiful self-image evaporates. Guests are seated around the huge, early American dining room table. It has all its leaves in place and appears quite regal in size.

The big window at the head of the room frames the view I had enjoyed only last week. The night is clear, and there is Market Street with its sparkling lights and traffic slashing through town to end at the Ferry Building. The bay is dark, spanned by the bridge, the lights of Oakland glittering in the far distance with the moon rising behind them.

Thankfully, Thom engaged in an animated conversation with a young woman at the dining table, a familiar face in this sea of strangers. There are men in business suits mingling about, still drinking rather than eating, and attractive, well-dressed women. I spy Dr. Burkhart in the living room, but he appears to ignore me.

"Well, how nice you look, Miss Botticelli. Good that you came. Let me get you a drink before dinner is served." I turn slightly to see Vincent Cooper smiling at me in a most charming manner. He appears to be the most gallant gentleman I have ever encountered, dismissing my terrible first impression of him. He is very handsome in a clean shirt with an expensive suit and a bowtie.

"Oh, hi, there. Uh … white wine would be fine," I manage to say. He unnerves me, somehow, but has partially restored my self-esteem.

He returns with my wine and ushers me to a place at the dining table. It is covered with a white linen tablecloth. There are two large vases of fresh daises and a candelabra, glowing with real candles. The wine and water goblets are cut crystal. The china plates all match, and only the flatware falters. It is stainless steel, but in a colonial pattern. Just a few steps up from my little studio apartment, and I am in a different world entirely.

The older man seated on one side of me turns, smiles engagingly, and introduces himself as Judge Morehouse of the Ninth Circuit Court. Vincent informs me that he is a great and old friend of his then excuses himself to set up card tables to serve the overflow of guests.

"And who might you be?" says the judge, his face a wrinkled smile.

I introduce myself as a neighbor in the building, living in the apartment below.

"Oh, yes, Dr. Kelley was telling me about you. You are the artist, and he says you are very good. He mentioned something about you working for him."

"Uh, yes, we talked about that the other day. He wants me to do medical illustration for him, but I am not sure. It's quite technical."

"Well, of course, you won't be able to throw paint all over the place ..." The judge chuckles at his perception of modern art.

Thom catches my eye across the table, smiles, and waves coyly. I wonder curiously what he is talking about to his companion. He loves to talk.

"Tell me," the judge continues, "do you exhibit your work in any of the galleries around San Francisco?"

"I am working to get enough pieces together, and then I will go around to the galleries. It is rather daunting, you know, facing possible rejection or likely rejection." He has this disarming fatherly appeal that allows me to confess my insecurities to this complete stranger.

"Yes, of course, rejection is painful, but it is something we all must go through and simply overcome in order to go on. You should probably think about facing it as soon as possible because there is always the chance of acceptance, eventual sales, exhibitions of your work. Think what that would do for your self-confidence, young lady!"

We both drink the wine, and I begin to feel *wonderful*. The pretty blonde woman who ignored me, she of the Austin-Healey, passes behind us with the wine bottle. The judge playfully commandeers her to fill our goblets, which she does unsmilingly. She appears angry as usual.

The Oriental man places plates filled with charcoal-broiled steak, potatoes, artichokes, and salad before us. 1940s big band dance music plays on the phonograph in the living room. Vincent sits down at the head of the table, the blonde woman next to him. Everyone looks to him expectantly.

He rises, holding his goblet of champagne. "Cheers to all. Let's drink to health, wealth, and happiness, and some luck to help us over life's rockier places. Welcome to you all to my first dinner party in our new home." He pats his companion on the shoulder, and everyone echoes his cheers as they drink up.

I had hardly eaten all day, so the food is most welcome. I make an effort to eat slowly and delicately so as not to show my hunger, but I finish before everyone else. The judge offers me another dinner roll and pours me more wine, except now it is champagne to accompany the dinner.

There is a very drunk man at the table who can barely speak. A pretty young woman who looks part Asian is trying to keep him propped up. She seems surprisingly tolerant of it all. He paws her continually, pressing slobbering kisses against her face. I wonder how she can stand it, but no one seems to be paying much attention.

The conversation rises and falls around me, laughter and gossip concerning people and subjects of which I have no knowledge. Talk of "personal injury law suits" and "ambulance chasing," controversial legal decisions, huge sums of money, juries, and judges, politics in San Francisco and Sacramento, and finally, ultimately, the reason for all of it seems to be aviation.

"So, Thom, you went for a spin in the Cub yesterday, I hear. How was it?" Vincent asks pointedly.

"Great, just great! Our little neighbor lady here from downstairs came along for the ride. Thought I'd initiate her into our private pilots' association. Yeah, we flew almost to Santa Rosa, but the fog was starting to roll in, you know. How'd you like it, Joanna?"

All eyes turn in my direction. I feel as though I am on stage and this is my first performance. I take a breath, clear my throat, smile at everyone, and find my voice. "Oh, it was wonderful! So beautiful up there! I loved every minute of it."

Vincent keeps at me, "I understand you want to learn to fly."

"Yes, I would *love* to fly," I gush as the guests silently take in this rather strained conversation.

"Well, we have everyone and everything at your disposal, so just say when and your classes begin."

The blonde woman turns her head away and stares out the window.

I giggle a little before responding. It is all so overwhelming. "I understand it is quite expensive, I will have to sell a few paintings first."

"Naw," says Thom, "Vincent and Burkhart are both licensed flight instructors and can give you a big discount."

"Well, thank you very much. I'll have to think about it. The man down at the airport said he might fit me into his training schedule, didn't he?" I look at Thom to affirm this.

"Jake?" says Burkhart.

"Yeah, he beat us to it." Vincent laughs.

The party resumes while I silently contemplate my blossoming new life. All these possibilities opening up before me in such a short time, the world could be mine. All I had to do was say yes. Maybe.

The Oriental man, the blonde woman, and the woman to whom Thom had been talking (who I later found out was his secretary) all did the cleanup while the rest of the guests continued drinking champagne in the living room.

A warm fire made with real firewood lights up the room and creates a flickering glow over everything. A feeling of professional cohesiveness and well-being permeates the atmosphere, something I have never experienced before at a social gathering.

Thom lights a cigarette and passes it to me. I accept is as though I see nothing unusual about this. Ordinarily, in my past life, a man offers a woman a cigarette, she puts it in her mouth, he strikes a match or a lighter, and she inhales in order to start the thing going. These do not seem to be ordinary times, however, so I puff and smile away, waiting to see what happens next.

Thom's face is quite red, and he seems pleased with himself. "Say, everyone's talking about our flight yesterday. You really got a kick out of it, didn't ya?"

"Very much. Whenever you want company when you fly, please don't hesitate to call."

"I also want you to know I am very serious about your work. I meant what I said last night. I think you're good. You probably don't know how good you are. You just need to knuckle down. This month, I'm pretty tied up with the divorce proceedings and a heavy surgery schedule, but as soon as I get all that out of the way, the divorce mostly, I'd like us to start working together. The first thing is to take you to the morgue at Saint Luke's."

"You were serious about taking me to the morgue?"

"Yeah, I was. If you're gonna be a great artist, you have to know anatomy from the inside out. This is going to really help your painting. Michelangelo dissected every corpse he could get his hands on to find out what goes on under the skin. For medical illustration, it is a requisite."

"I may get sick to my stomach or faint or something. Really, Thom, I can't stand to see too much blood. Maybe I'm superficial or something like that. Even needles make me dizzy, and I can't stand to watch bullfights. I ... uh ..."

"Forget all that. You won't get sick. You just look at it all as a problem to be solved, objectively, something to understand, no sentiment involved, and you soon find yourself following nerves to where they connect to the vertebrae and which muscles they serve. Then there is the circulatory system, the skeletal system. It's a marvelous learning experience that will aid you all your life. You will have to leave all your weak-kneed emotions outside the door of the morgue, you understand me?"

"Thom, I don't know if I have the capacity to do what you ask. I studied art and art education …"

"That's the big problem: they don't teach teachers anything except how to teach. There is a saying that those who can't do it teach it. Open your mind, girl. Most people only use a fraction of the intelligence they were born with. Life is all work and learning. You can never stop, or you *die!*"

He was like a sociological bulldozer, tumbling common cultural conceptions where ever they lay in his path, trying to rebuild it all with his nuggets of truth. He passed his hand along the side of his face wearily. "I need to sit down. Been on my feet all day." He reclines on one of the early American flowered-chintz-covered lounge chairs, and I sit on the foot rest, eager to continue our conversation.

"Thom, I can't believe *all* teachers are incompetent. I had some very dedicated professors in college, and I don't think they made too much money."

I continue enthusiastically, happy to have found someone to talk to, "But you are right about current standards. I lasted one month in the San Francisco school system. In truth, it was more like a jail system than an educational system. Imagine, I taught art in junior high in Forest Knoll, Illinois, and they almost cried when I left after three years. I taught school another year here in Haynesville, across the bay, and they wanted me to stay on, but I wanted to work closer to home here in the city. They put me in Lincoln Elementary School, and the principal gave me the worst class there was, kids no one could handle or wanted to handle, with no backup from the administration. Now I was a teacher, not a policewoman or a form-filler-outer. All they wanted me to do was to keep those kids in line during the school day and to fill out their endless forms based on average daily attendance, which is how they got part of their funding. While I am filling out these infernal forms instead of teaching, these kids are practically killing each other. It was fifth grade, but some of them were big enough to be in high school. Trying to present a lesson, like history or spelling or math, was next to impossible. Spitballs, ink balls, fights breaking out, swearing, street theater behind my back, mocking me and everything I was trying to do, it was a nightmare. And when I went to the principal for help, she said I was not meant to be a teacher! I cried over that but took her at her word, and I quit."

Thom wanted to say something, but I had to finish. "But you know, the great tragedy wasn't me quitting, although that may be part of the greater tragedy. Multiplying my experience by hundreds, maybe, of other discouraged, idealistic teachers was what really got to me. Some of those kids were hungry for education, maybe only two or three, but you could see it in their eyes, a starving intelligence longing for knowledge. Like you say, knowledge makes us free. Well, there was no hope there. They were mostly black kids, and I don't like to think what has become of them."

"Yeah, yeah," he says, "that's what I'm saying. All they do is put in their time, no commitment to education. Most of them want the most money for doing the least amount of work. My daughter teaches in Berkeley, and she says if you are a dedicated teacher by putting in overtime to help your students, the other teachers put you down because in their little brains you are making them look bad, and they come out against you. That's kind of what your experience was, although you didn't get very far."

"The kids lose."

"And society. Don't forget, the kids are the future, and we will have to pay for our lapses one way or another." He lights two cigarettes and hands me one. He stands up and throws another oak log on the fire. People are gathering up their coats and things to leave. "Say, I'm going to take my secretary, Nancy, to her car. You can get downstairs okay by yourself?"

"Of course, and the steaks?"

"Oh, those, keep them for yourself for a rainy day. Remember, just keep working, and do it well. There is nothing else."

I slip out the kitchen door, down the stairs into my apartment to a deep enriching sleep, absorbing my lesson on life into the marrow of my bones.

Upstairs, the drama continues. Vincent knocks softly on his locked bedroom door. "Oh, Steve, sorry to bother you. How you doing in there?" He hears some shuffling around, and Suzy Wong, wrapped only in a sheet, opens the door a crack.

"Oh, Suzy, excuse me. Dr. Kelley's secretary is leaving, and her purse is somewhere there in the bedroom."

"What color is it?" asks Suzy.

"Yellow," says Nancy, standing behind Vincent.

"Uh, Nancy, why don't you change the record. There's some Guy Lombardo in the stacks. I'll have your purse in a jiffy."

Vincent slips into the bedroom and locks the door behind him. Stephen Purcell, respected California State auditor, is naked in the bed. He struggles to sit up, his paunch chastely obscuring his penis. He is very drunk. Vincent suffers a slight pang of guilt. He sits down next to him on the bed, adopting a very conciliatory manner with this important man in a now very compromising situation.

"Hi, there, Cooper ole man. How ya doin'?"

"I'm okay. How are *you* doing?"

"Ta tell ya god's truth, I'm in love with this beautiful girl here. Hey, I fergit yer name."

"Suzy." She stands holding the yellow handbag.

"Yeah, Suzy, the most wunnerful girl in the world. Hones' to Chris', Vince, I almost got it off with her. You can't imagine the trouble I have with my damn pecker." Tears fill his eyes and begin running down his cheeks through the stubble of his beard. "Couldja please get me another drink? I hope I don't lose my job for this. Didja call Sacramento for me to tell 'em I'd be a little late?"

"Suzy, get dressed and take that purse to Nancy. Enough drinks for you, old man. Great lovers don't drink too much. Makes peckers worse instead of better." Vincent begins to assemble the auditor's clothing and tries to persuade him to put it on.

The man continues to ramble drunkenly and refuses to dress. "I tell you the truth, Vince. I love that girl. I want her to stay with me all night until I do it. Goddammit, ya hear me? My wife says I'm no man anymore, but she's so mean and fat, what does she expect? I'm gonna divorce her the first chance I get, but what female broad is gonna have me if this thing don't work?" Tears continue to run down his face as he shakes his flaccid penis back and forth in anger, as though the sad, fleshy appendage was responsible for his profound unhappiness.

Vincent found it hard to understand this man's impotence. His own problem was one of almost constant, low lying lust, a pervasive horniness that got him into no end of trouble. He was blessed or cursed with a super abundant virility. He loved women, and they loved him back. It had been this way all of his life.

Suzy appears at the door with a tray of steaming coffee, sugar, and milk. Purcell retreats under the covers, his face blotchy and bleary eyed from his emotional catharsis. The strains of Guy Lombardo playing "Blue Hawaii" filter through the apartment. Everyone has left. Mary Belle and Ham are busy cleaning up.

"Suzy, come with me a minute. I want to talk to you."

He leads her into the bathroom and locks the door. Suzie looks at him curiously. Her face is wan and tired. She brushes back her black bangs off her forehead, out of her eyes.

"Suzie, you have to stay here tonight. You have to spend the night with Purcell until he makes love to you. I'll give you an extra hundred."

Her head sags. "I'm so tired. I've done everything to him, blow job, you name it. Nothing works. It is like he is almost going to get off, and then all of a sudden it collapses. I can't go on."

"You got to do it. Mary Belle and I will sleep on the couch tonight. Ham sleeps on the floor in a sleeping bag. You go back in there and spend the night. Don't give him anything more to drink. The guy sleeps, and then in the morning, wham! That does it, like that. I will pay you double overtime. This man is very important to us in the office. Big problems. I need him to feel he owes me *something*. Can you understand?" Unwittingly, desperation has seeped into his voice.

She runs her fingers through her thick black, hair, shakes her head, shrugs her shoulders, and finally agrees. "Okay, I'll do it for you, Vincent. You have helped me a lot. If only it was you. Let me phone the babysitter." Her face was rather pitiful at the moment.

She was almost thirty with a small child to care for. She worked as a temporary office girl by day and a call girl at night. On occasion, she had worked in Vincent's office. He rather admired her courage for not having had an abortion, insisting on keeping the baby. But she only too eagerly recited her litany of woes and problems: sick baby, unreliable child care, fatigue, overwork, abusive clients.

But he cannot resist taking advantage of the situation and slips his hand under her blouse and gently fondles her small breast. Her nipple grows hard to his touch, and he feels the beginning of an erection. He pulls her toward him and kisses her, but he must resist. Mary Belle is right outside the door, and Vincent is negotiating Suzy's favors for another man.

"Oh, Vince, if it only were you, it would be so easy," she sighs as she backs away from him.

"Unfortunately, nothing is easy, baby. Let's get back to your true love, who is snoring away in my bed."

But Stephen Purcell was not sleeping, "Suzzzieee," he brays from the bedroom, "I am waiting for you!" Vincent opens the door, and the woman returns to work. "You are going to make me jealous," says the accountant. "Come here right now, and don't leave me again. Let me look at you."

Vincent quietly closes the door on the scene and returns to the kitchen to supervise the cleanup.

I am in foreign territory.

CHAPTER SEVEN

Work & Play

I make a conscious decision to stay away from men and concentrate on my work. The men distract me. They take my time and energy. They consume me. And I seek respite from them and my ambiguous feeling about the male sex. Of course, I realize I can never give up men entirely, but I need them in moderation. The past weekend had saturated and filled to overflowing the vacuum of male attention that had existed in me.

I struggle with my art. I can't seriously paint abstractions. I feel fraudulent about slathering paint willy-nilly on my canvases. My inner dialogue eases my conflict, and I go ahead with what I want to do. The children, do I paint them because I don't have any? Is my art the "cry of the unfulfilled womb"? Who knows? They are quite charming subjects, their expressions open and honest. They still have not learned to hide their feelings for the sake of social approval.

Yes, it does bother me that I have no children. I face that. I wanted children during my marriage, but it turned out that my husband was hopelessly sterile. No one's fault, but it caused our breakup.

For weeks, I immerse myself in painting, willfully ignoring the comings and goings in the building. Thinking that it is all terribly interesting and exciting, I still doggedly keep to myself, knowing, perhaps subconsciously, that that makes *me* more interesting.

I have an old Kodak camera that my mother had given me. It slides out of its leather case on tiny rails, with an accordion-like construct following along behind the lens to capture the image. I flip up a little monocle and sight my subject.

An Oriental child is leaning against a cyclone fence in a school yard in Chinatown. Her thumb in her mouth and her silky black hair falling partly over her face, she looks at me and the camera enigmatically. I click the shutter. She turns her head slightly. I back off a bit and click the shutter again.

Walking the busy sidewalks of the city, I seek art treasures in the babble of daily life. Street urchins look at me curiously or arrogantly or with hostility. I click the shutter. Children are fighting, playing hopscotch, and an older girl comforts a young child who is crying. Another is happily licking an ice cream cone. I see rage, cunning, hate, fear, and love in miniature. I click the shutter. Later, in my small studio, I will study my photos, my stolen art treasure, and work them up into Impressionistic-like paintings.

I take long walks in the afternoons to quell my nervous tensions. The city streets, Ashbury Heights, Twin Peaks, and down into the Haight-Ashbury. Strange activities are taking place on this once solid middle-class shopping street. Young people who look like beatniks are strolling around dressed like gypsies, or how I would imagine gypsies would dress.

Beatniks were the social rebels of the generation just before me. I was too young to belong to the "beat" generation, the beaten down generation that lived for the moment since there was no hope for a future. But I was informed that these new young social phenomena were called *hippies*. They were of the generation just behind me. They were the "hip" generation, the ones who knew it all, the progeny of the beatniks, but I was too old for them.

Thom phones me almost every day to invite me here or there, but I say I am too busy with my work. I struggle to get the rent money together. My $2,000 a year alimony is rapidly depleted. I cannot face teaching school again, so I call my mother for help. My mother sends me $200. which helps stave off bankruptcy for the time being.

My beautiful aunt from Chicago arrives to see how I am doing. We hit Union Street one evening for dinner and then out to Pier 19 to listen to music. She orders martinis for us both, and we settle back, talking above the rhythms of the small rock band. "Do you think you'll be coming back to Chicago to live?" she asks pointedly. "You know, we all miss you." She smiles sweetly at me. We are both a bit boozy by now.

"I don't think so, Aunt Henrietta. It's so exciting living here! It is lonely at times, not having family around, but I just want to see if I can make it here in San Francisco. And it's so beautiful here compared to you know where."

"Oh, Chicago is really not that bad. It's just that you are such a rebel, my dear. Most people put up with the weather, the dirty snow, the flatness, but you want something better, right?" She sips her martini then nibbles on the olive, doing it all with style, the old rustic farm ways totally erased from her being. I imagine she would be a very elegant drunk, her blonde hair falling over her big blue eyes, a devastating woman.

"Right," I reply, "but I'm not sure what it is I want. I just know what I don't want."

There is a group of raucous young men at the table across from us, and they keep looking at us and whispering. They are cute. Maybe I am ready for a cute, young man.

The waiter brings us fresh drinks.

"Hey, we didn't order these," my aunt protests.

"Compliments of the gentlemen over at the other table." The waiter smirks a bit as he awaits our reaction. Will we refuse them, or will we drink them? Aunt Henrietta glances over at the men, who are smiling broadly, nodding, and waving agreeably toward us. She lifts the fresh martini, mouths the words "thank you," and takes a delicate sip.

I do the same, and almost immediately two of them bring their chairs over to our table, introduce themselves, and begin a typical San Francisco pickup conversation. "Hello, there. My, but it's rare to meet two such pretty gals around town! What's your name? Where are you from? My name is Bob Watterson, and this is my pal, Dick William. How long you here for? What's your phone number?"

And so it goes. I give Bob Watterson my phone number. He gives me his card, which lists him as assistant vice-president in the brokerage company of Blatt & Sons, member of the New York, San Francisco, and Chicago stock exchanges.

After my aunt returns to Chicago. Bob Watterson phones, and we make a date to go out. He takes me to Union Street, of course, where he seems to know everyone in the bars we hop through. They are packed with well-fed men and well-dressed, skinny women breathing into each other's faces. We drink heavily while assessing each other's sexual potential in the moment.

Bob is attractive, though not handsome in a movie star way. He has thick, wavy blonde hair, a high forehead, wide-set blue eyes, and a sensuous, full mouth. He might be inclined to be on the chubby side and not very tall. But he smiles a lot, and is very nice to me. I turn to jelly under his kindly little attentions.

He holds my hand and jokes a lot with the men that come to join us. They talk about ski trips to Squaw Valley almost every weekend during the winter season. I find myself desperately wanting to go with him to these exciting, unknown places. I feel I am falling in love with this young man who seems to know his way around the city. It is very seductive to be the female part of a couple again, passively accepting the admiration of his many friends.

He pays the bar bill, which seems astronomical to me, then buys me a substantial dinner of red snapper with wild rice and salad with lots of Chenin Blanc wine, all of which I consume with relish. I feel loved and cared for, and by the time he pulls his car up to his apartment house on Telegraph Hill, there is no doubt in either of our minds what will happen next.

He makes love to me while his roommate snores in the next bedroom. Afterward, I study the bedroom. Two pair of Head skis are resting against one wall. A large framed map of the world is on the wall above the bed, and he talks of places he has been and places he wants to go. Of course, I think he must be in love with me and we will go to all these wonderful places together. The radio is playing "Moon River" softly in the background. I am happy and relaxed, confident I have finally found true love.

We sleep. Then toward morning, he awakens me and indicates that we should dress quietly. We tiptoe past the door of the sleeping roommate and down to his car, some sort of a sports car. We kiss goodbye passionately in front of my apartment as the sun rises over the East Bay Hills. He promises to phone me soon. Besides my ex-husband, he is the only other man I have ever had sex with in all my twenty-six years.

He doesn't phone.

I was raised not to phone a boyfriend unless it was a matter of life or death. I try to distract myself in my work while more than a month passes waiting to hear from him. I hate the phone that doesn't ring, and I hate myself for being so foolish.

Then finally he calls! "Hi, there! Remember me, Bob Watterson?" he says gaily.

I set down my paintbrush with a trembling hand. He does love me after all. Our night of passionate love is as meaningful to him as it is to me. Why am I so nervous? I mumble a dim response.

"Hey, if you feel like getting out and having some fun, there's a dance at the Palace Hotel this weekend—great society shindig, the Spinster's Ball. All the unmarried society girls get to invite a man. The gals pay for it all. Great fun if you feel up to it."

"Well, sure, I'd love to. Sounds like fun."

During the days before the dance, I agonize about what to wear. I finally reach into the back of my closet for a knee-length black crepe dress with a white off-the-shoulder bodice dotted with rhinestones. It has a flesh-colored net that reaches up to my neck. There is no choice of jewelry; there are only the pearls from the past and some inexpensive earrings. It will all have to do since I have barely enough money to cover my rent and gas for my little sports car.

The night of the traditional San Francisco Spinster's Ball, the Palace Hotel is blazing with light. A big-band orchestra is playing while superbly coifed and tuxedoed couples swirl around the dance floor. All the women are in long formal gowns. I am the only one in a street-length dress. My date essentially ignores me. He seems very distracted, and I can think of nothing interesting to say as we breeze about the tables and the dance floor. Everyone seems to know everyone else. The gossip is thick, and the champagne cold and plentiful.

Bob shows me to the ladies room, still barely acknowledging me. I wonder what is going on with him.

I am amazed at the luxury of the lounge I enter. A crystal chandelier glimmers from a high ceiling, and the walls are papered in a velvety, gold-flocked French design. The mirrors are framed in gold-leaf scrollwork, and the elegant tables support shining, marble tops.

I attend to my needs in the bathroom, also a Baroque designer's dream of marble and gold leaf, then repair my makeup while wealthy society women regard me curiously as the existential "other." As I brush out my hair, the mirror on the wall assures me that I am still beautiful, but my self-esteem is shattered miserably, and I wish the evening were over. Beauty doesn't seem to count tonight.

I emerge from the ladies' lounge and look for my date at the pillar where he left me. He is nowhere to be seen, so I sit in one of the overstuffed, dark-blue velvet chairs in the huge hall and wait.

Time passes. It has been an hour, and Bob is not appearing. I summon my courage and walk into the ballroom and look for him. I see him dancing with a woman, chattering happily. When he sees me, they suddenly dance out of sight among the couples. I grit my teeth, try to keep my head up as I wonder what I should do next.

"Looks like you lost something—or someone. Now, don't start crying there." A tall fellow in a pink tuxedo is standing next to me, smiling. He has lots of reddish blonde hair, freckles, and green eyes.

These men ooze self-confidence. I wonder where it comes from, where I might get some.

"Yes, I lost my date." I take a deep breath and manage a smile, grateful for this man's attention.

"You came with Watterson. Too bad. He is in love with the boss's daughter, Sylvia Blatt, and she invited another guy, so now he's got the chance to dance with her, and he doesn't want to blow it. She is super, creamy rich and not too bad looking. It's a shame these rich ladies can't be as beautiful as they are loaded. Come on! Let's dance. I'll take you home then. I came with my sister and her date. I'm Porter Hanson, and who may you be?"

It is past three in the morning when he drives me home through the foggy streets.

My meager conversational skills have been mortified out of existence by the past events, so I sit in brooding silence until we reach my apartment. "Thank you," I say to Porter, shrinking away as he plants both his hands squarely on my breasts over the white crepe and rhinestones.

I hear him chuckling to himself as I rush into the relative security of my little apartment. His car roars down the street, and some secret part of me wishes he and all his friends would go to hell.

The day finally arrives when I decide to take some of my paintings around to galleries to see if they are interested in exhibiting them. I select three pieces that I consider to be the best of my recent work. One is a mother tying a hair bow on a child on a windswept, grassy hillside. Another is the little Chinese girl in the school yard sucking her thumb, her face partly obscured by her straight black hair falling forward. The third is a street urchin of unknown origin staring out angrily from the canvas at the world.

I take the top down on my TR3 and carefully stack the canvases in the jump seat. I slide into the driver's seat praying the car will start. It does, which seems to be a good omen. The air is fresh and clear, and I feel happy about my prospects. The past months have been long and hard with the ongoing emotional struggle against feelings of despair and futility, aside from the sparse economic circumstances of my life.

First, I go to a furniture and decoration outlet near the financial district. They say no, thank you. Then I head toward Union Street, find parking, and feed the meter.

I walk into the first gallery I come to. Smiling as pleasantly as possible, I arrange the three canvases along the wall. The work in this gallery is non-objective—a bad sign for me—abstractions, large canvases painted in one solid color, sculptures of found, throw-away items, collages, and so forth. The woman I assume owns the gallery appraises my work briefly and shakes her head negatively.

I collect my paintings and continue working the galleries along both sides of the street, bumping into tourists with my unwieldy burden, and finally reach the end without any success whatsoever. By now, it is late in the morning, almost afternoon, and the air is getting chilly. The fog is coming in early, and I am very hungry and tired.

At a corner grocery, I set the paintings down and buy some cheese, lettuce, tomatoes, and some bread then drive to my apartment on Mount Olympus. I fix a simple lunch then retreat to my bed wondering how to deal with my sense of failure. What do I do next?

The phone rings. "Hi, there. This is Thom. I hope I am not disturbing you now. Am I?"

"No, not at all. I'm just resting. How are you?" The note of defeat in my voice travels through the phone line.

"I'm fine, but you don't sound so good. What's wrong? Got your period?"

"No, no, it's not that." I sniff. "It's just that I went to some of the galleries this morning on Sansome Street and Union Street, and no one, absolutely no one, was interested in my work. If I can't sell my work, what will I do? I'll die, I guess. I can't do anything else." I do not want to cry, but I am close to tears.

He chuckles into the phone as if pleased somehow. "Cheer up, old girl! You just started making the rounds. It happens to everyone. Why don't you take your paintings to some of the galleries downtown here on Sutter Street where I have my offices? These are the best galleries in the city, not like Union Street with all that tourist crap. Your work is better than that. Tell ya what, you go around to the galleries here this afternoon then come up to my office, which is right off Union Square, 450 Sutter, and we'll go out. I'll buy you a drink to cheer you up or maybe to celebrate."

"Well, I don't know."

"Don't give up, ya hear me? I'll see you at my office around seven."

"Okay, Thom. Of course, you are right. I'll see you later and hope I have better news."

I decide to take just two paintings, the one of the Mother and Child and the Chinese girl.

As I drive down Bush Street, I think how fragile this all is, how many artists do become discouraged and give up, succumb to depression and never do anything important, work that they love, that gives meaning to their lives. I resolve to keep going no matter what. There is nothing else to do. I silently thank Thom for his moral support. How important that is, I think.

I park in the underground garage and once again set out with a painting under each arm, my purse slung across my shoulder. It is starting to drizzle slightly.

Randomly, as is my habit, I walk into the first gallery I come to. Glancing at the walls, I know I have made a mistake—this much I have learned today—collages of burnt photographs, highly erotic paintings, old crumpled newspapers spray painted and stuck on canvases, and rotting pieces of wood hanging from irregularly shaped slabs of plywood.

Against the far wall is an almost life-sized, crudely drawn naked woman. She has breasts made of a baseball, cut in halves and glued onto the Masonite, and a Chore Boy pot scraper at her crotch representing her pubic hair, I surmise. The title is "Domestic Sport." There is a painting composed of dripped acrylic colors, a copy of Pollack. Others are Mondrian-like geometric squares and rectangles of color slashed through with black stripes of varying widths. There is a huge six-cent postage stamp perfectly reproduced in oil on canvas.

A slim young man is sitting at a desk to one side of the softly lit, elegantly carpeted gallery. He is talking on the phone. Another young man emerges from somewhere in the depths of the gallery carrying a piece of abstract sculpture labeled "Found Materials."

Much cheaper than having to go to Flax to buy them, I think.

"Oh, Rodney, where the hell do I put this piece of junk?" Then, upon seeing me, he corrects himself. "I mean this masterpiece of contemporary art."

Rodney hangs up the phone and walks over to me. He smells wonderful from what must be a very expensive perfume. "And what may I do for you, dearie?" he asks with a slight smirk. He has a thin mustache that doesn't do much for his male image. I am in foreign territory.

"I ... I'm an artist, and I am interested in finding a gallery here in San Francisco that might be interested in showing my work." I don't bother to set my paintings against a wall, rather, I balance them against my knees while they are scrutinized.

"Sweet," says the man who has set down the contemporary sculpture next to a construction made out of plumbing pipes and an old cracked toilet. It almost seems as though the toilet smells are competing with Rodney's perfume. Nothing looks promising.

"Rather Impressionistic in style—not too bad, actually." Rodney draws himself up and flashes me a forced smile. "Sorry, dear, awfully sorry, but it's not the sort of art we handle, as you can see by looking around you. Thanks ever so much for coming by." He turns abruptly to his desk and begins dialing his phone.

The other man looks at me sadly. "You would be better getting your subject matter from the garbage cans if you want to make a name for yourself in today's art world. Forget painting figuratively. Women and children won't sell, too sentimental for the market."

I just look at him morosely as I gather up my work.

"Look, dearie, don't start crying about it. I'm just trying to help you."

I go on. No luck either in the next two establishments, although one gallery official says he does like my work and I should keep at it and come back at a later date.

With this morsel of encouragement, I stop before a brightly lit display window and there I see a Renoir and a Degas. I peer closer into the place and see paintings of people, animals, landscapes, scenes of dance halls, something like Toulouse-Lautrec. I catch my breath and plunge into the gallery, feeling surrounded by friends at last. The sign over the entrance says, "Aldrich Galleries, Fine Art."

I set down my canvases and study the well-lit walls. There are sensitive palette knife renderings of portraits, boating scenes in soft, blending colors, and more Impressionism. There are works of art that revere the human form and expression; wild jungle paintings in bright viridian greens, cadmium yellows, ochres, lavenders and purples, classical still lifes, and actual seascapes with pounding surf and salt spray. I feel I am now in an art gallery. Maybe here, maybe …

A raven-haired woman, designer clothed and coifed, comes forward smiling, what seems to my hopeful expectations, an authentic smile.

"Hello, there." She glances knowingly at the canvases scrunched up under my armpits. "And what may we do for you this evening?"

"I have some paintings I'd like to show you. Perhaps your gallery may be interested in …"

"Oh, here, let me help you. Let's see what we have here."

We set the two paintings against a pillar. They don't look too bad, I think to myself, nothing to be ashamed of.

"Hmm, they are nice. They would fit in here quite comfortably. Oh, let me introduce myself. I am Marie Worthman. I run the gallery for Mr. Aldrich, who unfortunately is in New York at the moment, but he should be back next week. He lets me make decisions in his absence. And who painted these?"

"I did," I say proudly.

The woman raises her eyebrows and smiles. "And who might you be?"

"My name is Joanna Botticelli. I sign my paintings "Botticelli." See there, in the lower right hand corner?"

"What a great and famous name for a painter! Are you by any chance related to the great fifteenth-century Italian artist Sandro Botticelli, who painted the *Birth of Venus*?"

"They say that I am, that my family is. My mother did a genealogical study, and she claims that my father's family was directly descended from Botticelli. Apparently, the family was not too prolific, so there are not many descendants."

"Well, it is hard to have a houseful of kids and be a successful artist, more so if you are a woman, which of course you are."

We giggle nervously at that, at my gender-compromised professional future.

"My family wasn't too sure of whether to be proud of him or not, all those nudes and so forth, and the church wasn't too pleased with him, I understand. Then, when my father was killed in the war, my mother remarried, so the matter became moot."

Marie considered this then said, "I was fortunate to study art in Europe. Here in the States, most people have not heard of Botticelli, Leonardo perhaps and Michelangelo, but not Botticelli."

She stands back from the paintings and studies them silently, cupping the side of her face with her hand. "They are rather pleasing, and I would like to hang them here and see what happens. We take new work on consignment. That means that if we find a buyer, we take care of the transaction and reimburse you for the painting. Our commission is 40 percent of your asking price. Mr. Aldrich is making a "young collector's" gallery in the back rooms. He means to help people who are just starting their collections of art and also young artists making their first sales. A few sales in the beginning can do wonders for artistic morale."

I nod in restrained agreement. "So, you are saying that I can leave these paintings here with you, and you will hang them in your gallery and make an effort to sell them?"

"Yes, exactly. Come over to my desk here so we can fill out the consignment forms."

It is unbelievable, but true. My work will be hanging here in this lovely gallery in the company of Renoir, Degas, Utrillo, and other illustrious painters of the past. She hands me a form to sign stipulating the amount of commission and other details over which I skim and sign.

She laughs gaily while doing this, accustomed to insecure artists making their first transaction, and she enjoys this tremendously. She takes the paintings. "We may put a simple frame on them to show them off a little better, you know. Call next week when Mr. Aldrich is here, and I'll let you know what he thinks, but I am sure he will like them."

I float out of the gallery.

Sutter Street is brightly lit and teeming with people pouring out of the high-rise office buildings. It is after seven, and 450 is across the street. The lobby smells medicinal. Checking the directory, I see the place is crammed with doctors and dentists. I take the elevator to the seventh floor and find the door number 707. Printed on the pebbled glass is "Dr. Thomas William Kelley, Orthopedic Surgeon." I am impressed. He really is a big deal doctor.

"Do you have an appointment, miss?" inquires the receptionist peering out from behind a glass partition in the wall.

"No, but Dr. Kelley is expecting me."

"Name?"

"Joanna Josephina Botticelli."

"How's that again? Could you spell that for me please?"

I sit down in the nicely furnished waiting room and scan through the latest issue of *Aviation News*.

Thom pokes his head out of his office. He is smiling broadly. "Hi, there! How'd it go?"

"Incredible! I have two paintings now hanging in the Aldrich Galleries and—"

"Hold on. Let me finish this last patient, and then we can get out of here. I'll buy you that drink, and we'll celebrate. I told ya so. You just don't realize how *good* you are."

The receptionist stares at me. I must look frightful. My hair is tangled and wild from walking in the drizzling rain in my jeans, tennis shoes, and old jacket. I look like a hippie or a street person. I go into the tiny bathroom for patients and arrange my hair, put on some lipstick, and decide I don't look too bad after all. The good fortune has brought color to my face, and I feel happy.

After a wait of almost an hour, the secretary who was at Vincent's party passes through and out, smiling at me courteously. Thom emerges at last, smoothing his hair with his right hand, adjusting his suit jacket and tie. His hair is very white under the neon light. "Sorry to keep you waiting so long. I had to get some X-rays for that last patient from the hospital, and delivery service seems to take forever, especially during the rush hour."

"Thom, I'm not dressed to go out for a drink."

"You're fine. They'll think you are my daughter. You look about fifteen years old at the moment."

We drive through the rain in his Thunderbird to the bar and restaurant on the wharf, Pier 19, where my aunt and I had gone. It is a wonderful conglomerate of people where the classes mingle in blissful intoxication in the old tradition of San Francisco. People turn to look at us as we make our way to a table. We must seem an odd couple. His daughter, well, that *could* be the truth, but it's *not*.

There are men and a few women shooting pool at tables along the wall. The lights of the bay and the bridge sparkle outside of the huge plate glass windows. A freighter is moving slowly through the dark waters. The fog horns intone their mournful notes while a jazz band plays softly on a small stage.

"These are people from all walks of life," Thom pronounces in his professorial manner as the waiter stands by patiently for our order, "longshoremen, stockbrokers, waiters from other restaurants, bankers, mechanics, secretaries, hookers, wives without their husbands, and husbands without their wives."

"Reminds me of jumping rope when I was a child."

"Huh? How's that?"

"The girls used to jump rope at recess and there were all these rhymes to jump rope with. One of them went, 'Rich man, poor man, beggar man, thief, doctor, lawyer, merchant, chief,' and if you missed a step and stopped the rope on one of them, that was the kind of man you would marry."

"Well, sounds as good a system as any I've heard of. So, what would you like to drink Miss Botticelli? Say, that name does go well for an artist."

"I'm not sure what to drink. What do you think?"

"What say we order a bottle of sparkling Burgundy to celebrate your good fortune and then maybe some hamburgers and fries? You're awfully thin, you know. It's not really too healthy to be a starving artist."

"I like being thin. I feel light. It's the style anyway."

"Well, kid, the way I see it, you're on your way. You're gonna be important someday, and I can say I knew you when. Art, Jeezus, that's what makes life worth living, good art, that is."

"Good art. Good god, you should have seen some of the stuff they call art these days. There was a toilet—"

"A toilet?"

"Yes, seriously, a toilet. I think it even smelled like a toilet, probably part of the aesthetic, you know. There was garbage tacked onto plywood with a price tag of thousands of dollars. What does this all mean? Do people actually pay money for shit like that? Pardon my language, but it was a bit of a shock to see what I must aspire to if I want to be a successful artist."

Thom smiles at my vehemence. "My mama used to say that most people don't know horseshit from ice cream if they ate a ton of each."

The waiter arrives carrying a silver bucket with our sparkling Burgundy, two chilled wine glasses, and a big bowl of popcorn, which I immediately dig in to.

"So, if your mama was right, then where is the human race headed for, I wonder." The popcorn is warm, salty, and very buttery.

"Good question," he says as the waiter fills the tall, thin stemmed goblets three-quarters full of the bubbling, deep red Burgundy. Beads of moisture form on the crystal, and all thoughts of the decline of civilization evaporate and I feel exquisite. "So, here's to your success!" We clink glasses and drink. The Burgundy is slightly sweet.

I set my glass down, and he hands me a lit cigarette. "Thanks Thom. I really want to thank you for your encouragement. It is so scarce in my life. I hardly know anyone in San Francisco. My ex-husband took all our mutual friends with him."

"That's pretty standard in a breakup. His friends were your friends as long as you were together. You never cultivated friendships on your own?"

"It was hard. I worked fulltime teaching. I had no time or energy. I would come home and do all the cleaning, cooking, shopping, and laundry."

"Why did you divorce him, anyway? He seemed like a decent enough guy?"

"Yeah, he was. We had our conflicts like any couple, but the heavy part was it turned out he was sterile. We could never have children."

"Shot blanks, huh? That's a crude way we doctors have of referring to a condition of spermless semen."

"Anyway," I continue, "there was no property, no children, and we came to an impasse over the fertility problem. He wanted to adopt children and I didn't. I wanted to bear my children.

I wanted the whole thing that is a woman's birthright after all—the growing belly, a life inside of me that I am sustaining. I want to sense the fear, pain, and exultation of childbirth. Breastfeeding an infant seems divine. It has to be a magnificent experience for a woman. I am strong, reasonably intelligent most of the time, healthy, why not get pregnant? I suggested artificial insemination to him—at least the child would be from me. But he would hear none of it."

"Probably just as well. Some of those med students who donate sperm are real creeps, I tell you. It's like Russian roulette. You don't know what you are going to get from the shot."

"So, to make a short story shorter, we split up. He stayed here in San Francisco, and he is doing well working in an office of certified public accountants. We're still on speaking terms, at least, and he is becoming one of those handsome bachelors around town the society pages like to feature."

Thom pours more Burgundy. The popcorn is almost gone. He signals for the waiter and orders hamburgers and French fries with a salad for us. He looks me straight in the eye and says, "You don't look like a particularly maternal type to me, despite what you say, and probably it is just as well you don't have a bunch of brats running around. It would really put a damper on your artistic ambition. Most successful women in the arts don't have children. Have you thought about that?"

"Maybe, but I don't dwell on it at the moment. I am concerned with my work and making some headway. But to me, giving birth also seems a grand endeavor. Maybe artistic women should have children and society help them so they can continue to create beauty, but for me the idea of children hovers somewhere in the distant future."

He looks at me strangely, dismissing the topic. "Doing medical illustration on the side will give you a more secure source of income. As far as my divorce goes, we are still in the negotiating stage because of the property involved. It's almost over. I get Upper Terrace and some other stuff. The ones who win in a divorce are the lawyers."

The food arrives, and we devour it quickly. Thom, amused, orders me another hamburger, which I can't finish. I feel a surge of energy as the edge goes off the initial inebriation, and Thom orders another bottle of sparkling Burgundy. I dismiss all concerns over calories at this abundance.

I study Thom's face as he talks, and he loves to talk, especially when he has such an avid listener. He has a long face, an aquiline nose. His blue eyes are a bit watery. Age? Cigarettes? Alcohol? His lips are thin, and his ears, though slightly large, are delicately formed. His hands are interesting—very white with faint brown freckles and long, tapering fingers. He uses his hands while speaking to emphasize his words. He intrigues me. I have never known anyone like him.

After the meal, the bill is presented. He takes out several credit cards for the waiter to accept.

He must be well-off, I think unwittingly. I feel the thrill of temporary release from money worries. Thom and I have been entirely absorbed in each other, and I have barely listened to the music or looked around me at the other people in the restaurant or exhilarated over the amazing views of the city. When I was married, I hardly paid serious attention to my husband when we were in unfamiliar places. I was always absorbing my surroundings like a sponge for future reference. For what, I had not been sure.

Thom signs the receipt with an almost unintelligible scrawl. He catches me watching him. "Kind of messy handwriting. You learn that in medical school—to write so no one can read it. It's part of the mystique of being a doctor, you know," he says with a chuckle.

I pick up my sports car from the underground garage. Thom waits for me at the exit and follows me home. As I turn into the last curve on Upper Terrace, I note against my will that the Austin-Healey and the white Buick are parked one in front of the other along the guardrail.

My curiosity about the love affair of my upstairs neighbors irritates me, and I try to ignore them. I rarely encounter the two since that initial outburst of party fervor when they moved in. In the morning and sometimes late at night, I hear their movements on the ceiling above me. The house is solid, old San Francisco construction, and voices do not penetrate the walls and floor as in the more recent construction. Occasionally, I see them leaving in the morning, at times going together in one vehicle and at others driving away separately. It all has to do with their legal work, I think.

Thom kisses me lightly on the mouth and is gone to his flat. I let myself into the apartment, click on the lights, and survey the disorder. I can't bear cleaning. It seems such a waste of time as it all gets dirty and disheveled again. I usually delay the task for months. Twice a year is all I can stand. After I get a glass of water, I sit down and look at my paintings. I decide I like my work and take mental notes of changes I might make, what I might eliminate, and new concepts to work up. Fatigue overtakes me. and I fall into bed naked, sleeping very soundly through the night.

During the next week, I resist the temptation to call Aldrich Galleries. I see Thom frequently, and he often invites me to his flat to have supper with him.

I wait another week and give in and call. "May I speak to Miss Marie Worthman, please?"

"Whom may I say is calling?"

"Joanna Josephina Botticelli."

"Uh, would you please repeat that?"

I repeat phonetically, "Bah-tah-chell-ie."

"Just a moment."

"Oh, Joanna, I'm so happy you called," gushes Ms. Worthman. "I misplaced your phone number. Mr. Aldrich returned a few days ago, and he just loves your paintings, and he wants you to do more. And the other great news is that I sold one. Yes, the one with the mother tying the bow in the hair of the child on the mountainside. I have a check here for you for one hundred dollars. It's no great fortune, I realize, but it will help pay the rent. You have to start somewhere, my dear. Shall I mail it to you, or do you want to come down and pick it up? Why don't you come down here to the Gallery and meet Malcolm Aldrich? And don't forget to bring more paintings."

I can hardly believe it, and for the moment I am speechless. "Oh, of course, thanks so much, Marie. I'll be down there in the morning between ten and eleven. Is that all right?"

"Fabulous, just fabulous. I can hardly wait until he meets you. You are so beautiful and talented. He's going to love you. See you tomorrow. Ciao!"

Ciao? How strange! I must remember to say *ciao* instead of goodbye in this my new life.

I stretch out over my unmade, not very clean bed, overwhelmed by all this. I savor my first taste of success in solitude. It's all true, the platitudes they throw at you: believe in yourself, work like hell, never give up, it will all come in time. The treasures of the world are just lying around out there. My parents will be shocked. They were never encouraging, their hope for me lying in my marrying someone with money and becoming a proper, dutiful housewife. Well, that will never happen. I know inside of me I will never, ever get married again.

No time to rest on my laurels. Back to work. Subject matter is my issue now. I decide to steal subjects. I dig into my old *National Geographics*. They have such great photographs. Ah, here is a worthy subject, an Asian child with an old army jacket on. He/she is holding a firecracker in one hand and a Popsicle in the other. The filthy, matted hair is sticking out in all directions like a diabolical halo, and the smile is happy and impish. A long, slimy drop of saliva extends from the lower lip to the chin, provoked by the Popsicle. I will paint her/him with a palette knife.

The next morning, once again saying a silent prayer to my guardian angel the TR3 will start, I load three more paintings into the jump seat. One is an angry Chinese street kid, his eyes narrow and hostile even at about nine years of age. Another is a teenager sitting on a park bench holding a child on her lap, and the third is the profile of a mother with her child, the high-rises of the city towering in the background.

The engine grinds but won't start. No one is in the building at this late hour of the morning, so very carefully I put the car in neutral and push it to where the street begins its downward slope. At the first hint of unaided forward motion, I leap into the driver's seat, drop it into second gear, give it some gas as it starts to roll, and the motor sputters to life. My particular guardian angel helps she who helps herself, I have noticed.

Malcolm Aldrich, dressed in a dark suit, is a short, stocky man, balding, with great bushy eyebrows and a well-trimmed mustache. One eyelid droops slightly over one eye. He is smiling graciously and appears to be a kindly person. We shake hands.

I am glad that I took pains with my appearance this morning to the extent of putting on nylons, low-heeled opera pumps, makeup, and a dress from college days I found in the back of the closet. The dress has a nice belt that shows off my narrow waist. I feel nervous about meeting someone who may be important to my future—that is, as an adult woman on her own instead of someone's wife. But I have gained much in the past months from my association with Thom, and I surprise myself with how easily I am handling this.

"Miss Botticelli, (he pronounces it perfectly) how delighted I am to meet you. I very much like your work. Oh, here, Marie, help her. Let's see what you have there. Charming, yes, perfectly charming. We will show them in the Young Collector's Gallery. People do like your work, I am happy to say. We may have a client for the other painting you left. I also may add that if things turn out well, we would like to include you in a group show I am planning."

"Thank you very much. I really appreciate—"

"It's nothing, my dear. Don't thank me. You work hard, and you are good, and that is what it's all about."

Everyone is beaming at me. I feel like a star, the center of adoring attention, which I have not felt since I was a small child. I like it a lot. I can get used to this, I think.

"Congratulations, Joanna! Here is your check. I assume from your reaction it is the first money you have earned from your work?" says Marie as she hands me an envelope with my name on it.

"Yes, it is," I reply quietly and tuck it into my purse.

Seated in the privacy of my sports car in the underground parking garage, I tear open the envelope. There it is: a check *in my name*, drawn on the Bank of America on the account of Aldrich Galleries. It is the sweetest money I have ever earned. I probably should not spend it but keep it in a frame. Unfortunately, that is impossible. I am already behind in the rent and need more oil paint and canvas to keep going. This is only a drop in the bucket of my need.

After that, I throw myself into my work with renewed strength and commitment. I improve my work habits, clean up my palette, and wash my sable brushes carefully. I take more care in stretching the canvases and in priming them with rabbit skin glue. I begin to think of myself as a professional artist and take myself seriously at last.

CHAPTER EIGHT

The Morgue

The downward movement of the rickety old elevator lurches to an uneven halt at the lowest level of Saint Luke's Hospital. Thom and I step into the chilly, dank corridor in the bowels of the building. The lights give off a cold, greenish glow. They are encased in a heavy wire mesh. Only God knows why. The walls are painted a dull, institutional green, peeling in many places, exposing the moldy plaster walls. The air smells stale.

Thom, checking his watch, walks briskly as I hurry to keep up. There are doors on both sides of the corridor marked with the functions of the room within: boiler room, laundry, waste, bathrooms, tools, electricity, gas, water. There are large carts filled with tangled dirty sheets, pillowcases, and towels, the dirty laundry of a hospital, bearing stained testimony to deep suffering, pain, and death in their twisted folds.

"Damn, I hope they're not all there waiting for me. I give 'em hell when they are late. And look, it's ten after eight, and I told them eight o'clock sharp," he moans. Thom has changed from an old friend into a professor and has become very formal. I respond in kind out of respect for his position here.

We are on our way to Saint Luke's subterranean morgue. I grip my drawing pad and pouch carrying my drawing pencils, eraser, and pen. My pencils are sharpened and ready to use. The drawing materials give me courage. They feel healthy, warm, and alive in these morbid surroundings.

"Not too cheery down here, is it?" Thom mutters with a chuckle. It seems to amuse him to introduce me to strange and exotic circumstances, starting with that first flight so many months ago. He often say he enjoys my reactions since I mask my feelings so poorly. In a way, he has begun to live vicariously through me. What had become boring and humdrum before has become a wild, mind-boggling, new experience.

"That is an understatement. This place is creepy. I expect the tombs to start opening and Frankenstein to come out at any moment."

"Silly, pretend you are a female Michelangelo. See everything as objective and a learning experience. Do not *allow* your fears or feelings to intrude on your mind. You are here to learn something. Do not forget that!"

Turning a corner, the corridor ends in a room with its doors open. The room is a large, cold space painted the same green and looks as though it had been used as an operating room in the past. Cabinets filled with surgical instruments line the walls. There are several sinks. High intensity lighting fixtures illuminate the center table.

As soon as we enter, a group of five young medical students, one a woman, move forward to greet the doctor. They are wearing white uniforms and carry clipboards holding a pen and reams of paper.

"Good morning, Dr. Kelley," they say almost as a chorus.

"Good morning, good morning. I hope I am not late, since I value punctuality highly, as you well know." He speaks rather gruffly. He is so different in these surroundings, like another person.

The students stare at me curiously.

"I'd like to introduce my new medical illustrator, Miss Joanna Botticelli, who is also a painter. She is going to make drawing notes as we dissect the area around the brachial plexus."

They nod politely in my direction. Everyone is extremely subdued. One senses another presence, but it is unmanifested.

"Is everyone here? Good, then we may start." Thom fumbles in his pocket for a key, which he hands to one of the students. "Here, Hanson, you wheel the subject out and lay it here on the table while I change."

A student with a name badge identifying him as Dr. Hanson and another student open a large metal door at the far end of the room. As it slowly swings open, the fetid smell of formaldehyde overwhelms whatever breathable air exists. As I stare into the dimness, the overhead lights are switched on to reveal two gurneys, side by side, the occupants covered by white sheets. I feel woozy.

"One is Matilda, and the other is Homer. We don't want anyone getting lonely down here at night," says Thom. The students smile courteously, accustomed to macabre medical jokes.

"You want her or him, Dr. Kelley?"

"Let's work on the lady today. Her upper thorax is in better shape than his for what we want to explore." Thom goes to a closet and takes out two white gowns, one for him and one for me and surgical gloves for him. After we wash up, he assembles the surgical instruments for the project on a tray: several scalpels, scissors, various sizes of tweezers, and some towels. He puts on thin rubber gloves and we move to the now waiting cadaver.

Hanson draws back the sheet slowly. There are small towels covering the face and genital area. Thom delicately draws back a skin flap consisting of the right breast, part of the lower neck, upper shoulder, and part of the upper arm. It looks like an enormous, day-old leftover turkey from Thanksgiving, grayish brown and hacked up here and there. The students lean forward for a better view. Thom sits on a high stool next to the area he will dissect.

Unbidden thoughts race through my mind. I wonder who this cadaver was in life. I see her going to a market to shop, coming home to prepare a meal for her children or husband, or else she works somewhere. A cleaning lady is all I can imagine considering her present circumstances, thrusting a mop back and forth over the shining floors of some executive suite, working until she is too old to—.

"I want to emphasize to you young people how much easier it is to open a live body than a dead one and the importance of dissection of the human body for the education of a medical student." Thom begins his lecture, waving the scalpel in the air as he speaks like a baton directing an operatic aria.

"And I am fully aware that firsthand knowledge of anatomy through dissections is no longer a primary part of the medical school studies the way it was when I was a student. Those of us in surgery spent a third of our class time on cadavers. I want you to know that in ancient Greece and Rome, only the butchers knew anatomy, and they were the ones called upon to do emergency surgery, bone setting, and so forth. This knowledge of anatomy is critical to the ethical practice of medicine. Of course, you all know the part of the Hippocratic Oath that states you never want to leave your patients worse for having treated them."

This is greeted with nervous laughter. These young men were already taking classes with financial advisors on how to best manage the fortunes they would soon be making.

Thom turns and motions me to come closer. With my drawing pad open to a clean page, I am hanging tightly to my #3 drawing pencil. My wooziness has changed into a strange, vacuous space located somewhere behind my eyes. The walls seem to be receding into the distance. I repeat my mental mantra over and over: I must not faint. I must not faint. I will embarrass the doctor. I must not faint. I will... After all, I am his special, his very own, medical illustrator.

Thom looks at me sternly. "You all right?" he growls.

"Yeah, I'm ... fine." I am leaning against the shoulder of one of the medical students, struggling to maintain consciousness. Then the student is holding me up, his arms under my arm pits, but I remain aware.

"Goddamn! Get her some ammonia salts quick! We've got work to do. Oh, my God, why do these things happen to me?" Thom is on the verge of hysteria, while I take slow, deep breaths of ammonium oxide, still more or less on my feet, trying to redeem myself before these strangers and uphold the reputation of Dr. Kelley.

Two students walk me to a chair and have me put my head down between my knees as I continue to breathe the noxious fumes. Oh, for a breath of sea-swept air from the Pacific, but I go on, and slowly the emergency treatment takes effect. There is no turning back, so with my head relatively clear they walk me back to the anatomy lesson.

Thom hands me my drawing pad and pencil and continues to lecture. "Oh, say, someone move that light a little closer and tilt this dame up so I can get at her upper back."

Thom slowly draws the scalpel through the epidermis from the back of the neck across the shoulder and down the arm so that the skin flap is entirely free of the body. The underlying muscles are exposed.

Then he begins to loosen the muscles carefully from the bone, taking care to show how the nerves are arranged. The nerves are thin, yellowish-white strands that look like heavy thread. He shows where they connect coming from the cervical vertebrae. I force myself to scribble something like a vertebra and find this helps control my faintness.

Thom clears his throat and continues, "The brachial plexus supplies the nerves to the upper torso. It is formed by the ventral primary divisions of the fifth to the eighth cervical vertebrae and first thoracic nerves. It lies in the lower lateral part of the neck and in the clavicular region extending from the scalenus anterior to the axilla."

I sigh inadvertently. The students are busy writing diligently in their notebooks. I can't relate to anything he is saying and begin to do quick studies of his hand holding the scalpel.

"We will now concentrate on the lateral and medial roots as I don't want to roll Matilda over on her belly just yet." Thom continues the dissection, talking rapidly, using highly technical language of anatomy to explain the interactions of the bones, nerves, muscles, and veins. He obviously expects everyone to remember every word he says.

I feel better and begin to make crude drawings of what he is demonstrating. He glances at me, and reflexively I cover my work, like a school girl ashamed of her efforts.

"Never mind how the drawings look," he says to me. "Just keep drawing and keep looking. I'll help you with them when we get back to the house. We can refer to *Gray's Anatomy* there to clarify all of this."

"I can hardly emphasize sufficiently how crucial it is in spinal surgery to totally understand the patterns and functions of the nervous system," he continues. "Next week, we will roll Matilda over and study the nervous system connections on her ventral aspect. Are there any questions?"

"I have a question, Dr. Kelley." It was the young woman.

Thom looks up in surprise. He appears not to have even realized this female presence among the students. He nods in her direction.

"I understand there can be several variations in the contribution of the spinal nerve roots to the plexus, but could you explain these a little more clearly and also which roots are the prime contributors to the functions of the brachial plexus?"

"Are you a nursing student or what?" he asks rudely.

The woman flushes. "No, Dr. Kelley, I am studying general surgery here at the university."

"What is your name?"

"Janette Murphy."

Thom takes a deep breath, pulls himself erect with his knuckles on his hips, and manages to speak, "Well, Janette, you can understand my surprise. Usually, girls study obstetrics or gynecology, not surgery or orthopedics."

No one says anything, and the silence is embarrassing. The young woman wears no makeup. Her brown hair is pulled tightly behind her head. She is slender, her eyes dark and intelligent, her nose a bit too prominent for conventional beauty standards. She waits silently under the harsh light for him to answer her question since his comment merits no response. There is about her the quiet pride of someone who is fully aware of her worth, impervious to denigration in any form. I can sense Thom bristling at her.

"Yes, you are quite right. There are always the possibilities of variations from the norm that can exist in the contributions of the spinal root nerves, the origin or combinations of the branches in relationship to the muscles involved. To answer the last part of your question, the fourth cervical nerves contribute to approximately two-thirds of the function of the plexus we are discussing, and the second thoracic nerves contribute about one-third of the stimuli under average circumstances."

There is a scarcely audible communal sigh of relief.

They all continue taking notes. I stare at the young woman and admire her courage. I wonder why Thom was angered by her question. She looks competent, even more so than some of the callow young men accompanying her, snickering ever so slightly at her boldness as though she were not supposed to exhibit intellectual curiosity. How strange! I think, of Thom and all of them. I will ponder all of this later.

Thom continues answering their questions while at the same time digging around in the gray-brown tissue of the cadaver. He becomes so engrossed in his explorations that he seems unaware of the restless young people around him. "Well?" He sits up in his stool abruptly. "Does that answer everything?" He speaks to no one in particular.

There is a murmur of agreement, an anxiousness to be gone and on to other things.

It is over. The cadaver is patched up, covered, and rolled back to eternity with her companion in death. The heavy door swings shut, is locked, and the key returned to Thom. The instruments cleaned, the student wash up and are off to continue their classes.

In the hospital cafeteria, Thom buys coffee for us both. I want to talk about everything that went on, but he appears irritable and distracted. The harsh brew hits my stomach. Thom takes out a small pill vial from his suit pocket, extracts two of the little white tablets, and swallows them with his coffee. They must hit his stomach like tiny boulders combined with the raging coffee. He looks over at me. "Here, take some. You'll feel better."

"I think not, Thom. I don't take pills."

"The fact that humans can take medicines to cure their aches and pains makes us superior to animals who just suffer. But I have already told you that, haven't I?"

"Thom, my mother is a naturalist. She believes in grinning and bearing it. My father had never spent a night in a hospital when he was alive. She has her new husband trained not to even take aspirin!"

"Spartan of them now, isn't it?" he says mockingly, but his mood seems to be lifting along with his spirits and perhaps now he will talk to me. "Women should not go into medicine except maybe pediatrics," he says on the way home. "Surgery is man's work. Women are too nervous to operate objectively. They get their periods and what not. Orthopedic surgery is totally out for a woman. There is a bit of carpentry involved in orthopedics, hacking and sawing at limbs. Ya gotta be strong to do that."

"Yes, Thom, but what about electric saws and drills? Anyone can handle that."

He doesn't answer me. He appears to be still peeved at the young woman medical student and her questions. I was rather impressed by her. The conversation has dead ended.

On our way home, I stare out from the speeding black Thunderbird at the beautiful palm trees marching down the center of Dolores Street and wonder vaguely whose idea it was to plant them there.

Cobalt blue gouache dissolves and spreads through the clear water in a jar to my right as I clean my fine, sable watercolor brush. A large sheet of illustration board is laid before me on the new drawing table I have just purchased from Flax. It is the first piece of artist's furniture I bought new. The table is slightly inclined. My art materials sit beside it on a board supported between two stools—another unsatisfactory arrangement, but one that has to do for the moment.

My studio/bedroom is cluttered with open anatomy books; pieces of human bone from the vertebrae, some lying loose, others wired together offering a semblance of reality. An authentic human skeleton dangles to the left of my drawing table, suspended from a clothes rack on loan from Thom.

Thom has informed me that the true reason for the anatomy session at Saint Luke's morgue had been to prepare *him* for a trial. As he explained to me, he is hired by local attorneys as an expert witness in various types of personal injury cases. He receives a substantial sum of money for this work.

In this case, the victim's arm has remained paralyzed from a neck injury sustained during an automobile accident. The insurance company representing the party at fault claims a paralyzed arm cannot occur as a result of a whiplash injury to the neck. Thom will demonstrate to the jury, through my graphics, the anatomy of the nervous system in order to prove that indeed a paralyzed arm can result from an injury to the neck.

I will be paid the grand sum of $450 for my work, most of which will go back to Thom for past due rent, and the rest to pay for art materials, car repairs, gas, and a little food.

There are three drawings in total: a frontal, back, and side view of the neck, upper shoulder area, and arm. I work long hours perfecting the shading of the underlying bone structure then superimposing the tiny yellow, threadlike nerves and the muscles they serve. The muscles are dense and sinewy, but one is able to see the bones as the supporting structure of it all.

I work from X-rays, the skeleton, and anatomy books. I use gouache, watercolor, India drawing ink, colored pencils, and drawing chalk. The work intrigues me. I am learning things that will be of tremendous importance to me in the future in ways that I cannot even imagine.

"This first one is damn good, Joanna," says Thom, holding the drawing up in both hands, his glasses firmly in place to study it. It is late afternoon, and the rays of the sun setting over the Pacific filter into my studio, bathing the chaos in a soft glow. "I like the way you can see right through the body. You got that right."

The work draws us together. I like what I am doing, and it is sure money, not like the gallery where art is all risk on consignment. Maybe you sell what you have worked on, but maybe you don't. More likely, you don't. However, I continue to paint for the gallery when Thom doesn't have me working on his medical drawings.

Thom leans over my shoulder as I shade the under curve of the biceps muscle and suggest fibers of the tissue.

"What color should the muscle be?" I ask.

"Jeezus, some shade of red is logical, I guess. The nerves are always yellow. Here, look at these drug pamphlets I brought you from CIBA." He thumbs through them illustrating the different techniques.

I cannot help but notice the faces of these figures depicted in the drawings. The colored drawings are done very realistically, but the faces do not reflect the suffering these individuals must be feeling.

Here is a man with amputated fingers; another has no hand. There were those with various degrees of disease, lacerated joints and other body parts ruptured, decaying inner organs. The people appear strangely calm, almost ethereal in the face of mortal agony.

But again, as in the morgue, I catch myself. I must not think of them as humans. I must only study the anatomy, the colors and techniques of representation.

Thom is amused and reiterates, "Medicine, my dear, consists of problems to be solved. A doctor can *never* become emotionally involved with his patients. It is an unwritten law of medicine that he can never operate on a family member. All illness, trauma, disease, and degeneration are abstract scientific problems to be solved and nothing more."

"Is that why the artist paints these benign faces on these poor suffering people? Do you suppose people with such physical trauma think their condition is simply 'a problem to be solved'?"

He chuckles and makes a show of looking once again at the faces. "Lemme see. You are right. They don't look too upset for the mess they're in."

I continue, "Whatever became of the old-fashioned doctor who took care of everyone, mentally and physically, who truly cared about his patients and probably delivered and buried the same individuals in their lifetimes? Who accepted chickens, homemade preserves, garden vegetables, and fruits for payment for services when there was no money?"

"You have answered you own question, my dear. Old-fashioned, like an outhouse before indoor plumbing, the family doctor has become obsolete, a relic from the past."

I turn over the cervical vertebrae in my hand, giving it to Thom to mark the exact spot where the muscle tendon attaches, to make the drawing as accurate as possible.

"I somehow don't like that idea, Thom."

"What idea?"

"The idea that operating and treating people is merely another form of problem-solving, as though people are machines. What about psychosomatic illnesses where people's emotions cause the sickness? Do you treat that as a mechanical problem, or do you try to find out what is troubling the poor person?"

"I send someone like that straight to a shrink—a psychiatrist, in case you don't know the slang. I prefer dealing with X-rays, like fixing a broken leg. You see the break. You go in and you put it back together, nice clean work."

"There's a lot of money in surgery, right?"

"Yep, but we don't talk about that. I don't even think I 'll tell you how much I make when I operate. You may hate me, with your idealistic little judgments."

"It almost seems like a last frontier. A poor kid with nothing but his medical license can make himself a fortune. Like those guys in the anatomy class the other day, most of them did not strike me as being very dedicated, rather cynical, in fact, about the whole process. Where is the art in practicing medicine that you are always talking about? You may have it, but I didn't see it in those students the other day."

"You are right in a way. They are even teaching business and investment management to medical students now since doctors are notoriously bad at managing their money. But hell, don't worry your pretty little head about medical ethics."

"I want you to come to UC Medical Center next week. I am operating on Gladys von Rohr, heiress to the hotel fortune. You've heard of her, I'm sure. She's madly in love with me, can't wait until I operate on her again. She has me set up for a research grant in spinal surgery on children. You'll love her, and at the same time, you'll see what a real, live vertebrae looks like, the same as the one you are working on."

"Really, I'd like that. I hope I won't pass out again."

He looks around at the canvases in various stages of development.

"Been working on your paintings, too, haven't you?"

"Yes. You probably think they are sentimental subjects: children laughing, crying real tears. I'm getting good at painting bodily fluids since working with you. Art is my life, Thom, my salvation. There is nothing else to live for. I can leave it for periods of time, but I will always come back to it. The sketchbooks, the canvases, paints, pens, brushes, it's my life-support system."

"You need your friends, too. You need me, and you know it, for better or for worse. Your parents don't give you the emotional support you need as an artist. They want you to be a nice, married housewife, right?"

"Aldrich Galleries sold another painting of mine."

"No kidding? That's great!" he says sincerely in the childlike way he sometime expresses himself. He keeps pacing behind me, and I get the feeling he wants me to stop working and concentrate on talking to him. I lay my pencil down, rinse out another brush then arrange the vertebrae in a neat line on the top of the drawing table. I turn to face him. He is rubbing his chin, a little habit he has. "I think you need a break. You've been working all day. Come upstairs to my place, and I'll fix us some cocktails."

"Okay. Let me clean up, and I'll be right up there. I have something else to tell you."

CHAPTER NINE

The Men

Thom's flat on the top of the building still looks camped in, but there are signs of returning environmental concerns. Swatches of decorator's fabric lie on the mantelpiece above the fireplace. A few *House & Garden* magazines are on the old coffee table, with a thumbed-through look about them. There are little pieces of paper sticking out of the magazines, marking the interior designs that Thom admired.

The pages are open to his favorite, a Spanish-styled neo-colonial in the hills of San Luis Obispo. The furniture is intricately carved, Art Nouveau with a Spanish twist. Huge wrought iron lighting fixtures hang on heavy chains from the high vaulted ceilings of the living and dining rooms. The colors are wine red and forest green. The dark wood tones and white adobe walls are accented with gold. It looks like a monastery should look.

Thom strides back from the kitchen with his gin and tonic and my chilled Chardonnay. He seems to be in a good mood, which I do enjoy. He often sulks and nothing I say can bring him out of it. I settle back on the on the old sofa with my wine, noticing my ink-stained fingers holding the stem of the goblet, the mark of my calling.

"Cheers!" he says, and we both take deep drinks, our reward at the end of another day of striving. "Oh, say, whaddya think of this spread—the house, I mean. Nice, huh?" He motions his glass over the photo layout of an interior that I had been looking at.

I think great for an archbishop, but I am loath to criticize his taste."Uh-huh, yeah, it's nice, Thom. It could work here, with the high ceilings and the fireplace."

"Gold, I want it all in gold. And this kind of refectory furniture reminds me of those grand receiving rooms of the seminaries in Berkeley where I went to school. Sloan's has it. Want to go with me someday this week to help me pick it out? And gold drapes, gold carpeting, and a pouf."

"A pouf?"

"A pouf is a round sofa, not too large. I want it covered in leopard skin, and someday I want you to pose naked on it for me—oh, hah, hah, just kidding."

I laugh appropriately, and we drink some more, rapidly. Thom leaves to replenish his drink, returning with an ice bucket containing my white wine. He sets it carefully on the coffee table next to the *House & Garden*. I wonder where all of this is leading. I know nothing about interior design and could care less, but it's what he wants from me, so …

"So, what exciting news do you have to tell me?" he asks as he lights two cigarettes for us.

"Well, you know, I have those two paintings in a group show down at Aldrich Galleries. So, I went down there to see how it was going. The opening was last week, but you were out of town. They sold another one of my paintings! Then, Malcolm Aldrich told me they would like to do a one-man show for me in April. I will need about thirty works. What do you think of that?"

"Great! Congratulations! You now belong to the aristocracy of the creative, like I always told you. The future is going to belong to people like you who value and cultivate their creative talents and instincts."

"I can hardly believe it, Thom—my own show in a fancy downtown gallery on Sutter Street."

"I told you so," he repeats, smiling with a trace of his old cynicism flickering about the edges of his smile. "Just keep at the old grindstone, and you can do whatever you want to in your life. Don't ever forget that."

Almost, I think to myself, except for the babies I want but don't have and don't seem close to ever having. I don't mention this, though, since he is hostile to the idea of motherhood. He claims I have been brainwashed into the pursuit of children. It seems people are throwing that word *brainwashed* around more than ever these days—convenient way to deal with something one does not agree with.

We return to the decorating magazines.

I hear a door slam somewhere in the building. It must be Vincent coming home for the night. I have seen very little of him lately. He doesn't always come here to sleep. A short while later, the phone rings. It is Vincent; he wants to come up and talk to Thom.

As he enters the hall and greets us, I am struck by how haggard he looks. He is not as buoyant as he was at first when I met him; he suddenly looks middle-aged. Before, he impressed me as being glamorously youthful for an older man.

Thom goes to fix him a drink, Tanqueray gin on the rocks with a twist of lemon. We sit silently for a few moments. I have no idea what to talk about with this man.

He breaks the ice. "So, how's the little artist doing these days?" he says pleasantly as he takes out a package of unfiltered Camel cigarettes. He offers me one. He lights them both on one match and looks directly into my eyes as though searching inside of me for something.

My breath catches and my heart pounds. I can't understand this strong physical reaction I have to this man and struggle to contain myself, to behave in a normal, friendly fashion. I take a long drag on the cigarette. It is terribly strong, and I resist the urge to cough. "I'm doing all right, I guess. Selling a bit of my work here and there. Thom has also been helping with the medical—"

Thom is back and hands Vincent his drink and sits down. "How are things going with your little problem down at the office these days?" he asks.

Vincent takes a big swallow of gin and sighs deeply. I sense him mentally debating if he should speak freely in front of me then deciding to go ahead as I am of no consequence. "Not good, Thom, not good at all, I'm sorry to say." He lifts one arm above his head and frowns, the cigarette smoke curling around him like a smoky halo above his thick gray hair. "Walters put his fancy Palo Alto mansion on the real estate market, but I'm afraid that isn't going to save us. He owes so much money, and no one wants to buy those big old, peninsula white elephants. Costs too damn much to keep them these days. I had to arrange a bank loan for the second payment on the trust deficit."

I sit quietly smoking my cigarette as they talk. Thom had mentioned something about Vincent's problems at his office, but I have trouble conceiving of such large amounts of money and know very little about the law. What bothers me is a strange sense of foreboding, a premonition of a cruel twist of fate that lay ahead for this charming, gifted man. It is gone in a moment and leaves in its wake a feeling of shared destiny for Vincent and me.

I scrunch out my cigarette and am aware of enjoying the company of these two men. I love their conversations, and they create an exciting masculine aura in this magical flat high above the city. Between them, they seem to touch different aspects of my own psyche, one continually engages me intellectually, and the other attracts me physically and emotionally.

We follow Thom into the kitchen to view a standing rib roast he has bought for supper. "Say, how about I cook this thing and we all eat here? You hanging around this joint, Vince?"

"Yeah, that sounds great! I have to get to the office early and need a good night's sleep." He appears to be alone. I wonder why.

Thom throws garlic salt and pepper on the roast and shoves it roughly into the oven with several potatoes. He seems to resent the responsibility of being the cook.

"I'll make a salad, Thom," I volunteer. Poking around his refrigerator for the basic materials, I find an old head of lettuce and strip the brownish outer leaves, then a cucumber, an onion, and a tomato, all in fairly good shape. I make the salad quickly, and we drift back into the living room.

Thom has become more animated, and he begins searching for paper and matches to light a fire. Soon, there is a cheerful fire going to illuminate our conversation. We three seem to draw together. I catch Vincent staring at my hand as I hold the stem of the wine glass.

"Italians like wine, right?" he says.

"Yes, I suppose so. My family always drank wine with meals."

"How are your flying lessons coming along?"

"I've been so busy. I haven't had a chance to go to Half Moon Bay."

"You should try to make time for it. I talked to Jake about you. It's good to learn to fly in a tail dragger, make stall landings. And once you get that down, you can fly anything. One of these days when I'm free, I'll take you up." He doesn't ask me; he tells me.

"How much do you charge for giving flying lessons?"

"I'm cheap. Nothing for you—you're a starving artist and a neighbor besides."

The smell of roasting meat wafts into the living room. I am definitely very hungry by now.

"I do hate being poor. It seems like everyone in San Francisco has lots of money," I say.

"Don't kid yourself. It just looks that way. The banks and the ex-wives have it all."

Thom comes back with more drinks. "Yeah, let's not talk about ex-wives—depressing subject. Veronica's about to take me to the cleaners. She gets the house in San Mateo. Thank God, I bought this place before we married. Otherwise, I'd be out on the street." Thom's face is glowing by the firelight. He seems calm, for the moment, despite his problems.

"How'd you come out on your divorce settlement, Joanna?" Vincent asks me pointedly.

"Oh, all right, I guess. We had no children or property to speak of, a note on some land not worth too much. I hated worrying about money and would just turn my paycheck over to him every month to do whatever. I got the sports car and the right to keep the little apartment downstairs. He didn't like it too much here—too isolated."

"Boy, oh, boy, what a great wife! Never paying attention to money, working your tail off to support him while he studies, hardly any alimony, either you are very stupid or else a saint," Thom says, chuckling.

Vincent continues my interrogation. "So, why the hell did you get divorced? You were just about ready to sit back and be a housewife while he works. Not too smart."

"Pardon me, but why don't we all go into the kitchen while I check the roast so I don't feel so lonesome?" says Thom, standing and stretching.

We follow Thom into the kitchen, and I make a salad dressing from olive oil, vinegar, and some garlic. Thom takes out some frozen dinner rolls and throws them into the oven. Frozen peas he pours into a pot and slams the lid on. "Hmm, just smell that roast. I like it kind of rare. Is that all right with everyone?" He pokes a fork into the meat, and bloody juice rises up around the prongs.

Vincent is waiting for more information. "I… I really don't know. It's a long story. I wanted the divorce. Yeah, maybe it was kind of dumb. He passes the board exams, and I leave him. Strange, I guess, but I couldn't help it."

"You probably liked bringing the money into the household, and when it came right down to it, you didn't want to be dependent on him. Rather go out and be a starving artist than a nice, fat, taken-care-of housewife."

I don't mention the baby problem. It seems too personal to get into under the circumstances. Besides, it remains painful for me to discuss. I toss the salad. "Maybe I should be psychoanalyzed or something. My parents did think me slightly crazy to leave him," I continue to explain.

"It would bother me a lot on Sunday afternoons when he and I would ride north to Sonoma and Napa. I found the hills and mountains of the coastal range fabulously beautiful and would take my watercolors along and do quick renderings.

"This made him very impatient. He would look at this mystical landscape before us with an eye to real estate development. He would comment how he would like to buy it all up cheap from some farmer and turn it into a tedious suburb like Daly City, lots of third-class construction so it lasts only thirty years, so he would become a millionaire many times over."

"So, what's wrong with that?" Vincent's eyes narrow, studying me.

I struggle to cut a tomato with a dull knife. He takes the knife from me gently and runs his thumb over the edge. It is very dull, so he sharpens it carefully on a stone from the doctor's kitchen cabinet.

"Well, nothing, I suppose, if that is all you value in life— money, money, money, and more money."

He returns the knife to me, which now slips through the tomato as if it were soft butter. "I could use some of that filthy lucre, money, right now," he says as I serve the salad on three plates with a garnish of a tomato on each.

"But ultimately, it becomes boring," I continue, "I mean, the moneyed environment. I was tired of expensive restaurants every night, the social life with his wealthy friends where all they talked about was their trips, clothes, makeup, beauty shops, their illnesses, their psychiatrists, their children, their diets—the women, I mean."

"So," Vincent says, "what it comes down to is that the prospect of an upper middle class married life would have bored you to death, and you're rather starve to death on your own terms."

"You really summed it up, but I don't really want to die being an artist. I can see why you do so well with a jury as Thom told me you do. I don't want to talk badly about my ex. He was doing what he was supposed to do, what he had been raised from childhood to do: make money. He couldn't understand me. When you get right down to it, it's more fun making money than cleaning house, cooking, washing clothes, ironing, washing dishes, shopping, for the rest of your life, now isn't it?"

Vincent pours me more wine and I notice the bottle is almost empty, and I am beginning to feel the effects, shooting my mouth off as my stepfather used to say.

"Why no children?" he persists.

My eyes are watering from the onion in the salad. I dab them with a paper napkin.

"Tell him the truth. We're all good friends, and there is no disgrace in your husband's failure. It happens a lot more than people realize," says Thom.

"Sterile, he was sterile, no sperm."

"Shot blanks!" exclaims Vincent.

Thom laughs. "That's what I said. Kinda crude now."

I think back to the pain. These men are joking without any idea of the trauma we suffered. I could have handled anything in my marriage— boredom, his constant criticizing, his dark moods of silence, his accusations that I had inflicted some terrible wrong upon him, our conflict of temperament and values, my Gentileness and his Jewishness—all of that could have been tolerated if we had had children. I would have ignored it all and lived for my children. I begin to cry. Thom whips out a crumpled handkerchief and hands it to me. I dab my eyes, embarrassed, but Vincent had taken it too far.

"He blamed me for his sterility and made me feel guilty for it, ungrateful, a bad woman. You may laugh about it. I guess it doesn't *sound* so horrible, but it ... ruined my life!" I declare dramatically.

It looks as though they are even more amused. "But your life isn't ruined," cajoles Thom kindly.

"Yes, it is," I say bitterly, turning away from the salad plates so as not to drop tears on the vinaigrette. I lean against the kitchen counter feeling miserable. "I just turned twenty-seven last week, and I have nothing—no family, just my art. That's all."

"My God, you are ancient! Wouldn't you give your left testicle to be twenty-seven years old again, Vince, just one now?"

"Well, now, dear, we will be your family—uncles, sort of ... a substitute family," says Vincent, unwilling to say *fathers*.

Where is this all going? I ask myself as I carry the plates into the dining room where Thom has set up a temporary table.

"What about the life of your poor ex-husband? Don't you feel a little sorry for him? He may have been quite as hurt as you by the situation," Vincent continues, eagerly waiting to see how I handle this one.

"Well, uh, yeah, he was pretty upset when he realized I meant it when I said I'd leave him. He never thought I would. But he kind of blamed me for his problems, and I had absolutely nothing to do with them. I could have just as easily been the sterile one until he was tested. But really, I think he is happier now without me and the pressure. He likes his comfort, his freedom, doing business, and yes, making money. He never really expressed an overwhelming desire to have a family."

"Men often don't until they are actually confronted with one of the little bastards they are responsible for. Then suddenly, you never know, they can become quite paternal. I've seen it happen. You just place the squalling little brat in their shaking arms, and like magic they are 'Daddy,'" Thom says as he rummages around in his messy cupboards looking for oregano. Thom turns to me. "Say, you don't happen to have oregano in your place now, do ya?"

"I may. I'll go look," I say, glad to have a break from all these painful memories Vincent insists on dredging up. "You need anything else?"

"Maybe some ketchup," says Thom, studying some grubby sauce bottles with streaked, illegible labels through his glasses in mock seriousness.

"Ketchup on prime rib? Kelley, you have no taste at all. What we should have is finely chopped horseradish in whipped cream, something truly gourmet, you know."

I hurry out the kitchen door into the stairwell, the fresh air reviving me and my spirits. I don't really regret my emotional display. It was real, and I have been learning to respect my real feelings. This might be the most difficult part of facing my life, it occurs to me peripherally.

The reassuring odor of linseed oil and turpentine assails my nostrils as I enter my chilly, dark apartment, the smell of my personal life-support system, my own place, for the first time in my life, a room of my own. The streetlamp shines into the tiny kitchen as I switch on the light. Behind me the skeleton sways in the studio, animated by my whirlwind motions, smiling at me with its eternal mocking grin.

Ah, there in my barren cupboard is a package of oregano and a bottle of ketchup one-quarter full. That's enough to get through the prime rib, I think. I race back up the stairs, my treasures in hand.

Thom is refreshing the drinks while Vincent begins carving the rare, bloody roast, skillfully drawing the chef's knife across the meat in neat, thin, even slices. We silently watch him perform the ancient rite of the hunter. "Goddamn, Cooper, you do everything so well. See, I told you the knife goes through raw meat easier than cooked meat." Thom laughs, and we settle down at the table in the dining room in front of the spectacular view of a city we all love.

I sit pensively sipping my wine and thinking about the food, the view, and the circumstances. Meat placed in elegant procession across the serving platter, a steaming bowl of peas, a basket of hot dinner rolls, ketchup, salt and pepper, a small plate of margarine (not butter like in my mother's home), and my salad.

Ah, yes, my family home, where everything was done on schedule— lunch at 12:30, supper a 6:00 PM—not spontaneous like here in my new life, where one never knows from one moment to the next if there is going to be a big dinner party, an intimate supper for two or three, an invitation to an interesting restaurant, or a stretch of long, lonely nights.

It is now 10:00 PM, a perfect time for dinner, Thom informs me. "Cheers!" and we sip our drinks.

"Good luck on your show. When will it be? April, you say?" inquires Thom.

"Thanks, yes, April, I believe, but I still have lots of work to do. I hope you can both come."

"Of course," says Vincent, "now about your flight lessons, Jake would like you to get started. As soon as I have time, I will continue with your lessons. Jake can be kind of rough at times." He smears margarine over a warm roll and places it delicately into his mouth.

I feel happy they are taking me seriously and are being so generous. Is it because of the sales of my paintings? I wonder. Without those sales, would they still consider me an artist? I decide not to think about that now. Too much thinking can ruin a nice evening, I have noticed, so I drink more wine.

The men settle in for some serious dinner table conversation covering topics such as law, medicine, aviation, women, divorce, and money. I am slowly becoming accustomed to all of this as I reach for another piece of rare prime rib and douse it with ketchup. No starving artist for me tonight.

On the law: Boils down to deal-making these days, doing briefs and taking depositions, and is mostly hum-drum work. Hardly anyone can do worthwhile trial work, and Vincent considers that to be the most interesting and important part of his law practice.

On medicine: Hardly anyone is ethical anymore. Gynecologists are 'pussy peekers.' Lots of competition from young students who want to make tons of money. Future is in technology and pharmaceuticals. Socialized medicine was going to save the medical profession by paying patients' bills but would lower the standards of practice. Malpractice suits were becoming a big problem for doctors, raising their insurance rate astronomically.

On women: Ugly women grow up to hate men. Don't understand them. Women shouldn't be so jealous, since a man should have the right to more than one woman. Women should be subservient to men, like the good squaw that follows behind the Indian brave. All women want is money. Can't live with 'em and can't live without 'em.

On aviation: They don't teach flying like they did in the good old days. Too much government control. Flying was the best way to get from here to there but becoming more expensive than ever.

On divorce: A necessary evil. The modern liberator, but more expensive than aviation.

On money: People do some awful things to get it. Government taking too much of it. Losing its value, and never enough of it in your pockets.

"Cheers! Let's change the subject and talk about *you*," says Vincent, shoving his plate aside and staring into me as though there were something intrinsically interesting there. He takes out his pack of Camels and, while Thom clears the table, lights one for me and one for him. We have suddenly become on more intimate terms with this strange custom.

Vincent inhales deeply and continues. "You should really take some time off to visit Old Mexico. I don't mean those trashy border towns. Great place for an artist. You should see Puerto de Las Peñas right down there on the west coast. A really beautiful spot. Costs practically nothing to stay there. Why, Indians living on the coast don't have *any* money at all. They live off the land, trade coconuts for canoes, fish for clothing. Sometimes, I think that wouldn't be all that bad."

Thom breaks out into a great guffawing laugh. "I can just see you now in your loincloth on the beach trading legal advice for fish or coconuts. But what about medical care? Now tell me, what do they do when they get sick out there on the tribal lands?"

"Don't laugh, Kelley. They looked pretty healthy to me. They use herbs, I think, and witch doctors for head problems. Roland was telling me about it once, but we were kind of drunk. But *no doctor bills!* Roland Adams goes to them when he is sick, I swear."

"Is it hot there?" I ask, fascinated by this description, lured into it, visualizing it already, wanting to hear more.

"Not terribly, depends on when you go. Warm, clean, blue ocean water, clear surf, and you can practically pick the fish out of the water with your bare hands they are so abundant. Lots and lots of rain in the rainy season, monsoon rains like in India. People are really nice to each other, not like here—that dog-eat-dog system we work under."

"Oh, come on, Vincent! No place is perfect like that. You go as a rich gringo tourist and see all the good parts, but you would be bored to death living in a place like that. Can you imagine year after year of nothing but calm surrounded by excessive amounts of natural beauty? You would be tired of that sort of thing."

"I could handle it, Kelley."

"I've been there, and I spent a bit of money— to tell the truth, a lot of money—and I got ripped off by a taxi driver once. It's not as Utopian as you think, so don't mislead our little lady here. Look, her eyes are glowing, and not just from the wine. Las Peñas is a nice place for a vacation, period."

"My mother always loved Mexico," I say dreamily. "She and my real father went there around 1939 on their second honeymoon and brought back all this interesting stuff. Then in 1948 my mother and her new husband packed us all into the new Lincoln that my stepfather bought after the war, and we drove all the way from Chicago down the east coast of Mexico to Mexico City and then on to Acapulco. I loved it. Then I spent last summer in Mexico City studying art with an old master, Raul Anguiano. He taught me so much about drawing. Why, we even had nude male models. And just like you teach, Thom, he taught the students to draw just what they see and not to make it all up."

"Sounds like a good teacher," says Thom with authority, "I really can't understand art education today. They should teach you classical painting and drawing. When you can knock off a Rembrandt and no one could tell the difference from the original, then it would be legitimate to express whatever. Not to give art students a solid base in drawing and painting is a crime in my book." He glowers typically, slamming the table with the palm of his hand for greater emphasis, then grabs the wine bottle and fills our glasses. I love him.

Vincent contemplates our host quizzically, a smile playing about his mouth as he exhales smoke and then douses his cigarette. "I really never thought you would become an art expert, Thom, but just listen to you. Say, I think I'm going to hit the sack right about now. Great dinner, great food and company, but I've got to get to the office early. Lots of heat to deal with. Thanks."

He rises, stretches, and yawns, politely places his chair back in place at the table, waves to us, and leaves by the kitchen door to his flat.

Thom goes to his bedroom and lies on his bed—exhausted, I presume. It is late. I continue the cleanup. "Don't do that," he calls out to me from the bedroom. "Come here." He has the sheet over him, his clothes tossed on a chair.

This is it, I think. Finally, it is going to happen. My diaphragm is in place, and I feel the months of oppressive celibacy lifting, flying away, leaving me in a state of breathless passion for this fascinating man.

"Turn off the lights. The cleaning lady will take care of the mess tomorrow. I'll give you a key to the place. Take off your clothes. Come here. I need you."

I am naked and fumbling for the bed in the darkness. He turns on his reading light. "I want to see you, to look at your body. You are so beautiful. Don't ever have children. You'll ruin your small, lovely breasts. Your stomach will hang down, and you'll get ugly stretch marks. Believe me, I know!"

I slip into bed next to him, and he turns out the light. His hands are cold on my flesh. We embrace. His mouth is on mine, hard. I am aroused. It has been so long since I made love. I feel myself writhing, wanting him. I reach down and touch his penis. It isn't very hard, so I begin to massage him with my hand, frantic to make this all work.

"Okay, okay," he says, "that's enough. Let's give it a try."

He mounts me. I am dying for it, my back arching. I feel his hand guiding it in. He is partially there, but not quite. I am so aroused I feel an orgasm on the way that I cannot suppress.

"Goddamned pecker," he murmurs in my ear as he continues to ride me in spite of his impotency. One thing about doctors, they know where the right buttons are. I climax with a loud cry, followed by moans as the waves of involuntary spasms play themselves out within my body.

We lie there, his thin body on mine, silent for the moment. I feel spent and calm.

"I hope the neighbors didn't hear me," I whisper as he rolls over.

"Don't worry about it. They'll think I'm the big stud on the block now. Sorry about my cock. I think it's the booze, and I have this damned arthritis that bothers the hell out of me." I feel I should say something reassuring, but don't know what. I am still rather in awe of this man.

He switches on the light, gets up, puts on his robe, and goes into the bathroom. I follow him and stand still in surprise at the sight of him injecting his shoulder with a big hypodermic needle. He laughs at my shocked expression. "Don't look at me like that. This is cortisone, I swear. Great relief for my arthritic shoulder. Now, don't you go and faint on me." He puts the needle into his medicine cabinet, which is big, shiny, and new. He is modernizing his bathroom.

He is naked again. He grabs me, puts his arms around me, then slips his hand down between my legs, and somehow we are back in bed again, his fingers fondling me in all the right places. "I'm sorry, I'll do better next time. You're still hot, aren't you? I promise you, next time. Maybe I'm too nervous. I wanted it to be perfect the first time. I'll get more rest—not so much booze maybe. I love you very much. You know that. You make me very happy."

He brings me to another climax, and then we fall into a deep sleep. I feel calm and at peace. My anxieties are pushed back to some dark, unacknowledged corner of my psyche by this paternalistic adoration—for the time being at least.

We begin spending almost every night together unless he has a meeting or is totally exhausted. His sexual problem persists despite more rest. However, his consumption of alcohol remains the same. I notice he takes various pills, but I think I am in love with him so I brush away any potential faults I may see in order to maintain the rosy glow of infatuation.

We talk incessantly about anything and everything and eventually arrive at a high point of intellectual understanding wherein I totally agree with everything he says. He is wonderfully supportive of my work, and I find I am painting and illustrating with renewed enthusiasm and dedication. For him and for us, work is the highest level of being, without which nothing else matters.

He begins work on redecorating his flat. The housepainters arrive, and the whole place is transformed into a soft, golden, glowing space. I help him with it as much as I can. At times, he seems desperate about the disorder and keeping up his office and operating schedule.

I go to Weinstein's department store basement on Market Street and buy yards and yards of yellow-gold-colored material and soft creamy lining to make drapes throughout the flat. All is half price since the fabric is sold as remnants or seconds.

I begin to sew floor-to-ceiling drapes for him. Together, almost like a newly wedded couple, we buy furniture at Sloane's, heavy, Spanish colonial pieces with plush damask covering. I find him a used dining room set at a Busvan sale of unclaimed furniture. He may not like it very much but at the moment I can do no wrong in his eyes. There are two poufs, the round upholstered sofas in fake leopard skin, like something out of *Playboy* magazine just waiting for a naked model to pose.

To my unsophisticated sense of interior decorating, it is all becoming bizarre, but we keep at it with a crazy, unstoppable fervor. Two colonial wrought-iron lamps with heavy iron chains hang from the ceiling at either end of the living room. The shades are thick amber glass, which contribute to the golden glow at night. The whole flat, including the one bedroom, has been carpeted wall to wall with a thick, plush, golden carpet. The effect is wild and unprofessional, but we revel in our creation and the new life it represents.

One evening, after taking a shower, my doorbell rings. I wrap a towel around my wet hair, pull on a robe, and go to the door. There, to my surprise, is Vincent with a coy smile on his handsome face. I don't know him too well, and he intimidates me in a way that is also challenging. Right at the moment, I don't want my delicate emotional equilibrium disturbed. He is dressed in a business suit and looks tired.

"Hi, there! Caught you in the shower, didn't I? How about coming up and having a drink with me in a little while? I'd like to get to know you and hear more about your work."

Innocent enough. "I'm sorry," I reply, "I can't. I have to go shopping and …"

"That's too bad. When are you having your show of paintings downtown?"

"Next month, and I have so much work to do. I'm sorry, I have to go."

"You'll catch cold standing out here in the fog all wet like that."

He leaves, and I gently close the door. Did I see a flicker of disappointment cross his face? But I have been saved, for the moment, from him or from myself I am not sure. He is a turn-on, this lawyer/pilot. He has a certain pathos about him that makes him an irresistible force. I feel a twinge of self-righteous pride that I was able to say no to him.

Thom has been giving me money to do his shopping. I stock his kitchen and mine but still pay rent to him. He is the good, kindly, chaste doctor, and Vincent the dangerous seducer in my simple analysis of them. Then come to think of it, I haven't seen much of Mary Belle around the premises lately. The yellow Austin-Healey is parked by the retaining wall, but I can't recall seeing her coming and going in recent weeks. I comment on this to Thom in the evening.

"Oh, her, she's become a problem to him. Jealous woman, and they fight all the time. Well, then, ya know, Vincent is such a ladies' man. Goes after anything in skirts."

"Oh." I feel I am being slowly sucked into an emotional vortex and am swimming frantically to escape but to no avail.

"Oh, hell, forget about Vincent. Sit down here and catch up on current events." He has his TV on and is watching the news.

It is coverage of the farmworkers strike in Delano County in central California. Several men are speaking from a platform about worker's rights.

"Jeezus, those liberal bastards won't leave well enough alone," Thom complains as a tall, good-looking, dark-haired man shouts into the microphone about the greed of the agricultural corporations and the exploitation of the mostly Mexican farm laborers. "First, it's Negro civil rights, now farm workers. Hell, the next thing you know, women will be demanding the right to be men or some goddamned thing."

"Who is the man speaking?"

"Oh, him, he's one of those bleeding hearts. I tell you, they are going to ruin San Francisco. He's a state senator at the moment, John Chiletti. Why should you care? You're not interested in politics now, are you?" He turns and glowers at me, his eyebrows lowered as if my interest in politics were a very serious transgression of who he wants me to be.

"Well, no, but maybe I should be."

"Leave politics to the guys, Joanna. Women shouldn't meddle in that sort of thing. They lose their femininity."

"Oh? But what if you are a woman and you sympathize with the exploited farm workers, for instance? What do you do about it if you don't speak out about it?" I take a lit cigarette from him and inhale deeply.

"Women just don't understand the economics involved, that's why. Cuz you just don't know what is really going on. They are too easily manipulated by these goddamned liberals, that's why."

And that is the end of his effort to enlighten me about women in politics. I sit back smoking, watching John Chiletti accepting gestures of gratitude from humbly dressed peons, many hunched over, their backs distorted from years of stoop labor in the produce fields of central California. I instinctively do not agree with my mentor of many months, in a way my savior, about this demonstration.

I see the state senator as heroic, defending the rights of the underdog, of the oppressed. He is handsome, and the executive officer of the agricultural farm corporation is short, fat, and balding with tiny, squinty, pig-like eyes. He reminds me of the school bully I had to contend with in fifth and sixth grades in my grammar school. I become aware of faint stirrings in my breast of the birth of political awakening.

In the weeks following, I notice that Vincent has been coming to his flat above me to sleep almost every night. I hear his footsteps overhead and wonder. He phones me occasionally to invite me up for a drink, but I make excuses not to be alone with him. I feel like little Red Riding Hood and don't like the feeling.

Friday evenings are usually party time in the building on Upper Terrace—TGIF, Thank god, it's Friday. One Friday evening, Thom brings home his brother, John, and his medical secretary, Nancy. I had met her at the first dinner party. She is a tall, Germanic-looking woman, plain and shy in her presentation of herself. She is indispensable to Thom in his office.

John is scrawny and flushed, his skin dry and flaky, his face lined and creased in a perpetual, self-effacing smile. He is a very toned down, compromised version of his more dynamic brother, Thom. John talks incessantly and drinks constantly. He flatters everyone, and I almost expect to see him crawling on the floor in his crumpled suit and tie. Thom abuses and insults the poor man, who doesn't seem to mind at all. I have never seen this side of Thom.

I had bought market steaks earlier in the afternoon at Petrini's, along with the usual sour dough bread, baking potatoes, and salad ingredients. Thom seems to be in a bad mood, so I retire to the kitchen to begin dinner.

Like a puppy, John follows me there. "Let me help you. my dear. What can I do? Oh, you look so beautiful. Thom is just crazy about you, you know, and poor Nancy, her husband walked out on her just the other day, poor thing. Thom is trying to pull her through the emotional trauma, dear or dear, such problems, I swear. Here, let me do that. Give me the knife. I'll make the salad, you just tell me what to do. A beautiful, talented girl like you shouldn't be stuck in the kitchen with stupid, ole me. You are a lifesaver. Go ahead, have fun out there with the folks. Let me do the cooking, I will set the table, everything. Where the hell did he put the vodka now, that absent-minded doctor brother of mine?" He didn't seem to stop for a breath between sentences.

"You saved," John continues while chopping up the tomatoes, "my brother's life, I mean, he was suicidal over this last breakup. And don't let him fool you, this wasn't his first-time divorce. It's the third time. Some people have the worst luck. And I tell you, those gals went after him for everything he's got, poor Thom, such a good, wonderful man. My mother is turning over in her grave right now with all of this. Oh, my, you are a pretty thing! Did I tell you Thom is nuts about you? Oh, I did, didn't I? Don't you do anything. Here, let me take care of the steaks and all of it. You go out there and cheer up those gloomy folks, dear. You know what I mean. Oh, you are sooo lovely."

I take a deep breath to level out my equilibrium after this onslaught of hollow flattery, grab some chilled Chardonnay and a wine glass, and go on to see what is new in life's ever-changing spectrum here on Mount Olympus.

Thom and Nancy are deep in conversation, seated on the plush, new, golden-beige sofa. I settle in on a pouf and pour myself a glass of wine, placing the bottle and my glass on the new marble cocktail table. Thom glances up at me briefly, nods, and resumes a conversation concerning the faults of the vanished husband. Nancy looks happy to me in spite of the departure of said husband.

Suddenly, Thom stands up and downs the rest of his drink. "This dump looks pretty good now, doesn't it? Nancy, here, thinks it is somewhere between a monks' monastery and a bordello. Now, tell me," he says to no one in particular, "should I be insulted or not?"

John shuffles in carrying another drink for his brother.

"Thanks. Oh, say, put some more ice in it, will ya?"

The brother shuffle-trots back to the kitchen to return with the ice-laden drink. Nancy and I look on, wondering whether to scorn this display, to laugh, or to pity the poor older brother.

Thom has his shirt sleeves rolled up and is leaning casually against the heavy wooden mantelpiece, the fire roaring behind him to his side casting its flickering light across the scene. He drapes his thin, absurdly white arm over the mantel, holding a drink in one hand and a cigarette in the other. He is becoming calmer and happier by the moment. One of the sets of windows in the corner still lacks drapes. I had promised to finish them quickly but have been frantic to get enough paintings together for the show at Aldrich Galleries next month.

"Well, well, well, aren't you ladies a pretty sight adorning my golden living room? You, Joanna, on the pouf, you should paint yourself naked like the Maja reclining, and you, Nancy, you actually seem happier than I have seen you in months."

"Oh, thank you, Thom. You know flattery will get you everywhere," comments Nancy with a sly smile. I sense a strong rapport between the two.

"Women should be like Cleopatra," Thom proclaims. "Yeah, she didn't sit around waiting to be pursued. She went after the guy she wanted, and she had two of the most famous heroes of the Roman Empire at her feet, Julius Caesar and Marcus Antonius, Mark Anthony to those of you lacking Latin. And do you know how she seduced Caesar? "

"No."

"She had herself wrapped in a Persian carpet meant as a gift for the emperor with orders to her slaves that the carpet must be delivered to the great man himself in his bedroom."

"Really now?" Nancy sips her vodka tonic, a bemused smile playing about her mouth.

"Yeah, quite a dame! The slave unrolled the carpet, and there she was, beautiful, with only a silk scarf covering her body. Can you imagine? And if I understand my ancient history, from this encounter she bore a male child."

"And what did Mark Anthony think of her having an affair with Caesar at the same time as with him?" I ask, considering this most monstrous transgression of the rules.

"Oh, who the hell knows? She was the queen of Egypt and could do any goddamned thing she wanted to."

John appears with the white wine, ice, and a pitcher of vodka tonics on a tray. His head is cocked whimsically to one side. He is wearing a white apron over his shirt and trousers. "Can I freshen anybody's drinkie now?" He dutifully performs his chores and returns to the kitchen to get the dinner ready.

"How interesting," I say. "What were they like, Caesar and Mark Anthony, I mean?"

"Caesar was the intellectual, gifted in mathematics and administration, and of course, he was the great military strategist of the time. He was rather a genius, as was Cleopatra, who excelled in mathematics, architecture, and astronomy. Caesar was the brains behind the empire and their conquests.

Mark Anthony was his general, and the man possessed the courage and physical stamina to lead the troops into battle. He commanded the respect of the lowliest of the soldiers. You might say, he was the brawn behind Caesar's brain. Together, they made quite a team, as history tells us."

"And Cleopatra loved and had them both." I speak staring into space, imagining myself as Cleopatra and having it all. "Maybe women need more than one man to be truly fulfilled."

Thom's expression changes abruptly. "Normal women are monogamous," he states with a twinge of reproach in his voice.

I look down into my wine glass, feeling chastised. Apparently, men could have their fantasies, but women could not.

Suddenly, Vincent Cooper walks in the front door with a woman I have never seen. His wife perhaps? No, she is all smiles from the moment she comes into the room.

"Hi, everyone! Here we are to liven up the party. Let me present a friend of mine, Annette. She's a stew on Pan Am," he announces.

The woman is as tall as Vincent, her face broad and beaming, her eyes a bit slanted, something Oriental about her. She wears her hair, the color of mine, a dark chestnut, coiled in a braid around her head, foreign somehow. She shakes hands with everyone in a friendly manner, John wiping his wet hands on his apron before greeting her.

John trots off for more drinks, especially a Tanqueray on the rocks with a twist of lemon for Mr. Cooper, and soon the flat is pulsating with conviviality. Unfortunately, John has tired of the kitchen by this time and plunks down on the sofa with his drink minus the white apron.

I begin to smell something burning from the kitchen stove. I run to remove a smoking pot of green beans from the flames, douse it with water, and take out another package of frozen beans from Thom's ample stores, start them cooking in another pot, and return to the group.

"Jes, I vas born in Lithuania," Annette is explaining with a heavy foreign accent. "Vee came here to the US as refugees from zee Russians. I studied English and became a stewardess on Pan Am."

"A *stew*," corrects Thom, chuckling at the slang.

"Vell, okay, a stew."

"I thought I'd bring her here, a kind of cultural experience to see what life is like in the hills of San Francisco," says Vincent, slowly sipping his Tanqueray.

"Great!" exclaims Thom. "We'll just haul out some more meat from the freezer. Say, John, can you take care of that? We better eat before we all get potted."

John nods and nods, with his perpetual smile, and does not move, nor does he appear to be capable of motion, his eyes glassy and half-closed.

Annette sits down next to me on the pouf.

"My parents were born in Europe," I say to her conversationally. "My mother is German and part Bohemian. From what I know of it, Bohemia no long exists. And my father, well, he was Italian from around Milan somewhere. I don't even know. He got killed in the war in North Africa somewhere. How sad that was!"

"Veddy interezzting," says Annette, gulping down her vodka tonic, smiling all the time. "I zink sat Bohemia is now a part of Czechoslovakia and Lithuania. Ees all part of zee Soviet Union. But vee mus never forget our roots. Zees men in power, zey never, never let zees zings stay zee same, alvays trying to conquer, get more of zee land from zee people. Eet does not change. Maybe someday eet will change back again to what eet used to be, who knows?"

Thom's face has turned grim, as it always does when the talk turns to war and conflict. "The Soviet Union will never change. That's why we *must* be strong militarily. If they could, why, they would even make the US part of the USSR."

"I absolutely agree with you, Thom. You never know when those commies are going to drop an atomic bomb right on top of the Mark Hopkins Hotel and the radiation is gonna cook us right here. Those Russians are terrible. Right now, they are trying to take over Asia." John's face was as grim and red as his brother's. He serves as Thom's personal Greek chorus.

"Hell, then I'll have to switch from gin to vodka, if that happens. Say, how is that vodka anyway?" Vincent laughs, unable to take anything seriously in public.

I leave for the kitchen since John is finished for the night. I turn off the beans, which are just about to burn again, throw the steaks into the broiler, chop up a salad, slice fresh sour dough bread, put butter (not margarine) on the steaming bread, take a jar of Italian salad dressing from the refrigerator, douse the salad greens, sip some more wine, all the time wondering if Annette is Vincent's new love and hating that I wonder.

The conversation continues in the living room while I swiftly set the table. Glancing out at the view I love of downtown San Francisco, I am feeling happy and excited for some reason. I then formally announce that dinner is about to be served.

"Thank god! I am starved. Let's eat." Thom leads the way to the table for the hungry, rather inebriated group and assigns seating to everyone like the patriarch that he is. We are six people, and we seem to break down into couples, odd couples: Thom with his secretary; Vincent with Annette, the stew; and me with John, I guess, who seems out of it completely. His head bobs slowly back and forth, and a silly smile is fixed on his pinched face. All at once, feeling the martyred housekeeper on the premises suddenly displaced by Nancy, I prepare the plates in the kitchen, put the ketchup on the table for Thom, with salt and pepper and whatever else is lacking.

"Oh, dear, don't work so hard," says Thom, rising as though to help me with it all.

"No, no, sit there," I say. "It's all done. If anyone wants seconds, there's more meat in the kitchen."

The women appear to eat more than the men. Thom picks at his food, seeming to fill up on a few morsels, and then turns back to the vodka tonic. John eats practically nothing. Thom passes me his unfinished steak, which I devour. These meals with him are keeping me well-nourished under difficult circumstances.

Annette wants more meat, so I take her plate to the kitchen and toss the remaining steak on it. She is talking about war and privation and how they had nothing to eat when the Russians took over their Lithuanian village, taking the farm animals, destroying the crops, and how the people were starving.

I unwrap more steaks from the freezer, put them under the broiler as I imagine what that must have been like not to have enough to eat, to see children starving. Then they talk about how great our country is, the power of America, how there is no hunger here because of our military strength, how we are more powerful than the Russians.

I think about that. I have known hunger lately, not serious hunger, just cutting down on what I could buy for my meals, which I did not have to do when I was married. They would say I knew hunger because I chose a hungry profession, but that should not be. Oh, damn, very depressing. I prefer the discussion of Cleopatra, Mark Anthony, and Julius Caesar and how she had herself wrapped in a—.

They are calling for more wine. I take another bottle of Chardonnay and one of Cabernet Sauvignon, along with Annette's plate back, to the dining room and sit down.

I feel pleasantly drunk after dinner and resolve not to touch another plate. Thom gets up, and we follow him into the living room, leaving the mess in the kitchen and dining room for the cleaning lady in the morning.

Thom serves some cheap cognac to make us more inebriated. I catch myself watching Vincent out of the corner of my eye as I talk to

Nancy about medical illustration. I am hyper aware of him, though he seems not to pay any attention to me, has said nothing about my proposed flying lessons, and appears to be deliberately ignoring me. This is particularly annoying as I think of all the times when he invited me for a drink and I refused. He could, at least, be friendly.

Annette and Nancy begin to talk about how medical examiners abuse their profession when giving medical exams to the stewardesses. "Jes, eet ees not vaht I like to do, to stand naked een front of zees man, doctor, to turn around while he ees looking at my body. Can ju imagine? Then, thees Dr. Burkhart, thees friend of yours, he ees supposed to be taking my heart beat, you know, weeth hees stethoscope, and then he does zees." She rolls her right hand over her left breast, pawing under the beige print blouse she is wearing.

The men laugh uncomfortably, embarrassed at her bold mimicry of their abusing friend.

"Annette is staying with me at my apartment tonight," announces Nancy. "I hate to be there alone."

"Jes, tomorrow vee are going to look for a new apartment for me. Mine ees so very, very, ugly," says Annette, shaking her head sadly. She is very expressive with her hands and face when she speaks. Even when speaking of something that saddens her, the smile is never far away. It must be a protective device of some kind, I think.

Thom arises from the new sofa. "Well, I guess I'll have to take you gals home then. Unless, Vince, you want to?"

"I, uh, I'm kinda tired, to tell the truth. Thom, if you don't mind." He yawns ostentatiously.

"Well, in that case, the pleasant duty falls to me." Thom smiles ironically as he gets his car keys to the T-Bird parked in the garage under the building. He orders his reluctant brother to the kitchen to do cleanup.

Thom and the two women leave, and Vincent and I find ourselves essentially alone. We sit at opposite ends of the living room. He is on the sofa, and I am on the leopard pouf.

He stares dreamily into the fire, now in its dying stages, one arm raised above his head holding an ever-present unfiltered Camel cigarette and the other his little snifter of cognac.

I stare at his profile in the dim light. He is quite handsome, and his profile almost perfect, like those Roman statues of heroes I used to study in the art institute.

There is an awkward tension in the room. I don't know what to say to this man, and he seems reluctant to open a conversation—not like Thom, when there was never enough time to discuss *everything*.

I think, maybe I should leave. But I don't. "Uh, Annette is a nice person, I think. She's had a difficult life," I venture, "I love her foreign accent."

"Yeah, San Francisco is like that. It attracts all kinds, real cosmopolitan. I was born here, you know, in a house a few blocks away, on Buena Vista."

"You mean, you were born in the house—your mother actually gave birth to you in her bed?" I gasp. The tension dissipates.

"Yeah, right there in the house, I'm not sure if she was in the bed or on the kitchen table, but that's how they did it then. I remember how it was."

"How what was?"

"Being born. Don't you remember how it was when you were born?" he asks me with a perfectly straight face, takes a sip of the cognac.

"You mean you can actually recall the experience of birth?" I ask incredulously.

"Yeah, you come down this long, long, dark tunnel, and you don't want to leave where you are—it is so warm and comfortable and nice—but in this tunnel you are being pushed along toward a light at the end. Finally, and it seems like it's forever, you come into this horrible bright light and this giant begins to slap your behind and you scream to go back where you came from, but they don't let you."

"I don't believe you," I say as I drain my cognac snifter, wanting to laugh except I don't want to be rude in case he is serious.

"It's all true," he says and jumps up, takes the cognac bottle from the tray, crosses the room, and fills my snifter, then turns to stir the coals of the fire, which flame up under his attention. "How'd you like to have a nightcap down in my place?" He looks at his watch. "This is just about the time the violinist starts to play."

"Oh, I'd better not. I have to work tomorrow, and it's almost midnight." I know what is going to happen. I try to stave it off, knowing it will consume me, my work, my will. My carefully wrought defenses are disintegrating, crashing all about me. There is no escape.

He finishes his cognac in one gulp, "Okay, as you wish. I'll walk you down the stairs. You don't want the bogey man to get you now, do you?"

"No."

We make our way down the familiar stairwell, past his kitchen door, through the guts of the building, and stop in front of my door, which lately is unlocked more than it is locked. I reach for the knob, and he takes my hand. Oh, I think, it's *now.* He gently turns me around to face him, pulls me against his body. His mouth closes on mine, and his tongue begins to explore my mouth. I feel a surge of sexual desire that I have never felt in my life.

"I've wanted you for so long," he murmurs into my hair then resumes the kiss, his hand moving up and down my back as I involuntarily cling to him. "Why did you make me wait?" he says and continues the kiss, making it impossible for me to respond.

He reaches down and pulls up my skirt, his hand groping between my legs. He unzips his trousers, and then I feel *it* moving back and forth between my thighs, not entering, just tantalizing me. "That's nothing, honey, just the hors d'oeuvres," he whispers. "The main course comes next. Come on, let's go to your bedroom. I have never seen it."

He closes the door behind us and inserts the chain lock, then sweeps me up into his arms and carries me to bed, just like Scarlett and Rhett. I am Jell-O. Then for more film references, he begins to slowly, delicately remove my clothing like King Kong holding Faye Wray in one hand while straddling the Empire State building.

He caresses me softly, running his hands up and down, in and around my body as though he were playing an instrument. He undresses and lies down next to me. We turn to each other and begin the ancient ritual. Our mouths, our hands, our genitals, our minds and spirits, all dedicated to sexual consummation.

I run my hand over his abdomen until I reach his penis. It is silky smooth and very hard. How wonderful! I think fleetingly. He moves down on me and puts his face and tongue between my legs. I pray I don't smell bad but recall I showered before going upstairs. But then the pleasure becomes so overwhelming, so intense, I don't care and just give myself up to him and receive his gift. I climax completely, voluptuously, and want it all to go on.

He enters me, and I know I have crossed a threshold into another dimension of sexual love, a place I probably will never be able to leave in my lifetime no matter what. I feel improbable tears running down the side of my face as he comes heavingly, gruntingly, moaningly inside of me. So, this is what it's all about! I think, nothing like that rapid coupling with the stockbroker so many months ago. I was so foolish.

"I love you. You know that. You have been driving me crazy for months now, always with Kelley. I haven't fallen in love for ages, and you make me afraid. You're still so young."

"I had no idea. I thought you were getting married to your secretary." I don't want him to know I am weeping. I just cling to him, feeling his skin, the rough stubble of a beard, and know that what has just passed between us is true and honest, the very integrity of it creating the ecstasy. The tears are for such divine, fleeting moments, for the beauty, the pleasure, and of course, ultimately, the pain.

Beneath the bed, I hear the creaking of the garage door as it opens to let in the T-Bird. Suddenly I feel a wild, irrational panic as though I am about to be caught in an illegal act as serious as murder.

"Thom's back," says Vincent. "I don't want to talk to him tonight. I just want to sleep here with you. I am so tired."

"What if he is angry? What if he finds out about us, about this? Will he throw us out?"

"Probably, but we'll find another place. We are both over twenty-one." Vincent rolls over on his side, and in a moment or two he is snoring.

The phone rings. I crawl over Vincent, grab the phone, which is on the floor next to the bed, and walk down the three steps into my studio, where it is quieter, then pick up the receiver.

"Hi, there! I'm back. It's drizzling outside. Thanks a lot for getting the dinner tonight. I'm sorry about my brother. He's such a horse's ass. Does that every time you need him. I thought you might like to come up here for a nightcap. There's still a little fire. Or are you too pooped?" Thom sounded tired himself.

"Oh, Thom, thanks. Don't worry about your brother—it was fun. But really I am exhausted." My heart is pounding, struggling to ward off a massive attack of guilt.

"I could come down there, bring a little wine, have a nip to warm your innards." He needs me, I can tell. He doesn't want to be alone.

"Oh, Thom, I'm half-asleep already. Really, another evening would be wonderful."

"Okay, if that's the case. I just have a bit of good news for you. With all the commotion this evening, I didn't get to tell you that we settled that case involving the brachial plexus that you drew for my testimony. It was very favorable, and I have some extra money for you, around five hundred dollars, sort of a tip for a job well done." He chuckles softly, but I can hear the loneliness in his voice.

Oh, my god, I think as I drop the phone into its place, now what am I going to do? I return to the bed next to my snoring lover and begin to count the days since my last menstruation. It should be about a week until my next period. I am safe tonight if the rhythm system holds, but from now on I must use contraception. The irony of life! I think as I drift off to sleep, after spending five years counting the days in order to become pregnant, now I must reverse the process.

Light is beginning to penetrate my bedroom when I awaken, assaulted by a sense of panic aside from the hangover. Dawn reveals the debris of unleashed passion: shoes scattered about the floor, underwear of both sexes in odd corners, inside-out men's trousers, the necktie, the suit jacket and shirt in a heap, cards and notes spilled out around the phone. The skeleton moves ever so slightly hanging from his head in the corner, his wicked smile taunting me.

Thom must not find out about this, I think. I need him, and I need this apartment. I have become—yes, let's face it—dependent on him. *Like a silver dollar goes from hand to hand, a woman goes from man to man,* as the song goes.

I realize what has awakened me: Vincent snores loudly.

My mind continues mulling unabated. I must not worry about what Thom thinks, I decide. After all, I am a free woman, am I not? And he admires Cleopatra, and look how many lovers she had. I realize I am not the queen of the Nile by a long shot, but still, the aristocracy of the creative, as Thom says, should give me some privilege. But no matter how I turn the situation around, I still feel fear of the future, of stepping out of line, the curse of the female sex.

Then this new/old man next to me is married and probably has a few other mistresses on the side.

And me? I barely have a pot to piss in, to quote Thom.

Thom. Thom. He is haunting me. He is like God. Can he see us now? Is he all around me, above and below in the garage, knowing and seeing everything I do, like that angry old man in the sky? His building. Zeus.

Better not to think about it anymore. I have to go to the bathroom. I slip quietly out from under the covers.

Vincent stirs. "Don't go. I have something for you, look." He uncovers his very erect penis and takes my hand and places it around him then gently guides my head down.

I am going to wet if he doesn't release me. I pull away from him. "Wait! I have to go to the bathroom."

He lies there on my bed, looking too big for it. He reminds me of a huge lion, a lovable, passionate, but still very dangerous animal. The room smells strongly of sex, surely an animal smell. The odor blends with that of the turpentine and linseed oil. In a way, they all become complementary smells.

"Here, this time, Joanna, you get on top of me. Forget the missionary position. Just sit down on me and do the work this time." He holds my hips in place, and we move in unison. I can control the feelings from on high. I have never done this before. This man is liberating me sexually, and I will never be the same. I can feel my own engorging, the spreading waves, and the ultimate implosion, each stroke bringing it closer until it happens. I cry out in ecstasy then collapse on top of him.

He rolls me over, a sweet smile on his face as he towers over me. He spreads my legs and slowly slides inside me, watching it all fondly as he does, his expression transfixed. Vincent climaxes strongly, powerfully, and I can almost feel the tiny sperm gleefully running through all my channels and folds, the stronger ones pushing the weaker ones out of the way in their mindless pursuit of my egg, which hopefully, if my calculations are correct, is still safe for the moment in my ovaries. I am certainly not ready for a baby.

We lay at rest, side by side, staring at the ceiling together. The rising sun is striking the multifaceted structures of the skeleton's face. These bones that support human life a witness to our acts, he seems to be leering at us now.

I feel hot and sticky juice running out of me. Thirsty, I go to the bathroom, wash, drink a glass of water, and bring one for Vincent. During the sex, I forgot my anxiety, but now in the aftermath, there still is Thom. I'm not married to him after all, but still … I have had no experience with all of this, have never read a book dealing with my plight of loving two men, essentially no advice or guidance on how to handle the situation. I am just feeling my way along from moment to moment. I have never felt more alive in my entire life, and there is a strange happiness underlying all my problems, which is even more frightening.

Vincent hands me the empty water glass. "Doesn't that damned skeleton scare you at night?"

"No, don't object to him/her/it. Feel sorry for it. It's been dead a long time and is just jealous that it can't make love like we can."

"I know people who look like they are alive, but inside they are dead and can't make love anymore. Hey, I better get dressed and get my ass upstairs before Thom comes around. He'll have us both out on the street in no time. Later, you come up for coffee like nothing happened." He dresses quickly and is gone.

My muse, my inner voice, my guardian angel speaks: *Your life has been irrevocably changed, never to be the same. You are on the right track. And how to handle all of this? You will see,* the voice continues. *Just listen to me when it all gets too much. Don't be afraid to stand back and reflect, to gather your powers around you. Men can steal your energy, so be careful.*

As soon as Vincent arrives in his flat, he takes off his clothes again and goes back to bed. Shortly after, Thom knocks on Vincent's kitchen door, but there is no answer, so he opens the unlocked door. He walks into the bedroom, and there is Vincent sound asleep. Thom feels disturbed. There is something amiss, though everything looks normal. Thom leans over the man. He smells of sex. Thom reaches over and shakes his shoulder roughly. "Hey, Vince! How about some coffee for that hangover?"

Vincent sits up in bed groggily. "Uh, yeah, Thom, yeah. Say, what time is it?"

"Ten thirty. Don't you have to work?"

"Sure, I do. Let me take a quick shower. Coffee would be great."

The two men have coffee on Vincent's terrace overlooking the city. They talk of the personal injury lawsuit settlement, then Thom leaves for his rounds at Saint Luke's Hospital.

I hear the garage door opening beneath me, the Thunderbird pulling out, and the closing of the door. A little later, Vincent walks into my bedroom. He is a bit puffy around the eyes and is dressed carefully in a different suit. He smells of shaving lotion. He sits on the bed next to me.

"Kelley doesn't know a thing. We're safe. Don't you worry. You rest and then work on your paintings. I want you to sell everything at your show, so you get rich and take care of me someday."

I laugh at the improbability of such a thing taking place, but little do I know. "When are you coming back?" I ask him pointedly.

"Soon. I don't know. Lots of work at the office. But we are just beginning, you and I. You know that." He kisses me quickly on the mouth, puts his hand on my breast momentarily, and is gone.

I feel an overwhelming loneliness, more acute than anything I have ever felt before. I want him here with me, always, to talk to, to make me laugh. He is the most exciting man I have met, the love of my life, I am sure.

I hear the revving of the Austin-Healey as it pulls away down the hill. How does he feel? I wonder, exultant? The conquering seducer?

Okay, I say to myself, you wanted him as much as he wanted you. Don't just sit around mooning and feeling sorry for yourself. Get something to eat and get to work. I have no idea when I will see him again, but I will see him. I know that.

I throw myself into my painting. I don't see Vincent, and Thom feels cool to me, or is it my imagination? Perhaps I am cool to him from a guilty conscience. Did they talk about me I wonder. The sex? Compare notes perhaps? I will never know.

Aldrich's says I need around thirty paintings for the show. That's a lot of work ahead. I need around twelve more to complete my obligation. No longer do I work in a leisurely manner; it becomes like a job. I use a palette knife because the paint goes on faster than with a brush, not an ethical, artistic reason but a style born of necessity, the way some artists paint in watercolor because they can't afford oil paint and canvas.

I take some finished work to the gallery. Marie, the gallery administrator, greets me enthusiastically. "Darling, where have you been? We have just a few weeks before the show. Here are some invitations. Take a pile to your friends."

"I really only need about five or so," considering my sparse social life.

She takes my work for framing to a shop behind the gallery.

I sit down wearily and stare at the paintings on the walls. There are some large, life-sized studies of people by Alice Neel, bright colors, very intense, expressive work and well done. She knows drawing and anatomy. An artist named Staprans also paints with a palette knife—boat and water scenes—thick, harmoniously toned colors. A palette knife goes faster for him, too.

A handsome young man carrying a painting under his arm strolls by and stops, looking at me curiously. "Don't I know you from somewhere?"

I look up at him and smile politely. "No, I don't think so."

"Well, now, if I don't, I would like to. My name is Winston Hoffman, and who might you be?"

"Botticelli, Joanna Botticelli. Nice to meet you."

"Now isn't that a great name for an artist. You are an artist. I can sense it."

"Yes, I am having a show here next week. Some of my work is hanging in the inner gallery for young collectors." I experience the pleasant feeling of being part of an elite inner circle.

He sets down the canvas he is carrying to show me. It is expressionistically done in strong slashes of color. Studying it more carefully, it is a nude woman lying back across the width of the canvas, her legs slight parted, erotic, provocative. But then she also looks like a landscape, her body part of the mountains behind her. She is part of the mountain. Her knees are hilltops, as are her breasts. She is an abstraction of the coastal range, with all the foliage, forests, and streams a part of her. The work is done in shades of green, yellow, black, ochre, white, and umber, woman as nature. I like it very much.

Winston is attractive in a very intense way, exuding nervous energy. He is tall and lean, dressed as an artist is supposed to dress: blue jeans, a scarf, and denim jacket. His eyes are large and deep-set, green, taking in everything; his hair thick and brown; his nose a bit large, with a slight hook, aristocratic, as Thom would say.

He laughs and smiles as he speaks, but there is a melancholy behind his sparkle. "Your painting is very interesting. A loose style, but you can obviously draw very well. I like it," he says, stroking his chin in contemplation of my work.

"But will you buy it? I am a 'starving artist' you know," I say, lowering my head in mock humility.

"It's a struggle for all of us. They sell off some of my work here and there, but, well, you know how it is. You don't look like a starving artist in that fur jacket you are wearing," he says, his eyes narrowing, appraising me.

"Oh, this, a holdover from better times, from when I was married. Maybe you know how that goes." I laugh lightly, as though unfazed by my catastrophic life.

"Actually, I don't. I have never been married. But why don't you invite me to your show? You are a fellow artist. There will be free champagne, maybe some cheese and crackers to hold body and soul together."

"Of course, this is my first—"

Marie returns with a stack of invitations. "Oh," she says, "I take it you two know each other?"

"No, just met, as a matter of fact, but I do hope to know more about Miss Botticelli. My Lord, what a name!"

"Great, isn't it?" Marie giggles as she takes out an invitation for us to see.

There is my name in big letters, the time and date of the show, and a big photo of one of my paintings. Inside, there are more photos of paintings and a paragraph I wrote stating my personal goals and thoughts on my work. I feel a thrill that is new to me, the prospect of impending success.

There follows a shiver of nerves. Will success bring happiness? Do I deserve success? Is success meant for women? Do men dislike successful women? Does success entail responsibility? Must it be repeated over and over again or else cease to exist? All this passes through my head in one millionth of a second.

"Very nice!" I exclaim breathlessly. I hand Winston an invitation.

He hands it back to me, very formally. "Please put it in an envelope and put my name on it."

Marie gives me the invitations and the envelopes. I take one and write Winston's name on the front in my best handwriting.

"Thank you very much. I would be most happy to attend the opening of your first exhibition of paintings, which I don't think will be your last. Now, can I invite you for a cup of coffee."

He is right. I don't look very arty with my old Persian lamb jacket, sheath dress, and high heels—probably the last fur jacket I will have in my lifetime, but the die has been cast. We slip into a booth in a corner coffee shop on Powell Street.

This man is interesting, I think, young, probably only a few years older than I am. He could take my mind off the tension of the "ménage a trois" that persists on Upper Terrace. He is the right age for me, probably middle thirties. But then, what is the right age for anyone? my other self says in its usual contentious manner.

He orders two cups of coffee. His hands clasped in front of him on the table, he begins the conversation. His fingers are long and bony. They are good hands for an artist. "As I was saying, Joanna, from what I could see of your work, you are talented, perhaps a bit sentimental in your choice of subject, but you will grow out of that. The main thing is that you can support yourself and keep painting."

He orders apple pie and ice cream, which I decline. He puts two teaspoons of sugar and half the cream into his coffee. I drink mine black.

"I also do sculpture," he says.

"Oh, really?"

"Yes. That doesn't sell either"

"Oh, it's so difficult," I say, sipping the bitter coffee and sensing my stomach rebelling. I tell him about my educational history, how I regret not having had a classical art education, that I got a teaching certificate because my mother convinced me artists can't earn a living.

"That's too bad. I mean, you didn't have a fundamental art education. That could have helped you in whatever direction you eventually take. When you have some time, I can teach you classical painting—things like how to do an underpainting, modeling, oil washes, the whole thing—so you can paint Venus being born, just like Botticelli."

"That would be wonderful. I am also scheduled for flying lessons after the show."

"Flying lessons?" he says in surprise. "I've never known a girl who takes flying lessons. You mean in a real airplane? Like a pilot?"

"Well, sure. It is unusual, I guess. I don't have any girlfriends who have taken flying lessons. But I have made up my mind I want to learn how to fly."

"It's expensive, isn't it?"

"I suppose so, but it's worth it. One of my neighbors is a flight instructor and has offered to teach me at a discount."

"Aren't you the lucky one? How come I never have neighbors like that?"

I finish my coffee. Winston's ice cream has melted all over the remains of his pie. He doesn't eat it all. The waitress comes with the bill: $2.70. Winston stands and fishes around in his jeans pocket and comes up with a small roll of bills. He peels off three and tells the waitress to keep the change. He appears generous in the face of hardship, a man of character.

"Would you condescend to give me your phone number? I would like to come and visit you, see your studio." He looks at me coyly, his smile a bit crooked, going up more on one side of his face than the other.

With a slight foreboding, I scribble my number on the back of the invitation envelope. Will this further complicate things?

He is attractive and logically a more suitable companion for me. He appears unattached, and I sense his interest. Oh well, I decide, I won't worry about it right now. We wave goodbye, and I retrieve my TR3 from the garage underneath Union Square and speed up Market Street to home.

The gallery is glowing with light,
there are many people inside, standing
around, talking, sipping champagne
and looking at my paintings.

CHAPTER TEN

The Show

I have turned in all the paintings I can muster to the Aldrich Galleries, and this evening, beginning at 5:00 o'clock, my first public exhibition begins. My mother and step-father have refused to attend and have made it clear they are not impressed with my achievement. I brush it off.

Carefully, I dress myself. I put on a longish, red crepe dress I made myself, brush my shiny, crimped, long, chestnut-colored hair and check my makeup—all of this is topped by my precious fur jacket, the pearls from my ex-mother-in-law (god bless her)—then hop into my sports car, praying it will start.

It doesn't.

I will have to push it down the hill to start it, longish red dress, high heels, fur coat, pearls, great hair, and all.

I turn on the ignition switch and check to see that it is in neutral. Hoping for help from my guardian angel, I hold the steering wheel in my right hand and push with my left, turning it downhill. And as it begins to gain momentum, I somehow leap into the driver's seat, press the clutch, and drag the gear into second hoping there is no one coming up the hill. There is, but the oncoming car is far enough away. So as I release the clutch slowly, the motor sputters into life and begins to move on its own. I brake against the tug of gravity and wonder why girls are not taught auto mechanics in school. It ought to be compulsory, I think as I swing onto 17th Street.

After parking, I toddle along the now familiar Sutter Street on my high heels, feeling rather elated. I stop for a moment in front of Aldrich's gallery. It is glowing with light, and already there are people inside standing around sipping champagne and looking at my work. They are all engrossed in conversation. Talking about my paintings? I wonder.

Taking a deep breath, I enter and head for the bathroom to comb my hair and touch up my lipstick. I want to be beautiful.

"Hey, there, Joanna!" I see Marie motioning to me.

I wave back and duck into the very elegant bathroom. There are fresh flowers on the countertop. What fun this is going to be! I think, and when I emerge, my wild hair is tamed just enough to retain its allure.

Marie grabs me by the arm and propels me about. A waiter in a white suit hands me a glass of champagne, which I take gratefully. I finish it in three gulps, and he hands me another fresh glass. This, I take my time with.

"And this is Mr. and Mrs. Wildensturm. They bought that first painting you brought in, remember?"

The woman who owns my first sale is tall and very thin. Her face is perfectly made up, her hair short and blonde in wisps about her face, her eye shadow the requisite shade of blue to go with her eyes. She is wearing—what looks to my inexperienced vision—a necklace, earrings, rings, and bracelets of gold, silver, pearls, and diamonds. I touch my single strand of real pearls unconsciously. This woman exudes wealth, while I, I barely have a pot to—.

She extends her hand to me. "Oh, darling, we are sooo happy to meet you. You are so lovely, as well as very, very talented. Everyone loves the painting. We have it hanging over our fireplace mantel. And you know what? We may even purchase another this evening so it has a companion."

I sigh deeply, smile gratefully at the woman as we move to greet Malcolm Aldrich. "Joanna, my dear, how wonderful! You were a bit late, and we were worried. Everyone loves to meet the artist. Better late than never!" He chuckles. "The show is beautiful." He embraces me, which is embarrassing as I am not accustomed to embraces of the professional sort.

"Car trouble," I murmur, but he isn't paying attention.

He motions toward a gray-haired, older gentleman to come and "meet the artist." Aldrich's eyes glitter beneath his bushy eyebrows. He looks wicked, but he is a wonderful, generous soul. "This is Alexis Sturgis," he says, "a very well-known collector of fine art. I want you to know each other."

"How do you do, Miss Botticelli? Wonderful name for an artist! I am very pleased to meet you, and I dare say, you do paint very well."

"Thank you very much, "I mumble, embarrassed by this man's suave, polite manner. He makes me feel barbaric by contrast. I resolve to become accustomed to this new way of life.

"However," he continues, "I would like you to become more daring, throw caution to the wind, experiment. You are too careful and self-conscious at this time in your work."

"You are probably right. I do need to—"

"Your major problem is that you are a woman!" he says. "Female artists have a hard time of it, Alice Neel tried to commit suicide, you know, when she was around fifty years old. O'Keefe is one of the few, and she owes a part of her success to a fortunate marriage. Look at your brochure. Look what it says."

"Joanna Botticelli in a one-*man* exhibition in the Young Collector's Gallery." It had never registered. Me a man?

He smiles a self-satisfied smirk, pleased that he has had the opportunity to awaken me to my second-class status as a female artist, to make me aware that no matter how much talent or effort I made, I could never be great because I was a member of the inferior gender. I am becoming aware of what had been only a faint, hovering black cloud off in my emotional distance, the dark cloud of women's oppression.

Malcolm Aldrich is again at my side, clinging to my arm. "And this is Mr. and Mrs. Handelman. They would very much like to meet the lady artist."

"With whom did you study?" Mr. Handelman questions me gravely.

I feel I am being interrogated. "Uh, with Henry Schnur."

"Who? Where did you study?"

"In Chicago, well, at the art institute and at Forest Glen College. That's a college to the east of—"

"Oh." The couple moves away. Are they laughing at me, or is it my imagination? I want to leave. There are people around and about me, all talking at once. I strive to be polite and answer each of their questions no matter how irrelevant they may be, but it is impossible. I try to make the best of it and hope I am not rude. They seem insincere to me for some reason. I sip my champagne, and the waiter brings me another. He appears to be a genuine person and empathizes with me.

Suddenly, I feel arms entwined around me from behind and a man's presence hovering at my neck.

It's Thom. "Congratulations, sweetie! The show is beautiful, and I see some "sold" signs going up." He kisses me lightly on the cheek.

"Let me introduce you to Malcom Aldrich," I say. The men shake hands.

People continue to mill about, talking laughing, consuming large quantities of champagne. The whole event becomes a brightly lit, colorful blur of faces, perfume, voices. I maintain a smile through it all until my face aches from the sustained effort. I don't want to look sad, and the champagne eases the pain, somewhat, that Mr. Sturgis has inflicted on my delicate ego.

I hear the word *sentimental* bandied about as criticism. Must be bad, I think, for an artist to be 'sentimental.' But I wonder why sentimentality is bad. Not to feel with one's senses would make one less human. My smile goes limp at this thought.

"Don't look so sad now. This is your evening. This is what you have worked for." Winston Hoffman looks down on me with his own sad smile. "You are doing well. Lots of the rich folk here tonight. Aldrich knows how to put on a show all right." The friendly waiter passes with the tray of champagne, and Winston manages to grab one, drink it all at once, and take another before it all vanishes into the crowd.

"Oh, Winston, I would like you to meet Dr. Thom Kelley. Winston is also an artist. He paints nudes that look like landscapes, and he also does kinetic sculpture, right?" I say, brightening up a bit with these friendly faces by my side.

"Happy to meetcha, Winston, another creative aristocrat." Thom offers him a cigarette, which he refuses, then lights one for me.

"If I am an aristocrat, I sure as hell don't feel like one. Artists don't even get unemployment when they don't sell, have to live on beans and rice," remarks Winston, reaching for several of the fancy hors d'oeuvres passing by.

Thom laughs, thoroughly amused by the agony of self-imposed poverty. "That's just a stage you are at Winston. Didn't I see an article about you in the *Sunday Chronicle* recently? There were photos of full-length portraits of some of your artist friends. Good work, as I recall."

"Thank you very much for your praise and encouragement, Dr. Kelley. I've heard about you, too, and your iconoclastic procedures and theories."

I wonder what "iconoclastic" means and make a mental note to look it up.

"Call me, Thom, please. You make me feel like an old fuddy-duddy with all that formality. You just have to be patient and keep at your art. You've got what it takes. That's what I keep telling the little lady here. I got her doing medical illustration."

I hate when he talks about me as though I weren't present.

"Oh, does she now? You didn't mention that to me, Joanna," says Winston.

"I forgot."

Then I spy John, Thom's brother, hovering behind him with his impish, ingratiating smile. He looks like an ancient, forest elf dressed in a business suit. His features are so sharp and pointed, his ears poking out, and his lined, flaking face constantly flushed. He never seems to stand still but hops and ducks about. He waves to me over Thom's head.

"Say, Winston, why don't you join us for dinner at the Barbary. Help celebrate the success of the artist Botticelli."

"Joanna doesn't fit well with 'Botticelli,'" notes Winston.

"We'll have to change your name for sure, something like Antonia or Sylvana."

""How about Giovanna?" I say ironically.

Thom takes control. "I like you, Winston. You're going to have to come to our house one of these days, on Mount Olympus."

"In Greece?" Winston pulls back incredulously.

"No, right here in the middle of San Francisco. You never knew? By the way, the Barbary serves great sweetbreads and steak."

"Love to! Wonderful, a decent meal!" Winston drifts away to talk to more people. He seems quite at home in this arty, social environment.

Thom continues to talk to Aldrich and then to Marie. He appears to be inviting them to dinner.

John is in front of me, his watery blue eyes shining gaily as if he were the most fortunate man in the world. I realize with a slight shock that he is very happy in his own world. "Darling girl, the show is beautiful, just beautiful! I can't believe you are so talented and that I *know* you," he gushes. He is maddening in his desire to please.

"Thanks in part to Thom and his encouragement."

"Say, do you think you could tell my brother to invite me

to dinner with all of you wonderful people? He thinks I am a pain in the ass, but maybe if you say something to him. He'll do anything you tell him to do, you know. Oh, look who is here, Mr. Cooper himself."

I turn to face Vincent.

"Hi! Remember me, or has success gone to your head?" he says, smiling his sweet, seductive smile.

"Yes, I mean no, of course not. I'm still plain ole me," I say. My heart begins thumping out of control. My voice catches in my throat. God damn him! How does he do this to me? I wonder while struggling to appear normal.

"I've been really busy," he continues. "Had to go to Whittier to try a case that took four days, but I made it back here for your show."

Come to dinner at the Barbary with us, Thom just announced that he was going to give me a little celebration party."

"He didn't invite me."

We stare into each other's eyes. No one else exists for the moment.

I catch my breath. "Because he hasn't seen you yet. I invite you. You two are best friends. Why wouldn't he invite you? Do you happen to have a cigarette?" I look away, unable to stand the intensity of my feelings for him.

John is giggling. "Heh, heh, we all want to be invited now, don't we?"

Vincent takes out his pack of Camels and offers one to each of us. Unlike Thom, he doesn't light it first for me but flicks on his lighter as I draw on the cigarette. "There is a difference now," he says as he puts the pack back inside the pocket of his suit jacket. I inhale deeply as I recall fleetingly what happened to cause the difference.

The Barbary restaurant is situated close to the waterfront, close to Chinatown and to the financial district. It is a dark wood, leather, and glass restaurant with candles in special little lanterns on the tables. It has a distinct masculine feeling, strong and elegant at the same time. Thom had taken me there before, and I liked it very much. The waiters begin pushing tables together to seat everyone.

Vincent has not yet arrived, and I find myself looking for him. Thom sits at the head of the table, reigning over it, and I sit to his right with Winston across from me. Marie and her husband are next to me then the couple that bought my first painting. Alexis Sturgis, who rained on my parade but apparently is acquainted with Thom. John is there, and Thom is furious with him. He ducks behind people gleefully when his brother glowers in his direction, like a naughty boy. I feel like getting drunk. It has all been too much.

"Well, Doll, what would you like to drink? And please ignore my pesty brother. He sticks to me like glue," says Thom.

"The sparkling Burgundy," I answer.

"You order whatever your little heart desires. The night is yours."

The drinks are served. The waiter pours my bubbling Burgundy into a large, high-stemmed crystal goblet. He goes on to pour wine for Thom and Winston. Suddenly, Winston stands up holding his goblet. He flicks his long brown hair back from his brow with his free hand and then announces, "I would hereby like to propose a toast to Miss Botticelli and to her fine work. May she become an ever more successful painter."

"Cheers, yea, yea!" Then everyone drinks and begins to talk at once.

I feel myself moving away from this scene as though I am watching the event from afar, sort of hovering above it all. I am feeling unsure about my commitment to my work. Everyone sees me as wildly ambitious, going for glory, money, and success, but they don't know about that nagging, unfulfilled womb that keeps reminding me of the childless years passing by. I feel fraudulent tonight, and I catch Alexis Sturgis contemplating me with an amused smile, as though he can read my thoughts. Damn him.

"Now, my dear, before you get totally plastered, what do you want to eat? The usual?" Thom is giggling. He has a big Cheshire Cat smile on his reddened face, his eyes glassy. I feel he senses some consternation within me. I doubt he suspects the truth, but perhaps he imagines I am deeply in love with him and dying to marry him or that I am contemplating suicide or I will one day be one of the most famous artists on the West Coast or I will become a drug addict and die an early death from an overdose. I don't know what he thinks.

Alexis Sturgis is babbling away at the other end of the table, very much in his element. I doubt he bought one of my paintings. Female artists are defeated before they even start just because of a uterus and ovaries that lay an egg every month. How unfair! Well, I'll just keep going, come what may. The hell with him! I watch as he stands and pulls out a chair for a newly arrived young man who squeezes in next to him. They kiss on the lips and hold hands briefly. Fairies, I think.

"I'll have steak and sweetbreads for the both of us," I hear Thom ordering through my reverie.

"I'll have the same," echoes Winston.

The others order chateaubriand, filet of huachinango, and even hamburger with French fries.

The green goddess salad comes first, with sour dough bread, breadsticks, and butter.

Winston, in spite of an effort to slow down, rapidly consumes his salad, two pieces of bread globbed with butter, and various breadsticks. He talks with Thom, and they seem to be hitting it off very well. "It's the big museums and their sponsors that control the art market," Winston says. "They decide who makes it and who doesn't, a real bitch of a situation. If you want to make it with them, you have to do what they want and kiss ass. It makes it tough for people who won't compromise their art. It's a hell of a shame, but a lot of really good artists are not going to develop under these circumstances."

Winston eyes the sour dough bread but restrains himself and continues. "After all, an artist needs a following. You don't just paint or sculpt to stack your work in a closet somewhere. You paint to be seen, to share your vision with others, to enlighten, and of course to sell, so you can keep going. If you don't have a wealthy patron, it is a hell of a game to play besides being goddamned lonely work, when you get right down to it." He reaches for another slice of sour dough.

"I don't think you should compromise yourself," says Thom, draining the last drops of sparkling Burgundy from his goblet and ordering a vodka tonic. (He always mixed up his drinks, claiming it was all just alcohol and you drink whatever combination suited you.) "Nothing has any value except what you give it. You must first give value to your work, and let the dumb bastards follow."

There are now ten people seated at the table, guests of Dr. Thom Kelley's beneficence. This is going to be costly, I think, and all for me. He must be in love with me, but he is so much older than I. Could I actually marry an older man just for security? He would probably be my patron and encourage me in my work, and he wouldn't think of it as competition.

Vincent has not yet arrived.

"How are you doing there, Doll? You must be starved! Time to feed you. Too skinny these days. All these starving artists around." Thom drags on his between-courses cigarette.

The plates come heaped with sweetbreads, steak on brochettes, fat, juicy mushrooms, wild rice, French sauce, Worcestershire, béarnaise, hot sauce, and ketchup for Thom. The chateaubriand is sliced, and the waiters serve each plate with the red, juicy meat. The conversation slows as we begin to eat. The background music hovers, old songs from the '40s: '"It

Had to Be You," "Red Roses for a Blue Lady," "Some Enchanted Evening." The food saves me from becoming terribly drunk.

After dinner, cognac and coffee are served.

I hear Marie comment to her pale, inexpressive husband, "What a wonderful place this is, darling! You must take me here again sometime." He grunts, barely acknowledging her words.

How can women marry such creeps? I wonder. "Marie, why didn't Malcolm Aldrich come?" I ask.

"Well, he's probably tired and went home to bed. He isn't too well, you know, so he rarely becomes involved socially with the artists, and not enough time I suppose. But he is a wonderful man, and if he likes you and your work, he will do everything he can for you."

Thom studies the bill under the little flashlight the waiter holds for his convenience. He adjusts his glasses and sniffs. It is about twice what he expected. "Nothing too good for my friends," he comments as he takes out his credit card and signs the bill.

Outside the Barbary, people bid each other goodnight in the chilly spring evening. The fog has descended and covers the city with its soft moisture wisping about the streetlights mysteriously.

"Oh, say, Winston, why don't you come up to the house for a nightcap? To Mount Olympus right in the heart of San Francisco," asks Thom.

"I'd like that, but I don't have wheels. My pickup truck is on the blink right now."

"Well, just come along with Joanna here. You can take a cab home. See you at the house, okay?"

John hovers behind Thom, trying to be inconspicuous for fear his brother will send him on his way. He lives somewhere in the East Bay and has a wife. They turn to get into Thom's Thunderbird. I hear them arguing vehemently as they are swallowed up by the city night and the fog.

Winston gallantly takes my arm as we make our way through the streets to Union Square. The walk clears my head. Winston is silent for the most part.

We find my little TR3, almost alone now in the cavernous garage, looking quite sporty. Winston squeezes his lanky frame into the tight seat.

I feel rather glamourous as we break from the garage into the bright lights of Powell Street. People are looking at us. What do they think of me and my companion? Tourists probably, from who knows where. We are bona fide residents of this magical place, and these poor souls will have to board a plane soon to return to their mundane existence. I have become a geographical snob.

We speed up Market Street, making most of the lights. "Thom is very much in love with you. You know that, don't you? Anyone can see. You could hurt him badly," says Winston, his hair flying in the wind, looking gorgeous.

"Well, I wouldn't want to do that. He has helped me enormously, given me the self-confidence I never had. He is really wonderful. He feeds me, houses me, and gives me work that pays."

"Does he give you anything else?"

"Like what?" I say.

Winston remains silent until we reach the house. The top flat is ablaze with light, while the middle flat and my little apartment remain dark. No sign of Vincent. Where is he? I wonder.

"Winston, do you want to come into my place for a minute, see my studio? It isn't much. I need to freshen up a bit." We enter my cold apartment. I switch on a light in the living room.

Winston clasps his hands behind his back, studying it all. "Nice for a young woman alone—great location and even a view. The studio?"

"Back here, the studio and the bedroom."

The skeleton dances about from its hook, grinning at us by the light from the street. Winston just laughs at my bony companion, while I go into the bathroom to take care of my needs, repair my makeup, and brush my hair. The face staring back at me from the mirror looks tired from too much excitement, booze, and unaccustomed socializing.

Winston follows me into the bathroom. Through the closed door, I hear his streaming, using my female, sit-down toilet in his upright, male way.

He emerges, his hair damp and combed carefully into place. "It's nice to live in, but you need more space for your art," he says. "You need a big garage or something that rambles. This is too tight to be able to work decently."

"I know," I respond. "It's okay for medical drawing but not for big canvases."

I take him upstairs through the back way. He is delighted by our clandestine entrance through the kitchen door.

"Well, so, you guys made it all right. Kind of chilly with that little sports car at night—no top." Thom is preparing drinks.

"We're tough," says Winston.

They seem like old friends. Their instant rapport surprises me. They almost seem like co-conspirators in an intriguing plot.

John is bustling about, wearing his apron. The fire is roaring in the living room, diminishing the church-like atmosphere of the room with its Spanish colonial furniture and the wrought iron lamps hanging from their heavy chains.

If there were a stained glass window, an altar, a cross, and no leopard skin poufs, the effect would be complete. Thom is an ex-Catholic, but religion must be ingrained there forever from his childhood. But instead of fearing God, he has become god. My thoughts surprise me, judging him like that. I would never have done that before. I feel myself changing.

"Great pad, Thom! So, this is Mount Olympus—great location, view, space, everything. Now, Joanna, this is what you need." Winston stretches out luxuriously on the sofa, very much at home amid luxury despite protests of his poverty. He looks tired also, his face pale from the chilling ride up the hill.

It is late, almost 1:00 o'clock in the morning. I sit on the sofa next to the fire. I yawn.

They are talking about art. Now, I know what draws them together. They absorb everything around them and construct their opinions. I feel satiated with art. I can't finish my drink. I want to sleep, I am going to drowse off. I can't help it. The fire, the warmth, the food. I have nothing to say. My eyelids feel like lead. From a distance, I hear Michelangelo, Da Vinci, the Etruscans, Cleopatra, the battle of Hastings, and Julius Caesar. I am asleep, dreaming of being wrapped in a wonderful Persian carpet and being delivered to ... to whom?

Thom, shaking my shoulders, awakens me.

I sit up drowsily on the sofa, trying to get my bearings. "And Winston?"

"We called a cab and sent him on his way. He knows where the house is now. He's a great fellow. I really like him. Talented."

The fire is now embers. Thom drags me to my feet and escorts me to his bathroom. "You want me to put you on the potty now, like a little girl?"

"I can manage, Thom." But he stays until I finish. I feel out of control and allow him to do whatever. He takes me into his bedroom, and as I fall across his bed, half-asleep, he carefully undresses me.

He whispers into my ear, "You are like a work of art to me. Your body is so beautiful, so lithe, like the Roman goddesses on the Etruscan vases." He runs his hands all over my body, and then inserts his middle finger into me. All I want to do is sleep, but I muster the energy to reach down and touch his cock. It is soft. We don't speak. He stops the lovemaking and draws the covers up and over us. We sleep soundly until morning.

It is around 10:30 in the morning when I awaken. Late for me. Thom is still snoring. I glance down at him to see his mouth is flecked with dry saliva and is half-open. I look away. The flat is very cold. I wonder if he took sleeping pills last night.

He stirs then reaches to me, drawing me against him. I am aware of pressure on my naked thigh. Could it be possible? "Help me!" he pleads. I do what I can and hear him moaning there among the pillows. I keep it up and notice that his pubic hair is sparse and gray-colored, not the thick, dark, curly bush that my much younger husband sported.

"Now! Now!" he cries out and turns me urgently on my back and with rapid thrusting movements tries to enter me. I arch my back and open up for him, desperately wanting him to succeed, wanting him to feel manly, to feel the sexual hedonist he imagines himself to be who doesn't need pills to live his life. I feel wanton, wanting him to be all these things, the man of intellect and spirit and the erotic man of carnal flesh all in one person.

But despite this frantic effort, I feel him going limp inside me. Oh no, I think, what in the world is wrong? He rolls over on his back, his hand across his eyes. He is suffering greatly. "Goddamn!" he exclaims, seemingly close to tears. There is nothing I can do. I know of nothing more to do. I simply feel profoundly sorry for him.

"You know what?" he says. "You and I have to go away on a little vacation, just a few days maybe, a change of scene. Go walking in the woods somewhere where I can relax, maybe go to Tomales Bay. There is this great hotel and restaurant there, Inverness. I would like to take you there and show you the way I used to be. That marriage of mine, that bitch literally castrated me, I'm so sorry, I have you all worked up and nothing."

"Don't worry about it, Thom," I say, putting on my clothes, "Maybe we should do that—go away somewhere, rest, a change of scene."

In the kitchen, I prepare instant coffee. Thom comes out on the terrace dressed in his suit and tie, ready to leave for rounds at Saint Luke's. He gives me money to buy groceries for us both, like a married couple, then leaves.

Back downstairs in my apartment, I feel a heavy depression. The walls seem to close in on me, and it needs a cleaning. I have no energy to clean. Maybe I am let down after the excitement of the show or maybe the problem with Thom.

I phone Aldrich's and Marie answers. "What a nice dinner party last night. I was happy to see you with a boyfriend. Winston is really a fine artist and would make a good companion for you. He is going places someday."

"Actually, I was with Dr. Kelley," I say.

"Oh? A charming man, a little old for you perhaps. By the way, I have some money for you when you come here, or should I mail you a check? It is rather substantial. You did well, and Malcom is very pleased." I hear her talking to someone in the gallery.

"I'll be there next week. Thanks for everything, Marie. The show was wonderful." After hanging up I feel the fog of depression pressing in on me even more heavily. I should be ecstatic with my success. What in the hell is wrong with me? I ask myself. Maybe I am a bit crazy, I think. I walk to the window of my living room and stare at the empty parking spaces—no Austin-Healey, no Buick.

In the weeks and months that follow, I settle into a routine, acting a surrogate wife to Thom while continuing to paint and doing his medical illustrations. I see nothing of Vincent Cooper. I imagine over and over that passionate lovemaking we had and think that maybe that is the end of it. Thom leads me to believe he has reconciled with his wife and moved back into their home in San Mateo. He owes rent on the flat according to Thom.

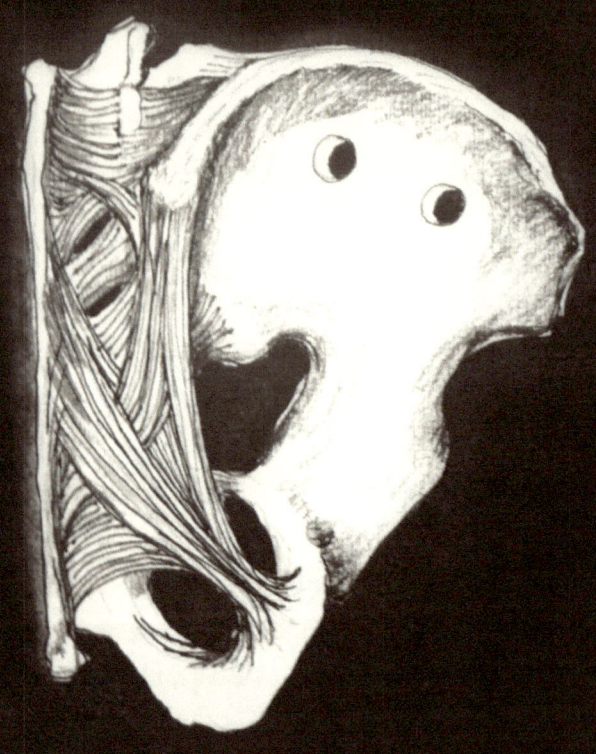

He decides he needs two bone plugs
from the hip in case one doesn't work.

CHAPTER ELEVEN

The Operation

Thom makes arrangements to have me observe his operation on the very wealthy woman who had acted as his patron on occasion. She has donated a large amount of money to the hospital for his research projects. He is going to do a procedure on her back—a laminectomy is what it is called. During the operation, he will take a plug of bone from the woman's hip and insert it between the vertebrae that have collapsed due to a slipped disc and are pressing on the nerves, which causes a great deal of pain to the patient.

The morning of the operation I wait for him in the kitchen. He wants me to take photos and to paint him operating, as well as illustrating the procedure.

"How about a little amphetamine there, Doll, to pick you up?" he says as he throws several pills into his mouth and washes them down with instant coffee.

I shake my head no, and I sense his annoyance. His pills affect me badly, temporarily energizing me but then suddenly leaving me feeling leaden.

Thom seems to function on a daily regimen of uppers and downers. At times, his mouth becomes foamy and his eyes glassy. I find it disturbing and wonder if he may be addicted to his pills.

It is a chilly late spring day in San Francisco. The fog hovers around the hills and valleys. It feels as though it will be one of those days where it never lifts. Thom presses his remote control garage door opener, and the Thunderbird is revealed in gleaming black, like a smaller, simpler version of the Batmobile. It is his macho symbol around town.

We slip into the leather seats, and he pulls out as the garage door closes behind us. I am beginning to cherish the whole ritual. We speed down Upper Terrace and over to Parnassus. He screeches to a halt in his special space in the UC Medical Center staff parking lot. It is marked, "Dr. Thomas W. Kelley," in large white letters.

"You'll have to scrub, put on a gown, cap and booties. And you should have gloves, but I know you can't draw with gloves on. Just don't get to close to the operating field, hear?" His face is tense, serious, and very professional.

We go in through the doctors' entrance to this sprawling, monolithic construction dedicated to modern medicine. Taking the elevator to the fourth floor, we enter a complex of rooms. First is the locker room, where we place our belonging. He points me toward the nurses room, where I take off my outer clothing and put on green cotton pants, a matching gown, a cap to cover my hair, booties, and a mask that covers my nose, mouth, and chin. I scrub my hands fiercely with an antibacterial soap to remove the contamination of the outer world. I place my camera around my neck and tuck my illustration pad and pencil under my arm.

Then, a nurse leads me to the operating room. Thom ignores my presence. I can see only his eyes, which are slightly reddened through his glasses. He is all business.

The patient is stretched out on the operating table, draped in sheets, illuminated by intense, merciless lighting. Behind the patient is the anesthesiologist working a machine that carefully monitors the anesthesia entering the woman's body. There is a table next to Thom laid out with myriad operating tools. A lot of it does look more related to the carpenter's trade; there are saws of differing sizes, drills, and things resembling screwdrivers.

I stay back of the group of doctors and nurses hovering about the area. I stand on tiptoe to get a glimpse of the scene, like something out of Rembrandt, but can't quite see over the tall shoulders of the interns. I am aware the camera is not sterile, and who knows what evil germs are clinging to its black carrying case? Better to take photos from a distance, I reason, and set it aside while I push forth to take a look at what he is doing.

Thom begins the first step of the procedure, which is to expose the hipbone. The very white skin is stretched thinly over ivory-like protruding bone. The woman is thin to the point of emaciation. The area has been thoroughly sterilized, the sheets folded back to feature the site of the incision. Thom begins to draw the finely honed scalpel across the skin, and as it parts neatly, blood oozes out, and I begin to feel the scene receding from view. I close my eyes and call to mind the dripping eucalyptus in the fog under the streetlight outside my kitchen window. Slowly, I regain enough of my equilibrium to open my eyes and watch what is going on.

"Notice that there is hardly any subcutaneous fat layer on this patient," he says. I sense he is talking to me sternly. I inhale deeply, organizing my brain, and step forward through the curtain of observers and peer down at the incision. There are catheters drawing blood away from the opening while Thom separates muscle from bone. This takes about twenty minutes. Fixing the scene in my mind, I back off, pleased with myself that I did not faint.

With my camera, I take a shot of Thom leaning over his work, hoping to capture the art inherent in this scene; the intent to cure, the transcendence of man over infirmity, the dedication of the profession, the drama of life and death being played out on the operating table. At the click of the shutter of the camera, one of the nurses jumps. The silence in the room is total except for the humming of the monitors.

Thom straightens up. "Oh, I forgot to introduce to you all my medical artist, Miss Botticelli. She has my authorization to take photos during the surgery from time to time."

Thanks, Thom, I say to myself silently, feeling the hostility of the nurses. They consider this their territory, but Thom is god and what he says goes, goddammit.

"Goddammit! Where the hell is the bit for the drill? Who's in charge of this?" he storms.

"Dr. Kelley, here it is." A nurse holds it in front of his eyes,

He squints at the thing through his glasses. "What size is it?"

"Point seventy millimeters."

"I need point sixty millimeters. Where the hell is it?"

Everyone leans away from the operating table except the nurse in charge of keeping the incision in good condition spraying the shiny, blue-white hipbone with a substance to keep it from drying. The search for the missing drill bit continues.

Thom, fuming on his stool, rips off his mask, and I snap a quick shot of "Doctor in Consternation." By now the personnel are hating me, since I am the easiest to hate and I am here on a vastly different mission than they are, but I have "god" on my side and they can't hurt me. So, I retreat to a different angle, circling the operating table, and shoot six frames in rapid succession.

Finally, the drill bit is found, rapidly sterilized for good measure, and inserted into the drill. Thom puts his mask back on. Holding the drill carefully, he makes a great effort to steady his hand, aims for a spot on the hip, and begins drilling. Smoke curls up from the penetrating bit, the area has to be kept wet. Slowly, he works his way into the bone with a screeching, grinding noise that is almost unbearable. The stench of burning organic matter permeates the room.

I focus on the grouping of figures to distract me from the shock of what is happening.

Thom continues swearing and cursing at his assistants, who seem oblivious to the harangue. I have never seen him like this. He decides he needs *two* bone plugs in case one doesn't work, so he needs to repeat the process at another point on the hipbone. The plugs are carefully placed on the sterile tray to be used for the second operation, the laminectomy, which will take place at a later time.

"Did ya get that angle I went in on the hip?" he growls at me. He motions me to come forward, and I lean over the two holes in the hip bone. I make a crude drawing of what I see. "This will be the first drawing of the series. You will have to study the vertebrae that we will be fusing for the second drawing. I visualize four drawings in all." I sketch the catheter draining the blood from the site.

"Doctor, we better sew her up soon. She's losing a lot of blood. We may have to give her another pint of plasma," says a young intern quietly, fearing our artistic motives are endangering the life of the patient.

"Oh, yeah, sure, let's get going on that." He begins his sutures then suddenly cries out. He has dropped something, maybe a sponge, into the open hip site. His hands go up in a gesture of helplessness while the interns gather around, peering into the incision. "Okay, you guys get it out. I'm through, goddammit! How many hours has it been?" he inquires of no one in particular as he heads toward the changing room.

The interns take over. They cauterize the blood vessels and begin to repair the muscles, suturing the layers of tissue and finally the outer skin. They murmur between themselves, occasionally snicker, and I imagine it has something to do with Thom. The whole operation has taken almost three hours. I feel exhausted by the tension and imagine how Thom must feel.

After changing back into my street clothes, I meet him in the hallway. He smiles broadly, although his face looks gray and tired. He pushes his white hair back across his head, puts his arm around me, and propels me toward the elevators. "Damn, that went great! I just hope those idiots don't lose those bone plugs. She's going to be happy as a clam when I tell her about it."

"Who?"

"Mrs. Von Rohr, the patient I was telling you about. Don't you listen to me?"

"Oh, that was her? It's just so anonymous there in the operating room."

"You could call it an operating theater. Let's see your drawings, hmm?" He takes my sketchbook in hand and flips the pages. "Rough, but you got the idea of the holes. You can use the skeleton for reference to get the proper curve of the hip and your *Gray's Anatomy* of course."

As we speed from the parking lot in the Thunderbird he asks me, "Do you want to go along on my rounds at Saint Luke's, or should I drop you off at the house? I would like to come home for lunch and take a little siesta before going to the office."

"I better go home and get started on the sketches, I'll work something up so we can begin."

"Okay, you're the boss, Doll. Thanks for coming along. Sorry about that scene I made, but it does get hairy in there. Lots of stuff can fall into the operating area, and it's hell sometimes to get it out. Sometimes, it even gets sewn up inside the patient. Not good, but that's just how it is."

He drops me off in front of the house on Upper Terrace, turns around, and goes on to the hospital and his busy day.

CHAPTER TWELVE

Complications

I stretch out on my bed, tired from the morning activities. It is 12:30. I should eat lunch, but I will wait for Thom.

The phone rings. "Hi!" announces a familiar, masculine voice. *Vincent!* Thump, thump, thump! "I've been calling you all morning. Where have you been?" There is a note of reproach in his voice, as though I had no business being away when he calls.

"At UC Medical Center. Orthopedic surgery, watching Thom perform."

"What are you doing now?"

"Nothing. I almost fell asleep."

"How about driving down to Half Moon Bay with me? I have to see Jake about the Staggerwing, pay him some money I owe. Maybe we can take a few turns around the airport in my Super Cub, have some lunch on the way down."

"Okay, that sounds like fun."

"I'll be there in about a half hour. Look beautiful for me. I've missed you."

My adrenaline surges and I totally forget my luncheon date with Thom. I shower quickly, put on some tight jeans, a pullover sweater, and a ski jacket left over from better days. I carefully put on makeup, brush my hair and let it fall around my shoulders. A final check in the mirror to make sure I am beautiful as ordered. The doorbell rings and I happily go forth to meet my destiny.

He stands in the door frame, handsome, his eyes twinkling and a seductive smile on his face. Older, distinguished, disheveled, I think of all the words to describe him. Unbearably attractive and desirable. He kisses me wetly on the mouth. I dismiss his years. He is more fun than anyone I have ever known in my life, and I am ready for fun.

There is the jaunty little Austin-Healey with the top down. He helps me in. Such a gentleman! This will be my first ride in this exotic yellow sports car. I am exhilarated, possessed and possessing. I own everything and everyone. Did Cleopatra feel like this when she seduced Mark Anthony?

The wind is cold off the Pacific as we speed past Daly City on Highway 1, the most beautiful highway on the North American continent. We hardly speak. Just our mutual proximity communicates. The sea roils and surges beneath us, the waves gigantic, smashing against the jagged rocks. The fog floats in the distance, ready to roll in. I am utterly happy.

"How do you feel?" he asks, placing his arm briefly around my shoulders.

"Wonderful! Do you think we could fly?"

"Looks like it. Fog's still out a way. A short flight will do. We'll grab one of Annie's hamburgers and see how it looks."

The airport office is deserted except for Annie at the desk pouring over an accounting ledger. She looks up. "Vincent, what a surprise! Jake was asking about you. He's in the hangar working on the Stearman. I'll call him." She nods politely to me as if to say, "Oh, another one of Vince's gals," or maybe she thinks I'm his secretary. But no, I have never been taken for a secretary.

Then again, she may remember me from my last time down here with Thom and wonder what is going on, that I am running around with them both—promiscuous, allowing myself to be passed around. She is judging me. People constantly are judging and being judged. Who determines the standard of perfection? I wonder.

"Annie, how about cooking us up a couple of hamburgers and fries? Coffee?" says Vincent as he slides into the booth. I sit across from him.

"Sure! Jake will be right here. Sit down, and I'll bring you some coffee in a jiff."

I have little appetite and cannot finish the whole hamburger, which is generously big.

Jake comes in, slides into the booth next to Vincent, takes one of his French fries and dips it into the ketchup and eats it with a smile.

"The Staggerwing is ready to fly, and of course, you know you owe me some money, my friend. Annie has your bill all itemized. You goin' up?" He takes another French fry, glances my way, but does not acknowledge me.

Vincent sighs deeply, scratches his head, and ignores the part about the money. "What do you think? Does the Cub have gas?"

"Yeah, I think so. I'll check it out. Just don't go too far away. Another hour or two and we'll be socked in here, and I can't afford to lose customers, especially when they owe me money," he snorts.

Vincent goes over to confer with Annie while Jake goes out to ready the Super Cub. I watch him write out a check. For how much? I wonder. He must really have a lot of money—a rich, older man. How much does it cost to own a plane? Will I ever be able to own a plane? I wonder. Impossible!

The Staggerwing sits in the hangar like a big magnificent bird ready to fly. We make our way through and around the other planes parked inside to Vincent's Super Cub. It is like a mosquito among monstrous moths. The plane is painted the same as the Staggerwing, international orange—the same color as the Golden Gate Bridge—and white. I am entering another world, like Alice stepping through the looking glass—from the operating room at the University of California to the world of aviation all in one day.

This world is more beautiful, without a doubt, than the one I left behind, I think as the men push and shove planes around to get to the Cub. Once outside, they check the oil and gas on the aircraft, draining the gas tanks of any condensed water that may have accumulated.

Vincent motions me to get into the back seat. It is identical to Thom's Cub. Jake gives the propeller a few turns by hand and then stands aside. We buckle our seatbelts, and Vincent shouts, "Clear!" then starts the engine. It turns over but doesn't start, like my sports car. On the second try, it leaps into action.

After letting it warm up, he taxis to the beginning of the runway. Holding down the brakes, he goes through the checklist: the controls, the ignition, the RPMs, the magnetos, ailerons, and rudder. He turns on the radio. "Hi, Annie. Taking off on 280. Give me the wind and pressure."

"Four knots out of the northwest. Not too much crosswind. Have fun," Annie's voice comes crackling over the radio.

He sets the altimeter for the air pressure and continues to hold the brakes while revving up the motor until the propeller becomes a blur. He slowly releases the brakes, and after about 150 yards we are airborne. The jackrabbits scurry out of the way alongside the runway and become mere specks as we gain altitude.

"You always want some runway left in case the engine quits!" he shouts back at me over his shoulder.

We climb in slow circles to around 2,000 feet then turn and bank toward the south, following the coast.

"I'll take you to Pescadero!" he shouts, reaching back with his right arm. He slides his hand up my inner thigh and turns around to looks at me, a sensual smile on his face as he continues to stroke me. "You know what my favorite things in life are?"

"No!" I exclaim, squirming around in the tight quarters as he continues to fondle me.

"The Three Fs: flying, fishing, and fucking, not necessarily in that order. I still haven't figured out how to fly and fuck at the same time, but I've heard it can be done."

He is outrageous, but he is irresistible. Why do I let him do this to me? I wonder if he respects me when I let him do whatever he wants. In high school, we always had to worry whether the boys respected us or not. Our reputations were paramount. The problem was how far to go with the guy. Now, in my new life, it's time for me to decide for myself what I want and don't want.

He takes his hand away, and we begin the descent and are soon over the water. "Look!" he shouts, pointing down to the water. Below us, churning about in the sea, is a large school of gray whales diving, spouting water, cavorting like a huge marine family at play. It is awe inspiring. He circles over the giant mammals until he indicates he is getting airsick, and the Cub begins to climb again. There are birds everywhere: albatross, sandpipers, gulls, cormorants, and others that I don't know their names. They swoop, scream, dive for food, or stand majestically still on the beach. Their cries are heard over the roar of the engine.

"What if the engine had quit back there? Where would we have landed?" I ask.

"In the drink, the water. Really, on the beach. This thing lands almost anywhere—pastures, roads, trees. When we get back close to the airport, I will show you what happens when the engine quits."

"Oh," I sigh, summoning up my perfect faith in this man's ability to fly.

As he does his turns and banks, the stick and the rudder next to my feet move under his guidance. The two sets of controls are interconnected so you can fly from either the front seat or the back seat. I back away from these instruments of flight, fearing my ignorance forbids me to touch them.

"Wanna fly back?" he asks me.

"Me?"

"Yeah. Here, I'm going to release the stick and rudder. You take over. You are going to fly. Grab the stick. Grab it! It's not going to bite. Grab the thing, goddammit!"

I grab hold of the fearsome stick. Nothing happens.

He is hanging over his seat, watching me to make sure I have it in hand. "Now, put your feet on the pedals for the rudder, both feet. Get the feeling of the plane."

He has my heart pounding, not from desire this time but from fear. This is something I have always dreamed of doing, and now I am doing it. I can't be afraid, or my dreams will be worthless.

"Okay, now push the stick from one side to the other. You are activating the ailerons—look up at the wings. They give us up and down motion. Now, push the rudder pedals." We go from side to side. "The rudder is on the tail. Keep doing it, and one day you will fly by the seat of your pants."

The seat of my *panties*, I think as I fly the plane up and down and back and forth.

He tells me to coordinate the ailerons with the rudder to make a controlled, banking turn. I put it into a steep dive. "Don't pull out of this dive too fast, or you'll tear off the wings. You're pulling too many Gs."

I gently apply back pressure to the ailerons so as not to tear off the wings, and I gradually feel myself in control of the little plane. It is wonderful. I begin to fly the airplane, the airplane isn't flying me.

"Try another turn, but first lower the wing in the direction you want to turn, then add rudder, or else you will slip. Once you are in the turn, you can slowly neutralize the rudder. It is all a matter of applying pressures, nothing rough or abrupt, like making love."

"Now, do a 180-degree turn. That's it, nice and slow." He is watching the compass and the altimeter while the plane slowly swings around and makes a half turn. I neutralize the rudder and we fly straight ahead, but the plane feels like it is bobbing up and down. "You are overcompensating. Get the feel of it. It's all pressure. Don't push back and forth. The idea is to fly straight and level."

I continue to fly south down the coast, and since he does not correct me, I assume everything is fine. This is easy, I think. We are almost to Monterey Bay.

"Okay, you're doing great! Do another 180 and let's head back to Half Moon Bay."

This time, the turn feels just right.

"Let me take it. We're going to do an emergency landing, and I want you to see just what happens when the engine does really quit." He begins climbing slowly, and by the time we return to Half Moon Bay we are at 5,000 feet. He turns off the engine, pulls back hard on the stick. The nose goes up, the propeller begins to slow down, and the plane stalls!

For a moment, it feels motionless in space, and then slowly it begins to fall off to the right and dive. The propeller is still. Vincent carefully works the craft out of the dive by pushing *forward* on the stick, regains control of the airspeed, and we are gliding slowly toward earth in large, lazy circles. Round and round, the vistas change from sea, beach, mountains, and bluffs. The airport and runway beneath us are coming closer with each turn.

When we are about 700 feet above the runway, he widens the circle so that we are lined up with the landing strip, facing into the wind. There is no power. I am fascinated and curiously without fear. I realize that I trust him implicitly.

He holds the Super Cub steady, and when we are just a few inches above the ground, he pulls back into a stall, and we settle onto the concrete. I barely feel our contact with the earth. I remember how Thom bounced us all over the place, but I don't mention it. Vincent turns around to smile at me. The late afternoon sun etches his profile; he has a noble head. "How'd you like them apples?"

"Really smooth, Vincent, not one bump."

"Not like Kelley, right? He can't fly worth a damn. You shouldn't go up with him, especially since he takes all those pills and injections. It's dangerous."

He starts the engine to taxi back to the hangar and turns on the radio. "Hi, Annie, we're back safe and sound. How'd you like my touchdown without power?"

I hear Annie's voice through the static and she is giggling. "Vincent Cooper, you are really something else!"

Jake helps him tie down the plane, and we go back to the office.

We sit in a booth in the restaurant drinking coffee. Vincent hands me a rectangular, hard-covered, black notebook. "This is your pilot's log book," he says. "You are going to be a good pilot. I know this was your first time at the controls, but I can tell you have the feel for it. You have a good speed sense. Remember, flying is the easiest part. The problem is getting back on the ground safely. "

I think of my stepfather, who would not teach me even to drive. I had to wait to get married to drive a car.

"I want you to get down here as soon as possible to start your lessons with Jake," says Vincent, lighting up two Camel cigarettes and passing one to me the way Thom does.

Jake, who acts like he hates me, I think. Oh well, I am too pleased with myself to harbor any doubts. I imagine myself in the Stearman's open cockpit, with my white silk scarf trailing behind me, goggles, and wisps of my sexy chestnut hair escaping from my flying helmet. I am devastatingly beautiful and brave. Cameras pop around me as I emerge in Moscow from my solo flight over the North Pole, the first woman pilot to achieve such a feat in an open-cockpit airplane. I laugh gaily, signing autographs while men fall adoringly at my feet—well, something like that.

"So, what do you think about that?" Vincent asks me, interrupting my reverie.

"Yes, of course! It is what I have always dreamed of doing, and now I have a little money from the sale of the paintings. I will come down here next week, definitely."

"We'll have Jake sign you up for lessons, and except for me, don't let anyone else teach you. He is the best."

I exhale smoke from my cigarette. It blows toward him and combines with his smoke and curls around us both in the fading light of the sun, a carcinogenic halo. "I don't think Jake likes me."

Vincent laughs. "He adores you. That's just the way he is. He is gruff, like a surly old bear. Just make him talk to you. Ask him questions. Make little jokes. He's just afraid of beautiful women."

As we leave, Vincent settles his account with Jake, and I am signed up for flying lessons next Tuesday at 11:00 AM.

As we drive along the coast, our hair whipping in the wind, conversation is difficult, and I sink into thought—how in a few moments one's life can change by saying yes. Yes, I will learn to fly. Yes, I will learn to live. Yes, I will make love with you. Yes, I will be an artist. And after all these yeses, nothing is the same again.

My family will not approve of any of this, of course. A waste of money to learn to fly. What good will it do you? Are you going to become an airline pilot or what? Get married again and have a family, they say. Cook and clean house like your mother. Who do you think you are anyway? But I don't want to get married again. I want to be free to do what I want to do, not what a husband dictates that I must do. I would rather be dead than married.

"What are you thinking about?" Vincent says to me, placing his hand familiarly on my thigh, sort of a possessive gesture. It is cold now, the fog has rolled in, and visibility is low. "Wanna stop for a drink at Dan's? Something to warm us up?"

I see the big red neon sign, "DAN'S," looming up ahead through the darkening night and the fog.

Without waiting for an answer, he turns off the highway onto the side road and into the restaurant parking lot. He jumps out of the car and comes around to my side and helps me out. For some reason, these trivial attentions embarrass me.

It feels nice and warm inside with its Italian country atmosphere along with a dose of aviation thrown in. The waiter smiles broadly and acts as though he knows me as he directs us to the bar.

"You been here before?" Vincent asks.

"Uh, yeah, a couple of times with Thom."

He doesn't seem to like that, but I am a free woman, and he is still a married man. He has no right to claim exclusive right to my activities. "Well, now, how about a Tanqueray on the rocks?"

"I'd like something warm."

"Hot buttered rum for you then. Myer's rum is the best. How does that sound to you, Joanna?" He reaches for my hand and holds it in both his hands.

"Wonderful," I reply, smiling warmly at him.

The bartender serves the drinks and puts a big bowl of hot buttered popcorn in front of us. It goes down quickly.

"Let me ask you something," says Vincent. "Are you in love with Thom Kelley?" He stares straight into my soul and continues to grip my hand. Except for the hand gripping, a technique he could not use when interrogating a witness, it would be hard not to tell the truth under that intense gaze.

"I…I don't know. He is most wonderful to me. I mean, he does everything to help me. Sometimes, I can't pay the rent, and he lets it go. I have never known anyone like him. And the experience of medical illustrating is fantastic. I admire him more than I can say."

"You think you might marry him? He wants to marry you. You know that."

"He mentioned something about that, but I'm not ready to get married again. I married too young. Nineteen years old is too young. I'd like to travel a bit, see the world on my terms."

Vincent lights our cigarettes, sighs, and drops my hand. I glance at our faces in the mirror behind the bar. Mine, youthful and smooth, long chestnut-colored hair flowing about my face and shoulders, alluring, as I want it to be. He looks his age, his face lined, but still handsome and distinguished. His hair is graying. His features are finely etched despite the creases of age. He must be in his late forties, I guess. His forehead is high and noble, like sculptures I have seen of the Roman warriors.

There is a sadness about him. His eyelids droop slightly over his blue eyes. Maybe that is why I love him and can't do anything about it except to make a concerted effort to keep him from knowing. Strange that should be the case, but there is that game to play whether I like it or not, and the one who is more in love is the least powerful in the relationship.

"Hungry?"

"A little."

"How about a small pizza? They are good here. They make everything from scratch, the dough, the sausage. Italian artists like you, only they are food artists."

We move to the dining room to await the pizza. The room is almost deserted on a weekday. He orders red wine, a local Cabernet, and we solemnly clink glasses. There is an awkward tension between us, as though Thom's spirit were sitting there at the table with us watching our every move and listening to our every word, like God.

The food is energizing and the wine relaxing, and we both are feeling good. "I want to talk to you about Thom," he says in a fatherly manner. "I know he is a great guy—we've been friends for ages—but he tends to take too many pharmaceutical drugs. He says he can handle them, but they can be addicting.

So, don't let him get you hooked, my girl. Sometimes, I see you looking a little dazed, kind of glassy eyed."

"I take them sometimes," I reply defensively, "for cramps or a hangover."

"Don't ever take anything like that for a hangover. Tea or soup, maybe, but not pills out of a bottle. It's really bad for your liver and kidneys."

"Well, if you say so, Vince. Your concern is touching. How do you know so much about what I do? You are hardly there in the building lately."

"I don't know. I've been trained to observe. I may have to give up the flat. It's expensive, and now that Mary Belle and I have broken up, it doesn't make much sense. Thom might even raise the rent to get rid of me, especially when he knows I took you up flying today."

"Oh, my god, I just remembered. He was coming back to the place for lunch with me this afternoon. I totally forgot. What a mess!"

"He doesn't own you. You may not have much financial security at the moment, but you are young, pretty, and talented. I like women who excel. Don't sell yourself short, my girl. You should marry again, a man near your age, and have a family, but keep painting. Don't give that up."

I want to ask him about his marriage but hold back. My future hangs about me like a gauzy gray cloud, unclear, uncertain. I don't know what I will do from one day to the other. I have *no* plans. "I don't know what I am going to do in the future, and what you say about continuing my art is about the future. But the other? In my brief experience in life, when men marry women they expect their wives to stay home and cook, clean, and take care of them and any children who happen along."

"Don't you think that's pretty normal? Don't knock your current freedom. Enjoy it while it lasts, because life can get pretty complicated real fast. Here, let's get a doggie bag for the rest of that pizza, and you can have it for breakfast. You really are too thin."

We drive back through the night to San Francisco. There is a light in the top flat I notice as Vincent parks the Healey alongside the retaining barrier on Upper Terrace.

He is going to hear us, I think as we enter my apartment. It is freezing cold. He is not giving me heat. I am being punished. Since he is on top and gets sun all day, his thermostat doesn't kick in, and my apartment is still connected to his gas furnace. I should complain, but he may be angry that I didn't stay here for lunch.

"Goddamn! This place is an icebox!" exclaims Vincent. "Take your clothes off and get into bed under the over before we both freeze."

His hands are so cold that when he touches my body I cry out.

"You are sooo warm," he says, nuzzling the side of my face.

"You stay there and warm up while I make us some tea with honey." I take a robe out of the closet next to my bed then go to the kitchen to scrounge around for teabags. I am waiting for the phone to ring as I put the water on to boil and chew a fingernail nervously.

The tea is prepared with fresh lemon juice and honey in steaming mugs left over from my marriage. I take them up the three steps to where my beloved lies waiting for me. Vincent takes his tea and begins to blow on it.

I set mine down next to the phone on the floor and wait on the edge of my bed. It rings. I pick it up. "Hello?"

It is Thom, of course. "Oh, hi, there, Doll! What are you up to? I heard you come in. By any chance is Vincent with you? I've got to talk to him."

"Oh, hello, Thom. How're you doin'? I heard all about the surgery this morning. Great experience for our gal here." Vincent speaks in his formal, unruffled voice. His control is amazing, something to emulate.

"Yeah, sure, I know." He rubs his chin with his forefinger, and I wonder what Thom is saying.

Silence for a few moments.

"Well, if you want, I can write a check right now. Just don't cash it until Monday. I know I owe you for two months, but you know how things are at the office right now with the problem of making payments on that bond we owe, my partner's debt, you know. Sorry if I have caused you an inconvenience."

A few moments more of silence.

"Oh, yeah, I took our girl to Half Moon Bay to get her feet wet in the Cub. She is going to start flying lessons, got her all signed up with Jake for next week. We're having a cup of tea right now if you can believe it. Say, it's cold as hell down here. Would you mind turning up your thermostat a bit to warm the place up, or this poor girl's gonna freeze her fanny tonight." His control is not total. I catch an unfamiliar edge to his voice.

He hangs up. "I'm going upstairs to talk to him. You rest here, sleep. I'll be back in a jiffy." And Vincent is gone.

Upstairs with Thom, Vincent sits at the dining room table and writes out a check.

Thom is pacing back and forth with a beer in one hand, his head cocked to one side, and a serious scowl on his face. "How about a martini? I got your Tanqueray gin somewhere in the cabinet" asks Thom.

"No, thanks." Vincent stands, hands Thom the check, then slips his checkbook into his inside breast pocket.

"Don't you think you're horning in here, Vincent? I mean, she is pretty young and inexperienced. You are back with your wife Phyllis, so why don't you just leave Joanna alone?"

"Why, listen to you! I thought she was up for grabs, Kelley. She's not stupid. She wants to learn to fly, and I like teaching aviation. Sure, she's cute and all that, but she knows what she is doing, and at twenty-seven years old, she's not exactly jail bait."

"No, no, of course not. She's a woman, and it's just that we're so damned old. We're all friends here. You know that. I don't want any problems between us and certainly not over some hot little wench, for god's sake. You sleeping with her?"

"Well, now, Dr. Kelley, you're getting kind of personal there. Don't forget I'm a lawyer, and a good lawyer never admits to anything that may be incriminating."

Thom laughs and throws back the beer can, draining the last drops into his mouth. "You win, Vincent. How's Phyllis these days?"

"Fine, just fine. Her brother is here visiting from Oregon, so she's pretty occupied for the time being."

"Leaves you fancy free to …"

"And remember, don't cash that check until Monday. Don't want the thing to bounce on us." He leaves by the kitchen door, hurrying down the wooden steps past the gas furnaces just as one kicks into action, and quietly enters my apartment.

I am almost asleep as he slips in beside me. The furnace is on, and soon warm air is flowing through my tiny apartment. "What happened up there?"

"Nothing. Just paid the back rent and two months up front so I can keep coming back here to see you."

He begins making love to me, and it is better than before because I know him now. He buries his head in my neck and hair, kissing me while his hands range over my whole body. I embrace him, loving the feel of his back, running my fingers through his hair. We can no longer wait. The urgency builds to intolerable levels. He mounts and enters me. His large, silky, thick penis penetrates my body, and I writhe in warm, oozing, wanton desire. "I want to go so far into you that I am a part of you," he murmurs in my ear. "I want to merge with you. I can't get enough, I could make love to you every day for a year and still not have enough."

I climax with an involuntary shriek that rises in ever expanding waves up to the top flat just as Dr. Thom Kelley is opening another can of beer. Then Vincent explodes in me. I am aware of the sensation of millions of tiny, aggressive spermatozoids fighting and shoving against each other in their frantic race up my vagina only to meet their death, hopelessly flailing against my diaphragm, struggling to merge with my eagerly awaiting egg on the other side of the rubber curtain with no turning back, the spermicide jelly that I had just placed in and around the diaphragm killing them by the hundreds of thousands, this month's egg destined to flush out, unfertilized, leaving my womb unfulfilled for the time being.

"How did you like that?" he whispers in my ear.

"Beautiful."

"I fuck as well as I fly, darling, don't you think? It all gets better with practice. Tomorrow I will go down on you, kiss you down *there*. You would like that, wouldn't you?"

"Goodnight, Vincent."

"Goodnight, Joanna."

I wake up in the middle of the night, sweating profusely. It must be over 90 degrees in my little apartment. The heat is on full blast. I jump out of bed and open windows since I cannot control the temperature.

Vincent stirs. "Watch doin', honey?"

"Opening the windows. Thom has the heat on all the way up. His thermostat, he hasn't turned it down at all."

"Goddamn Kelley! It's *his* gas bill. Come on, get back in here with me. I like the way you smell … like sex."

"Do you think he left the heat on like that on purpose?"

"Probably. Wants us to burn in hell, punish us for our sins."

"But he's not a Christian, or I mean a Catholic, anymore. He told me he doesn't believe in any of it, that there is no such thing as sin."

"It depends on who is doing the sinning. Deep down, he is still a Catholic. I can tell."

"What are you, Vincent?" I say as I curl in next to him, my arm across his chest.

"I'm a Baptist. My granddaddy was a Southern Baptist minister in Kansas." He rolls over to embrace me in the dark.

"Really? I never knew anyone who was a Baptist. I'm Presbyterian. My parents were both Catholics, but after my father was killed in the war, Mom remarried and she changed to Presbyterian like my stepfather. The Presbyterian Church was right down the street, only a block away. So, that is what we all became. I sang in the choir and taught Sunday school to the little children."

"And now you are here in sinful San Francisco being an artist, learning to fly airplanes, and—"

"And having sex with you."

"Don't say 'having sex.' It sounds so cold, like having the flu or having lunch. Say 'making love' because that is what we are doing."

We fall asleep, too tired to talk further about our lives.

In the morning, it is freezing again. The morning fog seems to have come in through the open windows, filling the apartment. The heat is off, and I have the feeling that it won't be on again all day.

Vincent dresses quickly, promising me more sexual delights in the near future and that he will phone me. After he leaves, I heat the pizza for breakfast and make instant coffee. I take a long, hot shower, put on many layers of clothing, and begin to work.

I persevere with the anatomical work through the week, concentrating on Thom's drawings of his laminectomy procedure. Vincent doesn't phone, and I resist the temptation to call him.

Saturday afternoon, Thom calls to ask how I am doing with the drawings for him. He asks me to bring up the rough sketches to his flat so he can critique them.

"Hi, Thom! How've you been?" I ask cheerily, hoping he has forgotten that I stood him up for lunch earlier in the week, and I fear he suspects I probably slept with Vincent that same night.

"Oh, just fine," he says coldly. He is drinking beer out of a can. "Wanna beer?" he asks me.

"Sure." I spread the drawings on his dining room table. He has the *Grays's Anatomy* open to the spinal column, a place marker on the hipbone, there are some loose vertebrae lying around.

"Hmm, they're not bad. I think you should change the angle on the view of the vertebrae and be sure they are correctly labeled. This procedure involves the twelfth thoracic and second lumbar vertebrae. Oh, and better study the transverse process on your skeleton. This is not exactly the way it is, how you have it drawn."

I take notes as he talks.

"And here, the articular processes should be painted a pale blue. I'll have to get you a bone drill so you can draw a convincing drill taking the bone plug out of the hip."

He continues the critique while I take notes. There will be five drawings in total. They will be photographed and made into slides, which will be presented at the Orthopedic Surgeons Convention that is going to be held in San Francisco this coming fall. He will combine my artwork with X-rays of the patient to aid in his verbal presentation.

"I'd also like you to make a drawing of a broken sternum. I am going to present a paper that says the effort to set a broken sternum is a waste of time, that the sternum will realign itself naturally with time. Draw a sternum emphasizing the jugular notch, lightly indicating the muscle attachments."

"Okay, Thom, with pleasure." I want to joke with him about needing an advance to pay my overdue rent, but his manner is forbidding, very businesslike in the extreme with none of the old camaraderie that we had enjoyed before. I roll up my sketches and start to leave.

"Don't you want your beer?"

"Oh, yeah, I forgot."

"Sit down and take a load off your feet."

I dutifully sit down, looking out at the view, fearing what is coming, like a naughty little girl caught in the act. I sip the cold beer out of the can like he does. He doesn't even offer me a glass like he used to. I have to light my own cigarette.

"You're sleeping with Vincent, aren't you?" he accuses me angrily.

"Uh, he's teaching me how to fly. Next week is my first official flying lesson with—"

"Don't bullshit with me, Josey. You're not the first girl to fall into bed with a guy at the first drop of a hat."

I can think of nothing to say. I feel an enormous guilt sweep over me, like I used to feel when I was married, as though I am the worst person that ever lived, a dirty female, wanton, sexual, doing it whenever I feel like it. I look down, using the moments of silence to gather a few shreds of self-respect, and say, "Please don't call me Josey."

This fuels him further. "Vincent goes after anything in skirts. You are not the first gal to fall for him. Look at Mary Belle. She got fed up with him and doesn't even want to work with him anymore. Then think about his poor suffering wife, Phyllis. He treats her so badly that her health is going to hell. She almost died a while back from high blood pressure because of Vincent's shenanigans. To be honest, she has talked to me about you, and at first, I thought you were a fine young woman. But in these last couple of months, I am beginning to see another side of you."

I want to tell him that I am seeing another side of him, also, but I need him too much. I need the nice, cheap apartment on this classy street with a view, and I need the money I get from him for the medical drawings, a job. It is necessary that I appear suitably chastised by his lecture on my morality or lack thereof. "I just don't know, Thom. He is so forceful. It is hard to resist him. What you say is probably true."

"It *is* true, goddammit!" And he slaps the table with his delicate white hand, his operating hand. "Just, please, promise me this—that you won't fall in love with him. Because that would be your undoing. You have so much talent. You are young and beautiful. You have your whole life ahead of you. Don't ruin it by getting messed up with this guy. He's an old friend of mine and all that, but it's always the same with him. He goes from one to another, gets bored, and then to another. That's how it is, Doll. I'm telling you this for your own good. And god forbid you should get pregnant carrying on like this."

Tears begin rolling down my cheeks. I don't want to cry, but it feels like the thing to do. Through my tears, I see a slight smile cross Thom's stern face. He is pleased with himself, vindicated. He comes to my chair and puts his arms around me, nuzzling his cheek against the side of my face.

I want to pull away from him, but he is trying to comfort me even though it was he who got me so upset with his damned lecture. My other voice speaks to me, and the practical tone is more comforting than anything Thom does. My inner voice says, I won't have to worry about the apartment or the drawing assignments for the time being. It's best to cry a little more and be more discreet in the future. I begin sobbing violently. It feels good, cathartic somehow, releasing all the tension and anxiety I have been feeling lately. Reality has been tough to face.

Thom becomes alarmed and shows genuine concern. "There, there, sweetie, don't cry, please. I can't stand this. I just had to tell you the truth about Vince. I want to save you because I care so much for you, and he is just playing with you. I can't bear to see you hurt like this. You can't imagine how much I love you and how much I have suffered lately worrying about you."

He hands me a crumpled handkerchief from his pocket. I blow my nose and wipe my tear-stained cheeks, sip some beer, and try to calm down.

"Tell ya what. I have some phone calls to make. You pull yourself together, and we'll eat out tonight—unless, of course, you have a hot date with one of those stockbrokers around town."

"No, nothing planned, just the apartment and the drawings."

"Good. Then you fix yourself up, take a shower, and look good. We'll go out to Chinatown—forget all this. How does that sound?"

Thoughts of Vincent intrude—how he hasn't called me and the struggle I have with myself not to phone him. Just to hear his voice would be so nice.

Thom and I agree on 7:30 in the evening.

I return to my apartment but find it impossible to concentrate on the drawings. All I can think about is Vincent—his profile that day against the afternoon sun dropping down to the Pacific, his hands on my body. I feel aroused just imagining us together. He is the most exciting man I have ever met in my life, the heroes of my dreams—Lancelot, Mark Anthony, Ivanhoe, Tristan, Vronsky, and Clark Gable—all wrapped up into one Vincent Franklyn Cooper.

I don't care about his other affairs. I sense he is sincere with me. Or am I just being foolish as Thom so emphatically told me? But why hasn't he phoned me? If he is sincere and actually divorced his wife, would I in fact marry him? He appears to be a man who needs a wife, someone who is there at home waiting for him when he needs her.

Ultimately, I stop thinking about it, as I am just going in circles. Better to let Thom distract me in Chinatown tonight.

CHAPTER THIRTEEN

The Flying Lesson

As I speed down Highway 1 along the coast to Half Moon Bay, I have a feeling of dread about what lies ahead. First, my instructor, Jake Morenetti, he is so brusque. He barely acknowledges my existence. I feel he disapproves of me, which is something I have begun to feel more often in my new life. Vincent says he adores me, but I don't buy it.

I need to communicate with Jake concerning this very foreign (to me) experience of learning to fly an airplane. Recently, I have become accustomed to a certain breathless male subservience and attention. Now, I have to deal with this man who appears not to care less whether I live or die, a man totally unaware of what others have said are my considerable charms.

Apart from my festering ego, it makes me nervous to think I will have to actually take the plane into the air myself. It is dangerous, more complicated than I had imagined, and I could panic and crash. Then whatever hopes I hold for my wonderful future would never come to pass.

But then there is the excitement of really fulfilling the dream of my childhood to be a pilot! I will be the one who flies the machines into the sky, like a bird, free.

Annie is busy at the grill in the airport coffee shop. A few people are seated in the booths talking, nibbling on doughnuts, and sipping coffee. The morning is bright and clear.

"Hi, there, Annie! Remember me, Vincent's friend?" I greet her lightly, wondering why I didn't say 'Thom's friend' and my stomach churns having reached this point of no return. "I believe I am scheduled for my first flight lesson this morning."

She nods politely, appears distracted, and opens the flight scheduling book, a large, black, ledger-like tome.

"Oh, yes, you are. Isn't this you? Botticelli? Oh, yes, I remember you. Italian? I'm Italian, too, you know. My father was born in the northern part of Italy, and my mother is from Sienna, in central Italy. Jake, my husband, now he's pure wop, Southern Italian. Very different people. Kind of barbaric compared to the northerners." She laughs at her ethnic prejudices.

"My Father was from Northern Italy, from somewhere around Milan as I recall, my Mother was born in Germany. My Father was killed in the war and Mother remarried an Englishman, but we never got along." I want to be friends with her, so I keep the conversation going.

Annie continues, "Oh, sorry about your father. So many good men died in that war! I lost an uncle, as a matter of fact. But so good that you are from northern Italy! Very intelligent, talented people come from the north. Being Italian and from the north, why, that practically makes us relatives. So, tell me, how do you know Dr. Kelley and Vincent Cooper?"

"We all live in the same apartment building on Upper Terrace in San Francisco. At least, the doctor and I do, and Vincent lives there part time."

"Oh!" Annie's eyebrows arch over her fluttering dark eyelashes and glistening, greenish-brown eyes.

She has very fair skin, her hair a light reddish brown fluffy around her face. Her body is what can be described as *hourglass*— large breasts, small waist, and wide, ample hips. My impression is one of a "good woman," hard-working, self-sacrificing, and long-suffering with her taciturn husband. Annie loves to talk, probably a result of living with an uncommunicative man unconcerned with anything that doesn't relate to aviation.

"If you want, why don't you go out to the hangar and familiarize yourself with the training plane? I'll call Jake that you are coming."

As I walk through the chilly air toward the hangar, the knot of fear in my stomach increases in size. I'm really going to do it. I've committed myself. I am going to fly an airplane, be a pilot, fly solo at some point, be able to fly whenever I feel like it, go wherever I want. The idea is mind boggling.

The hangar smells of aviation fuel and oil. It's cold inside the cavernous area inhabited only by the parked aircraft, the owners of which are either renting protected indoor space or awaiting mechanical service designed to prevent failure in flight. There is Jake working at a bench along the wall where an array of tools are kept. An overhead light illuminates his work.

I carefully thread my way toward him through the maze of wings, propellers, tails, rudders, and balloon tires. "Hello, Jake," I say in my most jaunty, self-confident voice.

He glances up briefly then returns to his work. "Yeah, hi, there. Annie said you were coming. Just let me finish adjusting this carburetor. Be with ya in a minute. Why doncha go over to the Cessna 140? It's parked right outside. Can't miss it—a little blue tail dragger. Begin checking it over. Get used to the plane." He barely raises his head from his work.

Obediently, I retrace my steps through the labyrinth and stand facing the plane. It is a mucky blue color with lots of dents and scratches. It has a high wing and a tail wheel. I remember Vincent telling me how much more difficult it is to fly a tail dragger. You have to stall the plane right above the field and drop down, all this without being able to see where you are going. Perhaps that is what he meant by saying I have to learn to fly by the seat of my pants. The Staggerwing and the Cub both have tail wheels.

I walk around the plane, jiggling an aileron here, the rudder there, then peer into the cabin. Unlike the Cub, the seating is side by side. There is no stick but a steering wheel with a gap in the top part of the wheel. Curious. Then the most worrisome part: the instrument panel. I recognize the compass and altimeter, but there are many more dials, gauges, knobs, and buttons to assimilate. Walking around the plane, the knot keeps growing inside, but there is no turning back. The humiliation of running back to my Triumph sports car and dashing home to safety is too painful to contemplate.

I must go through with this, my inner voice chides. Don't be a coward, a timid female. Be a daring courageous woman! Jake probably thinks I am going to chicken out, that I am a person playing games with men, flighty, hmm. No, I'll show them all. I will master this little, mucky blue airplane—no, not *master*, that is for men to do. I will *mistress* this mucky blue little airplane, not only the plane but my unruly gut that refuses to unknot itself.

Eventually, Jake appears, blowing his nose into a handkerchief loudly—*barbarous* said his wife Annie. "Whaddya think of the plane, huh?"

"Well, it looks fine to me. Of course, I don't know too much about airplanes, only what Thom and Vincent have shown me."

"The first thing is to check the outside of the plane, and then we'll get in the damned thing." I circle it warily as he shows where the cables are connected to the ailerons and the rudder. He drains the gas tanks of any accumulated condensed water then opens the cowling to check the oil levels.

"Very important, so watch what I'm doing, cuz next time, *you* gotta do it." He takes out the oil dipstick, wipes it clean, re-plunges it into the motor, pulls it out, and reads the level. "All this is critical, and you do it every single time you fly the aircraft."

He apparently had taken me seriously when I signed up for the lesson because the plane is ready to fly. The pleasure of that thought helps to reduce the knot of fear in my stomach.

"Now, get in," he orders gruffly.

I am becoming accustomed to his manner, a rustic, Old World male style that brings back dim memories of my father. He's probably a real nice man underneath his tough crust, like good Italian bread.

I slide into the left seat, the pilot's place. Jake gives the propeller a few turns, I imagine to help it get started, then gets in next to me and locks the door tightly. We buckle up.

He instructs me to hold the brakes down, push the starter button, and slide the throttle forward slightly. The prop makes a few turns but doesn't start. I repeat this, and suddenly the engine springs to life, the prop spinning and the motor roaring. Jake pulls my hand back on the throttle, and it all settles down. I started it! I press the brakes down for dear life, afraid the thing is going to leap into the air by itself.

"Now, release the brakes slowly. We are going to taxi out to the runway," he commands. "You are going to steer with the rudder— not the wheel in front of you that you probably think is a steering wheel like in a goddamned car—down there, with your feet on the pedals. The ailerons don't count until you are in the air."

"Oh." I press back and forth on the pedals, turning to look at what the rudder is doing behind me. I slowly release the brakes and give it some throttle. We lurch forward faster and faster, right toward all the parked airplanes.

"Give it left rudder!" he screams. "Pull back on the throttle! Don't accelerate too much, just enough to steer. Get the feeling of the plane on the ground. Make it do what you want it to do."

I give it left rudder, and the plane swings all the way around, and now we are heading straight for the coffee shop and the big plate glass windows. I see us crashing through the windows into the coffee shop and out the other side and ending up in the foothills behind.

He says nothing as our doom approaches, but takes over. I am to keep my feet lightly on the controls while he taxies to the runway. I am embarrassed at my ineptness, but it is my first time trying to taxi a plane. I wonder if Amelia Earhart did the same thing the first time she took over an aircraft. Was she born to fly?

"Okay, now I want you to get this bird under control, ya hear me? None of this pushing back and forth on the controls, or you'll go slithering down the runway like a goddamned snake. It's all about pressure, easy, with feeling. You need to compensate for the wind when you taxi. The rudder works off the wind and your ground speed."

He has the plane pointed into the wind, so I take a deep breath and very slowly push in the throttle, keeping even pressure on the rudder pedals. We begin to move forward slowly, more or less in a straight line.

"You will have more control if you accelerate a bit." He lights a cigarette and opens a small vent in the window. I imagine he hates me for my incompetence. We go faster, and I begin to get the feel of the rudder, I struggle to make the plane go straight, to go where I want it to go.

"All right, turn it around and take it to the beginning of the runway. Keep looking around for other aircraft," he says, exhaling luxuriously. I make two 90-degree turns and take it to the beginning of the runway. We are now in a position to *take off.*

Jake takes over. "Let's first go through the check list. You want to test your magnetos, your carburetor pressure, oil pressure and RPMs, set your altimeter according to air pressure, test your ailerons, rudder, and flaps if your plane has them."

He does all this while I watch, then he turns on the radio. "Annie, you there?" he growls into the transmitter.

"Yeah honey, I'm here. Pressure is 30.06. Wind is 7 knots at 320. Temperature is 68 degrees"

Jake sets the altimeter. "Fine, we are going to do touch and go's for the next half hour. Let me know if any aircraft are planning to land during that time."

"A Beech Baron radioed he's due here in about half an hour from Bakersfield. I'll let you know when I hear from him again and give you his position."

"Over and out."

He straightens the plane. "Now, look out around you. See how the horizon is in relation to the interior of the plane. That is close to how it is going to look when you are about to land. You will be right above the concrete and still flying. Okay, watch what I do. Keep your hands and feet lightly on the controls and go through the takeoff with me."

The small plane starts to roll forward, gathering speed, and suddenly we are airborne. We climb up over the small village of Half Moon Bay, then he banks to the right over the foothills. While making the slow turn, he calls my attention to the altimeter so I get accustomed to the feeling of altitude.

I look back out toward the ocean and below to the tiny building and runway at the airport.

"Quit looking at the goddamned view like some tourist, cuz next time you are gonna do this," he snarls.

The craft rises and falls on the air currents sweeping in from the Pacific and wafting up and over the coastal range mountains.

The radio crackles and Jake tunes in.

"Hi, honey. That Beech Baron is on its way in. You should be picking it up approximately at 110 degrees coming from the southeast. He's going to make a direct-approach landing."

"Okay. Tell him we are here. We're going up to 1200 feet."

We climb in lazy circles. He points down toward the mountains, and I spot the plane making a direct approach, aligning itself with the landing field, and touching down. It is mesmerizing, like living in another world entirely.

We go down in dizzying circles until we are once again at the regulation 700 feet. He prepares to touch down. The horizon drops in my line of vision as we approach the runway. I feel we are sinking. The controls are mushy. The power is off, and the nose rises. We are hovering over the pavement. The stall warning goes off, and he pulls back further on the ailerons. We touch down tail first and then on the main landing gear, a perfect landing. He turns to me and smiles. I believe it is the first time I have seen this man smile, especially at me.

"Okay, kid, now it's your turn. Push in that throttle. Hold her steady, and you are going to take off. Push that thing, goddammit! Go ahead! It won't bite. Do it! Make it do what you want. You are in command, not the plane, *you!*" He is screaming at me as we gather speed, and I do as I am told.

We go down the runway, careening from side to side. It is an enormous struggle for me to go straight. It takes all my strength, as well as my five or six senses dedicated to what I am doing.

"Pressure!" he yells over the whine of the engine. "Don't push back and forth! Hold your feet steady on the rudder pedals!"

My breath is coming in short spurts as I feel the plane tugging at the runway, ready to fly. I pull back slightly on the ailerons, and we are in the air. I pull more, and the nose goes up and we lose speed. We are about ten feet above the runway.

"Not too high or you will stall! Make a slow climb out of here!" he yells in my ear. "Back off on the throttle! You don't need so much speed once you are off the ground. Now take it to pattern altitude."

"My god, I did it! I took off!" I shout, elated.

At 700 feet, I try to level out, but I put too much forward pressure on the stick, and we drop 20 feet. When I pull back, we go too high, to almost 750 feet.

"Gently," he repeats, and gradually I am able to keep it straight. "Watch your goddamned airspeed! You're going too slow. Division of attention, remember? You have to be on top of everything at once—airspeed, altitude, and where you are in relation to the field. Look! You're letting it drift to the east because of the wind."

Sure enough, we are over the foothills. The airport is to the right. I adjust with the rudder and notice we have dropped 50 feet again. It is maddening, and now it is time for the banked turn to enter the base leg of the pattern, then the approach. The knot in my stomach returns as I consider getting this thing on the ground without killing us.

The turn goes well, and I am on base leg, then I make the turn for the approach, losing altitude but not fast enough. As I fly over the end of the runway, we are 15 feet too high to land and the landing strip passes below us.

Jake takes over and repeats the pattern. I keep my hands on the controls while he lands then takes off. He turns it over to me. This time, he says, I *have* to land it.

Nervously, I line the aircraft up with the field on my approach. I cut the engine and we are gliding, but too fast. "Pull up the nose to lose speed!" he shouts at me. We are above the pavement, about halfway down the field. I try to remember everything, how the horizon looks in relation to the inside of the plane. I feverishly work the ailerons and rudder, concentrating all my energy on the task. We sink onto the concrete, bounce a bit, and then settle down.

To my chagrin, he pushes full throttle, grins at me, indicating I should immediately take off again. I feel exhausted by what I have just done, but his smile of approval provides the impetus to do it again, only I will do it better this time, no bouncing.

I repeat the pattern until we are about five feet over the runway, feeling more in control this time. I sense the pavement beneath the plane, and as I pull back, the stall warning goes off and we touch down. I push the nose gently forward, apply the brakes, and we come to a stop. I have landed myself!

"Jake, did you touch anything?" I ask anxiously, wiping the perspiration from my forehead with the sleeve of my blouse.

"No, nothing. You landed it on your first lesson. You are going to be a good pilot someday, but you have to keep at it, kid. Now, do it once more, and then we head back to the hangar."

I feel wonderful after my second landing, and as I taxi back to the hangar, I am bursting with self-esteem. Jake ties down the aircraft, and I walk back to the office, my legs feeling wobbly. He fills out my logbook and signs it. Thirty-five minutes of touch and go.

"Well, congratulations!" says Annie as she flips over some hamburgers on the grill. "Jake says you landed it yourself on your first lesson. That's pretty good, you know."

"Thanks, Annie."

I lean over the glass display case where a variety of aviation knick-knacks are offered for sale. There are compasses, books on flying, calculators, goggles, logbooks, watches, maps, and gold-plated trophies of antique airplanes with blank nameplates.

I pay for my lesson and head back to the city. I'm exhilarated by what I have done, but at the same time puzzled by it. Where is this going to lead? I wonder, certainly not to becoming a professional pilot. Perhaps it is my lesson in life that I never got from my parents. It is about taking control, not depending on someone else to do it, making happen what you want to happen—facing real life?

CHAPTER FOURTEEN

Fading Illusions

It is late in the afternoon when I arrive at my apartment. The aviation lesson has exhausted me, so after a sandwich, I lie down and nap.

The phone awakens me. "Hi, honey! Heard you did well on your first flying lesson. Good for you," says Vincent in a strangely subdued voice.

"Oh, thanks. Yes, I was pretty nervous, but—"

"Say, I've got a bad stiff neck going here, slipped cervical disc or something like that, says Kelley. May have to operate. I'm coming by there to rest up. Kelley's going to fix me up with some traction equipment to see if that will help. How about fixing me some coffee? I need some tender, loving care right now."

"Sure," I murmur, part of me excited to see him but the other part realizing I won't be getting any work done the rest of the day. My love needs me, no matter that I am a terrible nurse.

"See you in a bit. Love you," says Vincent.

He hangs up the phone and leans back in his well-worn, leather-upholstered attorney's chair. The pain in his neck is almost intolerable. It had come on suddenly. Maybe he'd slept wrong last night or making love to Phyllis was a bad move. He hates illness.

Kelley suggested that he had calcium spurs on his cervical vertebrae that were pressing on his nerves—goddamned Kelley, just dying to get him under the knife.

He knew he had to face getting old, but it was too painful. His youth had been too glorious for him to happily accept aging—mostly the women. The time would come when he couldn't pick and choose. He passes his hand over his face to obliterate the thought.

He takes a pain pill, tells his secretary he is leaving early, and heads for Mount Olympus. As he drives up 17th Street, he has to hold his head at a slight angle to accommodate the pain in his neck.

He wants to see her, his little artist. Surprisingly, she is going to be a fine pilot, good speed sense, talented person, but so young. Imagine, she was just born when he graduated law school, only ten years older than his daughter, Alice. Being with her makes him feel youthful. Oh, what the hell he thinks. This isn't the first time for this sort of thing. Look at Kelley. Nuts about her.

He stops for a light at Castro. He notices the young people dressed in exotic, unusual clothing—girls in long skirts with wreathes of flowers in their long flowing hair, young men with long hair walking around in sandals, some of them playing music on a flute or a guitar, dancing with each other spontaneously on the street. Some of the men are in dresses, for god's sake. "Hippies," they are calling them, and there are more and more all the time, especially on Haight Street. They carry rough, homemade signs that say, "Free Food," "Free Housing," "Free Love."

Looks like they are smoking something weird, probably reefers, he thinks as he presses down on the gas pedal to propel the reluctant old Buick up the hill to his haven. Curious that they have to go through all that trouble! He has always enjoyed "free love."

The engine labors painfully up the steep hill. Needs work, he thinks, but he is worse off with every passing day. His partner finally sold his mansion on the peninsula, but for a lot less than he was asking. After paying off the construction debts, there wasn't enough money left to totally cover what was owed to the bonding company. The pain in his neck is torture. He parks the old Buick and slowly gets out of the car, careful not to move his head too much.

He rings the doorbell on Joanna's apartment.

"Vincent, are you all right?" I ask, as he enters, concerned by his haggard expression. He is pale and crooked-looking, with bags under his blue eyes. His disheveled look is not one of charming nonchalance but a sad indication of a fall from grace.

"No, I'm not all right. Coffee ready?" he asks as he collapses onto my bed and throws his tie down onto the floor. "Take care of me."

He sits up in agony to sip the black instant coffee. "Oh, my god, this is awful! Help me get up to my place. Kelley should be here in about an hour to put me into traction. How is it up there in my flat? I haven't been around for a while."

"Okay, I guess. I haven't been there either. Busy with my work. What did you do to your neck?"

"Nothing that I know of. Maybe God is punishing me for something." He manages a wicked smile. "Help me up the back stairs."

We go to his bedroom with him leaning on me, and I help him undress. The sheets on the bed look rumpled and soiled. The smell is musty, neglected, abandoned. But somehow

Vincent appears to my addled, romantic mind as a wounded hero, a warrior who needs me, and I like the feeling. I am in control now. We get to his undershorts, and as I expected, his male member is swelling, ready for action despite his slipped cervical disk.

His hand slips down, and he begins massaging himself and brings it to full maturity. He stretches out naked on the bed. "Honey, please, just do me a little before the doctor comes. Oh, turn up the thermostat first. It's freezing in here."

He guides my head down, and I do him until he ejaculates. "Don't spit that out!" he commands me, my mouth full. "Swallow it. It's good for you. Seriously, it's chockfull of vitamins, proteins, minerals, and hormones that will keep you young and healthy, believe me."

I gulp it down as he says. It tastes like thick, warm egg whites seasoned with some salt. I rush to the kitchen for some water to get it all down. At least going in from this end, I won't get pregnant—poor, unfortunate spermatozoa battling their way down my esophagus searching for the elusive egg, only to land in my stomach, and dying a miserable death in all that stomach acid. The hallowed egg is tucked away down below all that, also doomed.

"What kind of vitamins?" I ask, pulling the covers over him and sitting down on the edge of the bed.

"Yeah, well, uh, vitamin A and vitamin B and vitamin P."

"P?"

"Believe me, it's all great for a woman. Why, those rich ladies on Pacific heights just gobble the stuff up—or down! They say it keeps them young-looking, and I believe them. Hell, I should probably bottle the stuff and sell it at some health food store. Make a fortune. The Elixir of Life, I could call it. Honey, bring me the telephone over here next to the bed, wouldja?"

"You are kidding me," I say as I untangle the phone line and place it on the bedside table.

He looks at me through half-closed eyes, a smile playing around his mouth, enjoying my consternation over him, my reaction to his unusual sexual practices and ideas.

"No, I'm not kidding. It's true. I would never lie to you. I love you too much. Semen is probably one of the richest fluids in the body, richer than blood maybe, and pee is sterile when it leaves the body. Ask Kelley about that sometime."

I have never imagined Vincent being sick. He seemed invulnerable to me, and now this, an ordinary, mundane stiff neck has brought him down. Terry of 'Terry and the Pirates" would be wounded every once in a while during combat missions and tended by his beautiful lover/nurse, but a stiff neck?

"Honey, that was beautiful. Sex is so wonderful. You can do everything. You cook. You sew your own clothes. You paint beautiful pictures that people actually buy. You can even fly an airplane! You are the woman I should have married twenty years ago, a woman I could be faithful to. Bring me some more coffee please."

I bring more coffee and see that he has fallen asleep. Twenty years ago, I was eight years old. He is snoring softly. I will go downstairs and get busy on my drawings.

As I start out the kitchen door, I hear him calling me. "Don't leave me alone!" he calls out. "Do you have a heating pad I could put on my neck?"

"I don't, but I think Thom does."

"Could you go up there and check? I think a heating pad with a damp towel would help the pain." His face is twisted in agony. He holds his arm above his head to alleviate it somewhat.

I enter through the unlocked kitchen door to Thom's flat. His linen closet is full of full of brand-new luxury towels and sheets. The heating pad is tucked away in the back. I hear the key turning in the front door lock. For some reason, the adrenaline shoots through my body, preparing to flee for stealing the heating pad. This is irrational. We are friends. I even have the key to this place. I put the heating pad under my arm, go to the front door, and with a big smile and a kiss welcome Thom into his home.

"Thom, hi, there! I was looking for your heating pad for Vincent's neck. He is really suffering downstairs. I hope you don't mind."

The man looks a bit startled, perhaps annoyed with me, clutching his heating pad for Vincent's neck. I sense his disapproval, but Vincent is his dear friend, is he not? "Oh, yeah, sure, take it. But that's not going to help him. He needs surgery—and soon. I brought this traction outfit from the office to give him some relief from the pain." He is dragging a big suitcase-like thing behind him.

We go down to Vincent's with all of our equipment in hand. He is dozing with his arm still above his head.

"Hey, wake up. Cooper!" he shakes Vincent roughly.

"Aghhh, don't do that! My neck, you're killing my neck!"

Thom laughs. "Okay, Vince, let me connect you to this traction apparatus and see if it eases your pain."

"And the heating pad?"

"Yeah, sure, Joanna has it right here."

"He wants a damp towel between the heating pad and his neck," I say as I plug the cord to the pad into the wall socket.

"Whatever. You be the little nurse while I try to figure out how this damn thing goes together," says Thom, emptying the suitcase on the floor of the bedroom. A heap of wood, springs, straps, and ropes lies there in an unceremonious jumble.

Thom screws one of the wooden pieces to the headboard of the bed, and from that a strap fits under Vincent's chin. Another strap that attaches to his feet is fixed in place, then a weight is attached. Another rope passes through an overhead pulley, and the whole thing is cranked up in order to stretch out Vincent's spinal column, with special attention to his neck, theoretically in order to relieve pressure on the affected nerve. He cannot speak. I tuck the heating pad in around the back of his neck with a damp towel, hoping it does not short out, electrocuting him after all of this. I know I am no Florence Nightingale, but go forth with all the best intentions anyway.

Thom stands back admiring his handiwork and smiling. "That looks just fine to me. Now, you just rest there, Vincent. Try to sleep. If you want, I can give you an injection."

Vincent can barely shake his head in the negative.

"Now, Joanna, let's go upstairs and relax, I'll fix you a drink while our patient rests. I hear you had a flying lesson today. I want you to tell me all about it."

It seems early to start drinking, not even 4:00 o'clock yet, but I have been living this semi-anarchic life long enough to accept the vodka tonic offered by my landlord. Thom has stopped buying me wine, since he attributes my so-called "bad behavior" to the effects of drinking wine. I miss the excellent Napa Valley Chardonnay but have been unable to convince him that my "bad behavior" has everything to do with Vincent Cooper and probably nothing to do with the Napa Valley Chardonnay.

Thom sets up his slide projector in the living room. He wants to show me the slides he has had made of my drawings of the brachial plexus. I sit back and admire them. They look very professional up there on the screen. He takes a pointer and becomes the professor. "And this is where I think Vincent's problem originates. We will need some new X-rays of his neck to be certain. And by the way, how is my drawing of the sternum coming along? I need it by next week. The convention begins Thursday at the Fairmont."

"Well, I was going to work on that this afternoon until this all happened with Vincent's neck. How many do you want?"

"Three: one of a young person lightly drawn with a broken sternum highlighted, then one of the sternum aligning itself, then one of the sternum joined with a ridge of bone where the parts adhere to each other. I have some old X-rays I am going to use. Nancy is looking all over hell in the files for them. I hope she finds them, since they will really tell the tale."

I stand up. "Let me go downstairs for my sketchbook before I get too drunk."

"Good idea."

Back in Thom's golden living room, drawing pencil in hand, *Gray's Anatomy* opened to the sternum, I draw a young man, waist up, with a transparent body. His sternum is badly broken, and his lightly drawn face, which slightly resembles Vincent, is grimacing in pain.

"Yeah, that's good, something like that," says Thom, his arms folded, his eyes squinting in close scrutiny through his glasses. "The kid sure looks miserable, not like Netter's drawings where all the faces are serene despite their broken bones and so forth. You know what I mean. You like to get arty on me, don't you?"

"Art is what makes life worth living. You told me that, you know, Thom."

"Yeah, yeah, of course. But remember, this is problem-solving."

"Can't you do both at the same time?" I ask as I roughly sketch the three concepts, note his labeling instructions and comments.

"Maybe. Haven't thought about it for some reason. Let me freshen your drink."

Finishing, I close the sketchbook and place the *Gray's Anatomy* on top of it, along with the drink. We go down to Vincent's.

Vincent has disengaged himself from the traction and is sitting up in bed talking on the phone. He covers the mouthpiece with one hand. "It's Burkhart. He says I probably need a drink, no injections. Bad for the booze." He is smiling. The brief rest has done him good. "Be a good girl and bring me a Tanqueray on the rocks," he pleads.

His kitchen is bare, almost nothing. An empty bottle of Tanqueray gin. "Thom, do you have any Tanqueray gin in your place?" I call out.

"Maybe, but give him vodka. It's better for him."

"No vodka. Gin—and the good stuff."

Vincent continues his phone conversation. "Yeah, come on over, Ted. Bring a bottle with you on the way and see what you think of my neck here. Kelley can't wait to get his hands on my cervical vertebrae and butcher me up. Probably let the knife slip and leave me paralyzed or decapitated. You know how friends can be."

Thom frowns at this.

I hurry up the back stairs, not wanting to miss any of the drama going on in Vincent's bedroom. I notice it is beginning to drizzle. The first rains of the fall. The stairs are damp. I will have to put the top on my TR3, I think as I push the bottles around in Thom's liquor cabinet.

There is a bottle of gin but the cheap stuff. Vincent won't notice if I throw in some olives and pickled onions. Searching frantically in the refrigerator, I spy a lone lemon and carefully cut off a curl of rind from its best side, give it a twist, and drop it into the glass over the ice cubes, gin, olive, and onion.

For a moment, I linger over Thom's refrigerator. Lately, he has stocked it with many gourmet offerings: caviar, exotic cheeses like Brie and Camembert, marmalades in little jars of different varieties, eggs, sour cream, horseradish, hearts of artichoke, a big jar of black olives, smoked oysters, herring in wine sauce, ham, and bacon. And there behind everything is a bottle of Chardonnay that he has been holding out on me. I sigh with pleasure, contemplating this vision of abundance, close the door, put the drink on a tray like a dutiful slave, and take it to my master.

There is deep male laughter coming from Vincent's bedroom. John, Thom's otherworldly brother, has arrived on the scene. "Oh, my gosh, darling, how are you? Oh, you are so lovely!" he gushes and kisses me wetly on the cheek as I narrowly avert my mouth.

He is dressed in an old pin-striped business suit, frayed in places, that hangs on his thin frame. His face is redder and flakier than ever, and the perpetual smile is still frozen in place. "I just love to come here and visit all you beautiful, interesting people, you know," he says. "Here, I brought some beer and wine. Oh, not the good kind that my rich doctor brother can afford, but it's good just the same. I'll just put it all in Vince's refrigerator if you don't mind. Anyone want a little drinkie while I'm in the kitchen?" He smiles ingratiatingly at us all and seemingly floats out of the room.

Thom throws his head back and stares at the ceiling. "I wish he'd shut up, but what can I do? He is my brother."

Vincent sips his gin on the rocks. "Yuck! What is this, some rotgut you keep around to poison your friends, Kelley?"

Thom smiles his little smirk of pleasure, "Now, Vincent, beggars can't be choosers now, can they?"

Vincent still owes several months of back rent. My love sighs, takes another sip, then sets the drink down and passively waits to be strapped back in the traction. He wears only a tee shirt and boxer shorts.

Physical infirmities are unfamiliar and unpleasant to me. My husband and I were rarely sick, maybe a cold now and then. Breakdowns were something that happened to other people you hear about or very old people. This situation stymies me. I don't know how to react. There is no nursing instinct in me. My mother taught us to take care of our health and nothing would go wrong.

Now, between Thom and his patients, Vincent and his cervical problem, I feel I am being assaulted daily by the reality of human frailty. Then there is the annoying romantic notion of the stalwart hero. I tend to shroud the object of my desire with this cloak of invincibility to the point that it even occurs to me that Vincent is faking this. But no, the pain he is expressing is too real, and he is not phony in any way.

If only I had the powers of sorcery, I could magically cure him, like in the fairy tales of my childhood, make him whole, even maybe a few years younger. But stop thinking that. Do what must be done, and he will most likely improve, counsels my inner voice.

Thom phones his office, cups his hand over the receiver, motions me over to him. "Say, I think you should get yourself downstairs to your studio and get busy on those drawings. I'd like to see the roughs by tomorrow morning." He then returns to his conversation with Nancy, his secretary, concerning the search for some missing X-rays.

Reluctantly, I go down to my studio, knowing Vincent would like me to stay with him, bring him his coffee or his drink or whatever he wants, then to slip into bed with him at night to keep him warm and to cure his ills with my love. But Zeus has commanded.

Before going to work, I rush outside into the rain to button down the top of my sports car. Several of the snaps are missing. Where will I ever get the money to replace this vehicle? I wonder, a vehicle left over from my terminated marriage. The rain feels fresh and clean on my body. It clears my brain and my soul to go ahead with what I must do.

After about an hour and a half, Thom phones me from Vincent's flat. "Hi, Doll! We all miss you." His voice is kind of slurry. "Wyncha come up here and have a drink with us? All work and no play will make you a dull doll." He giggles at his little joke. "Burkhart and Annette are here drinking to the health of our lawyer friend."

"Give me another half hour, Thom. I'm on the last drawing, so you can go over them."

Annette, the Lithuanian stewardess, greets me affectionately, her face beaming.

"Oh, Joanna, y'all are as beautiful as evuh." Dr. Burkhart kisses me on the lips, his tongue about to pass into my mouth as I draw back. I barely know this man.

Annette declares with her charming, Eastern European accent, "Oh, ju people make a party out of everything! How vonderful! I luf to come here!"

Thom hands her a drink and chuckles. "Why, we love you, too, Annette! This is your house. *Mi casa es tu casa*, as they say in Old Mexico."

He says nothing about owing the rent; however, he covets the monthly payments and is very annoyed at Vincent for getting behind. But then there is something about Vincent's incapacitation that appears to have lifted Thom's spirits, dissipating his frequent depression.

"Say," he continues brightly, "why don't I call the Chinaman on the corner to send up some market steaks? I don't know about you all, but I am starved."

Ted Burkhart grins his devilish grin. "Me, too, hungry as a bear in March. Let me pay for the steaks, and order more booze while y'all are at it."

After ordering, Thom sits down with me in the chintz-covered chesterfield in the living room, and we go over the drawings. He likes them, makes a few changes, some notes in the margins, and we are done. I put the drawings aside in a safe corner since no more serious work will take place this evening on Mount Olympus. Zeus has declared "party time."

Annette follows me into Vincent's desolate kitchen. Months of accumulated dust covers the early American furniture, the complete set of crystal goblets, and the dining room table. Even the painting of the violinist seems dulled, as though the musician has become blocked by neglect. Somehow, it is all the more depressing for the attempt Vincent made to simulate middle-class propriety than when I lived my sparse, bohemian existence here without furniture or pretense as to the purpose of my life. But maybe I am being harsh on him. Perhaps he really did want a nice, stable, acceptable way of life here with his girlfriend.

"Let's us make sumzing goot. Is zer rice? I can make it vedy, vedy goot," declares Annette as I fix another drink for Vincent. She finds a dusty box half full of wild rice in the back of a cupboard. "Wow, vut luck! Vee can mix zat wiz brown rice and stretch eet. I pick out zee few bugs from zees grains. No vun vill know zee difference." Annette cleans the rice, puts in some water, salt, and butter and starts cooking it.

I deliver the drink to my wounded warrior. The men are discussing World War II and pay me no attention.

Annette and I go upstairs for a serious raid on Thom's wonderfully stocked kitchen. We load a grocery box with condiments, frozen vegetables, butter, olive oil and olives, balsamic vinegar, capers, spices, onions, garlic, dried chives, parsley and basil, frozen sour dough bread, potatoes, and anchovies. Thom will not object until tomorrow morning when he appraises his loss. For the moment, he will be very happy with the wonderful dinner we are going to prepare.

We become inspired. The steaks arrive, several pounds of choice market steaks, beautifully marbled with white fat. Annette and I fly between the kitchen and the dining room. We scrub months of grunge from the crystal wine and water goblets, polish the silverware, dust the table and chairs. We chop, mince, and mix.

I find some surviving flowers in the planter boxes on the terrace, a few ferns, and arrange a tiny bouquet for the table. Annette discovers a beautiful white linen tablecloth and embroidered napkins in the buffet and spreads it all over the table.

John makes his humble service available and is put in charge of changing records on the phonograph, lighting the fire in the fireplace, keeping it going and serving drinks to everyone.

We prepare béarnaise sauce from scratch for the steaks. We make green goddess salad dressing for the romaine lettuce. I decide against sour dough bread and go ahead with corn muffins. The kitchen becomes a blur of flashing knives over chopping blocks, whirling egg beaters, dishtowels flapping in their drying processes. We are spreading, cutting, pouring, dusting, chopping, greasing, draining, mashing, and mincing. John is dispatched to bring us more wine, the good Chardonnay, to fuel our labor.

"I theenk zee needle is stuck in zee record," Annette tells me as I place the muffins into the hot oven. I rush to the living room and lift the arm of the phonograph off the very scratched Montovani record and replace it with Vincent's favorite, Al Jolson.

"Donchu like jazz?" Annette asks, her mouth turned down in displeasure as the strains of "Swanee" waft into the busy kitchen.

"No, but I will go downstairs and get some of my Mexican records. You will love Pedro Infante. Latins are so romantic."

As I climb back up the stairs clutching my records, the noise of the dinner party is increasing in direct proportion to the alcohol consumed. Are we celebrating my first flying lesson I wonder? Or maybe I am celebrating the two men I love in my life or maybe that Vincent has returned to Upper Terrace. Or maybe Thom is celebrating Vincent's incapacitation, which would be very neurotic of him, or that Ted Burkhart and Annette are lovers, or what? No matter, for the moment everyone is happy.

It is almost 9:00 o'clock by the time dinner is ready and we gather in the dining room to admire the beautifully set table, the china, silver, crystal, and lovely furniture hardly having been used since Vincent bought it all almost a year ago.

Vincent sits regally at the head of the table in his blue terrycloth bathrobe. The only sign of his discomfort is his arm suspended over his head, which is cocked at an unusual angle.

The windows are so steamy from all the cooking on the inside and coated by the salt air on the outside that the view is barely visible. John pours the wine, giggling constantly with pleasure over amusements only he is aware of.

Back in the kitchen, Annette and I fill the plates with French-cut green beans topped with slivered almonds toasted in butter; thick, rather rare market steaks oozing fat and juices; baked potatoes slathered with sour cream, chives, and bacon bits. I carefully remove the corn muffins from the oven, place them in a basket, and cover them with a beautiful, flower-embroidered linen towel. Annette takes the plates to the table while I serve individual helpings of green goddess salad.

"God almighty," exclaims Vincent, "what a spread we have before us! I almost feel like saying grace like my Southern Baptist granny used to. And look, corn muffins! From a mix?" He looks at me directly, wanting the truth.

"No," I reply demurely. "I made them from scratch just for you." I glance quickly at Thom, concerned he may have heard that, but he is arguing about something with his brother.

Burkhart intervenes. "Holy shit! And y'all took yer first flying lesson today, and Jake says ya did good. My goodness gracious, the gal can do just about any ole thing now, right, there, honey?" Burkhart's southern drawl is soupier than ever.

"Well, now, harrumph, I think the little lady needs a toast to her future in the air," announces Thom grandly. But for some reason, it doesn't sound sincere to me. A touch of sarcasm taints his words. They all raise their glasses and toast to my impending pilot-hood, downing the Chardonnay rapidly and forcing John to jump up, open more bottles, put more ice in the bucket, and refill everyone's crystal goblet.

I am next to Vincent, with Thom on the other side of me. Annette is across the table, while Ted Burkhart is to her side. John is seated next to Burkhart so he can more easily attend to us. It all feels quite comfortable as we pass plates of sauces, salt and pepper, butter, and the wine bottle back and forth among us. It is almost tribal, atavistic in feeling, nothing like the formal family dinners at home in Tucson. The strains of Glenn Miller's big band serenade us as we eat.

Dr. Burkhart is halfway through his steak when he sets down his knife and fork loudly on his plate. "Say, Vince, y'all look mighty fine to me. What's all this talk about cervical fusion?"

Thom reacts immediately. "He may have a remission in pain, but those spurs on the fourth and fifth will never go away without surg—"

Vincent interrupts, "No way! I told you, Thom, no neck surgery. I admit I am a coward, scared to death of surgeons with their knives. Let's face it, I don't even like the way you carve a roast, Kelley, for god's sake."

"Modern medicine is what separates man from animals. We are able to treat ourselves with advanced science," Thom repeats his mantra of medical justification pompously.

"I like zee animals," adds Annette drunkenly. "Zey are much nizer zan zee people."

"Is that why you like me so much, baby?" Burkhart buries his head in the back of her neck, and she collapses, giggling.

"I would rather stick with the rest and exercises. Let's see how it all goes," sighs Vincent, his face slightly grimaced in pain.

We finish dinner with cognac and coffee.

Vincent beckons me to help him. "Joanna, honey, take me to my bedroom and my torture rack. It's been a long day." He stands with difficulty, his hand on his neck, his face twisted.

He throws his other arm over my shoulder, and we make our way to his bedroom. I seat him on the edge of the bed, and he slowly reclines. "Honey," he says softly, almost in a whisper, pulling my head down to his mouth, "Please bring me some water and leave it here on the table with the aspirin, and then when they all leave come back. Promise me you'll come back here and sleep with me. This bed is so cold at night, and I feel so bad. I need you. Please, honey, promise me. Forget about Kelley. He's just a jealous old fart."

"But what if he finds out about us?"

"So what? He already knows. He doesn't own you ..." His voice fades away. He seems to be talking in his sleep, exhausted.

Back in the dining room, the conversation ebbs and flows like a riptide among rocks, moving erratically from one subject to another.

Burkhart is talking about his ranch in Texas, how he needs a woman to help him work it. He has been divorced twice so far. Annette, who is now smashed, hanging on his shoulder, is passionately volunteering for the job.

A pall of unwelcome sobriety hangs over me in the midst of all this. I have strong feeling of great, imminent responsibility ahead of me, which is a further sobering phenomenon.

CHAPTER FIFTEEN

Responsibility

Responsibility to what? to whom? to my landlord? to my lover? to Aldrich Art Gallery, or to myself? For the time being, I divide it between myself and my lover, Vincent, who seems especially vulnerable now. Then there is my reproductive responsibility to those miraculous little eggs that drop one by one into my womb every month seething with passive desire to connect with those rascally, miniscule sperm. What if one day they do connect? What would my life be like then?

No one notices as I begin to fill a part of my female destiny of cleaning plates from the table. Thom and his brother are suddenly locked in a family argument concerning their long-dead mother.

Conscientiously, I scrape the leftovers from the plates into the garbage. There is a lot of good food going to waste, my mother's voice echoes in my head, 'waste not, want not', a kind of old-fashioned mantra utterly ignored during these times of economic and material abundance. But what if it is correct after all, and we someday live with scarcity for having wasted so much? I put the corn muffins into a plastic bag and into the freezer, I'll be damned if I will throw away perfectly good muffins.

Annette staggers in, her eyes glazed and a silly grin on her face, carrying my half-empty glass of wine. "Here, jou left jour wine at zee table. Dreenk eet!" she commands. She leans on the kitchen counter, her mouth forming a half smile, her eyelids drooping, and her head wobbling slightly. She watches me drink my wine. "Vhy jou not marry Thom, zee doctor? He ees very reech. He luves jou, and jou treet heem like sheet."

I feel drunk just watching and listening to her. I adjust the hot tap water with a little cold so it won't burn my artist's hands. Look at me washing dishes like any ordinary housewife. How disgusting I think.

"Annette, I am not ready to be married again. I really did not like being married for those five years. I may never marry again. Besides, I feel like playing around a little, see what it is like to have a few affairs here and there. I never had a chance to do that."

Her eyes droop farther, and her head nods slowly up and down. She pours more wine into my glass. "Hmm," she croons, "jes, jou are playing around reel goot, fucking wiz zee both of zem, huh? Jou are having a reel goot time zees days, no?"

How can she know that? The walls of this building must speak, speak to their owner, who must be aware of everything that happens here and then *talks about it.*

"Why do you say that? You don't know."

Her mouth breaks into a full smile, covering her whole face. "Jes, I know. I know zat jou loff two mens at the same time, very good zat, lots of big fun. Zey get reel mad becuz zey know eet, but jou have zee control, not zem … beeg, beeg, fun!" Her English suffers from a surfeit of wine, but it does communicate her profound amusement at my situation.

She wanders off while I continue to heap up the garbage. Starving children in Europe, I think, or now it's Bangladesh or Africa. The image of my Aunt Minerva is before me, collecting all the leftovers from the kitchen table, the cuttings from the fruit and vegetables, the weeds from the garden, and the whey from the cheese into a big bucket and taking it to the voracious pigs that would hungrily and snortingly devour the nutritious mess. Here, it will all just go into the scavenger's truck in the morning.

I leave the kitchen fairly well-organized and cleaned up, possibly hoping to atone for my sexual behavior, then join the others in the living room. There the argument rages on, with the usually self-effacing John, seething with fury, yelling at his brother Thom!

"You never, never cared about her, and she did everything for you. She loved you more than any of us, and you didn't even have the decency to go to her funeral, you miserable, ungrateful …" His crooked, aged finger points at his brother, accusing him like a vengeful troll about to pounce. The man struggles for words, oblivious of the rest of us, those years of living in subjugation to his arrogant brother all culminating in this unleashed fury. His face is red and contorted. He is frightening to watch, a diminutive, raging demon. Then, he seems to grow larger and appears on the edge of committing some violent act.

Thom is smiling, "That's enough, John, old boy. You are embarrassing the girls."

"It's not enough!" John screams. He won't be shut up. "They should all know what a godforsaken, thankless son you were, and you know it. You got big and famous because she sacrificed everything so you could study medicine, then you never came to see her, like you were embarrassed of her, of the rest of us. She died before her time because of that, because of you, you thankless bastard. You'll burn in hell for that!"

Thom's face turns sour. "That's enough out of you. You get upstairs now and go to bed, you farty, old, stupid drunk." Thom turns to us. "Just ignore him. He's drunk, and he gets like that when he drinks too much. Don't pay any attention to him, and he'll go away."

Suddenly, John flings the rest of his drink into Thom's face! The drops glisten in the firelight as they run down the doctor's cheeks, his chin, and onto his shirt.

Thom takes his handkerchief from his pocket and wipes his face, staring in cold fury at his brother, who returns the stare, his chest heaving, his fists clenched, his jaw set, the veins on his scrawny neck standing out, pulsating rapidly. They are children again, acting out their still unresolved sibling rivalry.

"John, I have had just about enough of you. Come along." Thom grabs his brother by the arm and fairly drags him from the room, through the kitchen, and up the back stairs to his flat. The door slams loudly. We hear screams then silence.

Burkhart is smiling, having thoroughly enjoyed the spectacle. "Don't look so shocked, ladies. John just drank too much. He is envious of Thom, and it just comes out when he drinks. Don't pay any attention to him. You know the story of their father, a train conductor who drank *himself* to death. Runs in the family. His mother worked as a cleaning lady at Berkeley in order to send Thom through school, and then—well, maybe John is right in a way because Thom never acknowledged his mother, kind of ashamed that she was a cleaning lady, you know, and he was going around with all the rich kids. He dropped his family when he became successful. Not too nice, but it happens all the time." Ted Burkhart raises his gin on the rocks to the rest of us in a sad sort of toast to human failing and drinks it all down.

We sip our wine reflectively. The god of Mount Olympus, Zeus—or in this case, Thom—has feet of clay. I imagine John either dead or heavily sedated, and I wonder if he was beaten by Thom. Thom will probably rejoin us to laugh at his poor, dumb brother.

And Thom, ashamed of his poor but courageous mother, blames all his problems on her—his depression, the fact that no matter how much money he has, he still feels poor and inferior. The ultimate emptiness of his success is the inner vacuum he is forced to live with, a vacuum no woman can fill no matter how beautiful or desirable or young or rich she may be.

The party is over. Thom does not reappear, so I say goodbye to Ted and Annette at the door, like the mistress of the house. To be safe, I go downstairs to my cave under the building and wait until the place is silent. Then, I stealthily tiptoe up the back stairs, open his kitchen door as quietly as possible, close it behind me, and *lock* it. I creep into Vincent's bedroom, pull down his bed covers, and crawl in next to him.

The next day, I finish the drawings for Thom. He immediately has slides made from them. I can tell he is pleased with my work.

The convention of orthopedic surgeons takes place at the Fairmont Hotel at the top of Nob Hill. The last day of the convention, Thom delivers his speech about the clavicle and his procedure to fuse spinal vertebrae to eliminate back pain. The speech receives extensive coverage in both the *Examiner* and the *Chronicle*. A photo of him smiling broadly is featured on the front pages and refers to him as an "iconoclast." I had to look the word up. Next to his photo is a reproduction of my drawing of the self-healing clavicle bone.

He phones me that he is bringing home friends, and would I order a standing rib roast from the Chinaman? He is jubilant, and I sense another big celebration in the works. Although the parties are beginning to weary me, he depends on me as his hostess, and I don't feel I am in a position to say no. Whatever sexual involvement we had has faded away, and we are now "friends" and working associates of a sort.

Winston Hoffman is invited, along with Thom's office staff; a doctor acquaintance from out of town, Jake and Annie from Half Moon Bay, Ham Sado, the Japanese flower farmer, Ted Burkhart and his friend Annette, Thom's daughter, and Vincent of course (now recovered). Thom decides to have the party professionally catered. He will contribute the roast while the caterers do the rest. I will be free to make conversation and look pretty for the now-more-famous Dr. Kelley.

Ultimately, there are over thirty people congregated in the golden flat on Mount Olympus. Thom holds court from his fake-leopard-skin-covered pouf.

His brother, John, now more self-effacing than ever, acts as butler and servant in conjunction with the catering people.

"Yeah," says Thom, downing the last drop of his vodka tonic and handing the empty glass to his brother for a refill, "most doctors today don't know their ass from a cup of tea. They over-treat. Broken bones just need to be realigned and taped. Bones have an affinity for each other. They *want* to unite, like separated lovers, something like that."

The crowd laughs politely at this notion. Thom's face is crimson, flushed with pleasure at his sudden fame. He is pleased with his role of the rebel against the medical establishment. He is a renegade, a bad boy, but now vindicated by his minor revolution.

I flit about the place in my homemade, red-flowered, Galanos-print dress, which came out beautifully this time. Thom often pulls me to his side to extoll my virtues. He needs me to complement him. He has even bought me a case of my favorite Chardonnay wine.

I sometimes wonder how he reconciles my ongoing affair with Vincent in his mind. Perhaps he pushes the thought to a dark corner of his brain, as though it doesn't exist, like a decaying tooth that doesn't hurt yet— unpleasant, yes—but ultimately has to be reckoned with.

Vincent and I barely acknowledge each other except toward the end of the evening. He approaches me and whispers, "I want to stay here with you tonight, but I have to go back to San Mateo. I promised. I love you. You know that, I will call you tomorrow."

After everyone leaves, I know I will have to stay with Thom. He gives me that desperate, needy look that I fully understand. In his bed, we repeat our doomed lovemaking.

He sits up in bed. "Stand by the lamp, Doll. I want to look at you naked. You have such a beautiful body, your lovely small breasts. Stay that way."

I start to cry.

"Hey, what's this? Why are you crying? What's wrong?"

"I ... I don't know. I feel empty inside. I think I very much want a baby."

He pulls me back into bed with him. His body is so white, thin, and fragile-looking. "Marry me," he says, "and I will give you all the babies you want. How many? ten? twelve? Whatever you want, I'll give you. I can make you the happiest girl in the world. This, uh, problem I have is just temporary, because of the divorce you know, that castrating bitch."

I listen in silence, wondering how temporary his problem is. We fall asleep, back to back.

In the morning, I wake with a start. I hear the kitchen door opening and know with a rapid sinking feeling in my chest that it is Vincent. There is no escape. Why don't we lock doors in this place? I wonder, fleetingly. In a few moments, he will enter the bedroom and see me lying naked in bed with the doctor.

I can already smell the cigarette smoke before I see him standing in the doorway, looking down on us, his mouth set hard in a straight line, smoke trailing from his nostrils like an angry bull. He looks so handsome to me.

"Good morning," he says flatly.

Thom sits up and swings his feet around to the floor, covering himself with the bed sheet. He laughs. "Sooo, caught us en flagrante delicto, huh, Vince?" I sense the pleasure in his voice at this situation.

Vincent turns and is gone. I hear the Buick start outside and pull away and I know I won't be seeing him for a while. Later that day, he phones Thom to tell him he is taking his things out of his flat and it will be vacant by the end of the month.

Winston Hoffman calls me frequently enough and comes to visit. I don't really lack companionship. He distracts me from the painful void inside of me, the ache over the loss of my dashing pilot. Winston sets up a painting project on my bathroom wall.

He will show me the fine points of classical painting, and we will paint a nude mural of the *Venus of Urbino*, by Titian, which we will copy from my old college art history text book. He loves champagne, and whenever he can afford to, he brings a couple of chilled bottles to help us in our work.

"Here, I will show you underpainting and glazing techniques used by the Old Masters. Unfortunately, nobody paints that way anymore, but it's good to know anyway."

I agree and scrub the bathroom wall vigorously, then he pencils in the reclining female form, her right hand modestly covering her crotch, and a seductive smile on her face. She is beautiful.

Thom comes to watch or to chaperone, I am not sure which. As he says, the wall and the building are his, so he has to approve.

Winston points out to me the warm and cool shadows of Venus's flesh. She becomes a problem to solve. "Yeah, just another problem to solve. Forget about her erotic pose. That's not important. She is a mass of warm and cool flesh tones, that's it," he says, brushing the color on rapidly.

Thom sits on a stool outside the bathroom sipping a glass of champagne, enjoying the spectacle of us poor, creative aristocrats working in our medium. Paint is dripping onto the floor, and I make an effort to clean it up, finally spreading newspapers all over the work area.

After several sessions, Venus is about two-thirds done. Thom becomes bored and goes upstairs to watch television and drink beer. The champagne has gone to my head, and I must force myself to concentrate.

Without warning, I feel Winston's arms around my waist, gently turning me toward him. His hands are stained with colors from the oil paint, his long, dark hair tousled, his eyes glistening, his face strangely contorted with that old demon *desire,* a moment of truth, but not *here*, not in Thom's castle where the walls, floors, and ceilings can see and hear everything I do and report it back to their owner. *Not here.*

In our awkward shuffling, I step on the paint palette. He knocks the turpentine off the top of the toilet seat. I am leaning against the mural, and my blouse absorbs the colors of Venus's plump, extended right leg. His lips are on mine, and he is trembling as his tongue explores the inside of my mouth. If Titian could see us now, he would probably be very pleased.

"Please," he begs, "forget about Thom, I know what you are thinking."

We pick our way out of the mess in the bathroom and lie on my bed. He takes off his shirt and begins to unbutton my blouse.

"I can't do this Winston. I really can't."

He sits up, angry, erect, his arms folded around his legs. "What is it with you? Are you engaged to the guy or what? He's old enough to be your father—or grandfather, probably."

"He has been very good to me and has helped me more than I can say. He's given me a sense of self-worth, something no one has ever given me. And maybe, I don't know, it has to be a gift from your family, your friends, society, somewhere, somehow, but it seems to me that it is something very difficult to obtain on your own. He has done that for me. And if you and I made love, I would feel I am betraying him. I don't want to suffer any more in my life. I want things to be easy and uncomplicated."

Winston snorts derisively. "You will never have a so-called easy life married to an old man. You are still young. You need someone like me."

"But if we married, we would fight. We would compete with one another, and eventually, you'd want me to just focus only on being a wife. We'd probably have a bunch of children, and I wouldn't be able to paint anymore. And besides, you are just starting out. You have no resources."

His face is contorted, no longer handsome, as he says, "I have what Thom has given you, and it's all I need. I know who I am, and I know I will be a famous artist someday. We could have such beautiful children together. Imagine." His face softens at the thought.

The phone rings. It is Thom.

"Winston, please, get dressed. He is coming down. Please, quickly! Go out through the living room window. Now, so he doesn't see you or hear you. I told him you left, hoping he wouldn't come down, but he is coming. He will think I am a liar, and he has a bad temper that he's barely able to control. Oh, Jeezus, I can't handle this!"

Winston pulls on his clothes, and we open the window to the little garden outside the living room, and I fairly push him through the sash. Hearing Thom's footsteps coming down the back stairs, I sit on the window seat catching my breath, struggling to calm my nerves as he knocks softly at the door. It all seems so futile since, no matter what precautions I take, he always seems to sense when I have been fooling around.

"Hi, there, Doll! Winston left didn't he?"

"Uh, yes, he left a while ago, like I told you. Do you, uh, want to see the painting?" The bathroom in total disarray. The turpentine spreads over the floor in an oily, yellow pool. Brushes are scattered about. The page in my art book with the *Venus of Urbino* is splattered with oil spots. There are tubes of oil paint oozing their contents, their caps scattered among the balls of wrinkled, dirty, stained paper towels. My tennis shoes, covered with the paint I had stepped in, are in one corner. What had begun as a serious, scholarly project has ended in erotic chaos.

"Well, well, well," comments Thom, stroking his chin with his sly, knowing half smile playing around his mouth, "you two really made a mess here. Too much champagne, huh? But the painting is nice. Her leg is kind of smudged. I hope you finish it. I'll keep it here for posterity."

Venus stares back at us, unfinished, her face is good though, echoing Thom's smile, sly and knowing but more sensual; definitely not a woman to throw a young, handsome, prospective lover out of her living room window.

We sit in my tiny living room, and he lights two cigarettes and hands me one. "You look tired," he says. "I won't take up too much of your time. You should sleep, sweetie. I just want to tell you that the San Francisco Sheriff's Air Squadron is having a fly-in picnic this Sunday, and I hope you can come with me in the Super Cub."

"You are a sheriff?"

"Yeah. Don't I look like a sheriff? Well, it's just an honorary position. Every county in California has an air squadron, volunteer usually, but since San Francisco is both a city and a county, you hardly need a plane for any kind of search and rescue here. It's mostly a men's party club. We usually meet once a month in some fancy restaurant to eat and drink a lot and tell exaggerated aviation stories. They say that once a small plane crashed into Sutro Forest, but before we could get to the airport, the fire department was on the scene, so our right to exist was co-opted. Most of the guys are professionals: doctors, lawyers, businessmen, mechanics, and the idle rich who inherited their money—good guys, though. Lots of fun, you know."

"Of course, Thom, I'll go with you. I love flying. Do we have to bring anything?"

"No, the guys get it all together and their wives. Now, you get some sleep, and I will talk to you in the morning." He kisses me lightly on the mouth and is gone.

My brain whirls reviewing recent events, trying to organize them into some coherency. My thoughts prevent me from falling asleep no matter how tired I am.

The pressure of monogamy—in a way I can understand the life of a harem woman, one king, or sheik, for all the women.

The women would have unlimited time when not bearing or nursing babies. They could make clay pots and decorate them, create mosaic designs, and design exotic clothing. They probably wove tapestries and rugs, maybe painted pictures, composed and performed music, poetry, and theater. They would have each other's companionship besides security, abundance, and leisure.

They might have been very contented or very bored. It would be hard to know the truth. Perhaps some were happy and some were not, depending on the woman. But who chooses the king? I wonder. Certainly not the harem women. Imagine, a grizzled, old, smelly monster!

But then there were the Amazon women. They would never be bored. They kept only men of the queen's choice to impregnate them when they so desired. The rest they killed. They spent their days hunting, living in harmony with the earth and its creatures. They may have been artists like the harem women, but much freer. They certainly were not lonely, oppressed, or alienated.

Thinking these forbidden thoughts, I finally drift off to sleep.

CHAPTER SIXTEEN

Air Squadron Picnic

The day of the Eel River San Francisco Sheriff's Air Squadron Picnic is cool and crisp. It is late autumn, and Thom and I are dressed warmly as we speed down the Coast Highway in his Thunderbird.

Jake Morenetti is in the coffee shop in the airport at Half Moon Bay. He will be flying up later because he has to get an old Air Force training plane, an AT-6, ready for a flying exhibition at the picnic. Jake leans across the countertop, a cigarette dangling from the corner of his mouth. "Listen, Kelley," he says in his usual gruff manner, "you need to make a right-hand approach to that landing strip there on the river. It's tricky and it's a short field. You can't mess up and go around again, got me? And be sure to check the wind direction."

"Yeah, yeah, sure, Jake," says Thom absently as he fills out his flight plan for the day.

We go out and check the Super Cub. I feel more comfortable with all of this as I have now completed ten hours of flight instruction and I am about to solo.

"You sure you don't want to fly this thing?" he asks me, "Jake says you are pretty hot on the stick."

"No, Thom, you fly. I want to watch the scenery go by."

The takeoff is wobbly, and I wonder if he took his usual amphetamine dose this morning. Unwittingly, I think of

Vincent's admonition concerning Thom's capacity as a pilot. Well, I could probably take over if he screws up, I think. Such is the dangerous thinking from a little knowledge.

The magic of flight never ceases to enchant me, the world unfolding all around us as we soar. I have the air chart open on my lap, but trying to study it makes me air sick, not a good sign.

Thom shouts back at me, "We are going to follow the Russian River till we get to Willits, and from there we'll follow the Eel River and hope to hell we find the guys and the party! You watch for other aircraft now!"

A little past Willits, the Russian River begins, then a little to the west we pick up the Eel, a smaller river.

"There they are!" he shouts.

Below, we see a dirt strip next to the river. The strip runs right into a dense forest at the end. It is on a large ranch owned by one of the members of the sheriff's air squadron and is made available once a year to the group for their outings. I see the planes parked alongside the strip, with people milling about. I imagine them all craning their necks to see who we are and to watch Thom's approach and his landing prowess. I sense his nervousness.

There are tall pine and redwood forests covering the undulating coastal mountains complicating the taking off and landing of small planes. I, too, am nervous as we descend, my eyes darting back and forth as we almost brush the tops of the trees. It somehow feels wrong.

Then the trees are next to us, and Thom is doing a sloppy slip. He is letting the plane fall sideways toward the ground. I feel him struggling with the controls, the stick and the rudder moving back and forth frantically as he tries to straighten out before we crash land on our side. He manages to level the plane before we hit the ground, but there is very little field left. A barbed wire fence and the forest loom ahead.

We hit and bounce. He presses hard on the brakes, and the plane does a ground loop at the end of the field, a disgraceful landing. but we are safe on the ground and can only hope that the plane is undamaged so that we can fly back in it. This whole event will be a subject for commentary today and far into the future of the San Francisco County Air Sheriff's Squadron and their lack of aviation competency.

He turns around to look at me, his face white with fear and dripping sweat. "You okay? Sorry about that. It happens sometimes." He taxis the fragile little aircraft over to where the others are parked. "A crosswind, we didn't check the wind, Doll. Lucky we made it." He is trembling, making an effort to appear unfazed as we get out of the plane.

The squadron members are laughing and joking about the near fatal landing. I feel calm for some reason. Our time had not come, or my guardian angel had taken charge at the last moment.

"You ain't gonna do much more bone surgery flying like that Doc Kelley," says a heavyset man with a florid, freckled face.

"Hey, Kelley, you almost bought the ranch on that one. How come you flew in over the river?" says another man.

"Cooper or Morenetti told me to make a right-hand approach, and then the wind—say, what direction is the goddamned wind?"

We walk over to the picnic tables, where women are setting out bowls of potato salad, chips, sliced tomatoes, pickles, ketchup, mustard, and mayonnaise. Hotdogs are sizzling on charcoal grills, with many hotdog buns piled on the sides warming up. There are ice chests filled with beer and soft drinks, but no hard liquor.

"Y'all landed downwind, you jerk," exclaims Burkhart, a beer in one hand and a cigarette in the other.

"But Jake said right."

"Yeah, usually the wind is out of the north. But for some reason, it switched and is coming out of the southeast today. You mean, you didn't check the wind direction before your approach?"

Thom is opening a beer for me, smiling sheepishly. "No. I forgot, I guess." He opens one for himself and drains half of it in one gulp. "I don't want to talk about it anymore with anyone, understand?"

Burkhart smiles at me, shaking his head as though to say we are alive only by some miraculous intervention.

I sit down on one of the picnic benches under the softly sighing redwoods of northern California, breathing the clean forest scented air, sipping my beer, and beginning to enjoy the day. I wonder what is to come. I attempt conversation with some of the wives, but they seem remote.

I realize we have nothing in common and give it up. It's as though we come from different planets or are a different species of females. They don't even seem too chummy with one another. There are no children around, and I miss seeing Annette, Burkhart's girlfriend. I realize I am waiting for Vincent, who I quickly noticed was not present. I munch a potato chip, and Thom hands me a lit cigarette, and I smoke. I make no attempt to be wifely and help with the lunch. I am, after all, a confirmed "other woman," and the women seem to smell it.

There is the sound of a plane overhead, and everyone looks skyward. "It's Perry Atkinson in Cooper's Staggerwing!" someone shouts. Atkinson is a partner in the famous personal injury law firm of Martin Barbusco. He is flying the plane of my beloved.

Everyone watches as the biplane makes a perfect into-the-wind landing and breathes a collective sigh of relief. The occupants step down—first, Perry helping his fiancée Barbara, a six-year-old daughter of Perry's from his second marriage, then a boy about eight years old, a completely normal San Francisco family. I find out that the boy is Vincent's from his second marriage. Everyone greets everyone else, and the children are soon stuffing hotdogs into their hungry little mouths.

Then Jake Morenetti lands in the open-cockpit Stearman and saunters over to the men, Annie following close behind him.

"Look, Jake, let me tell you all about it before anyone else does, that I made a stupid downwind landing and almost bit the dust, but I don't want to hear about it anymore from anyone else, is that clear?" declares Thom, swigging his second beer, which should be his last if he is going to fly back. He is sitting next to me, and I continue munching potato chips, reluctant to help myself to a hotdog.

"There he is!" someone shouts. All eyes focus on the sky. Roaring, convoluting, and diving high above us is Vincent in the AT-6. He is doing an aerobatics exhibition of barrel rolls, loops, and spirals, the plane soaring and plunging in a performance of sheer madness, of play, of total competence and control. I have never seen anything like it. He is flirting with death and destruction before our eyes. The plane descends and approaches the field when I realize he is upside down!

"Hey, look at Vince, goddamn!" they shout as the AT-6 roars upside down over the runway, the pilot not more than six feet above the ground. I can hardly breathe watching the spectacle. He climbs, does a slow roll while gaining altitude, then drops down for another approach, this time right side up, lands, and rolls to a halt.

His friends rush to help him down. He has redeemed the honor of the San Francisco Sheriff's Air Squadron after Thom's debacle. They crowd around him, joking, congratulating him on his skill, admiring him. He basks in it all, tearing off his helmet and goggles, the white scarf around his neck drifting in the breeze as he strolls over to the picnic area with his entourage of peers.

Our eyes meet, but we do not speak.

"How'd you like them apples?" he asks his son Billy, ruffling up the boy's hair.

Billy's mouth is full of hotdog, mustard clings to his lips, and he seems unimpressed. "Oh, great, Dad, real good." He takes another bite of his hotdog.

I sit demurely, waiting for him.

Eventually he slides in next to me, swinging his leg over the wooden bench. Thom is off talking to another flying physician. "Did you like my aerobatics? Did I impress you?" he asks, smiling at me, his face reddened from the wind, his hair tousled, handsome, heroic.

My poor heart begins pounding again—love, fear, uncertainty, desire. I wonder if he has missed me in these weeks following the excruciating scene in Thom's bedroom. I find my voice. "It was beautiful, Vincent, but very dangerous. What if the engine quits and you are upside down six feet over the field?"

He hands me a lit, unfiltered Camel cigarette. There is no one here but the two of us. The rest of the crowd recedes to some unknown dimension as we look into each other. I have missed him terribly.

"To answer your question, you die a quick uncomplicated death. Better than wasting away in a hospital full of machines and tubes, and people remember you for a long time."

"Hmm, but you checked it all out yourself, didn't you? The mechanical part of the plane, I mean."

"Yeah, I know what I'm doing, not like Kelley. I told you not to fly with him. He landed downwind and almost killed you both. Dumb thing to do, not check the wind direction before making a landing. Look at him over there, laughing about it, drinking more beer, which is a no-no, especially for him."

I sit silently. He is right. And I have to fly back with Thom, and I know without a doubt it's not safe. All those pills and injections he takes have impaired his judgement and coordination.

There is a barrier between Vincent and me, and we both know who and what it is. I am the only one who can remove the wall, and I am afraid to make the decision, so I go on doing nothing about the situation.

Vincent excuses himself from the picnic table. "See you around San Francisco. Be careful." He goes over to talk to his friends and leaves a painful vacuum next to me. My whole predicament is unsettling. I want to flee, to avoid making more mistakes. My inner self speaks, loud, that I am twenty-seven years old, and it is time to grow up and face reality, become a *woman*! How scary that is!

Thom brings Perry Atkinson and his girlfriend, Barbara, over to meet me. The attorney looks like an attorney, heavyset with thick, bushy eyebrows, large glasses, and longish, straight black hair. He appears formidable but has a wide, amused grin on his face that neutralizes his bearish appearance. She is tall, lean, and bony, strong. She is also an attorney. She moves and speaks with total confidence. They are getting married soon, according to Thom, the second time for her and the third time for him.

She greets me warmly. "Hi, there! So, you are the famous artist of Upper Terrace that all the men are talking about. Pretty, aren't you? When are you going to invite us to one of Thom's famous dinner parties on the hill?"

Her utter equanimity embarrasses me. She wears little makeup and laughs a lot, tossing her long dark hair. A smart woman *who knows what she wants* and goes after it, not like me, I think.

I shake myself out of my funk of morose self-pity and begin to make light conversation with her. Of course, they are invited to the next dinner party, and yes, I still do medical illustration and I'd be happy to do jobs for her future husband. We exchange phone numbers.

"And you must visit us in our new home in Sausalito. We are already living there, you know." She smiles. "It is so comfortable and spacious after the city apartment, and it's quiet. Our wedding will be in two months, and I hope you can come."

I drink more beer, preparing myself for the return trip and wishing there were something stronger.

Vincent and I avoid each other for the rest of the afternoon. He sits with Perry Atkinson and Barbara and the two children. Burkhart sits with Thom and me, Jake, and another couple I don't know.

After lunch, the women clean up, repack the picnic baskets, and gather the garbage. The sun is beginning its descent, and the shadows of the forest lengthen across the field. The pilots begin to check out their planes, load up their things. The first one begins to taxi into place.

Quickly, I sneak off to go to the bathroom in the bushes, brush my hair, and apply a little lipstick. If I die in a plane crash, I still want to look good if anything is left of my face. This macabre thought occupies me as I trudge back to Thom, to whom I belong for the remainder of the day for better or for worse.

One by one, the planes take off according to some preordained plan I can only imagine. As Thom goes through his checklist on the Super Cub, I see Vincent in the AT-6 pulling on his helmet, adjusting his flying goggles. His son will fly back with Perry Atkinson. My heart melts with love for him. The distance between us is sweet misery. He looks so handsome as the plane begins its forward roll. He is soon out of my sight. The melodrama is aching.

I decide I will never love another as much as love him. I don't realize it at the moment, but this kind of love seldom happens in life. He is the man I will never have because I don't think he can be faithful, and he will not tolerate my infidelity. And then, of course, he is still married. But do I want to marry again? I wallow in my romantic quandary, almost hoping to die on the way back and be done with it all.

"Okay, Doll, buckle up. You ready to fly back? You aren't scared now, are ya?" Thom gets into the plane after me and looks back smiling, trying to reassure me.

"No, no, of course not, Thom. Just be careful, please." I am not so eager to crash after all.

"Clear!" he shouts and guns the motor as we taxi to the beginning of the runway, heading into wind, the forest behind us. He is a little tight from the beer—I can tell, now that I know him so well—the flushed face, the shining eyes, and amusement at every little thing. What had been charming before, his breaking of the rules, has now become an alarming trait. He disparages everything, even flight safety rules. The man is dangerous.

We take off and retrace our route back over the Eel to the Russian River and approach the Golden Gate Bridge. He is descending, and he plans to fly *under* the bridge, I am trapped in the plane.

"Hang on there, Doll! We're going under!" he shouts, and indeed, we do go under. We skim over the tops of small boats sailing back into the bay. A huge oil tanker blows its horn. I can look down into its exhaust stacks. The underside of the bridge is above us, with all the weekend traffic flowing over head.

If the engine quits now, there is nowhere to go except crashing into those wild, thrashing tidal waters flowing with tremendous force into San Francisco Bay. If we go in, I will swim as long as I can, hoping a shark doesn't get me, and maybe one of those sailboats will pick me up if I am lucky. But how could they stop in the tidal stream?

Then, thankfully, we emerge from under the bridge, start climbing, and head for Half Moon Bay Airport. The sun is low, and the fog forms bits and pieces of gauzy mist beneath us.

Thom makes his approach after checking the windsock, bouncing on the landing, which is usual for him. Then we taxi to the tie-down. We did not crash. I see the AT-6 tied down with a canvas cover over it, but as we drive out of the parking lot, I see no sign of Vincent's car.

"You know it is against the law to fly under the Golden Gate Bridge," he says, chuckling, immensely pleased with himself.

"Really," I mumble into the wind as we drive along the coast, exhausted by the past harrowing experiences and my own quandries. I feel a need to escape, but to where? I am essentially penniless, living from one art sale or one medical drawing to the next. It is all sporadic. Whatever comes in goes out immediately for rent, groceries, flight school, or car repairs, that sort of thing. There is never any extra money. I long to go somewhere totally different from San Francisco, someplace exotic by the sea, the warm sea, any sea, I don't care.

Thom parks the Thunderbird, and as we emerge, I can sense he wants me to go upstairs with him. I don't want to go. "Thom, I am tired. I need to sleep. Tomorrow, I am going to see Perry Atkinson about a drawing assignment. You know I need the money. I owe you a month's rent, and I think I am going to fly solo next week. The money it just goes."

"Forget the rent. Come and have a nightcap with me. I want to talk to you."

I obediently trudge up the green carpeted stairs to his chilly flat. He flicks on the thermostat, and the gas heaters kick in, warming the place. I follow him into the kitchen, and he begins to panfry some steaks and makes us drinks. I feel trapped again.

I put an album on his record player, old-fashioned love songs of the '40s. Songs that Vincent enjoys of eternal love, falling in love at first sight across a crowded room, of the eternal beauty and pain of being in love.

After Thom gets the fire going, we sit on the sofa and sip our drinks.

"You better forget about him, Doll. Like I told you, he is back with his wife. He has never been faithful to a woman for a moment in his life. He will only make you suffer. I can do so much for you if you only let me."

I am going to cry again, I fight it, take a long sip of the vodka tonic, and stare into the flames, seeing him there, imagining our bodies entwined in love.

Thom won't quit. "Concentrate on your work. Hell, I know I'm no great stud in bed but there are other things in life besides sex. Sex won't save you, but your work will. Believe me."

"I know, Thom. You are right," I sniffle a bit and toss down the rest of the drink, struggling to erase my erotic vision.

We go to the kitchen to make more drinks and check the steaks in the broiler. There is some sour dough bread in the freezer and succotash, which I cook up in a pot. We are hungry from the trip. Hotdogs just don't take the place of a good steak medium rare. I set the dining table, and we eat like an old married couple who hardly feel the need for communication—bored.

"Vincent is quite a pilot, isn't he? You finally got to see him in action at the fly-in. He is impressive. To change the subject, where do you plan to spend Christmas?" he asks.

"I think I'll go to Tucson with my family. My brother is on his fourth marriage, and I'd like to meet my new sister-in-law. There is a succession of them." I absently butter a piece of bread and put it in my mouth, wanting to be asleep in my bed.

"If you like, I'll fly you there in the Cub. Okay, don't look at me like that. I promise to check the wind direction. Really I don't usually foul up like that. It's pressure from my work, the divorce, or maybe I'm just incompetent as a pilot. Trust me, Doll, please."

He is looking at me directly, demanding my attention. His face is tired, need written all over it.

I look down at my plate feeling guilty. All I can think of is Vincent. My thoughts betray the love of this tired, older doctor who to me now feels irrelevant. Will I ever be faithful again to a man? I wonder. I am like Vincent in a way, swept up in the moment, wanting what I can't have until I get it, loving the conquest.

He hands me a lit cigarette, and we inhale, the smoke circling around in the dim light. "I'll think about it, Thom. I'll phone them to see what is happening over the holidays."

He walks me down the back steps and waits until I unlock the door to my apartment. The heat comes blasting out at us. "I'll turn down the thermostat. You sleep tight now, hear? I'll phone you tomorrow afternoon. I love you." He kisses me lightly on the cheek and retreats into the darkness and back up to his place.

I open the window and let in the fresh sea air. The foghorns moan on the buoys in the distance. I change into pajamas without bothering to shower and slip into bed, cuddling under my down comforter, tired from my head to my feet, feeling more ambiguous than ever about my life. Work, love, what does it mean? We all die eventually anyway, so why get so hot and bothered? With that morbid, spiritually castrating thought, I drift off into a troubled sleep.

CHAPTER SEVENTEEN

Solo

I work all day Monday. Thom calls, but I tell him I can't spend the evening with him as I must catch up on my work, keep my appointment downtown, and be rested for my flight lesson tomorrow. I need to go to bed early and *not drink*. He should understand that.

Tuesday, I get up quivering with excitement as I dress and drive to Half Moon Bay for my flying lesson. Will I or won't I solo? I have lots of hours of instruction, twelve, I think. Will I crash flying that Cessna 140 all by myself?

It is a sparkling, bright, cool day in early December. My lesson is scheduled for 11:00 AM. The Pacific shimmers off to my right as I speed along the Coast Highway 1 in my Triumph. It is cold. My leather top has been deteriorating. The snaps are falling off, and I can no longer cover the passenger seat. Things are going to get a lot worse, but blissfully, I am unaware. On the contrary, I feel wonderful, better than I have in months, as though I can do anything I want, that the world is *mine*.

I arrive early, and Jake is still out with another student.

"Sit down and have a cup of coffee. Jake will be back in a few minutes," says Annie, pouring me a cup as I slide onto the leather seat at the counter. The coffee hits the knot in my stomach. Damn knot, go away.

Soon, Jake saunters in wearing his creased, leather aviation jacket, a cigarette dangling from his mouth. He nods in my direction and takes the student over to the desk to settle up and he fills out the logbook.

He walks to the middle of the coffee shop and looks at me. I set down my coffee and return his stare, the knot growing. He jerks his head in the direction of the plane and says, "Okay, let's fly."

We go through the checklist of the cables, the oil, the gas, then I get into the pilot's seat as he slides in next to me, locking the door securely. He smells of leather, cigarettes, and aviation fuel. I start the engine and taxi to the beginning of the runway. Annie gives me the wind direction, velocity, and air pressure on the radio. I adjust the instruments accordingly then do the run-up. I check the sky for other planes approaching. There are none, so I release the brakes slowly, push in the throttle, and we start running along the concrete strip. Gaining speed, I gently pull back on the stick and we become airborne.

Conditions are ideal: visibility for 50 miles, wind northwesterly at 330 degrees, 7 knots, straight down the runway.

I do the flight pattern almost automatically: 700 feet straight and level, parallel to the field, 90-degree turn to base leg, another 90-degree turn for the approach. I cut the power at about 50 feet, and we glide to the beginning of the runway, where I let it hover briefly a few inches over the concrete before settling into a stall landing. We roll to a halt, the motor still purring.

Jake and I look at each other and smile, a perfect landing.

"Okay, I'm getting out now. I got work in the office to do. It's all yours." He jumps down onto the runway, indicates I should secure the door, waves goodbye, and walks to the side of the concrete.

Oh, my god, I am alone in this thing! I have to do it alone. No man to help if things go wrong, it's all up to me. I sit here for a moment, numb with unrealistic terror—psychic terror, actually—and mentally go through everything I must do to fly. It's like life; I could sit here and do nothing, get out of the plane, and give it all up, fail from fear when I know perfectly well what to do and how to do it. It's just because there is no *man* next to me.

Well, my inner voice says sarcastically, what are you, woman or wimp?

Woman, I answer back, push full throttle, and take off. The panic is controlled. I go through everything automatically, as I have done many times before. It is easy. It is nothing. If the engine quits, it is me and only me who must make the emergency landing. But I can do it. I know I can. And by the time I make my approach, I feel the sweet pleasure of control, of dominating the plane, but most of all, myself.

The landing is good, not quite perfect due to a bit of a tremor still there, but good enough. I roll to a halt and see that Jake is not alone. There is Vincent, waving at me, clasping his hands in a victory salute. The big white Buick is parked behind them. I feel overwhelmed. I am drenched in perspiration and hurriedly take out a handkerchief from my bag and wipe my face.

Vincent comes to the door of the aircraft. I release the lock. "Beautiful, honey! You are going to be a great pilot. Do one more stop-and-go around the field, and I'll meet you in the office. I have a surprise for you. We are going to celebrate."

I do another takeoff and landing, this time more calmly, thinking of Amelia Earhart and how proud of me she would be. I am enjoying the exhilaration of flight. After landing, I taxi to the hangar, where Jake takes over the plane.

In the office, I pay for the lesson. Annie congratulates me and tells me lessons will be cheaper now since I don't pay the instructor until I get to solo cross-country flying. Jake signs my logbook, and Vincent and I leave. We get into his Buick, leaving my TR3 in the lot. I lean back on the leather seats and sigh deeply as he moves over to me and kisses me hard and long on the mouth and in my mouth.

"Look on the back seat, honey," he says as he swings the car out onto Highway 1. There is a big corrugated bucket filled with ice and two bottles of champagne chilling. Next to that is a grocery box from Petrini's Market filled with what? I can hardly see into it—caviar, maybe, or French Brie, some lovely crystal goblets, special for the occasion. He never ceases to surprise me. Just when Thom had me convinced that Vincent couldn't care less about me, now this!

This is a day made in heaven, and I decide to lose myself in each moment, keep everything indelibly in my consciousness. A day like this is rare. I know that much at this point about real life.

We soon swing off the highway and are on to a rough blacktop road that winds up into the hills. "Where are we going?" I ask, not really caring.

"Ham's Canyon. Yeah, Ham Sado. He is the Japanese flower gardener, a good friend of mine. I think you met him at one of the parties. His family was quarantined during World War II because they thought that the Japanese nationals living here were going to lead the Japanese army into California, if you can comprehend such a thing. Anyway, he's a good guy. Wouldn't hurt a fly, and he raises the most beautiful flowers you could ever imagine, lots of daisies, all different colors, and in the spring it's tulips and lilies. They go on for acres and acres. Wait till you see it! We are going to celebrate among the flowers that you, my dear girl, are now a bona fide pilot. I have all kinds of treats for you, especially this."

He takes my hand, puts it on his crotch, moving it back and forth over his swelling erection. We drive like this up the canyon. I am distracted from his sexual foreplay by the sudden view of the flowers. The gentle slopes are carpeted with daisies in colors of pink, white, yellow, and blue. It appears to be a magical place I never noticed from the air, considering we are right below the air traffic pattern.

He turns the Buick onto a dirt road that enters the field of flowers and parks under a tree. There is no one around. We are alone to indulge our erotic celebration of my achievement. Just God, the sky, and the flower-covered earth surround us.

Vincent carefully spreads an old Indian blanket on the ground, and I sit passively while he arranges the ice bucket with the champagne and shines up the chilled crystal wine goblets. He has small plastic plates, napkins, and a spotless white towel.

Is that his wife's towel? I wonder, then as soon as possible, squash that inappropriate thought. I recline on the blanket, like a modern Venus of Urbino, sensual, secure in the authenticity of my wantonness. I await the libation that will totally liberate my lust for Vincent Cooper.

He smiles at me as he opens a jar of Beluga caviar from the grocery box then a carton of sour cream and then some exotic-looking round crackers. Mesmerized by the ritual, I watch as he smears the tiny, greasy black eggs of caviar over the crackers with his Swiss Army knife then plops a glob of sour cream on top of it. He arranges them on two plates then continues his preparations.

He cleans his hands and the knife on napkins then takes the white towel and pops the cork on the first bottle of champagne. The bubbly wine overflows the bottle happily, and all that pent-up tension is released. He pours champagne in the two large wine goblets I recognize from his collection on Upper Terrace.

"*Salud*," he says in Spanish, "health, without which nothing else much matters." We drink quickly. He pours more. We don't say much to each other, just eat and drink. He takes my glass and sets it aside, draws another blanket over us.

We lie prone among the flowers swaying gently in the breeze, looking at the blue sky and the bits of fog beginning to move in over the hills. Slowly, we undress, and he begins to make love to me, slower, calmer than before, more serious somehow. He insists I climax.

"When you come, it is like me coming again. I feel what you feel," he whispers to me, and my body totally gives over to our mutual passion. "I could make love to you over and over. I can't get enough of you. I miss you so much. What are we going to do?" he says.

I turn to him and am shocked to see tears in his eyes.

"It's Thom. He says I shouldn't trust you. He says you will just love me, and then when I finally love you back, you will drop me just like that." I snap my fingers in the air the way Thom does when he lectures me.

Vincent sits up angrily. "The hell with Thom! You are your own person. You must trust me!"

"But your wife, what about her?"

"Forget her."

"Oh?"

He waves his hand in the air as if dismissing his wife like a troublesome mosquito. "I want to take you away, be with you all the time, to Mexico. I want to show you how beautiful Mexico is. You could paint, and I would go fishing. That's all we would do, and make love two or three times a day—or more if you want."

I take my champagne and sip it dreamily, picturing our life. "Yes, I would love that, I know Mexico City but not much more of the country. Maybe next spring we could go."

Vincent wants to leave this minute. "I'll take you to Puerto de las Peñas. You'll love it there. My friends and I go there all the time. No roads, just one hotel downtown, and we could cruise the beaches in a *panga* like the Indians. You can only get there by boat, by plane, or by burro."

"What's a *panga*?"

"It's a dugout canoe. The Indians hollow out a log by hand, you know, like you used to read about in your history books. Only there, they still live like that. Up in the mountains there are huge ranches, haciendas they call them, where people go around on horses and live in adobe houses with dirt floors, hardly any housecleaning to speak of. Chickens, dogs, cats, pigs, horses, all over the place, lots of children running around. They treat us like gods when we come flying in there from *el nor*te."

I am melting with desire, desire to go and partake of this fabulous place, Elysian Fields, paradise, nirvana, Shangri-La, heaven on earth.

His hand rests on my breast while he speaks. "Will you go with me?" He leans over and takes my nipple in his mouth.

"Yes," I answer breathlessly, "right now if you want."

He raises his head, laughing. "We'll have to organize it."

He opens the other bottle of champagne, and we drink more. He lies back and begins to doze while I watch the sky, dreaming of changing into an Indian maiden and living off the land and sea, with no rent to pay every month, no traffic, no boring job, no supermarkets, no need for money. I will paint on sheets of bark like the Indians used to do, make my paints from colored clay and plants. We will be divinely happy and make lots of little Indians to keep us company.

Then, somehow, Thom's image intrudes on my fantasy, his stern face disapproving, like an angry Zeus. Thom recently moved a friend of his into Vincent's vacant flat, a bureaucrat who runs the San Francisco Municipal Transit Authority. The bureaucrat is dull, and I am beginning to admit that I have become tired of the whole situation on Upper Terrace.

I am tired of feeling sorry for Thom. I am tired of feeling guilty for betraying him. And I am bored by his constant lecturing. Just because he is no longer sexually dynamic doesn't give him the right to condemn those of us who are, I reason to myself.

As for his intellect that I have found so intriguing, it is a though he has revealed everything worthwhile and interesting, leaving nothing more. Rather than be repetitious, he is becoming despotic. He can no longer keep me entertained. And his rebellious attitude, which I had found rather romantic, now seems more like repressed anger, pompous, even pathetic.

What does he want to do with the rest of his life? I wonder. He must be close to sixty, which seems ancient to me. He should have about twenty more years left to him if he takes care of his health.

But he injects cortisone and whatever else, has all those bottles of pills crammed into his medicine cabinet. He often foams around his mouth. And he drinks all that booze on top of all that. So, what is going to become of him? *Salud* (health), Vincent said earlier. How could a doctor be so negligent of his health? It seems to contradict the whole medical profession.

The air is colder as the winter sun dips lower over the ocean and a wind picks up off the sea. A few daisy petals float by, and the scent of the earth is refreshing. Vincent is snoring contentedly under the warm blanket, cozy.

I pour myself more of the deliciously dry champagne— he buys the best it seems—and sip it thoughtfully. Should I insist on a divorce? I really can't imagine doing such a thing, destroying his marriage for the "other woman," me. But then the present wife destroyed the previous marriage. She was the "other woman," and now it is coming back to her. He marries the exciting mistress, makes her a housewife, and then gets bored. It didn't seem right, destroying someone else's life for the sake of your own.

Maybe Thom is right, I think reluctantly, Vincent needs the conquest, and once he wins, loses interest. Perhaps it is better not to encourage him to divorce but rather remain the other woman in his life, his mistress. That status is far more interesting, and it would allow me to pursue my career, preserve our precious love, and offers many more possibilities, not the least of which is freedom from housework.

But then I hear the faraway cry of my unborn children, and with that my inner voice intervenes, really, now, haven't you known from the time you were ten years old, you don't need to be married to have children, no matter what your mother told you?

Vincent begins to stir, so I drain the last drops of champagne and begin to gather up our picnic things for the return drive to San Francisco.

To be continued in
Book II: Escaping Real Life.